SERRA ROSE

Bloodsong

To all those who encouraged and inspired me during the writing of this book. You know who you are. You were with me through the delirium of late nights and endured random outpourings of ideas for this book and these characters.

To all those who have an obsession with vampires: Same. I wrote this for us.

Contents

Content Warning   iv

Authors note   vi

Glossary   vii

Chapter 1   1

Chapter 2   7

Chapter 3   13

Chapter 4   19

Chapter 5   29

Chapter 6   37

Chapter 7   45

Chapter 8   53

Chapter 9   58

Chapter 10   62

Chapter 11   71

Chapter 12   75

Chapter 13   80

Chapter 14   85

Chapter 15   90

Chapter 16   96

Chapter 17   107

Chapter 18   114

Chapter 19   119

Chapter 20   124

Chapter 21   129

Chapter 22   136
Chapter 23   141
Chapter 24   149
Chapter 25   155
Chapter 26   160
Chapter 27   169
Chapter 28   175
Chapter 29   185
Chapter 30   191
Chapter 31   197
Chapter 32   204
Chapter 33   210
Chapter 34   216
Chapter 35   222
Chapter 36   230
Chapter 37   236
Chapter 38   242
Chapter 39   247
Chapter 40   254
Chapter 41   261
Chapter 42   268
Chapter 43   276
Chapter 44   281
Chapter 45   286
Chapter 46   295
Chapter 47   304
Chapter 48   310
Chapter 49   317
Chapter 50   323
Chapter 51   330
Chapter 52   335

Chapter 53   342
Chapter 54   347
Chapter 55   353
Chapter 56   360
Chapter 57   368
Chapter 58   375
Chapter 59   385
Chapter 60   389
Chapter 61   397
Chapter 62   401
Chapter 63   407
Chapter 64   418
Chapter 65   424
Chapter 66   432
Chapter 67   436
Bonus Chapter   442
Epilogue   450
Dark Eyes of a Stranger   458
Acknowledgements   459
About the Author   460
Also by Serra Rose   462

Content Warning

Bloodsong is a spicy dark romance with themes that may trigger some readers. These include but are not limited to:
  Post break-up depression
  Knife play
  Blood play
  Stalking
  Arson
  Death of a child (off page)
  Death of a sibling (off page)
  Violence
  Murder
  Torture
  Starvation
  Sexual manipulation
  Mind control
  Abuse of power
  Drunk aggression
  Instances of dubious consent
  Death of a spouse
  Profanity - This book is set in Australia, and it would be unnatural to not have my characters use normal everyday language.

Be kind to yourself; your mental health matters.

Authors note

Bloodsong is set in Melbourne, Australia, and it includes Australia and New Zealand lingo. A glossary of Aussie terms, and Italian and Te Reo language translations, have been provided.

Some things may *seem* inaccurate to those in the northern hemisphere, such as it being winter in June. Believe me, Melbourne was very cold here in June while I was writing Bloodsong!

The book itself is written in British English. We use U a lot in words, and sometimes S instead of Z, such as in recognise.

Glossary

Australia and New Zealand Glossary

Journos – Journalists

Rando - random person

Yeah nah – no

Keen as - eager, enthusiastic

Bench – counter

Mobile phone - cell phone

My shout - My treat

Bonnet - Hood of the car

Te Reo Māori - Native language of Aotearoa (New Zealand)

Ponaumu - Green stone

Too easy - no worries

Doona - blanket/duvet

Lift - Elevator

Italian Glossary

Amico - friend

Cantante – Singer

Vita mia - my life

Mi amore - my love

Ti amo - I love you

Stronzo - Asshole

Il mio piccolo cantante - my little singer

Sei mio. - You're mine.

Merda! - Shit!

Vampiro Veneziano - The Vampire of Venice

Te Reo Glossary

Kia ora - Hello, or Thank you.

Tēnā koe– Hello (to one person) or thank you. It is considered more formal than kia ora.

Chapter 1

Quinn

As I stepped back into the studio for the first time in months, the shadow of heartbreak and grief hung over me. Hands shaking, I grasped the headphones, pulling them over my ears. I glanced over at Mia and Lilith. Both gave me a smile of encouragement. It had been six months since my whole life imploded, and coming back was like coming home.

My bassist, Mia, was a Japanese Australian with a red balayage on shoulder-length black hair. Donning knee-high leather boots and a short red skirt, her white tee-shirt and denim jacket was her usual wear when we played.

Lilith's Italian line was still visible with her olive skin. She had short, spiky, white-blonde hair, a black sleeveless vest over her tee-shirt, with jeans that were full of rips. Around her neck she wore a wide black ribbon. She was covered in tattoos with a nose ring, and her eyes were lined heavily, with smoky eye shadow.

Finally, I reached for the mic. Singing always brought me such joy, and holding the mic felt right. I took in a deep breath and let it out slowly.

"How do you feel?" Lilith asked, her eyes showing her concern.

I gave her a small smile. "Like it's been too long."

Mia's face brightened. "So, you're ready?" she asked with hope in her voice.

I took in another shaky breath and exhaled. "I think so."

Lilith nodded. "Okay, we'll be in the booth with Gavin. Take your time."

They left, closing the door with a soft click. I shut my eyes, allowing the silence to envelop me. Music was my life. Singing was my life, but I'd walked away, much to my ex-boyfriend's pleasure. Lilith had been working hard to bring me to the studio for months. It got to the point that I missed it enough to give in, so I'd allowed her to book a time to record the lyrics to music she and Mia had already recorded.

"Let me know when you're ready," Lilith's voice came through the headphones, gently.

I opened my eyes, glancing at her on the other side of the glass with Mia. Next to them, our sound mixer, Gavin, watched me. I gave them a nod.

Music came through the headphones. I closed my eyes

again, letting it in. The sound of Mia's bass blended in with Lilith's drums washed over me, and a smile crept across my face. My heart thudded in time with the drums. It had been too long, and I became energised, letting the track play through. I hummed to the tune that I'd sing, taking joy as the words returned.

At the end, I opened my eyes. "Play it again, I'm ready to sing."

Mia and Lilith's faces lit up; and I couldn't hear them, but I could tell they were cheering. Lilith fist-pumped the air. I couldn't help but laugh.

The track started over, and as I started to sing, the pain of the last six months faded away. The break-up, and all that followed, held no meaning in that moment. He'd forced me to give up singing, and he gaslit me to the point that I believed it was my idea to quit. But song burst forth from me, healing and energising me.

I knew these words like I knew my own heart. I'd written them. I sang along, overwhelmed by the urge to cry. It was joy that filled me, and peace. My life was chaos without music, and I let myself go. It carried me to a deep part within myself where only music existed. The centre of my being rejoiced. This was my world, and I would never let myself be pulled from it again.

Silence came through the headphones, deafening. I opened my eyes to find the three of them staring at me, open-mouthed, through the glass.

"Again," I requested.

"We've already played it three times," Lilith countered. "We have everything we need. You were perfect."

Three times? I'd gotten so lost in the music that I hadn't

even noticed. "One more time?"

It started to play, and my chest ached as I released my fear of singing. My voice never wavered; it was as if no time had passed at all. As the last of the chords died down, Mia and Lilith burst through the door and wrapped me in tight hugs.

"I'm so proud of you!" Lilith's excitement lit up her eyes. "You did it, Quinn."

I pulled the headphones off, hanging them up. "I'm sorry it took so long."

"It's okay," Mia said. "You needed time."

"Time to celebrate!" Lilith said. "I'm going to buy you the biggest serving of 'Death by Chocolate'!"

I grabbed my jacket, but before we left, I turned, scanning the studio. "When can we book in again?" I asked. "We still have the rest of the album to record."

They both looped their arms around mine.

"Already taken care of," Lilith said. "When you were singing that last time, I told Gavin that you were ready. We're booked in for next week."

"Thank you," I said, almost choking on emotion. "I don't know where I'd be without you three."

Lilith stopped, her serious face on. "Just, please talk it over with us next time? We can't see you walk away from the music in your soul again. If I knew where Steven was, I'd kick his ass."

I choked back a laugh as we stepped outside into the bright sun. It was chilly, and the beginning of Autumn, but for once Melbourne had given us sunshine. A cold breeze pulled at my jacket, and I zipped it up, pulling a beanie over my head. "Don't worry, I'm not looking to go down that road for a *looong* time. Let's just focus on our career for a while."

A man walked by with dark sunglasses over his eyes, alongside a blonde woman who looked like a model. He had black hair with olive skin, maybe Mediterranean. His chest and shoulders were broad, and his arms were all muscle. A hint of stubble lined his jaw. He wore black jeans and a black tee-shirt. His face moved enough for me to feel like he was looking me over, but he kept walking. I caught what I thought was a whiff of cedarwood and sea, which only made me think of my sister. Pain pierced my chest, but I pushed it down.

I didn't realise I'd stopped until Mia burst into giggles. "And for a second there I thought you were ready to swear off men."

I cast a look over my shoulder at the same time he did. My cheeks heated, and his lips twitched slightly as if he were holding off a smile. Then he walked away with the blonde.

"I can still look," I quipped, ignoring the inner voice chanting, *'Yes, yes, yes! Him!'*

I resisted the urge to look back again, following my friends to the cafe.

"So, I have some news," Lilith revealed as we walked in, the strong aroma of coffee beans filling me with relief.

I grabbed menus on our way past, and we sat down at our usual corner table. My fingers wrapped around my dolphin pendant as I waited for her to say more. "Why do I feel like you're gauging my reaction before you continue?" I asked.

"Because she is," Mia laughed.

"Out with it," I glared at Lilith, but then grinned.

"I got a call this morning from Pete at The Underground. Someone sent him our music video, and he listened to our album."

5

The Underground was a bar where the owner hosted live bands. I'd gone there for plenty of gigs before, but never to sing. "And?"

"He wants to give us a trial. Once a month. If we draw in enough of a crowd, he'd be willing to discuss something a bit more frequent. I told him I'd have to clear it with my band first." She smiled at me with hope in her eyes.

Excitement bubbled up. "Oh wow. When's our first gig?"

Lilith gave me her widest smile. "This weekend."

Chapter 2

Matteo

I lit candles, placing them around the studio, casting a soft glow on the subject. She was a beautiful woman, already bare for our session. The scent of her blood mixed with a floral fragrance of her perfume. I ran my fingers over paint brushes, calm settling over me, the beast within quiet. Painting had always created a sense of peace, holding my feral nature at bay. In the last century, it had become harder to control, so I'd sought to paint more in the hopes it would still work.

"Are you comfortable?" I asked.

"I didn't realise it would be this dark," she murmured.

"How can you see what you're painting?"

The candlelight showed enough of her shape, reflecting over her cheek, and the curves of her neck and breasts, for what I would paint. Blonde hair lit up like a halo around her head. Even if it were pitch black, though, I would still see her perfectly. I moved towards her with human slowness, so as not to startle her.

"I'm focusing on light and shadow." I brushed my fingers across her cheek. "We don't need to see every detail for it to be sensual. The way the light touches you here." I lowered my fingers to her throat, my canines aching to sink into the soft flesh. "From the curve here," careful not to touch her breast, I lowered my hand again. "To the softness of your body. The candles behind you help create that silhouette, while the others cast enough light and shadow for what's needed."

My eyes lifted to her throat again, the feral part of my mind stirring. I returned to my easel to put distance between us.

Soft breaths whispered from her lips, and her heart thumped with a quickened pace, sounds that even across the room I could hear as if she were right next to me, my head to her chest. I used the strokes of brush upon canvas to focus on, letting myself relax into the mind of an artist. The outline of her body started to take shape on the white background as my hand moved in slow rhythms. Bristles slid over canvas, and contentment bubbled up, allowing me to smile.

In dark colours, shadows played across the planes of her face and body, the background completely black. Softer colours in paint showed light dancing in her eyes, highlighting one side of her. The rise and fall of her chest became hypnotic, but the pulse in her throat was impossible to look away from. I yearned to caress her cheek, murmur to her until she begged me to bite her.

I sucked in a breath, hit both at once by two hungers. We'd met only three days before, but it was obvious she desired me. Her perfume did nothing to hide that distinct fragrance of arousal, which awakened my own lust.

"Would you like to take a break?" I asked, my voice husky. "You've been still for a long time. Perhaps you'd like to stretch."

She rose from the seat, stretching out her body in such a way that it was clear that she wanted me to see her. I'd been staring at her naked body for a while, yet she still wanted to draw my eyes to her. But it was her throat that pulled me in. I considered giving in, letting her desire be what overrode mine.

She met my eyes, and I averted my gaze quickly.

"You don't have to be polite," she said with a smile on her soft lips. "I'm naked. I think we're beyond the need to look away." She glided towards me with a deliberate movement of her hips.

There was no denying what I wanted. The hunger that had long since taken root inside of me. I could hide behind the artist all I liked, but my feral nature would always rear up. I should have been more careful, fed more before I'd allowed her into my home, my studio. She stopped in front of me, unaware that her attraction to me was a simple part of her human brain responding to my presence. The allure of the vampire. She couldn't resist me if she tried.

I reached for her, stroking the soft flesh on the underside of her breast with my thumb. Her lips parted with an intake of air. Rising to my feet, I pulled her to me. Fangs lengthened, at the promise of her blood. A low growl rumbled from my chest as my lips brushed hers. Inside me, the beast stretched out, knowing it was about to get what it wanted.

"Offer me your throat," I murmured, waiting for her to say yes. "It won't hurt; in fact, you'll quite enjoy my vampire's kiss."

Her eyes widened. "Vampire?" Fear surged in her, reaching to me.

I lifted her chin to meet my eyes. "Do not be afraid. You'll know nothing of this afterwards, just that you posed for an artist. I will not take much."

"I'm not afraid," she said, under my sway.

I had no desire to hurt her, and my hunger rolled out as she tilted her head, exposing the long vein in her neck, blood pulsing beneath her skin. I wrapped my arms around her, running my tongue over her throat, coating it with my venom.

A shiver tore through her. "Did you mean it when you said it wouldn't hurt?" she asked.

"All you'll feel is pleasure." I sunk my fangs in, letting my venom into her system.

She let out a moan, and when her blood hit my tongue it took everything to hold back my own. I stroked the back of her head, forcing down the part of me that yearned for the chase, the screams. Her heartbeat thundered in my ears, quicker than my own.

Once I'd taken what I needed, I lifted my head. Her eyes were closed, and she clung to me.

"More," she whispered, her voice heavy with desire.

"I've taken enough," I told her, but I kept my arms around

10

her. If I was to release her, it was likely she'd fall.

"No, not that. *More*." She ground herself against me.

I wanted to take her body, as hungry for that as I had been to feed. But I wouldn't force myself. "Is that what you really want?" I asked her.

She laughed. "Do you honestly think I volunteered to pose naked for you without wanting that?" Her hand pressed against the crotch in my jeans, rubbing over my erection. "Looks like I'm not the only one."

She reached for my belt. Satisfied that this was her desire, and not an effect of my sway over her, I let her. Soft lips pressed against mine. She tasted like strawberries, her lip gloss. I lifted her effortlessly and took her to my bedroom, laying her on my bed. She looked around. "Do you have protection?"

It was my turn to laugh. "That's not something I've had to worry about for a long time. Worry not, we don't need it." I pulled my tee-shirt over my head, then removed my jeans and briefs.

Her eyes widened as they darted over my chest, down my torso, stopping on my cock. I dipped into her mind, curious.

'Holy fucking shit, he's built like a god.'

I didn't try to hold back my grin as I crawled over the bed towards her, a growl rising from my chest. Her hands slid over my abdomen, her arousal overpowering. I lowered myself over her, letting myself slide in slowly. With gentle motions I thrust in and out, her sounds of pleasure fuelling me on. She clung to me, her fingernails digging into my back. I maintained the rhythm, sinking in deep and eliciting gasps and moans from her.

My own pleasure rose in waves, warmth spreading

through me as I became aware of every little movement and breath. I felt all of it. The feel of her skin against mine, soft as silk. Her muscles clenched around me as I moved in and out, her head thrown back. As I rocked against her, unable to take my eyes from the softness of her throat, I couldn't resist. I struck fast, taking pleasure again in her sweet blood. Delicious, hot and satisfying as I drank.

In that moment, her blood filled me, and her body belonged to me. My own moans filled the room alongside hers. I grabbed her arms, pinning them above her head, and I lifted my mouth from her throat to her lips. I raced towards my release and quickened my rhythm, chasing it. Her moans increased in volume, her eyes on mine as we came together.

Her heart raced, and I let her catch her breath, pulling out of her.

"Wow," she breathed. "I could get used to that."

I stiffened. There would be no getting used to it. I tended to avoid taking a human's blood or body more than once. Humans sought out connection, often desiring more. I saw no reason to continue any kind of relationship, happy to feed and move on. Blood and sex went hand in hand for vampires, but we were not suited for humans or their lives in the light. We were meant for the shadows.

I held her in my arms, giving her time to recover.

Her eyes remained on my face. "Strong silent type, huh?"

I gave her a smile. "How about we get back to the painting?"

Chapter 3

Quinn

Two months later, we readied our instruments on the stage inside The Underground for our third gig. Word had gotten around. Chatter inside the bar rose to a crescendo. Lilith settled herself behind her drums and glanced over at me. Excitement gleamed in her eyes, and she spun a drumstick around. I turned my focus to Mia.

"Ready when you are," Mia said.

The entire bar went quiet, as if they knew we were ready to start, waiting. All eyes turned to us. Lilith smacked her drumsticks together and started to play, followed by Mia.

My fingers tightened around the microphone, and my heart soared. The music flowed through me with a life of its own. I imagined that everyone's hearts beat in time to the drums, alongside my own. Empowered by the energy of the bar, I let my song surge forth, my voice rising and falling. It was a full house tonight. I was giddy from the buzz of being on stage and performing. I chased that feeling, holding on to it. This was where I belonged. This was what made the ground steady beneath my feet.

The bar had a real underground feeling, with stone walls and dim lights. Heaters warmed the entire room, and people danced in front of the stage. Under the heat of the lights, a trickle of sweat slid down my neck. A strange sensation jolted through my chest, leaving me breathless. I opened my eyes, my focus drawn towards a silhouette standing in the doorway. His face was in shadow, yet I somehow knew he was staring right at me. A gaze that pierced my soul, leaving behind sparks of desire and excitement. Warmth flooded me, as I stared back.

His presence offered peace from thorns of trauma still wrapped around my heart. The intense urge to drop my mic and run into his embrace had my chest squeezing hard. In his arms, I could find a part of myself that I had lost. Confused by the rushing feelings, I forced myself to look away from him. Instead I focused on the crowd around the bar, as entranced by the music as I was by the energy surging through me.

Removing the mic from its stand, I held it towards the room. They took that as an invitation to sing. Their voices were awful, but I didn't care. They knew my lyrics, and it made my heart soar. As someone walked past the stage, hot chips and a pint of beer in his hands, the scents wafted around me.

I caught the dark figure still watching me, this time closer.

Everything around me slowed as our eyes locked. The way he looked at me was as if I were the only one in the bar. My focus wavered. I felt like I'd seen him before, and everything about him pulled at me. The longer we stared at each other, the more it seemed as if I were reaching out to him. Calling to him. I brought the mic back towards my mouth and felt like I was singing to him.

I sang, in a dreamlike state. A drum solo was coming up, and I loved to stand beside Lilith and air drum as she did her thing. After a viral video from our last gig, I could tell the crowd was waiting for it. His eyes only left mine to move down my body. I raked mine down *his* body, surprised to find myself wondering what he would look like naked. I shivered, unable to look away from his wide chest, shoulders, and bulky arms. A wall of muscle that I could almost feel pressed against me. I was trapped in his gaze again. A spark of deep hunger shone through his dark eyes.

"Quinn!" Mia's stage whisper pulled me from my trance.

I had missed the solo, much to the disappointment of our audience and my own. Lilith looked over at me with concern.

Oh, shit! I shot her an apologetic smile.

"You done drooling over Mr tall, dark and mysterious?" Mia asked.

I cast a glance back, and he was smiling as if he'd heard her words. I replaced the mic and grabbed my guitar, ready for my solo, waiting for Mia to play through hers first. Then I started, the strings alive beneath my fingers. I sought out the stranger again, and he hadn't moved. He watched my hands, as if in a trance.

We finished the song and started another. When we finished the last one, everyone broke into applause and cheers. I grinned and sought out the stranger, only to find him gone. Relief filled me. The intensity of his stare and of my reaction to him was at a level I was not prepared for. Way too much.

"What happened?" Lilith asked above the din as we started to pack up. "You've never missed the solo."

"A hottie caught her eye," Mia said. "The way they were eyeing each other, I thought they were going to *do it* right there. She's really getting her perv on, she's practically dripping on the stage right now." She stuck her tongue out and started panting at me.

"Mia!" My face was getting hotter by the second.

"Oh, don't look now!" She winked.

The stranger picked that time to approach the stage. I clenched my jaw, eyeing him warily. His black hair was slightly wavy, with expensive looking sunglasses resting on top of his head. I had a sense of deja vu. It was June, and despite it being winter, he maintained colour. Perhaps Mediterranean. He wore a black tee-shirt and no jacket. Ballsy with Melbourne weather at this time of year. Just thinking about that made me cold. I suppressed a shiver.

"You have quite a hypnotic voice." He had a heavy accent, possibly Italian. Mia nudged me. She loved to remind me of my inability to resist men with accents. Stubble lined his jaw, and a slight smile curved his lips as he met my eyes.

"Is that a compliment?" I asked, frowning at Mia. She gave me a smile and turned away, leaving me with the stranger. *Thanks, Mia.*

"So, where are you from?" I asked, suddenly awkward under his stare.

"Venice," he said. "But I left a long time ago."

16

I caught a twitch of pain pass over his face. As if the subject bothered him.

"What brought you all the way to Australia?" My tone was of disbelief, and I was probably being rude.

Unsettled by the effect his presence had on me, I didn't know how to get rid of him. I hated small talk.

He half smiled. "A change of scenery. I arrived here with family."

His hand was cool and firm as he grasped mine, raised it to his mouth and kissed my fingers. The contact with his soft lips sent a shiver through me.

"Your fingers were just as mesmerising as your voice," he murmured. "I heard you from outside and was drawn in. You are a beauty, *mi amore.*"

I didn't speak Italian but had seen enough movies to know that phrase.

"Yeah, nah, slow down there, Casanova." I pulled my hand back. "While I appreciate your attempts to flirt, I'm not your love."

My rejection did nothing to affect his smile. He gazed down at me.

"What *do* I call you then?" he asked.

"Quinn," I said without thinking.

"Quinn, a beautiful name, fitting for such a voice. I'm Matteo."

I was torn between wanting those soft lips on mine, our bodies pressed together, and to turn my back on him, hoping he'd get the hint. My entire world no longer felt steady; the ground beneath me had shaken. I watched him, trying to recall where I'd seen him before.

He was still staring at me. I gave him a small smile. "Sorry,

I have to pack up. Nice to meet you, Matteo. I'm glad you enjoyed our music."

I turned to put my guitar away and glanced over my shoulder. He was gone, and I couldn't help but wonder if I'd ever see him again. I hoped I would.

Chapter 4

Quinn

"Quinn? You awake in there?" Mia waved her hand in front of my face, and I realised I'd zoned out, staring after Matteo.

"I'm awake," I murmured and let out a sigh. "Unless I dreamed him up. Damn."

I grinned at her, and she beamed back. "She's checking out men again!" she fake-whispered to Lilith.

"He was hot," Lilith noted with amusement, spinning a drumstick through her fingers.

"A new admirer," Mia laughed. "Quinn's playing hard-to-get, though."

Lilith grinned. "Good, although that dark hair, if you don't want him—"

"He has an accent," Mia noted, rolling her eyes at Lilith's obvious attempt to annoy her.

"Ohhh." Lilith held her hands up. "He's all yours, then, Quinn." She grinned at Mia. "My dark-haired girlfriend is enough for me."

The pair gazed at each other with dopey grins.

Mia pretended to pout. "You only say that because Quinn has called dibs on him."

"I haven't called dibs on anyone," I laughed.

"No, just any man with an accent." Lilith put her drumsticks away.

"Hey, you like anyone with dark hair, Mia likes tattoos, I like accents. We all have our thing." I shrugged. "Why do I feel like I've seen him somewhere before?"

I glanced back at the crowd, relieved that I saw no sign of him. An intriguing interaction, but I couldn't stop thinking about it. Or his lips. *Ugh, snap out of it, Quinn!*

Pete, the owner came over, cash in hand.

"Here's your cut for tonight," he said, and then passed an extra wad to me. "Some guy left this as a tip."

"A tip?" I asked, dumbfounded. "Who leaves tips here?" There had to be five hundred dollars in his hand.

He shrugged. "He gave it to Jazz, so I didn't see him. He told her to make sure it got to the red-haired beauty on stage with the hypnotic voice."

Mia grinned. "It's your mystery admirer!"

"Not a mystery if I know what he looks like and his name," I offered, staring at the cash.

"Of course you already know his name!" Lilith laughed.

Part of me loved his gesture yet felt a bit disquiet about

some random guy walking in off the street, flirting with me, and giving me such a large amount of cash. I split the money three ways and pocketed mine anyway. Everything we earned we shared.

"You drew a larger crowd tonight than we've seen in here for a couple of years," Pete said. "How would you like to discuss playing on a weekly basis?"

I met Lilith's eyes. She nodded once, as did Mia. "What's your offer?" I asked.

"Five hundred, every Friday night," Pete said. "Only I'd ask that you not be half an hour late like you were tonight."

I winced, knowing it was my fault. I'd never been good with deadlines, and my indecision about what to wear, followed by the need to eat, had delayed us. "Sorry about that," I said.

He shrugged. "It didn't bother anyone tonight, but it cannot be a repeat occurrence." He turned, motioning to someone. "Lisa here is going to film your gigs. We're going to put the footage on our website. You'll really draw the crowds."

"Is there going to be a contract?" Lilith asked. "Or is this just a week-by-week thing?"

His eyes were on her in an instant. Lilith, our negotiator. "I can have something drafted up. Drop by on Monday; you and I can talk."

He walked away, calling out to someone across the bar. I helped Lilith and Mia carry their equipment up the stairs. Outside, cold air surrounded me, wind pulling at my hair.

"You want a ride?" Lilith asked when we were done.

"Yeah, nah, I'm all good. It's a five-minute walk." I laughed.

"Walk safely." Mia got into the car.

21

Lilith studied me. "You sure? It's no problem."

"Lil, go. I'm okay," I said.

It was a cold night, so I zipped my jacket up, grateful that it wasn't raining. I waved to Mia and Lilith before heading towards my apartment. They lived together in the suburbs. I'd given up my beachfront one-bedroom a year ago, the sound of the sea too much of a reminder of the sister it had taken from me. Now, I am a city girl. It was a clear night, with an almost full moon, and the drunks were out.

I walked past an alleyway and almost gagged. It reeked of vomit. Graffiti covered the walls, and shadowed figures pressed against each other in an intimate embrace. One single street lamp lit up the woman's blue hair. She had her head thrown back, the man nuzzling her neck. A low moan echoed from the woman. He had one hand around the woman's waist, pulling her to him, the other behind her head. *Get a room.* I rolled my eyes and hurried past.

"Where ya goin?" a man in a dark hoodie approached me.

"I'm going *home,*" I said tersely, a sliver of fear raising the hairs on my arms.

"What's your hurry?" He stepped in my way.

Now my heart was pounding, fear becoming icy fingers down my spine. I loved the city, but there were creeps around, and until then, I had been lucky to not be confronted by one. I wished I had taken Lilith's offer of a ride. "I just want to go home," I said, working to keep my voice steady. "Please, let me pass."

His smirk suggested he wasn't going to move. I took a step back, ready to run.

"Quinn?" My heart skipped at the familiar voice behind me. Matteo from the bar. "Is everything okay here?" His

22

eyes glinted like steel under the street light, a hard look that he gave to the guy in the hoodie.

"Mind your business," the one in front of me said.

"Now why would I do that? Move on, *Amico*."

If I weren't so relieved at his appearance, I would have melted at his use of Italian.

"Make me," the mugger challenged.

Matteo slammed the other into a glass window with a loud crack. I hadn't even seen him move. "I told you to move on." His voice changed, touching a fear deep inside of me.

In shock, I turned around, glancing up the street I had just walked down. He'd come out of nowhere. *Was he following me?* I frowned at Matteo with thoughts of stalkers.

The would-be mugger tried to push Matteo off him, but my rescuer didn't budge.

"You'll leave her alone," Matteo's voice sent a shudder through me.

"I'll leave her alone," the hoodie guy said. Then he gasped. "What?"

I caught their reflections in the darkened window and took a step back. Something was very, very wrong. My instinct told me to run. I sucked in a breath, and Matteo looked over his shoulder. It was just a flash, but enough for me to catch. His eyes were red. I dropped my guitar case and bolted, the spike of fear gripping my throat. I loved my guitar, but at that moment, I valued my life more. My shoes pounded the footpath, and I focused on steady breathing. Adrenaline flooded through me as I fought against the urge to look over my shoulder. *Don't look, just run.* I had been an idiot, stupidly thinking the five-minute walk home wouldn't be a problem.

I made it home, yet I couldn't shake the feeling that

23

someone had followed me. I stood at the door for a moment, relieved to find no one. The guy at the concierge desk gave me a strange look as I ran past him to the lift.

Safely in my apartment, I leaned against the door, out of breath, a trickle of sweat sliding down my neck. *Did I really see that?* My teachers in school had always said I had an overactive imagination. Maybe my fear was playing tricks on me. He had stepped in to help me, after all.

I hung up my jacket, kicked off my shoes, and swapped my silver hoop earrings for smaller studs. Once done, I pulled on my dressing gown and grabbed a notebook before opening the door to my balcony, looking over the city. Taking a seat, with the light over my shoulder, I started to write in my notebook. Despite what I thought I had seen, I couldn't stop thinking about the dark eyes on mine in the bar. I wished I could draw, and I kept seeing his lips, curved into a smile, his jawline, and the way his hand had grasped mine.

I could no longer focus, so I put down my pen. I sighed and read over what I had written. Lovey crap about Matteo.

"Ugh, you've got it bad," I groaned, but could feel a new song coming. It had been a long time since I'd felt that creativity.

I spent the next hour writing lines that came to me, crossing some out as I re-wrote them differently.

I flicked through the pages, reading and humming, already knowing the tune. There was a lower tone to it, and I couldn't help but wonder what Mia and Lilith would add to it. It would need work before I could call it a song, but it was a good start. I hadn't written a song in at least twelve months. 'Dark Eyes of a Stranger' seemed like a good title, so I wrote it at the top and underlined it before standing. I dropped the notebook on the chair and leaned against the railing.

I hugged myself in the cold. I'd been so engrossed in writing that I hadn't felt anything. I took in the sight of the city. Dark clouds had moved in, and the city lights shone, my favourite view. Twenty storeys below, people went about their night.

"Wherever you are, Matteo, thank you," I murmured. "Sorry you had to rescue someone as hysterical as me." I couldn't help but feel disappointed at the thought of not seeing him again. Lilith had been right, he was hot. It had been months since I'd even looked at another man after the mess of my last relationship.

The idea that I had seen red eyes just seemed ridiculous in the light of my apartment. I wasn't usually one to panic like that. Now I'd need to buy a new guitar. *Idiot*.

My phone rang, startling me. I stared at the screen. Mia.

"What's wrong?" I answered, moving inside. She would never call this late.

"I was just making sure you were okay." Voices in the background sounded like she was watching TV.

"Uh, why wouldn't I be?" Apart from the fact that I hallucinated red eyes on a man trying to help me. But she didn't need to know that.

"Two people were attacked down Little Lonsdale St tonight, and you walk that way to get home."

"An attack?" I grabbed my remote. "I didn't hear anything."

"It's all over the news," she said.

I turned on the TV. A cordoned-off alleyway came up on the screen. "I was just there," I murmured. I wondered if the police had found my guitar.

"Quinn, next week we're taking you home. I know it's only

25

five minutes up the road, but the city isn't safe anymore," Lilith's voice through the phone was tinged with worry. "This was a vicious attack; you need to be careful."

A picture of a woman's face appeared on the screen, and I frowned. The alley had been dark, but the blue hair was unmistakable. "It's her!" I gasped as the reporter said the name 'Leah Jackson.'

"Her who?" Mia asked through the phone.

"I saw her and a guy when I walked past."

"You saw a guy?" Lilith asked. "What was he doing?"

"Maybe the guy is the other body they found," Mia said.

Lilith's voice came through the phone, but faint. "Who's she talking to at this time of night?" I asked.

"Her family. They've been calling for the last hour. Non-stop," Mia said.

A second picture took up the screen then. "The second victim was found nearby. Both appear to have fatal and gruesome wounds to the throat. Suspected animal attack. He's been identified as Grant Cooke."

The phone slipped from my fingers. The man who would have attacked me had it not been for Matteo. I stared at the screen in shock, the muffled voice of Mia calling me through my phone. Heart pounding, I bent down to pick it up with a shaking hand.

"Quinn?" her voice rose in panic.

I swapped the phone to my other ear. "I'm here."

"What happened?" she asked

I tried to calm down. "That man, I saw him tonight."

"With the woman, yeah you said," Mia reminded me.

"No, I don't think he was the one in the alley. He…" *Do I tell her?* "He tried to mug me, or…" I trailed off. "What kind of animal would attack them in the middle of the city?"

"Wait, he tried to mug you?" There was her panic again.

I hesitated. "Yes."

"What happened?" she pressed. "I *knew* we should have dropped you off at home!"

"The guy from the bar, Matteo showed up," I explained.

The silence through the phone was deafening.

"He showed up? And?" Mia's voice rang with barely contained excitement. "I want all the details!"

"What? No!" I laughed. "Nothing happened."

"You mean he didn't save you from being mugged or worse to get invited back to your place? Is he still there?"

My face heated and I was glad Mia couldn't see me. "No and no."

"Quinn, straight single women everywhere are swooning over what you have just walked away from." Mia laughed.

"That doesn't make any sense!" I said.

"It does to her," Lilith said, returning to the conversation. "What did I miss?"

"Matteo showed up to rescue her from a mugger," Mia said. "So what happened?"

"Nothing." I rolled my eyes.

"Did he at least walk you home?" Lilith sounded distracted, which meant she and Mia were more focused on each other.

"No."

The sounds of kissing came through the line.

"Mia, Lil, I'm still here. How about you let me go, so you can get back to each other," I said with a smile.

Lilith hummed in agreement. "Laters!"

"Wait! Are we meeting up tomorrow?" Mia asked.

"Yeah, I'll text you. Bye." I hung up.

I watched the news, irritated. I had left my guitar, and it wouldn't be long before the cops came knocking on my door. My business card was taped to the inside, so it wouldn't take them long. The reporter named the victims and spoke about an anonymous source of the Police Department saying that the woman had bite marks on her throat, wrist, and inner thigh, but the man's throat had been torn out, only to be on the ground next to him. They had no leads and were calling for witnesses to come forward.

My hands shook as I changed the channel. I needed to distract myself. Thoughts of Matteo kept creeping in. Regret and embarrassment over the way I'd run from a man who'd only stepped in to help me. Cross-legged, I flicked through for a movie that might distract me.

I settled on a musical. I sang along as I watched it, feeling a bit more at ease. Music in any form always calmed me.

'*Quinn,*' a voice whispered inside my head. '*Come to me.*'

Chapter 5

Matteo

As I fed, I kept picturing a red-haired, green-eyed singer. Her lips were inviting, the black lipstick something women seemed to like in this time, with large silver hoop earrings. She'd had a slight scattering of freckles across her face. Her green shirt showed the curve of her breasts, and black jeans hugged her hips. I'd memorised everything about her and longed to taste her.

The blue-haired woman currently pressed against me was drunk on the effects of my venom. I moved from her throat, lifting her skirt. Dropping to my knees, I bit into her inner thigh. She trembled, a loud moan filling the alley around us, the scent of her arousal overpowering. I closed my eyes, biting back my own growl, the taste of her blood divine. Laced with alcohol, the sweet flavour of her desire only made my own lust soar. She smelled of jasmine and wine. I was already hard, and the urge to take her body right there against the wall surged. I stood, wrapping my arms around her.

"Do you want more?" I whispered, pressing myself against her so she could feel what I meant. Careful to not pull her under my sway, I lifted her chin to look at me. This had to be her decision. I may be what humans would call a monster, but I wasn't *that* kind of a monster.

"More," she whispered, throwing her head back and dropping one hand to lift her skirt.

She was inviting me to bite her again, and to have her. I lowered my mouth to her throat and withdrew before fangs entered flesh. A delicious scent pulled at me. One that called to the feral beast in me to hunt. *Fear.* I turned my head towards the entrance of the alley, a low growl rumbling from me.

"Don't stop," she pleaded.

Her eyes met mine again, and she was unable to look away as I *did* pull her into my power this time, to compel her.

"Forget me. Sleep." My voice was soft, and she gave in to my command, slumping in my arms.

I lowered her to the ground. Anyone who came across her would think she was drunk. My fang marks would heal soon enough.

Tempted by the tantalising scent of fear, I paused at the end of the alley ready to attack. The strong odour of urine right next to me and a dark patch on the ground irritated me. *Yet somehow, I'm the feral.* I moved away from it. Nearby,

30

someone had vomited, the sick smell worse than the urine.

A man advanced on a woman, his intention clear in his face; enough to bring another growl from me. I recognised the woman as the singer from earlier, her enchanting voice echoing in my mind. Two natures battled in me. One that reacted to fear, bringing out the urge to give chase. The other; a protectiveness I had never known other than with my clan. Not with humans.

Forcing down the rising growl, I stepped in to help. Quinn had intrigued me from our first meeting, not just her voice but everything about her drawing me in. Normally, I was the one who drew human women in, but she'd been irresistible, and already I wanted her in my arms, head back, throat exposed, inviting me to drink. Now, she stared at me wide-eyed, and I knew her attacker would not live to see the sun rise.

What I hadn't counted on was for her to see my eyes as anger and protectiveness swept through me. She fled, leaving behind her instrument. I let her go, keeping my grip on her attacker to stop from going after her. I dragged him into the alley, and a knife came out of nowhere. I let out a hiss of pain as his blade punched into my gut. Bleeding, fury rose up and I bit into his throat to feed as I healed. His blood wasn't anywhere as sweet as the woman I'd fed from who lay unconscious nearby, wrapped in a pleasure dream.

My bite didn't give him the same effect it had given that woman. I made sure of that. He screamed in agony. Yet he refused to give up, the human nature to fight for life strong as he stabbed me again and again. Everything became a red haze, and I tore out his throat. His knife clattered to the ground, and his body an instant after. I spat his throat at him.

"Merda!" I lifted my tee-shirt, dark blood seeping from four wounds, which closed quickly. But my tee-shirt was ruined. Hunger turned to bloodlust as I returned to the blue-haired woman, lifting her with my hand around her neck, pressing her against the wall. "Sorry, " I murmured. "But I need more." Her eyes opened a slit, a smile on her face. "Dream of me."

Her eyes closed again. I struck fast, biting into the untouched side of her throat. Despite being unconscious, she moaned. Each swallow of her blood took me closer to bliss. I detached from her throat with difficulty, licking her from my lips and letting her go.

The mugger had bled out on the ground, his clothes soaked in blood, the tang of it making my mouth water.

"You stink," I muttered, kicking his body as I stepped past him. Both his bladder and bowels had emptied upon his death. "It's only fitting that you die on the ground the same way you would have left her." I returned to the street.

Unable to resist, I picked up Quinn's case and slowly followed her scent to an apartment building not far away. I stood in an alley at the foot of the building, separating her heartbeat from those of the rest of the humans around her. I could smell her out on the balcony, and I listened to the scratching of pen on paper, as well as a low hum that seemed to resonate deep within me. My hunger for her washed over me, blazing.

"Wherever you are, Matteo, thank you." Her voice drew my smile. "Sorry you had to rescue someone as hysterical as me." She was questioning what she'd seen, as they often did.

When the door slid shut, I leapt into the air, between

balconies until I found hers. In the darkest corner of her balcony, I watched her as she watched the news, talking to her friends. Their voices were those of the other women I'd seen her with at the bar. As she stared at the screen, I caught sight of the woman I'd fed from. *Dead.* I frowned, sure I'd left her alive. *How can she be dead? Did I lose control again?* Perhaps I'd needed more blood than I thought. I regretted ripping out the mugger's throat. I should have fed from him and made him suffer.

The next photo on the screen was that of the mugger. Quinn's heart pounded, and the delicious spike of fear made my canines ache.

"Yes, I killed him for what he was about to do to you," I whispered.

I closed my eyes for a moment, listening to her heartbeat, taking in her scent. She'd sat out here, on the chair next to me. She started to watch a movie, singing along. Her voice once again drew me in. I wanted to speak with her. I whispered to her, luring her out to me, coaxing away any fear. She moved as if in a dream and would probably think this to be one later. At the glass, she stared at me.

"What are you doing?" she asked. "How did you get out there?"

"Open the door." I knew the effect my voice would have on her, and she would do as I asked. As soon as the door opened, I lifted my hand, inviting her to take it. She didn't fight me as I pulled her body to mine.

"How are you on my balcony?" she frowned. "We're twenty storeys up."

While she didn't resist my control, she still had enough awareness to question me.

My fingers brushed her throat, and I wished to press my lips against the softness of her neck. To sink my fangs in, to mark her. "You're safe," I told her. "You have no reason to fear me."

She was deep under my sway. "I'm not afraid."

I wanted to kiss her. The yearning to do so was so strong I could almost taste her lips. I longed to devour her, to taste her blood. I'd seen her before, two months ago. We'd passed each other in the street, and I'd never given it another thought until I saw her on the stage tonight. I released her from my compulsion and stepped back.

She gazed up at me.

"Please let me kiss you," I murmured. "Even if it's only once, I will have tasted you, and I'll leave you in peace."

It was more than her lips I wanted. The desire to claim her as mine took me by surprise. I'd *never* claimed a human before, and it would only end one way for her. I didn't hate what I was; in fact, I took great pleasure in being a vampire. The feralness in me was a nature most vampires didn't have, my lack of control my only struggle. I'd been turned unwillingly; I wouldn't do that to her. Why would I want to claim someone I'd only just met?

"One kiss?" she asked.

"One kiss." I lifted her chin. "Then you'll never see me again." This human woman confused me. I'd already killed for her, and I would do so again. I couldn't blame my inner beast, either; this was all me.

She turned her face away from me, towards the city. I could appreciate that my presence on her balcony would be confusing.

A shiver passed through her, and I reached out, rubbing

34

her arms. "You're cold."

"No shit," she laughed. "It's winter."

She frowned at my bare arms. I saw no need to wear jackets; the cold didn't affect me as it did humans. Perhaps I should, so I didn't draw attention.

"One kiss," she made up her mind. "Then you should go."

I pulled her to me, and I softly caressed her cheek with my fingers. Her lips parted, and I leaned in. There was nothing gentle, our kiss ferocious and full of a deep yearning. From her as well as from me. She let in my tongue and pressed herself hard against me, her hands on both sides of my face.

The beat of her heart pounded against my chest. I didn't expect my own heart to race, nor the familiarity of having her in my arms. I wanted everything about her. Not just her lips, but her body, her blood. Her. The feral in me awoke. My hunger for her surged, and I dropped my mouth, running my tongue over her throat, fangs lengthening, ready to bite into her. I shuddered as I fought against the rising red haze. She moaned, just as she would with my fangs in her.

Claim her. Turn her.

"Go inside," I compelled her before I gave in to my desires. "Go to sleep. This was nothing but a dream."

She didn't resist, simply returned to her apartment, a smile on her face. This woman had as much sway over me as I had over her. I closed the door behind her as she sat down on the chair, her head back. The musical continued to play, but she fell into a deep sleep.

The guitar case at my feet would be a surprise when she awoke. I caught sight of a notebook and pen on the chair. She'd written words of her desire, and my name. The words 'Dark Eyes of a Stranger' were scrawled across the top. My smile widened as I glanced back at her asleep inside.

"Are you writing about me, little *cantante*?" I murmured to myself.

Her scrawled handwriting revealed her innermost thoughts: She wanted me as much as I yearned for her. I closed the notebook into her guitar case and pushed it up against the glass. Rain was a common occurrence in this city, so this would keep them dry at least. I gazed back one more time at her sleeping form before dropping from the balcony.

I landed below, absorbing the impact that would have killed a human. No one saw or heard my drop from above. I glanced up once more before walking away, listening to the city around me, the presence of drunk humans hard to ignore. Cities were hard to live in these days with the amount of smog and noise. I didn't know how humans did it. Not one single member of my clan lived in the city, with good reason.

A steady rain started, hissing as it hit the ground, soaking me in seconds. People ran to get out of the rain, laughing, their footsteps hurried. Someone dared push past me, and I fought the urge to growl. He had stale beer on his breath, the wool of his jacket brushing my arm. This was usually a feeding ground for me, but I'd already had my fill, and my hunger for a red-haired seductress called to me over all else. I needed to leave the city, to return to my home by the sea before I found myself back on her balcony.

Chapter 6

Quinn

I woke up with the sun inching around my blinds and groaned. I'd awoken in the early hours in the morning in my chair after strange dreams about Matteo. I could almost taste his lips, a searing kiss that lit a blaze deep within me. To be thinking this hard about a guy, to be desiring him this much left me feeling unsettled.

Never one to rise early, this day was no exception. My bed was warm and inviting. I pulled my blankets over my head, not ready to get up. But my thoughts turned to the dark eyes, and the fiery kiss again, and I kicked the covers back. Staying in bed wasn't helping. I left behind the comfort and changed into gym clothes. *Maybe running will get my mind off such things.*

As I entered the lounge, I froze. A dark shape sat on my balcony, against the door. My heart skipped. I opened the door, staring at my guitar case in confusion. I'd left it and had run, and I was on the twentieth floor.

"This makes no sense," I muttered.

I opened the case to make sure that my guitar wasn't damaged. My notebook was tucked inside. Unsure how it had ended up there, I pulled it inside, shoving aside confusion and worry. I headed down to the gym, ready to push myself. I couldn't stop thinking about Matteo. The dream kiss, and what I thought I'd seen last night.

The gym was quiet, a couple of guys using the weights, their voices low as they spoke to each other. Music came from someone's phone speaker. I found Dan about to step onto the treadmill, and I smiled when he saw me.

"Quinn, I had almost given up hope of you showing up," Dan said.

"Never." I grinned at him. "I'm going to speed it up a little today, do you think you can keep up?"

His eyes glinted and he started his treadmill. "Is that a challenge?"

Dan was attractive with a lean body, brown eyes, sandy blonde hair, and a goatee. His grin was always one of mischief, and he worked in the sun, as evident in his tan. There was an attraction between us, and I wondered if I should just have some no-strings-attached fun. I wasn't ready for a relationship but wouldn't mind having sex. I'd only known him for a year and thought it likely I'd give in sooner or later. He seemed to have the same expectation.

I took the treadmill next to Dan's. As my feet pounded on the belt, I started to relax. My focus switched to running and breathing. We faced a window that looked out over the city.

I would have practise with the girls later and started to look forward to it. I longed for the day I would find myself on the stage of a bigger venue, with thousands cheering my name. It was likely an unrealistic dream, but one I would always have. Perhaps one day I'd travel beyond Australia. Despite that, life was comfortable, and I was content.

We ran for half an hour, side by side, and I felt I could have gone longer, but I stopped anyway. I wiped my face with the towel I'd brought with me.

"Someone needs a shower," Dan joked.

"And breakfast," I commented.

My words only made his eyes light up. "I cook a mean breakfast," he offered.

I only smiled as we got into the lift, even when he stood too close. I knew he'd never force himself on me. Unlike…

I froze. The man who had wanted to last night. I still didn't know if he wanted to rob me or rape me, but either way, it could have been me in that alley. I had been lucky.

"You all good?" Dan asked.

I forced a smile. "Yeah, sweet as. I'll see you in a couple of days."

"Too easy!" He got out on the eighteenth floor, and I returned to my apartment on the twentieth to have a shower.

As I towelled off, I turned music on. Once dressed, I danced and sang as I pulled eggs from the fridge. The run had given me the energy I needed, and I was ready to face whatever the day threw at me. I wanted to start the day with a large breakfast.

I arrived at Lilith and Mia's place just before ten.

"We're going out for coffee first," Mia told me when she greeted me at the door. "Lil hasn't had one yet, and you know what she's like."

Lilith would only drink cafe coffee and was not approachable before she'd had her first cup. She always insisted how much instant coffee was an insult to coffee, so we just went with it.

"How have you not managed to get coffee into her yet?" I laughed.

"It was a late night, and she's only just got out of bed." Mia's grin suggested the reason for the late night. I burst out laughing.

"Uh huh. Okay, then let's go. I want to go to that place we went to last time; they had a really good 'Death by Chocolate.'"

"Isn't it a bit early for a sweet tooth?" Lilith asked, walking into the room.

She didn't smile, and likely wouldn't until she had her

coffee.

"It's ten," I told her with a shrug. "You have your vices, I have mine."

"Doesn't it undo the run you had this morning?" Mia's eyes lit up. "Oh! How was *Daaan*?" She winked. "Or is it all about Matteo now?"

I had spent most of the morning trying not to think about Matteo. I knew my face was pink as my cheeks heated.

"Come on." I urged. "Put your boots on and let's go."

"She doesn't want to talk about Matteo," Mia said to Lilith and turned back to me. "Did something happen?"

I opened my mouth and frowned. "I dreamed about him."

Mia led us outside, and I pulled on my sunnies. "Tell me all about your dream," she insisted, delighted as we walked to the coffee shop.

I shrugged, trying to play it down. "He was on my balcony and called me out to him. There was kissing and…" I stopped, aroused by the dream again. The feel of his tongue as he licked my throat as if tasting me. I suppressed a shiver.

"You've gone red again," Mia laughed. "And I know that look: You're hot for him, aren't you? From a dream! Quinn!"

"Can we talk about something else?" I asked. "I'm not ready for that."

"She's only just returned to music. Maybe we should lay off with pushing her onto men," Lilith muttered.

Mia lost her smile. "Sorry Quinn, I didn't mean to."

I nodded. "It's okay. You're okay. I doubt I'll ever see him again anyway. It was a one-off meeting. He looks like a bad boy type, so he's probably already off with some woman, completely unaware that I'm having dreams of him."

The idea of him with someone hurt, and I didn't understand my growing obsession. *Forget him.* Instead I turned my focus on the streets around us. People hurried by, going about their Saturday morning. I let myself soak up the sunshine. As we entered the cafe, a man walked out and smiled at me.

Mia nudged me. "Ten bucks says he'll check out your ass," she murmured.

I glanced over my shoulder, and sure enough he was doing so. He caught me looking and smiled again, without shame.

"I'm not giving you my money," I told her.

"You draw their attention no matter where we go. Especially when you sing," she said, and I knew she was talking about Matteo.

We sat at our usual table and hung our jackets on the back of the chairs. Mia ordered for us. Caramel macchiato for me, long black for Lilith and a jasmine tea for herself.

"I thought we were going out for coffee," I said.

"I'm trying to lay off the coffee." She shrugged. "It makes me jittery."

Lilith's moody silence remained as Mia talked for the both of them.

"There's a new art gallery opening up near your place next week," she mentioned. "We should go."

I raised my eyebrow. "You're kidding, right? You hate art."

Her laughter was infectious. "You think I go for the art? Hello, have you met me? It's all about the free food and alcohol."

"Nothing about checking out the artists?" I asked.

"Actually, Lil read an article about the owner. He really seems genuine in wanting to help unknown artists. But no one has seen him, nor what he looks like. No one even knows his name."

"You want to go to an opening to check out some guy who helps artists?" I frowned. "How long before you get bored?"

Our drinks arrived and Lilith took a sip, sighing in relief. "I'll give her an hour. I wouldn't mind seeing the opening, though."

I'd taken a course in art while studying music at uni, so the idea had appeal.

"I'm keen as!" I agreed and flinched. I'd picked up my dad's use of phrases.

An elderly couple walked past, glaring at Lilith's tattoos. Lilith's arms were covered. A small crossbow on her wrist, with music notes and lyrics twisted around her arm from our first song that we'd recorded together. Above that, an armband of roses intertwined with thorns. The other arm had the first lines of the Iliad on her forearm, a roman helmet on her shoulder and movie characters, around her arm, above her elbow.

I was glad they couldn't see mine.

I breathed in the strong coffee smell, savouring the sweet notes of caramel and let out a deep sigh. Lilith rolled her eyes but stuck her nose in her coffee cup. Next, my food arrived. Chocolate cake heated and covered in chocolate sauce with a dollop of ice cream.

"My teeth hurt just looking at that," Lilith commented.

"Just as well you're not eating it, then." I bit into the cake, almost moaning at the rich chocolate flavour. "Oh, chocolatey goodness."

Lilith scoffed. "I think our album will be ready next week."

Mia grinned. "So I was thinking, we should start filming a new music video." She held up her phone. "We're getting some serious views on the last one we did. Last night at The Underground showed that people are interested. We need to give them more."

"As long as we avoid the beach, though," I said. "Maybe we can film in the city this time."

Lilith nodded, understanding my reason.

Lilith grabbed the phone from Mia. "Woah, a hundred thousand views?" her voice rose. I couldn't blame her; we'd never had that many views on anything before.

"Not only that, but I also uploaded the video from the sound booth of Quinn singing…" Mia grabbed her phone back and pulled up the new video. "Ten thousand views. I think we should do more behind-the-scenes videos and pics. Views have increased since your return."

"You should put social media personality extraordinaire under your name on the business card." I laughed. "Okay, how about a photo of us with our coffee. It can be a 'before practice' promo."

"Perfect." Mia opened her camera, and we shifted around the table. "Say roses and thorns."

Chapter 7

Matteo

I had been summoned to Gabriela's den. She was the Queen of our clan, and it was her responsibility to remind me of the accords. This was not unexpected after I'd killed two people. She had not caged me yet, but she still punished me every time I lost control. After all this time, I still didn't know her reason for taking me in, when she could have left me where she found me. As I approached the house that she resided in, I recalled the first time I'd seen her.

I was feral, lost in the haze of bloodlust and hunger, after having killed the one who turned me. I hunted with an appetite fuelled by rage and confusion. I had torn through my wife and told my daughter to run, then proceeded to cause great terror in Venice. A shadow in the dark, snatching people off the street to satisfy my hunger. Their screams as much a joy as the hunt and the kill. I hid in my villa during the day, stalking the city at night.

Buried deep under my feeding frenzy, I was vaguely aware that the human's screams had become whimpers as she cried in pain and fear. At the sound of a footstep, I moved to protect my meal, hissing in warning, blood dripping down my chin. A black-haired woman stood over me, watching me with curiosity, but showed no fear. She didn't smell human.

"So, you're the vampire of Venice I've heard about. Aren't you a wild little monster?" she asked, flashing red eyes at me. "I'm not here to take your meal. Perhaps you'd share it, though." She lowered herself to my level, fangs bared.

"You're like me," I said, the words strange in my mouth. I couldn't remember the last time I'd spoken out loud.

"You're surprised by this?" she asked, moving towards me.

"I've only seen one other. I killed her after she turned me into this." I didn't even know what I was.

Her eyes widened in surprise "You killed your maker? That's not something I've heard of before. The blood bond is usually too strong for a newly turned to raise a hand against them." She tilted her head, studying me. "Quite a hungry little vampire, aren't you? Ruthless."

"Vampire," I echoed, "Is that what we are?"

She started laughing. "You didn't know you were a vampire? Did your maker not teach you anything before you killed her?"

Angered by her laughter, I growled. "Who are you?" I demanded "Why are you here?"

"I've come to help you. Word of your existence has spread. The humans have summoned hunters, so your presence here is well

worn out," she said. Her eyes lowered to the human below me. "Share it with me; then we can leave."

"I don't share," I told her. "Find your own."

Her delight rang out as she laughed. "What's your name, little feral?"

I hadn't spoken my name in the three years I'd been turned. "Matteo."

"I am Gabriela." She moved fast then, closing the space between us. "Give me a taste," she murmured, and licked blood from my chin. I froze, baffled by her action. It filled me with pleasure, and I growled from deep in my chest, a sound of satisfaction.

"Oh, I think he likes that." She followed me as I tried to back away from her, until I realised she'd claimed my meal, her body over it. Before I could do anything, she dropped her mouth to the human's throat. A moan escaped from the person I'd been feeding on, one of pleasure, not pain.

"How did you do that?" I asked.

She looked up at me, blood dripping from her mouth. "You have a lot to learn about what we can do. Your maker should have been the one to teach you. What you've become in absence of such guidance, you are quite an animal. Surviving and nothing else. Come with me, and I will show you how to enjoy the hunt, and how to make them enjoy it."

"I'm not going anywhere." I insisted. "Get away from my meal."

"Share her with me," Gabriela repeated. "Join my clan. You might find you like being around others of your kind."

I was intrigued, and my hunger got the best of me. As she fed, I bit into the other side of the human's throat. Gabriela's hand stroked the back of my head, and again, the sensation of satisfaction flooded through me. I'd never fed with anyone before, and I had to admit it was pleasing.

47

A hand touched my shoulder, pulling me back from my memory. I turned to find piercing blue eyes, full of concern. He was slightly shorter than me, and leaner. His curly brown hair was messy, windblown. "Carlos, I'm glad you're here." Relief washed over me. Whatever Gabriela was going to serve out, at least there was someone in my corner.

"The whole clan's here," he said. Despite being fluent in Italian, Carlos was Spanish, but never spoke of his life as a human. He'd once told me he didn't miss being human, and that looking at his life was pointless.

"You're her second; how bad does it look?" I wondered if this would be the time she caged me.

A human walked past us, from Gabriela's den. He bore the twin puncture marks of fangs, his eyes glazed over, a smile on his face.

Carlos watched him. "Matteo, you didn't..." he winced, growling. "It wasn't..." He let out a sigh.

I frowned. "What?"

"Nothing." His eyes avoided mine. I sensed unease and remorse through our blood bond. He wasn't one to feel guilt often, so my own concern grew.

I stopped, grabbing him. "Carlos, what are you trying to say?"

He shook his head. "Nothing. Let's just get this over with, I have three lovely human women waiting for me at home, and Celeste isn't happy that we got disturbed."

Three human women who were probably chained up for him and Celeste to feed on while they had sex.

I grinned. "Your house is no doubt filled with the delicious scent of fear right now."

Laughter boomed from him. "I do enjoy the spice of fear,

48

but I released them from their terror while they await my return. I can't have their hearts give out in my absence."

I paused before we opened the door. "I don't remember killing the woman," I admitted. "The man, yes, I tore out his throat after he stabbed me. After what he was about to do to Quinn, he deserved worse. But the woman, I must have needed more than I thought."

Carlos froze, his hand on the door handle. "Who's Quinn?"

I groaned inwardly at the slip of her name. "It's not important."

His eyes turned red. "Have you found us a human to play with?" His smile widened. "It's been a few years since we did that. Although I must admit the last one broke a little too quickly for my liking."

A low growl rose from me.

He raised an eyebrow. "You're possessive over a human? That isn't like you at all. When did this occur?"

Our conversation was interrupted by the tug from Gabriela, her impatience clear.

"We'll talk about this after," Carlos told me. "I'd like to meet the human that elicits that response. Especially knowing that you killed for her."

I followed him into the house. Thirty vampires awaited. My clan turned to face us, ceasing their conversations as we entered. A few surrounded me, showing their support. I hated that I lacked the control they were all capable of.

'It's not your fault,' Carlos spoke through the blood bond that Gabriela had once forced on us. It had been something she'd done in an attempt to stabilise my feral nature, giving Carlos a maker-like bond with me. If not for that, I may have fallen deeper into the feral madness.

'*In a way, it is,*' I responded. '*I killed my maker. If not for that, I'd be like the rest of you.*'

'*It's also likely you would not have joined our clan,*' It hurt him at the thought as much as it hurt me. While we had hated each other to start with, and tried to kill each other many times, we soon developed a friendship closer than any in the clan.

"Matteo Barone, you know why you're here." Gabriela's tone demanded our attention.

'*Whatever you do, do not tell her you killed for a human.*' Carlos instructed me silently.

"I know why I'm here." I confirmed.

"Do you have any defence for your actions?" she demanded.

"I lost my temper with the human male," I admitted. "He stabbed me. I killed him willingly."

She glared at me, her anger heavy in the room. "What of the female?"

Carlos stepped in. "Matteo has admitted to me that he doesn't remember killing her. It is likely it wasn't him."

His own anger struck against me through our bond as he stared down Gabriela and she growled in warning. Lorenzo glanced across at me with a frown. I shrugged. Carlos backed down, submitting to her with a bow of his head.

"Well, seeing as he is aware of the first body left in that same location, I think it's safe to assume the woman was his too." Gabriela met the gaze of everyone in the clan. "Does anyone disagree?"

No one spoke.

"I want nothing more than to cage you. Each time you lose control, I feel The Bloodking's anger. We made the accords with the first hunters, and their descendants have the right to claim your life. Your latest slip-up has gained the attention of hunters; many have seen them in the streets, seeking our presence. It makes our own hunting difficult." She glared across at Carlos. "My second however, has informed me that your absence now would raise concern in the human community. You have established yourself as an artist and intend to open an art gallery next week. Is that correct?"

"It is, my Queen," I muttered. "To not attend the grand opening would—"

"Kneel," she commanded.

I fell to my knees, succumbing to her power; one only Kings and Queens had over their clan.

"I sentence you to three days of starvation," she declared.

My heart skipped. "Starvation?" Starvation was the most painful punishment she could give me. Three days with no blood. I sought out Carlos, but he had nothing to offer for help.

"You're lucky I don't defang you." She approached me, and vampires moved out of her way.

She smiled down at me, hunger in her eyes. I knew what was coming next and braced myself. The small smile she gave me was enough for me to know she would enjoy this. Her fangs were in my throat. Venom spread through me, stronger than that of normal vampires. My eyes rolled back, and I strained to hold back the moan. Already hard, my fangs lengthened, and despite my best efforts, I groaned. Hands pressed against my back, my clan holding me up.

Flesh tore as she jerked her head. Pain flared through me, and I let out a scream. She released me and moved away, a low chuckle rumbling from her.

51

"Was that necessary?" Carlos asked in a hard tone.

"Are you questioning me?" she demanded.

Blind with pain, I could only listen, my body spasming. Hands pressed against the gaping wound in my throat, vampires whispering to comfort me. My screams became whimpers.

"You never used to be this cruel," Carlos's voice softened. "To take joy from the pain of another vampire, that's not who we are. Gabriela—"

"Silence!" her voice boomed across the room. Carlos swore under his breath. "For that, you will be the one to watch over him. You'll be with him to ensure he doesn't feed. Then, to help him maintain control, he will not feed without you present." She let out a sound of disgust. "Get him out of here so I don't have to listen to that."

Chapter 8

Quinn

I walked towards the camera, singing. People around us stopped to watch, their chatter distracting me. Lights were set up under cover, and I was dressed in a winter jacket, the wool of a scarf warm against my skin. Gavin had a camera on a tripod, and his assistant held a portable fan to my face.

"Ok, try again, but don't flinch with the fan," he instructed.

I gritted my teeth together. "It's winter, Gavin. She's been blowing cold air onto my face for the last hour. It's hard not to flinch."

"Is it needed?" Lilith asked. "You want her to smile, then give her something to smile at." She glanced at the growing crowd. "You!" She pointed at a guy. "Have you ever wanted to be in a music video?"

He blinked. "Uhh…sure."

"Great!" She grabbed his arm and pulled him next to Gavin and the camera. "Walk towards Quinn. You don't have to do anything else. Just walk." She turned to me. "When he's walked past, glance over your shoulder once, and smile as you continue walking."

We did another take, and I did as Lilith asked. She and Gavin looked at the footage.

"I love when she gets all bossy," Mia murmured, and laughter burst from me.

A couple of drops hit my cheek. "Uh-oh," I held out my hand, glancing up. "There's the rain."

The rain had held off for the morning but didn't look like it would much longer.

"Umbrellas!" Gavin called out, and someone shoved an umbrella into my hand. I held it above my head as more drops fell from the sky.

He and Lilith talked in low voices. "Ok, next shot!" she shouted.

My guitar was brought to me.

"Um, Lil, how am I supposed to play the guitar while holding an umbrella?" I asked.

"You're not," Gavin said.

"Nope. Hell no!" I pointed to the person holding my case. "I am not playing this in the rain. Bring me that." I glared at Gavin. "You're a sound tech, you should know better."

With my guitar safely away I sighed. We'd been at this all morning, and I was getting tired. "Maybe we can stop for food?" I directed my question at Lilith. "I'm a little hungry."

"Agreed. I could do with some coffee," Lilith said.

The sky opened up, and rain bucketed down, drumming against my umbrella. Gavin's assistant held an umbrella over him.

"Maybe we should do some filming in the studio." Mia suggested, standing with me. "I don't think anyone wants to work in this. We've only gotten half of the shots we have planned.

"Let's finish this off tomorrow," Lilith suggested to Gavin. "It's too cold to be filming in the rain."

"Okay, let's pack it up!" Gavin instructed everyone around us.

"Um, do you need me tomorrow, too?" the guy Lilith had pulled into the video asked.

"Nah, you're all good." Lilith said. "Can you talk to Yvonne over there, though? We'll need you to sign a couple of forms."

He followed the direction she was pointing. Thunder rumbled overhead. Lilith joined Mia and me under my umbrella.

"That's the shot!" Gavin said and lifted the camera to us. A photographer took photos for Mia to add to our social media.

"I thought we were finished for the day," I muttered.

"Humour me," Gavin grinned. "This is a good shot. Sing your chorus."

"Do you want us splashing in puddles and singing at the top of our voices, too?" Mia asked.

"Oh! Or tap dancing!" I chimed in.

Despite her role in directing us for the day and trying to be serious, Lilith gave us a wide grin. She left the cover of my umbrella and threw her arms open wide, spinning around.

"Oh my god, Lil!" Mia laughed.

"Fuck it!" I handed the umbrella to Mia and stepped into the rain. It was freezing and drenched me in seconds. I danced, grabbing Lilith. We laughed as we spun around. Mia joined in, the umbrella discarded on the ground.

Gavin recorded us, and more photos were taken. Most of the onlookers dispersed. Joy bubbled up from deep inside me. Those who remained were taking photos. My hair was plastered to my head, my clothes stuck to me, but I was overcome with jubilation. I'd spent months hiding in my apartment, and in that moment everything in my world fit.

"Okay, you girls should probably get some dry clothes," Gavin recommended. "We can't have you sick for the shoot tomorrow."

The crew finished packing up. My apartment was nearby, so I led Lilith and Mia back home. We walked into the building and got strange looks from other tenants.

"I'll come back with a towel," I promised the concierge.

"Don't worry about it, Quinn; I'll get a mop. Did you get caught in this?" the concierge replied.

Mia laughed. "Nah, we danced in it."

Back in my apartment, I threw towels at them.

"I'm going to have first shower. Please don't sit on my furniture. I won't be long."

I showered quickly and let them clean up. Switching the TV on, I sat down when the news came on.

"Breaking news. Another body has been found. This one a woman in her twenties, in her own car in Brighton. Her body drained of blood."

Lilith walked from the bathroom, dressed in dry clothes, her eyes on the TV, her expression unreadable.

"What is wrong with people?" I muttered. "Some sicko's been watching too many movies."

"There are definitely monsters this world could do without," she agreed.

Chapter 9

Matteo

"Matteo," Carlos's voice reached me from far away. "You only have another day to go. You have the worst of it to go. I'm here."

Two days. Two days of no blood, and it was taking all my strength to remain myself. To not fall into the red haze. I'd already attacked Carlos numerous times in an effort to escape. I lay on my back with him sitting next to me, leaning against the wall. Chains rattled as I dropped my arm over my eyes. I could smell the blood from his recent meal.

"Can you brush your teeth or something, so I don't have to smell that?" I grumbled.

He chuckled. "Tell me about your human," he requested.

"You killed for her, you endure this because of her, so I want to know more."

Her face appeared before me, a hallucination. Her eyes that lit up as she sang, her voice that had pulled me in. I sighed. "She's not my human."

"But you *want* her to be, don't you? I want to meet her," he said in a low voice.

I growled. Carlos's hand pressed down onto my forehead. "Worry not, Matteo. I will not fight you for a human. Talk about her to get your mind off your hunger. How did you come across her?"

I smiled then. "She was singing, and her voice pulled me from mid-hunt. Human or vampire, I've never seen, nor heard, a creature so beautiful."

Carlos took a while to respond. "She must be something," he marvelled. Through our bond I showed him her face. "She is stunning, I can see why you're already possessive of her. Imagine how she'd look as a vampire. She'd be irresistible."

I sat up, meeting his eyes. "No. I won't take her life from her as mine was."

He smiled. "If she chose you? Loved you? Would you bring her into our world?"

I yearned to say the words, but instead I shook my head. "She would never love someone as feral as me. To a human, any vampire would not be easy to accept, but a feral? To invite me into her bed, I'd be just as likely to rip *her* throat out."

"Why not let her decide that? You won't take her choice away about being a vampire, yet it seems like you already have as to whether she would open her heart to you."

Another wave of hunger washed over me. I groaned,

squeezing my eyes closed.

"I hate seeing you like this, Matteo." He sighed. "When this is over, I'll bring you a party. You'll need a lot of blood."

The hunger burned through my veins. "You speak as if I won't rip anyone apart. Or that I won't end up on the street, taken by the feral." The image of Quinn filled my head again. But this time it was of her walking towards me, unaware of the danger she approached. "Don't let me hurt her," I pleaded, still not understanding my obsession with a human.

"It won't come to that," he promised.

I fought down the urge to attack Carlos again, rip into his throat. His blood would do me no good.

"I have an idea." Carlos rose from the ground. "Wait here."

I lifted my arm and rattled the chains, growling. He laughed and left the room. No sooner had he left than he returned with an easel and canvas. He vanished again, returning with paints and brushes.

"You have these here?" I stared in shock.

"I've always seen how much it calms you, so I thought to have some on hand in case of emergencies." He moved the easel and canvas closer to me, then the paints and brushes.

I reached for a brush, the shackles restricting movement.

"If I unlock one shackle, I have to leave the other one on," Carlos approached me. "Don't try to escape."

I nodded, holding out my right arm.

The weight of iron dropped from my wrist. I contemplated what to paint. "Would you let me paint you?" I asked.

Carlos laughed. "Why don't you paint your human?"

Quinn. Once again, her face appeared before me. She would be easy to paint from memory. I'd memorised every part of her. I set up the paints, knowing what colours I'd need. Finally, ready to paint, I let myself go. I fell into calm, my hunger forgotten for the moment, my feral allowing me the peace I needed.

Carlos watched over my shoulder as my work took shape on the canvas. He said nothing, his presence as much a comfort as my work.

Finally, I put down the brush, staring at my masterpiece. Quinn, along with her band on stage. I'd painted a glow around her. The fire that burned within her, a strength that I'd seen. I could almost hear her singing, could almost smell her, feel her warmth. Her soul shone through her eyes from the canvas.

Carlos stood beside me. "I do believe she already has your heart, Matteo. That is quite the masterpiece."

"*She* is the masterpiece," I countered, realising that while painting, the feral within had calmed, almost as if painting her had soothed my darker self. "You knew this would help."

Carlos smirked. "Of course I knew. In the moments you were lost to the feral, I brought you back by talking about her."

"You did?" I didn't remember any of that.

"Normally I would say don't start anything with humans. But something tells me this human woman will be in our world before long."

I gazed at the painting again. Her eyes really felt like they were watching me, staring into my very being. "This will be the front and centre of my display at the gallery,"

Chapter 10

Quinn

T he line for the opening of the art gallery was long. Not wanting to be late, Lilith had dragged us to line up two hours before it opened.

"Remind me why I signed up for this?" Mia asked, shivering.

"At least it's not raining," I offered, wishing the gallery would open already.

A tram went past, breaking up our conversation briefly.

"Maybe hot food would help?" Lilith asked. "There's a fish and chip shop around the corner."

"I'll go; maybe walking will keep me warm," Mia left, hands in her jacket pocket.

Our conversation turned to the unknown owner.

"I bet he's hot," Lilith said. "That sexy artistic look. Maybe he has a leather jacket. Long hair."

"That's very specific," I laughed.

I'd seen an article written about the gallery. The owner was something of an artist, and rumours flew about him also being a collector of art. Whoever he was, he'd wanted to remain anonymous until opening night. I spotted half a dozen journos and photographers in line, amused that they were not automatically granted special treatment.

"Do you think the owner's already there? Or will we see him arrive?" someone nearby asked.

"It's likely they're already in there," I said in response. "Someone who wants to remain anonymous, we probably won't even know who they are." I imagined looking at art and some mysterious art collector watching everyone, the entire room clueless to who he was.

The woman looked over at me and gasped, her eyes widening.

"You're Quinn Bailey and Lilith De Micheli! I saw you play on Friday night! You're amazing!"

"Quinn and Lilith? No way!" a voice behind us gasped and I hid my smile. "Can I get your photo!"

The woman who'd recognised me looked at Mia. "Oh my god, and Mia Wallace."

A man spoke up. "I love your music! You have such a unique sound."

"Thank you!" The three of us said in unison.

The heavenly smell of hot chips made me hungry. Mia handed us a carton each. They were still hot, and delicious, flavoured with chicken salt.

"I want to work with that new song you wrote this Friday," Lilith said to me.

My scrawling had turned to lyrics over the last couple of days.

I shook my head. "It still needs some more work."

Lilith's eyes met mine. "You're doing it again."

"Doing what?" I asked.

"You're letting your imposter syndrome hold you back. Why don't you come over tomorrow and see what we can come up with for music? Maybe try playing it on Friday, see how people react to it."

Before we could continue, the door to the gallery opened, and people started to move in. Looking forward to the showing, I followed them.

Inside, artists stood by their art, food and drink was handed around, and no one had identified the owner yet. I loved the display, and spoke to all the artists, some of whom recognised us. But I was drawn to a piece that stood out from the rest. It looked older, similar to those of the renaissance period. Water with the colours of a sunset dancing across its surface with what looked like Venice in the background. I stood there so long, Lilith and Mia gave up on trying to move me to the next display. They left me alone at the painting.

"You've been here for quite some time," a male asked from behind me. "I see your friends left you, I'd love to know what you see."

I tensed, annoyed that some guy had decided to try to get his flirt on with me the moment I was alone. But I couldn't turn down talking about the art. "It's a beautiful piece," I expressed, lost in the painting. "I can almost feel sadness in it, like it's the last time the artist saw this and they wanted to

64

hold on to it."

"You have a good eye," he noted. "A singer *and* an art connoisseur, that is unexpected."

This time I recognised the voice and glanced up, Matteo's dark eyes met mine. Then I realised I was staring. "Um, hi!" I knew I was doing a bad job of hiding my embarrassment. "I studied art in uni. I wouldn't say I'm a connoisseur, though. I just appreciate a good painting when I see it."

His eyes passed over my face, and he smiled. "Thank you."

"Wait, this is your art? *You* did this?" I gaped at the painting again. "Mysterious Italian guy and artist. That's not what I expected."

His face lit up. "*And* gallery owner."

Gallery owner. I tried to work out what the chances were that the hot guy who I'd dreamed of kissing would be the owner of the gallery. "Gallery owner? Wow. You really are full of surprises."

I caught sight of Lilith and Mia watching us from the other side of the room.

He held his arm up in an old-fashioned way, as if waiting for me to loop my arm around his. "I'd be honoured to show you the rest of my collection and hear your thoughts."

I saw no reason to be rude, so I wrapped my arm around his. A quiver ran through me, his skin through the shirt cooler than expected. He led me across the room, showing me his paintings. Most of which I had seen, unaware he had painted them. I couldn't deny I was enjoying his company, though. He was merely an artist excited about showing his work. I couldn't blame him for that. We spent some time before each painting, him asking for my thoughts as we went.

"You're really talented," I enthused, his presence the only

thing I could focus on. The painting in front of us was a nude woman, with light dancing across her face and neck, as well as one of her breasts. But most of her was in shadow enough to conceal her body. "Tasteful, and elegant," I said. "A nice combination of light and shadow."

"You know your art." He sounded impressed. His hand slid over mine. "I have one more piece, I'm not certain how to prepare you for it. I hope you don't consider me..." he paused as if searching for a word. "Creepy."

I met his gaze. "Creepy?" Laughter burst from me. "You worry about that now, after kidnapping me to force me to look at all this incredible work you've clearly put a lot of effort into."

"Uh, kidnapping?" Horror flicked from within his eyes.

I gave him a warm smile, holding back laughter. "I was joking. Lead the way, Mr gallery owner. Show me the piece you've clearly been saving for last."

People crowded around us, questions being shouted at him. He answered them, but his eyes never left mine. Then we were alone again.

"This is my most recent work. I was inspired in a way I haven't been for a long time. I finished it a couple of days ago. I hope you don't mind."

We stopped in front of a painting of a stage with three women. A 'Not for sale' sign had been placed in front of it. I had missed this painting on my earlier circuit of the gallery. A single shaft of light shone down through the painting on to the singer, red hair with a glow around her. I stared, speechless. I didn't know how I felt about art *of me* being on display. Or about the fact that he'd painted me in the first place. His use of the word, 'creepy' was accurate.

"You painted me." I couldn't look at him.

"You don't like it." Hurt reflected in his voice.

"This is a serious invasion of my…" I didn't know how to finish the sentence. Privacy? "Not only to paint me without my knowledge, but to put it on display. You didn't think to ask me?"

His silence only made it worse. Frustration flared. I opened my mouth, but before I could say more, something stopped me. Fear curled around my spine, ice fingers sliding over the skin on my back.

"Thank you for your company," Matteo's voice was low. I'd hurt him. "If you'll excuse me." Without another word, he walked away, leaving me in front of the painting of myself.

Fuming, I turned to leave, almost walking straight into a man I didn't realise was there. "Sorry, excuse me," I muttered, stepping around him.

He stepped to the side, into my path. I glanced up at him, confused. He had curly brown hair, and his eyes were so blue I could have sworn they saw into my soul. He was dressed in black jeans, a white tee-shirt and black leather jacket. But there was something unsettling about him. I forced down the urge to run. "Excuse me," I said again.

"Perhaps it is your manners that need excusing," he spoke with an accent.

My heart sank. Great, a friend of Matteo's had stepped in to say his piece.

"I don't think so," I snapped. "This is-"

"Stop talking," his voice was so low, it was almost a growl, and I immediately shut my mouth. "Before you make snap judgements, perhaps you should appreciate the art. He painted this from seeing you one time. He didn't stalk you,

67

merely painted from memory."

I wanted to argue, for him to understand my point, but I couldn't find the words. This guy was clearly protective of his friend.

"Matteo is taken by you, and now that I've met you, I see why. However, you should know that the past week has been a difficult time for him. Art has been his peace for a long time. When he's in pain, or struggling to contain…himself, art helps to calm him. And this time, you did that. Painting you was what it took to centre himself."

"I didn't know," I said, my shoulders slumping.

"Of course you didn't. You made up your mind that you didn't want to look under the surface." He turned to face me then, his eyes moving from my eyes down my body and back up to my face. "There is pain in you, deep pain. I think you two might be good for each other. But you're afraid."

"I suppose you're going to tell me there's nothing to be scared of." I rolled my eyes. The feeling of uneasiness slid across my skin, and I wondered if it was his presence that was giving me the creeps.

A smile slid across his face. "Oh on the contrary. You have a lot to be afraid of. But wouldn't life be boring without a little fear every now and again?" He winked at me.

I took in the painting again. He was right, I hadn't given any thought to the why. I'd just seen that some rando I'd met once had painted me.

"I do like you, Quinn Bailey. You have a fire in you that I don't see all that often these days," he said with admiration

I tried not to flinch that he knew my name. Matteo had probably told him. "Who are y-" I stopped, realising he was gone.

Mia and Lilith joined me as I was searching the crowd. There was no sign of him.

"So, he's an artist," Mia noted as we stared at the painting.

"He also owns the gallery," I said.

"Whatever you said to him, it really looked like you hurt him," Lilith observed, "You got angry about this, didn't you?"

I scoffed. "Can you blame me?" The feeling of being watched ticked between my shoulder blades, but I couldn't see anyone in the crowd facing us.

"I think it's romantic," Mia gushed.

"You think everything's romantic, babe," Lilith laughed.

Mia hit her playfully. "It is good art. Maybe we can ask him to use the image on our website or something."

"I think I screwed up," I admitted. "He was nothing but a gentleman, and I overreacted."

"What are you going to do?" Mia nudged me gently.

I let my shoulders slump. "I think I'm going to find him and apologise. His friend seemed to think that painting it was therapeutic for him."

"You want us to wait for you?" Lilith asked, pulling Mia's hand into hers.

I shook my head. "Nah, I'm okay. My apartment is just around the corner."

Lilith's eyes lingered on me. "Are you sure?"

I gave her a reassuring smile. "Go. I'll be careful, I promise."

Mia grinned. "Maybe when you've apologised, you can let him walk you home and…" She grinned. I burst out laughing.

We said our goodbyes, and I set out to find Matteo. He was nowhere in the gallery. A 'Staff Only' sign on a door challenged me. I glanced around before opening it and walked down a dark hallway. I had no idea where to go.

I asked myself how I was going to explain being where I shouldn't be when I heard a moan. I stopped at the door to an office and found him in an intimate embrace with one of the artists. It looked like he was kissing her neck. My heart fell. I let out a small sigh.

He lifted his head and hissed at me. I took a step back as the room around us darkened, spinning. His eyes were bright red, as was the blood that dribbled down his chin, but the fangs were terrifying. A scream bubbled up as I took a step back, unable to look away. The woman fell from his arms, hitting the ground with a thud, groaning.

Recognition crossed his face. "Quinn." The eyes remained red, but his fangs retracted, and he licked at his lips.

He wasn't human. I had seen those red eyes that first night and convinced myself it wasn't real. I turned to run, and he was there, right in front of me. "Don't," he pleaded. "Please don't be scared. I can't control myself with fear."

I took a step away from him, unable to speak. I could only stare, my heart racing as he took a step towards me. I'd read plenty of vampire books and watched enough movies to know exactly what he was, but I didn't want to believe it. My gaze lowered to his mouth, the lips I'd fantasised about, red with blood dripping down his chin.

"Are you going to kill me?" I asked finally, my voice betraying my fear.

He didn't hesitate. "No. Just please, don't run. Or scream."

A growl rumbled as I took a step back. Darkness swelled and swallowed me whole.

Chapter 11

Matteo

Quinn fainted, and I caught her before she hit the ground. Unsure how she'd found her way into my office, I laid her on the couch and moved to clean myself up. I'd been enjoying the feed a bit much after a night of being surrounded by the scent of blood and desire. So caught up in it, I hadn't even sensed or heard her until she gasped. The third time she'd pulled me from feeding. She'd seen me. Red eyes, fangs, and blood dripping from my mouth. To make matters worse, I had hissed at her.

The fear in her as she turned to run was dangerous. I'd moved to stop her escape, fighting against the call of the hunt. Desire and pleasure were one thing, but fear was a guaranteed draw for me to give chase.

I glanced in the mirror, making sure all traces of blood were gone, licking my lips and teeth. The artist groaned and lifted her head. "What happened?" she asked.

My fang marks in her throat were already healing, assisted along by my venom. Not only did it inject humans with pure pleasure when we fed, but it also contained healing enzymes that quickened the healing process. A useful necessity to avoid dozens of humans walking around with twin punctures in their throat.

"You had too much to drink and wandered in and passed out," I said.

Her mind accepted my words without a fight. She'd already forgotten that I'd been feeding from her.

"I'm sorry." She seemed horrified, I almost felt sorry for her.

"No harm," I told her. "Maybe go home and get some sleep. I hope you had a good time tonight. Congratulations on your first art show."

Her eyes fell to Quinn, passed out on my couch. She paled. "Is she okay?"

"She passed out, too." Her questions were starting to get on my nerves. I pulled her under my sway. "Go home."

She left without another word, her footsteps echoing in the hallway.

I turned back to Quinn, taking in her scent, looking at her face, her red hair, unable to resist gazing over her body. She had seen what I was, and I needed to get her out of the gallery before she awoke and started screaming *vampire.*

She whimpered, the scent of fear a temptation. My fangs ached. I dipped into her mind to see what she was dreaming about. Quinn faced off with a dream version of myself. Red eyes that glowed, fangs longer than my own. Already she was warping her own memory of what she'd seen.

I needed to calm her, to take away her fear. Even if she never wanted to see me again, I didn't want her to be afraid of me.

"Don't be afraid," I whispered.

"I'm not afraid," she said, deep under my power.

I hoped it would hold but thought it unlikely. If the fear was deep enough, it would claw its way back.

Carlos would know what to do. I considered reaching out to him but dismissed the idea. He didn't trust humans all that much and would not react well to her knowing about us. The only way would be to compel her to forget. I left her dream, pacing my office. Could I do that to her? Once she got over her initial shock, would she accept me, or turn from me?

I picked up the phone. My assistant answered after one ring. "Hello?"

"I'm leaving for the night," I told her, eyeing Quinn. "Make sure you lock up when everyone's gone." I hung up before waiting for an answer.

I picked her up in my arms easily and let myself out the back door. Using my vampiric speed, I passed by people in the streets, unseen. It was a cold night, and I wanted to get her inside quickly. At the foot of her building, I pushed myself from the ground until I found her balcony again. The door was unlocked.

I looked down at her face, eyes still closed. "I usually wait to be invited in, but I'm not about to leave you out here in the cold," I whispered, and I entered her apartment.

The room was tidy. Her guitar stood in the corner, her guitar picks were on the coffee table, and she had a collection of candles. Photos hung on the walls of what I could only assume to be her family, as well as the friends I'd seen her with. In her bookshelves were travel books, journals, and art from ancient cultures. I paused when I caught sight of a ceramic Venetian mask decorated with blue and gold paint.

I was surrounded by her scent, and I breathed in deeply, not realising I'd lowered my nose to her throat until my fangs emerged. I wanted to bite her, to taste her blood, for her to whisper my name, to scream it in ecstasy. But I wanted her to be awake, to be the one to ask me to kiss her. After what she'd seen, I wasn't sure I'd be welcome anywhere near her. I placed her on the bed, listening to her heart beat.

"What is it about you?" I murmured. "I should leave you here, but I yearn to stay."

I knelt by her bed, unable to leave. Her breathing was steady, and I pushed a lock of hair from her face. She moved as if she were about to wake.

"Sleep a while longer," I urged.

I moved towards the door, but I paused, turning back towards her. I wanted Quinn. I was drawn to her; something within her soul had called to me when I'd heard her sing. I wanted the chase, to make her mine. For her to give in to me, to ask me to kiss her. To bite her.

Chapter 12

Quinn

I did not expect to wake up in my bed. The events of the gallery washed over me, and I sat up. Still wearing the clothes from the gallery, I stripped them off and pulled a robe around me. As I walked into the lounge, my eyes fell to the guitar case. At least now I knew how it had ended up on my balcony. He'd probably flown or something. Fear gripped my heart. A vampire knew where I lived and probably wanted my blood.

I pressed a hand to my neck, looking for bite marks. Nothing. That didn't mean he wouldn't try. Tears streamed down my face as the realisation hit me.

"Oh my god, I'm going to die." I panicked. I'd attracted the attention of a vampire and had quickly been drawn to him. I couldn't deny I'd felt something in that first meeting. Or the second.

I headed towards my kitchen, needing a glass of water. I flicked the light switch, bright light filling the room. An uneasiness prickled at the back of my neck, and I recognised the sound of my door sliding open. Heart pounding, I grabbed a knife and turned around. With slow steps, I moved towards the living room. He stood there on my balcony, watching me. I froze, and he came towards me.

"Stop," my voice trembled, as did my hand when I held the knife out in front of me.

"I'm not here to hurt you." He held his hands up and took another step towards me. "I wanted to make sure you were okay."

Hysterical laughter bubbled up. "No, I'm not okay, I saw what you are. You're a ..." I shook my head not wanting to say the word. To say it made it real.

He stopped advancing. "Yes, Quinn, I'm a vampire."

"Are you here to kill me?" My voice verged on hysteria, tears welling up.

I tightened my grip on the knife.

His eyes softened. "No, I could never hurt you, little *cantante*." He glanced at the knife. "Can you put that down? It can't kill me, and I don't want you to accidentally hurt yourself with it."

"Not a chance," I glared, trying to act like I wasn't terrified.

We eyed each other in silence. I couldn't move, couldn't look away. There was a vampire in my living room. A hot one that I was attracted to.

"I saw your eyes, that night," I said finally. "I thought I was imagining things, but I saw. They were red. That was real."

"You weren't supposed to see them. You weren't supposed to find out," his voice was soft, calming. "That you have is dangerous. If you tell anyone, she might come for you."

"Who?" I asked, dread sinking in. He was threatening me, and I didn't know how to react.

He gave me a smile that made my heart melt. "You don't need to worry about her. Just don't tell anyone what you saw,"

"I won't." I frowned. "No one would believe me, anyway." Realisation dawned on me. "You killed him. You killed them."

"He got what he deserved," he said, taking another step forward. I raised the knife higher, as if to remind him to stay back. "The things he would have done to you had I not intervened, he faced an easy death. Unfortunately, he stabbed me."

This was a heavy burden he was laying on me. "What am I supposed to do with that? You killed someone, because of me? You're the one the police are looking for, and you just made me an accomplice." I took a step towards him, fear turning to anger. "What about the woman? Did she deserve it too?"

He put his hands down and lowered his head. "I thought she was alive when I left her." At least he had the decency to look ashamed. "I was wounded, and she had what I needed to heal."

I forced down the urge to whimper, or cry. "Is that why you're here?" I asked. "I have what you need? Is this a game of torment? Pursue me, then drink my blood?" My heart raced.

"Please, your fear…" his eyes flashed red again.

Panic bolted through me. I waved the knife. "Stay away." I threatened.

"I'm sorry, fear is…please be calm," he seemed to beg.

A strange feeling passed through me, as a soft whisper brushed against my mind.

"What are you doing?" I demanded.

A line appeared in his forehead, his eyebrows furrowed.

"I'm trying to calm you," he replied. "You can feel that?"

I shook my head as if to clear it. "Are you in my head?" I asked. "How?"

"We can sway humans," he said. "I have the power to calm you, compel you."

"Compel?" I gasped. "I dreamed of you last week. But you told me it was a dream. That kiss, was it real?"

He nodded. "It was real."

He'd licked my throat. The knife slipped from my fingers. I'd had a vampire with his mouth to my throat, probably wanting my blood. I was so attracted to him I probably would have let him. I wondered if I was going to pass out again.

His movement was too fast for me to see. He was across the room, right in front of me, and he caressed my cheek. I couldn't move. "You don't have to be afraid of me," he affirmed. "I will not hurt you. Yes, I hunger to taste you, your blood. But I will not drink from you unless you ask me to. I promise you that."

This close, I could smell cedarwood and sea, and it had a calming effect on me. But not enough.

"And I'll never ask you to do that." I told him, horrified at the thought. "You're a killer." All the fight left me, leaving only absolute terror.

He continued to stroke my cheek, his eyes pulling me in again. "You don't have to be afraid of me," he repeated. "I'm not going to hurt you, Quinn."

Calm washed over me. This time I gave in to his sway, and my fear melted away. "I'm not afraid," I stated.

"I killed to protect you, and I would do it again," he said. "But you, you have nothing to worry about. I've been unable to think about anything else since I heard you sing."

That wasn't the comfort that I think he wanted it to be. "What do you want?" I asked.

His fingers were warm, calming as he caressed my cheek, and it took everything not to close my eyes and lean into his touch.

"I want you, Quinn." His voice was soft, soothing like his fingers. "I want to know you. There was a moment tonight when I know that you enjoyed my company just as much as I enjoyed yours. Was I wrong?"

Is he serious? "No," I stepped out of his reach. "You weren't wrong. I enjoyed you showing me your art. In fact, I was looking for you to apologise. I was rude about your painting. But that was before." I pointed to my teeth and did an imitation of him hissing.

"You won't see past that. Can you?" His shoulders slumped with disappointment.

"I can't," I whispered. "This is too much. Please leave, or I'll call triple zero." I hoped he'd fall for my bluff. Explaining that an intruder had entered from my balcony would not be believed easily.

Without another word, he was gone. For the first time since I'd moved to the apartment, I locked the door and closed the blinds.

Chapter 13

Quinn

The moment I woke up, the events of last night settled over me. I pulled my doona over my head. Vampires were real, and Matteo was one. I'd barely slept a wink since he left. Every sound had me worried that vampires were trying to break into my apartment. I'd even dreamed he was on my balcony, with fangs and blood dripping from his mouth, red eyes watching me. I brushed my tears and sat up. Determined to not let the existence of vampires get in the way of life, I dragged myself out of bed.

My reflection gazed back at me with dark shadows under my bloodshot eyes, my face pale. I pulled my hair into a braid and changed into gym clothes. I didn't feel very energetic as I took the lift down to the gym. Unable to stop yawning, I found Dan already on the treadmill. I set the speed and incline and focused on running.

'Don't run,' Matteo's voice was so clear that I stumbled.

"Quinn?" Dan's worried eyes met mine. "You okay?"

I mumbled and slowed down the treadmill, taking an easier pace.

Dan left his treadmill and reached over to press stop. "You're not in the right headspace to run today, I can see it clear as day."

"I'm fine," I muttered and started running again.

"Quinn, stop. Maybe you should go back to bed or something. You shouldn't be here. It's okay to take a day off." He pulled me from the treadmill and wrapped his arms around me. "Sorry, you look like you need a hug."

I fought against the urge to cry into his shoulder. Dan, who'd tried to get me into his bed, was suddenly the safe option.

"You're right." I pulled out of his arms. "I'm going home. Sorry, I'll see you in a couple of days."

I left the gym, but not before I caught his reflection in the door. He was watching me. I returned to my apartment and contemplated returning to bed. Instead I sent a text to Lilith and Mia, asking them to come over.

Mia replied quickly. <On our way.>

I opened my blinds. In the light of day it seemed stupid that I would shut out such a view. My apartment had never been absent of sunlight shining through in the mornings.

Horror seeped into every cell in my body as I caught sight of something on the balcony, leaning against my chair. I stared at it, not daring to move as I searched for signs of him.

He came back.

Finally, I stepped forward, curiosity compelling me to open the door. It was something flat, wrapped in brown paper, with a note taped to the front. I reached for it with shaking hands.

Quinn, I saw how you were drawn to this tonight, and you were able to see the pain behind my brush strokes. You were right, it is a memory of my last day in Venice as a human, in the fourteen hundreds. Please take this gift. If you ever change your mind about seeing me, please allow me to answer any questions you have over dinner. I promise to keep the fangs out of sight...unless you ask. Until then, I will respect your wishes and leave you alone. - Matteo.

"You're persistent, I'll give you that," I muttered.

Re-reading the note, I shook my head in disbelief. *Six hundred years?!* I moved the painting inside and removed the paper wrapping. Once again, the strokes saddened me, almost as if I could feel his pain as he painted. His last day as a human. I surprised myself when a tear slid down my face. This painting had to be worth at least a couple million dollars, and he'd just left it on my balcony. Despite my fear, my heart melted slightly at his gesture. He'd taken a risk with a piece of art that clearly had meaning to him. Especially with the weather of Melbourne. If it had rained, this would have been ruined.

I leaned the painting against the wall and sat in my chair, staring at it. Lilith and Mia walked in then, and I quickly hid the note.

"Is that...?" Lilith stared at the painting. "Quinn, where did that come from?"

"He left it as a gift," I admitted. She didn't need to know

exactly where he'd left it.

"He must really be trying to impress you. That is quite a gesture." She moved over to the painting, kneeling down. "This is the one you kept going back to. Clearly he noticed."

I didn't want to talk about this with them. They didn't know what he was, and they wouldn't believe me.

"So, did you speak to him, then?" Mia asked hopefully.

I took a deep breath, trying to work out what to tell them. They were trying to push me into the arms of a vampire. It made Steven's emotional abuse, narcissism, and cheating look mild in comparison. I needed to pick my words carefully.

"I'm scared," I frowned. "I get myself into messes that take a long time to recover from. What if he's like that?" I sat down next to Lilith, Mia on the other side of me.

"Then we'll be here to help you through it, as we were last time. But you don't know he's going to do that to you. He's willing to give you such a gift," Lilith paused, glancing across at the painting. "Which looks incredibly expensive, by the way."

Mia hummed in agreement.

"We know nothing about him," I protested. "I'm tired of the whole 'bad boy' thing." I'd initially been attracted to Steven because of his 'bad boy' look.

"I get it," Lilith said. "You want *safe*. You want boring."

I nodded, relieved that she understood.

"Oh, like Dan!" Mia giggled. "Then why don't you go for him?"

Surprised at my rejection of the idea, I laughed. "No!"

Lilith turned around to face me on the couch. "Look, we saw the way you looked at him, and the way he looked at you.

All you were doing was talking about art, but you looked so happy. I haven't seen you look at a guy like that in months. There's definite attraction there; how can you not want to find out if there's more?"

"What if he's worse than Steven?" I asked, tears welling up. "I can't go through that again." *What if he's a killer who drinks blood?* I pushed back the panic at the idea that he wanted my blood.

Lilith's hand rested on my calf. "I know. We just want to see you happy." She lifted her phone to face me. "And that's the happiest we've seen you in a long time."

There was a photo of me clutching Matteo's arm as we stood in front of a painting. We were deep in conversation, both of us smiling. The headline above it read, 'New gallery owner Matteo Barone seen entertaining rising star Quinn Bailey. Love interest or just a shared interest in art?'

Chapter 14

Matteo

I stood in front of the painting of Quinn, waiting for Carlos. In my art, I'd captured her likeness but had not foreseen the strength that woman possessed. In the face of a nightmare, she had refused to give in to fear. Instead, she'd pulled a knife on me, asked questions, and asked me to leave. It only made me more curious about knowing her. Most humans would have been quivering in the corner, but she'd stood tall. I should have compelled her to forget what she'd seen, but I hadn't been able to bring myself to do so. Which added to my curiosity of her.

I could smell the moment Carlos walked in through my office. He wasn't alone; a human woman was with him. His arm was around her waist as he stopped a few meters away from me, eyeing my art.

"Hand-feeding me again?" I asked, my mood shifting.

He turned to face me, sympathy in his face. "I know you hate it, but Gabriela made it clear to you that you were to be—"

"Babysat," I grumbled, interrupting him. "You got burdened with watching me like a child, because of my inability to control my nature."

His eyes hardened, and a look of fury swept across his face. "Dammit, it's not…" he stopped, and let out a sigh. "You're not a burden. You never have been. Despite what I would have had you believe in the beginning." He pointed at the painting. "How was opening night? Was it what you hoped for?"

I crossed my arms, staring at the painting again. "There were a lot of people here. More than I expected."

"I know." He smirked. "I attended. Quite the lavish event."

"You were here?" I asked in surprise. I hadn't sensed him at all.

"I met the beautiful Quinn. Did you know the two of you made the front page?"

I'd seen the newspaper and had spent the day talking myself out of racing to Quinn's. Australia already thought she was mine; why not make it official?

"How long were you here for?" I asked, curious as to whether he was aware of how the night had ended.

"Not long." His eyes flashed red. "The soft and pretty throats became a temptation I could resist no longer. So I went hunting. Did you at least feed?"

The feeding that had resulted in a human seeing me in my

true nature. "I did. No one died."

Carlos glanced around. "Where's your sunset painting?"

"I gave it to her," I revealed, nodding to the art of Quinn.

Carlos's fingers brushed the human's throat. The movement made my canines ache. She smelled like cinnamon. Her eyes were wide, unblinking, a clear sign of the trance Carlos had her in. She would wake up in some dark corner of the city with no idea how she got there. Her heartbeat echoed through my head.

"She saw it for what it was," I said.

His fingers stilled. "You've had that painting for hundreds of years and gave it to a human. She must really be something."

"She saw me," I blurted out. "She walked into my office when I was in mid-feed."

Carlos frowned. "Did you compel her?"

I averted my eyes. "No."

He sighed. "You know the rules. As beautiful as she is, she'll become a problem if she starts screaming 'vampire'. Especially if a hunter takes notice."

"I don't think she'll do that." She'd said she wouldn't, but humans did strange things when they were afraid. I couldn't know for sure how she'd react to the existence of vampires.

Carlos studied me. "You're infatuated by her. Not that I blame you. It's risky, Matteo. Especially if Gabriela gets a hint of a human knowing about us." He licked the human's throat, a low growl of satisfaction rumbling from him. "You must turn her, then. There is no other way. Or claim her; it will at least grant her protection."

I wanted to turn Quinn, but I couldn't do that to someone against their will. "I want her. She's not ready," I told Carlos.

"She fears me."

"Then get her ready. I can feel how much you want her. That is dangerous, for her *and* for you." A slow smile crept across his features. "She *does* desire you, though." He pointed to the painting "As angry as she was that you'd painted this, I could feel it in her. Once she gets past her fear of vampires, she may be more willing to admit that. Claim her; you'll both be happier for it. *Then* turn her."

I moved towards the human, licking the other side of her throat. We both gave into our hunger and struck at the same time. I hated that I'd been placed under supervised feeding but appreciated that Carlos had been the one to be chosen for that role. The two of us had hunted together for a long time now.

I resisted the bloodlust that threatened to claim me and released the human. She fell to the floor. She let out a sigh, no longer under Carlos's will, but still under the effects of our venom.

"You once told me that I'd be a maker and have a blood bond with another. I never thought there would be one that drew me in as she does. She calls to me. I want her more than I've wanted any human, and not for her blood. Everything in me wants to claim her as my own. I want to hunt with her," I turned back to the painting. "But she must make the decision naturally. That won't happen while she's afraid of me, of what I am."

He faced the painting, too, crossing his arms over his chest. "Then you have to help her past her fear of vampires. The rest will fall into place. She will be yours, Matteo. You can be sure of that."

He'd likely attempt involvement of some kind. "Her

choice," I reminded him. "Not influenced by your sway."

He grunted in disgust, moving away to look at the other art, and I followed him. "Very well." He flashed fang. "She'll soon ask you to bite her. Mmm, I can almost taste her myself." His eyes closed and he breathed in deep. "She smelled like coffee and chocolate with the sweet aroma of desire."

I bared my fangs and growled before I could help myself, the deep rumble vibrating from my chest.

Laughter burst from him. "You have not growled at me like that since we first met. This human really has her claws stuck in." A glint of lust shone through his eyes. "I will not seek her for myself, but I won't be opposed to sharing her with you. I do love the red-haired women; they're usually so fiery."

With a deep breath, I forced myself to calm down. "Sorry, I cannot help myself. The idea of another vampire anywhere near her, even my feral nature doesn't like it."

He continued examining paintings. "The fact that your feral half is as possessive as you are, is a good sign. All of you wants her and will likely protect her with everything. You know what you must do."

Chapter 15

Quinn

T he article about Matteo and me was followed by a couple of emails asking for interviews. Mia had replied and set a time to meet.

"They want to know more about your relationship with him." Mia said as we headed to the interview.

I scoffed. "I don't have a relationship with him. He was showing me his art." There would never be a relationship with him. I wasn't his love interest; I was his food source. "I'm a musician with an art degree. That's all. I'm allowed to talk to male artists without there being more to it."

Mia giggled. "You had your arm tucked into his. We can't blame them for thinking there was something romantic. You two were so wrapped up in each other, it's as if no one else existed."

It bothered me that it was already at the level that I had to handle it. Curious as to whether Matteo had seen the article, I sighed.

Lilith tapped my arm lightly. "Something good can come of this. Trust me. We can use this as promo. Get word of our existence out there. People read the article, next thing they're looking up who Roses and Thorns are and buying our albums." Her eyes lit up. "Albums. Plural. Gavin should be finished with the music video in the next couple of days, too."

Mia cleared her throat. "You know, it's very likely Matteo saw that article. What will you do if he's there, too? They could have invited him. Put you in the room together."

My heart kicked against my ribs. It wasn't as if I'd be alone with him. "I don't know. I'll deal with that if I need to."

"We should probably pick up our pace," Lilith quickened her steps. "We're twenty minutes late."

We stopped outside the magazine office. "Okay, here goes nothing." I uttered.

Inside, we waited for the journalist who'd emailed us.

"Thank you for agreeing to meet," she said. "I'm Natalie. We'll get started soon." She walked out of the room, leaving me with Mia and Lilith.

"Don't look so terrified," Lilith whispered. "It's okay. She'll probably just ask how you know him, all that stuff."

I took a sip of coffee, my foot tapping. Mia pushed my leg to make me stop. "You really have no reason to be nervous," she said. "You keep doing that, she'll think you're hiding something."

91

Five minutes passed, and I started to get impatient.

"Do you reckon she's making us wait because I was late?" I asked.

Two people were talking as they neared the office. Natalie's voice was one, the other a male with an Italian accent. I knew that voice.

"Shit!" I cursed, "No fucking way!"

"What?" Mia and Lilith asked in unison.

Panic swept over me, and I made way for the door. It opened, and Matteo stood in the doorway, wearing his usual black jeans and black tee-shirt. Only this time he wore a jacket. His brown eyes met mine and he showed genuine joy, his mouth widening into a smile. That damn mouth! I tore my focus away but found myself trapped in his gaze again.

"Quinn." His voice was warm and friendly, and my heart melted slightly.

In the light of day, with him standing right in front of me, I could almost forget he was a vampire. *Almost.* I stepped back, trying to force down my absolute terror. *Please don't hurt me.*

He reached for my face, his thumb stroking my cheek. "Be calm," he whispered so softly I wasn't sure I had really heard him.

No sooner had he spoken the words when a wave of peace washed over me, spreading outward from my chest. I took a deep breath. Someone cleared their throat, and I glanced up to find Natalie watching us.

"Should we start, then?" Natalie asked.

"Okay," my mind was foggy, and I wasn't sure if I was going into shock, or what had just happened. I backed away, licking my lips as I took my seat again.

'I'm sorry, little cantante, I had no choice but to calm you.' His voice was inside my head.

I should have felt anger that he'd invaded my mind like that. But I couldn't find it in me to. He'd removed my fear or something and I felt perfectly calm. He sat opposite me.

Lilith, on the other hand, was not impressed. "You ambushed her," she accused Natalie. "You spoke nothing of this when we agreed to meet with you."

"You didn't know?" Matteo frowned. "I'm sorry, I thought you had agreed to all of us meeting."

The way his eyes focused on my face and softened, I believed him.

"It's fine," I claimed. "Ask your questions."

Natalie grabbed a notebook and pen, crossing one leg over the other. "Thank you both for coming in today." She eyed Lilith and Mia. "And I appreciate you two being here as well. I've heard that the three of you are a close band."

"Lilith handles the business side of things, and Mia social media." I explained. "Anything band-related involves all of us." I resisted the urge to glance at Matteo again. Instead, I focused on Natalie, while his gaze burned into me.

"Have you known Matteo Barone for long?" she pressed.

"I can't say I actually really know him," I admitted. "We've met twice. The first time at The Underground, where my band was playing. I was surprised to see him again at the gallery. Even more so to find out he was an artist and owned the place." I shot a smile across at Matteo then. "He wanted to show off his work, and I had studied art at uni. I wasn't about to say no. I could talk about music and art all day with anyone." *And his eyes.*

Natalie stared at me, and I thought I saw disappointment

in her. "You'd never seen him before?"

I tried not to let out an impatient sigh. She was clearly unhappy over the lack of excitement in her story.

"I'm sorry, Natalie, I don't know what else to tell you. I don't really know the guy." I addressed Matteo. "No offence." I was impressed with my ability to sound so flippant.

"None taken," he said, his voice sending shivers down my spine.

"So you only met twice, but he's clearly thought of you after your first meeting and taken the time to paint you."

Oh shit. That painting. I'd forgotten about that. The very reason I'd gone to find him, only to interrupt him drinking some poor artist's blood.

"I was inspired," he said. "I saw a fellow artist and couldn't resist painting her afterwards." He gave me a small smile. "I learned afterwards that I should have asked, both before I painted her, and before I put the painting on display. We did not part on happy terms that night, and I do regret the upset that I caused."

"Aww," Mia's reaction almost made me laugh.

I melted at his words. "All good," I said. "I think I could have reacted better that night."

Natalie was watching us closely. "For two people who don't know each other, there are some deep vibes here," she challenged. She was still digging for a story that wasn't there. She glared at Matteo. "You're telling me, there was nothing more than inspiration after you met her, and that you didn't know she'd be at your opening where a painting of her was on display."

"She said it herself," he replied in a calm tone. "We met twice, and I do not know her. I'm an artist, I paint what I'm drawn to paint."

I wondered if Natalie was about to lose it. Her face had reddened, and she returned her notebook to the table.

"But I'd like to get to know you." I had not expected those words, and my mouth dropped open. He continued. "Please accept my invitation and let me take you out for dinner. I promise I won't bite."

Chapter 16

Quinn

I lay in bed staring at the ceiling. It had been a week since the interview. The article printed had resulted in more emails requesting meetings. I declined them all. His invitation to dinner had floored me. While everyone else in the room had thought it romantic, I hadn't been so impressed. His proposition had felt like an ambush, and I'd told him no. The hurt in his eyes had affected me more than I would have liked.

I climbed out of bed. Not only did I know a vampire, but he also wanted to take me out for dinner. I was sure his idea of dinner involved his lips on my neck taking my blood.

"Let me take you out for dinner, where you'll be my meal,"

I mocked, walking into the living room after my shower.

On my balcony, a red rose had been left sitting on the chair. He'd done it every day in the past week, and I'd thrown them all out. I couldn't deny it was a sweet gesture, if it weren't for the fact that my balcony was twenty floors up, making it a little unsettling. A reminder of his inhumanness. Before I could throw the latest gift in the rubbish bin, the intercom buzzed.

Lilith and Mia smiled and waved at the camera.

"Come on up," I unlocked the door for them, and I realised there was a note attached to this rose.

'Quinn, I do hope you'll reconsider and accept my invitation.- Matteo.'

"Why are you so insistent?" I pondered. "You've got to stop leaving gifts on my balcony."

Lilith and Mia walked in then.

"Ohh, another rose." Mia gushed. "He's really into you."

"Come on, let's go," I said instead, dropping the rose to my kitchen bench. "We don't want to be late."

Lilith pressed her lips together but couldn't hold back the grin. "You, telling us we don't want to be late? Who are you, what have you done with Quinn?"

I laughed and pulled on my jacket. "I've laid in bed for an hour, so I suppose I feel like I'm on time."

"By your standards?" Lilith raised her eyebrow. "Or are you just trying to avoid talking about Matteo? I mean, if he's what it takes for you to be on time, we should have him show up in random places more often."

I groaned as I locked my door. "Or never."

"You can only say no for so long," Lilith pressed the button to the lift. "You had a moment when he walked in last week.

I still don't get why you're fooling yourself that you're not into him."

I clenched my jaw. *Maybe because he's a vampire?* I had no one to talk to about what I'd discovered, and I really wanted to tell them. I'd never thought it was possible to feel so alone as I did then.

"We know nothing about him," I repeated what I'd been telling them since the night of the gallery opening.

"Ugh, I think you're using that as an excuse," Lilith put her hand on my arm. "It's okay to be scared, no one can blame you for that. What you went through with Steven is going to make you cautious. But you can't hide from men forever."

"She's right," Mia agreed. "You'll eventually need something other than your vibrator to get you off."

"Say my bi and lesbian besties." Laughter burst from all of us.

"No, but what if Matteo's *the one*," Mia burst with excitement again.

"You sound like my sister. Niamh believed in all that 'the one' stuff. I don't. He's just a normal guy, pursuing someone who's already told him no." *Normal guy.* I wasn't sure if I wanted to laugh or cry.

"Your mouth says no, but your eyes say something else altogether." The lift arrived with a ding. Lilith narrowed her eyes at me as we entered the lift "You're *terrified*. There's something you're not telling us."

Mia glanced at me with curiosity.

"I'm not terrified," I lied. "Can you stop pushing me on this? I'll date when I'm ready. Just not him."

Lilith studied my face, and her expression softened. "Sorry, you're right. Ok, today's your birthday; you're supposed to be smiling. We have a fun day planned. This is your last year of your twenties, so you have to make the most of it. Live life and all that." Her grin was wide.

"Uh-oh, what do you have planned?" I asked as we reached the ground floor.

We walked outside into the cold wind, dark clouds overhead. I zipped up my jacket.

"That would be telling." Lilith winked.

My trepidation melted away when we arrived at Chocolate Trail. "Chocolate tasting? It's almost as if you know me!" I laughed.

Our first tasting was marshmallows dipped in melted chocolate. I took a bite and moaned in satisfaction.

"I know you love chocolate, but try not to have an orgasm over it," Lilith whispered, her eyes dancing with amusement.

Mia nudged me. "Next time you do have a sexual partner, tell him you like chocolate. Having chocolate sauce licked off your body is enough to—" she stopped when Lilith elbowed her hard in the ribs. "Ow, that hurt!"

"I'm sure Quinn doesn't need to know that!" Lilith said.

"Too late," I laughed, my mouth full of chocolate and marshmallows. "Cannot be unheard." I had to admit the thought of having chocolate licked off me did have appeal. I could almost visualise it. Except it was Matteo who I imagined. I stopped chewing, my core tightening.

"You okay?" Lilith asked. "You look like you're enjoying that chocolate, but try not to choke on it."

I snorted and did start to choke then. Mia and Lilith burst out laughing, which drew the attention of the three other people on the tasting. Lilith's phone rang, and she answered. I ignored her conversation, taking another marshmallow and swirling it in the chocolate.

Her excited tone drew my interest. "Yes, of course, I'm with them right now."

Excitement reflected in Mia's eyes as she met mine. This was something music-related. I hoped it was good news. We were gaining recognition as more of our content had started to go viral. If the number of magazines and newspapers taking interest in my non-love-life was anything to go by, I could only hope someone in the industry would notice us. A few years ago, we'd been the opening band at a big concert, but not much had really happened since.

"Thank you, I appreciate that." Lilith smiled and hung up.

Not saying a word, she put her chocolate marshmallow into her mouth, aware that Mia and I were staring.

"So, are you going to tell us what that was about?" I asked.

A slow smile crept across her face. "Not much."

Mia let out a frustrated sigh. "Then why are you grinning as if you've won the lotto?"

"Because we have," Lilith said in a way that I knew she was

trying to keep her voice calm.

"Lil, just spit it out already, you're torturing us!" I rolled my eyes.

"We just booked our first tour," she said, her voice strangely calm.

Her words settled over me and I squealed. "Are you serious? An actual tour?" My reaction gained looks from everyone around us again. "Sorry!"

Lilith's joy broke across her face. "An actual tour. Melbourne, Sydney, Brisbane, Adelaide, and Perth."

The world spun, and overjoyed, I couldn't hold back my own smile. "Well, shit!"

Mia grabbed my arm and Lilith's. "Let's remember this moment, girls! It will be how it all started for us. Quinn, happy birthday!"

Overwhelming excitement rose up and I fought to contain it. We were in public and had already called attention.

"Let's not get ahead of ourselves," Lilith said. "It's just one tour."

"Yeah, but it's our first! We'll never have another first tour." Mia grinned at me. "Now you'll have your pick of groupies."

I scoffed, still weirded out by my reaction to the fantasy of Matteo licking chocolate from me.

"Okay, next we have caramel-filled chocolates," our tour guide announced, and a new tray of chocolates was laid on the table in front of us.

"So when is the tour?" Mia asked.

Lilith bit into her chocolate and chewed deliberately slowly as we waited. "January," she said, finally. "Tickets go on sale next month."

Six months!

101

"Oh my god, we have to post about this!" Mia pulled out her phone.

Lilith grabbed Mia's arm. "Wait, let's play this smart. Take a photo but tease our followers. We're at The Underground tonight. Tell them there is a big announcement *there*."

I smirked. "Lil, for someone who hates social media, you're pretty clued in as to how to create intrigue."

Mia took our photo and spoke out loud as she typed. "Chocolate tour for birthday girl Quinn. See you all tonight at The Underground. Big announcement, so make sure you're there!" She kept typing, probably putting in all the hashtags.

I put a new caramel chocolate into my mouth, loving the burst of caramel as I bit down. "Oh, my favourite!" I enthused.

We all sent our parents messages to let them know and were immediately invited to Lilith's family's home to celebrate. They lived on a farm, and it had been a few years since I'd been out there.

The rest of the tasting went by in a blur as we were more focused on our tour. It was raining when we left. To avoid walking in the rain, we jumped on the tram, getting out near Melbourne Central.

"Movies," Mia said, excited. "We're seeing one about a singer who receives her second chance at love where she least expects it." Her excitement was clear on her face, she smiled at me.

Mia was a true romantic at heart and would take us to a romance movie any chance she got. Not that I minded. But the topic of this movie hit a little close to home. We found our seats and relaxed, waiting for the movie to start. Lilith sat in the middle. It was the middle of the day on a Friday, so there weren't many people. I caught Lilith grabbing Mia's hand out of the corner of my eye and smiled to myself. We've known each other for most of our lives, but the two had only connected romantically in the last three or four years, and I couldn't be happier for them.

We were only part way through the movie when I thought I heard a moan behind me.

"I think someone's enjoying the movie a little too much," Mia whispered loudly.

I resisted the urge to turn around. The second moan sounded more muffled, and this time I did turn around, ready to tell them to take it to their bedroom. In the back row were three people. A woman with two men on either side of her, both kissing her neck. Only it would have looked like that if I hadn't recently seen a vampire in mid-feed.

I gasped and both men pulled away, looking at me. In the light of the movie, their eyes were red, blood on their lips. Matteo, and the one who'd spoken to me at his gallery. The woman slumped in her seat.

'*Quinn, please don't scream,*' his voice whispered in my mind.

"Don't look!" Lilith whispered to me. "Voyeur, jeez!"

"I need to get a drink!" I said. "I'll be back."

"Bring me one!" Mia called out as I bolted for the door, keeping my eyes down as I passed their row.

In the foyer, I rubbed my hand over my face. I'd just seen two vampires feeding, and my heart was hammering hard.

"Quinn," he spoke behind me in a soft voice and placed a hand on my shoulder.

I clamped down on a scream. Behind him, I met the eyes of his friend who was watching me warily.

103

"Breathe, we won't hurt you," Matteo spoke as if speaking to a child. "You're safe. The woman is alive, just under the effects of our venom, and a little light-headed. She'll be passed out for the rest of the movie."

Venom?

"Are you following me?" I asked. "Keeping an eye on me? And who is he? I knew he had to be a va-" His hand covered my mouth, muffling the word vampire. I caught panic in his eyes. I forced myself to relax, realising that I'd been about to blab more than I should in public. "Sorry," I mumbled against his palm, meeting his eyes so he could see I meant it.

He let me go, stepping away from me yet still watchful. He and his friend exchanged a worried look, their eyebrows drawn down. It occurred to me that I was as much their source of fear as they were mine. That allowed me to take a deep breath and let it out slowly.

"Quinn, this is Carlos," Matteo relaxed. "I believe you've met."

I eyed Carlos, his presence as chilling as the first time I'd met him. He inclined his head to me in acknowledgement with a smirk. I got the feeling that was his permanent facial expression.

"It's the middle of the day," I whispered. "How are you walking about?"

Carlos chuckled. "Humans!" he murmured to Matteo, his voice low. "Sweet, naive Quinn, you shouldn't believe everything you see in movies. We don't burn in the sun, nor do we sparkle." His lip curled in disgust.

I turned my attention to Matteo, deciding that he was less menacing than Carlos. "So, you're here to what, catch a movie over lunch?" I asked, trying to sound casual and not accusatory.

Carlos laughed, loud and booming, drawing attention from those in the foyer. "She has a sense of humour, despite the fact that you frighten her." He clapped Matteo on the back and pulled sunglasses from the top of his head to cover his eyes. A matching set to the pair on Matteo's head. "I'll be outside." He left, leaving me alone with Matteo.

His hand lifted as if he were about to touch my face, and he stopped himself. "I wasn't following you," he answered my earlier question. "But I'm happy to see you." His smile appeared genuine.

Mia chose that moment to walk into the foyer. "Quinn, you're missing the mov…oh." She grinned at Matteo. "That explains what was taking her so long. You're not stalking her, or anything are you?"

"No, he's not stalking me." I didn't look away from Matteo, our gazes locked.

"Oh, for crying out loud." Mia grumbled "It's her birthday, you know!"

"I did not know that," he said to me. "Happy birthday."

"Are you just going to stare at her all day?" Mia asked. She knew exactly what she was doing. *Sneaky, Mia.*

"I'll let you go back to your movie," Matteo said. "On the condition that you let me take you out for dinner tonight for your birthday. We can go wherever you want. What do you like?"

I opened my mouth and paused. He was really going out of his way to get me to agree to go to dinner with him. I wondered if I should just try to get to know him.

"Not tonight, sorry lover-boy, we're playing at The Underground. But she's free tomorrow. And she loves Italian!"

I forced down the urge to roll my eyes at Mia. *Subtle, Mia, real subtle.*

"Perhaps I can have your phone number?" he asked with hope in his eyes. "That's if you're in agreement?"

I let my breath out slowly, my heart pounding. "You're persistent. But sure." I pulled out a business card, handing it to him. "It has all our numbers on it, but that's mine." I pointed.

"So I can call you?" he asked, pocketing the card.

I nodded, entranced in the way his lips curved, his eyes never leaving mine.

He shot a glance at Mia before his eyes returned to mine. "I know of an Italian restaurant with the finest red wines from Tuscany. I can meet you outside your building at seven o'clock?"

"Oh, she'll probably be late." Mia laughed.

I elbowed her. "Seven is fine."

His face lit up, and he lifted my hand, lowering his head to kiss my fingers. "Then I shall see you tomorrow, Quinn Bailey."

Then he was gone. And I had a dinner date. With a vampire.

Chapter 17

Quinn

I was still terrified. But Lilith and Mia had spent the afternoon telling me to just enjoy his company over dinner. I couldn't deny I was also curious. There was an attraction to him, despite what he was, and maybe in public I could find out more about what kind of man he really was. And why he had picked me to pursue.

The Underground was packed. We set up and I searched the room. "Looks like your little teaser worked." I told Lilith.

"You doubted me?" She scoffed. "Of course it worked. I sometimes know what I'm talking about."

I adjusted the mic stand. "Only sometimes?"

"Shut your face." She laughed.

Pete greeted us at the stage. "I don't know what this announcement is that you've got planned, but we have people lining up around the block to get in. We're already at full capacity. You're really bringing in the cash tonight, girls. I've already made a grand. Maybe you can play a couple of songs from your new album, as I'm sure they'd love to hear something new."

"Sure thing, Pete!" I smiled at him, already giddy from the buzz of the bar.

"Have you given any thought to adding Dark Eyes of a Stranger to our set?" Lilith whispered.

I recalled the painting. How upset I'd been to find it on display. To sing Dark Eyes would be doing exactly the same thing. "No. I think I should tell him I wrote a song about him before I sing it." I had no idea how I was going to do that.

I tuned my guitar and happened to glance up in time to see Matteo and Carlos at the door. "Oh, this can't be good," I muttered.

They both lifted their gazes to my face as if they'd heard me. Of course they had. Carlos smiled across the bar at me. It was not a smile that set me at ease. In fact, his entire presence sent a chill through me. When I'd seen them feeding at the movie, he'd shown no shame over being caught feeding. Matteo's expression had been different, with more compunction.

I tore my gaze from Carlos and met Matteo's. While I still didn't like the idea of what he was, there was something warmer about his eyes. His presence felt familiar, I just couldn't quite place it. A part of him spoke to me, and once again the urge to run to him, let him wrap me in his embrace overcame me. When he met my eyes, the shiver that passed through me was different. A slow smile spread across his face, and I couldn't hold back my own grin.

"Aww look, your first groupie," Mia called over to me.

Matteo's shoulders shook as he laughed. He'd clearly heard *that.*

"Looks like you've thawed slightly towards him," Lilith noted.

I didn't break eye contact, choosing my words carefully for him while I spoke to Lilith. "I thought I'd give him a chance. Get to know him a little, before I judge who he is."

He inclined his head slightly to acknowledge my words.

"He looks like a real gentleman," Mia observed. "I bet he's a real animal in bed."

He raised his eyebrows and met my eyes unflinching, his smug smile unmistakable. My face, neck, and ears were hot enough for me to know I'd gone bright red.

"How about we not talk about him like that when he's right there," I said to Mia, forcing myself to turn away from him.

Mia laughed, but let it go.

Ready to start, I glanced over at Lilith. Behind the drums, she spun the drum sticks. Mia gave me a nod. We went straight into playing. The audience was anticipating our announcement, but we'd agreed to make them wait for it.

Every face in that bar was turned towards us. I let the music fill me with joy, putting it into my song. As I finished, Mia approached me.

I turned, confused. "You okay?"

The smile on her face told me she was up to something. "Move over." I stepped out of the way, and she grabbed the mic speaking into it. "Hello!"

Cheers and whistles rose up around the bar.

"What are you doing?" I asked. "I thought we were going to wait before announcing anything."

She ignored me. "Tonight is a special night, and all of you get to share it with us."

Oh crap. "Mia, no, we're here to play."

"Quinn here will make an announcement later that I know you're all excited for, but first, it's her birthday, so let's show some appreciation to our amazingly talented singer!"

The entire room started to sing happy birthday, and I felt like a five-year-old. I sought out Matteo, to find him watching the room carefully. Carlos was no longer beside him, and nowhere in sight. A cold fist of horror gripped my heart, followed by a wave of fury.

I turned my back on the crowd, busying myself with my guitar. "While I didn't say anything at the movies, I will now. These people are here for me and did not come here to be fed on. Off limits. That's all I ask. Please." I was either being really brave, or really stupid to make demands of vampires.

Mia moved away from the mic, allowing me to take my place again. Carlos stood next to Matteo as if he'd never left. The two looked to be in a deep conversation, and both of them turned their faces towards me.

'You have claimed this as your territory. We acknowledge your demand.' Matteo's voice whispered in my head, his mind a soft brushing against mine. *'We will not feed in here. You have our word.'*

I wasn't sure what he meant by claiming territory, or whether to trust the word of a vampire. I shook myself out of my daze and started into the next song. Everyone in the bar watched; some even sang along. A few moved to the dance floor. Eyes burned into me. Matteo's. Unblinking.

Just as I had been the first time I met him, I was captivated. Only the two of us existed.

"Quinn, solo," Mia whispered, breaking me from my trance.

With a grin I took my place next to Lilith just in time. As she pounded her way through, I pulled the perfect air drums. Each thud beat through my entire body, energising and intense. Breathless when it finished, I returned to the mic, picking up my guitar as Mia played through her solo.

A man climbed on stage, and I glanced over at Mia and Lilith, concerned, moving away.

"Hey! Get off the stage!" Lilith shouted over the noise. Across the room, Pete yelled for Security.

"Dance with me, beautiful," the man said, his eyes on me.

I shuddered. He was drunk and stunk of beer and vomit. A bouncer started to make his way through the crowd. "Move! Get out of my way!" He pushed people aside.

I stepped away from the drunk, my heart pounding as I recalled the guy who'd tried to mug me weeks ago. "You should get off the stage," I said, annoyed that our set had been interrupted.

Lilith was there, standing between us. "Back the fuck off! We're playing here." Her voice was like ice.

The drunk shoved Lilith, pushing her to the ground, and advanced on me again. "I said dance with me," he demanded and grabbed my wrist and pulled me towards him. I stumbled forward.

Matteo stepped onto the stage. "Get your hands off her," he said, his voice sharp with warning.

The drunk let me go, and I fell forward hitting the stage hard. Matteo towered over him, his face dark and eyes glinting with unrestrained fury.

"Okay, break it up!" The bouncer arrived with two others. "You, out. Now," he said to the drunk and shoved him from the stage. He glanced at Matteo. "Are you going to be a problem?"

"Only if he isn't immediately removed from her presence," Matteo asserted.

"Oh believe me, he's going." The bouncer grabbed the drunk by the arm, leading him away.

Matteo crouched. "Are you hurt?" He helped me stand, his hand cool and firm around mine.

"Fucking drunks. Ugh." I grasped his arm for balance, shaken. "I'm okay. Thanks."

His gaze remained on mine, full of concern. I realised I still hadn't moved my hand, nor had he pulled away from my grip. The bouncer's voice boomed across the bar, the entire crowd silent, watching.

Another bouncer helped Lilith to her feet, and Mia reached for her. The two comforted each other in low voices.

"Thank you," I said to Matteo, not understanding why him stepping in had made me feel safe. That I never had to be afraid ever again. He was a vampire, and I should be terrified. But it was not me he'd given the death glare to. Confused, I pulled away from him and turned my focus to Lilith and Mia. "Are you all good?" I asked, curious as to how she hadn't kicked his ass when he laid hands on her.

"Yeah, let's just keep playing," Lilith muttered, returning to her drums. Without waiting, she started from her solo, her eyes clouded with humiliation and rage.

"Would you have hurt him?" I didn't have to raise my voice, knowing he'd hear me over Lilith's angry drumming, but wasn't sure I'd like the answer.

"Yes, I don't like that he tried to touch what's mine," he glanced over his shoulder at Carlos.

My heart jumped at the word 'mine.' I wanted to be his, but I didn't know what came with that.

"But I'm not yours," I said.

His eyes met mine with a spark of determination. "You will be, little *cantante.* Heart, body, and soul."

Chapter 18

Matteo

I watched her from the shadows. Next to me, Carlos's silence was deafening.

"I know you're dying to share your thoughts." I said, keeping my eyes on Quinn.

"You're following her from the shadows instead of at her side. You helped her tonight, you should not be trailing behind her," he grumbled.

"She tends to get in trouble when she walks home, I'm just making sure she gets home safely. Especially after what that drunk human did." The desire to tear him apart for daring to touch her had been great. I still wanted to hunt him down but knew that Carlos wouldn't allow me.

"You want to escort her home, then escort her home," he muttered. "This, following behind like a puppy, is beneath us."

I waited for a human woman to walk past us. Carlos turned around to watch her with a hungry smile.

"Not for her." I continued watching Quinn. "Nothing is beneath me when it comes to her. I will protect her from the shadows if it'll keep her safe."

She reached her apartment building and hesitated before going in. Her head turned slightly towards our direction. "I don't know if I'm imagining things, but I feel you there. Thank you. I'm home, safe. See you tomorrow night."

I watched her walk inside, fighting the desire to follow her. She'd sensed me, an intriguing revelation. Was she drawn to me as much as I was to her? No matter where I was, all I could feel was her presence.

"Come on," Carlos's words pulled me back. "You walked her home. I'm hungry, and I know you are too. Her little declaration that we must not feed there has me a little irritated. She already interrupted our earlier feeding."

I followed him and we fell into a slow walk, seeking out a human for the hunt. Carlos targeted a human man, and we trailed him into Flagstaff Gardens.

'I want fear,' Carlos whispered to me through our bond. 'I'm tired of them being without flavour. I want him running and terrified.'

Before I responded, he cut off the human's path, baring fangs, his eyes red. "Look what we have here," he growled. "A human, all alone. Have you ever had reason to fear the dark as you do now?" With vampire speed, he moved to the shadows. To the human, Carlos would have simply

115

disappeared.

The human's heart raced as he looked around. The distinct scent of fear rose, calling me forward. Unable to resist, my fangs lengthened, and I released a savage growl.

'Wait,' Carlos commanded me. 'Not yet. Scare him first.'

He wanted to draw it out. I smiled, enjoying the slower chase as much as him. I forced back my hunger and tapped the human on the shoulder, only to smile, showing him what I was as he turned around.

"What are you?" his voice trembled.

I chuckled. "We are exactly what you think we are."

"Run," Carlos whispered from the shadows, and he released a deep growl. He moved forward. "Let me breathe in your fear as you try to escape."

The human froze, his eyes wide, flashing with terror. The feral in me rose, responding to the delicious scent of fear. The feral was hungry. I was hungry.

"He said run," I growled.

Finally he ran, stumbling as he fled from us. Gasps escaped his mouth as panic roared to life in his chest. We let him get halfway across the garden before I could no longer hold back.

"Remember, don't kill him." Carlos was right next to me as we gave chase.

The fear made it hard to control my nature, and it would be so easy to let myself go. To let the feral take over. So I pulled up something to help gain control, to force back the enticement. I didn't expect it to be Quinn. Her face, her voice. Her smile. I took a deep breath and nodded to Carlos. I was in control.

Carlos stopped in front of the human, who turned around,

running straight into me.

"Please don't kill me," he begged.

The two of us laughed. I struck first, coating his throat, with a slow lick of my tongue before sinking my fangs in. The taste of his blood had me groaning as he also let out a moan from the effects of my bite. Pinned between Carlos and me, he couldn't move. Not that he wanted to, with the desire and pleasure currently gripping him.

With effort, I lifted my head, warm blood trickling from my chin.

"Forget you saw us, go home," Carlos compelled him, evidence of our bites in his throat already closing.

I watched as the human left, oblivious to the fact that he'd just fed two hungry vampires. He'd most likely feel fatigue over the next few days. The scent of his blood and the thunder of his heartbeat called to me.

Carlos grabbed my jaw. "Stop watching him, let him leave," he warned.

I wrenched my gaze away. He then leaned forward, his tongue sliding over the blood on my chin, cleaning me. A growl of contentment rumbled in my chest. When he was finished he waited as I licked away the blood that dripped from his jaw.

"I much prefer them like that," he said. We left the park. "That fear really adds a kick to the blood that I became accustomed to, long ago. This hunting in cities is a nuisance; we need to be careful they don't scream. It draws too much attention."

I grinned. "I don't know, I do like when they scream. There's just something about it. Music to my ears."

Laughter burst from him. "That's because you didn't know

how to release venom into your bite until I taught you. All you had were their screams."

The two of us walked through the quiet streets of Melbourne. A few drunks wandered past us on their way to the next bar. Even sated, I could easily have another. I couldn't remember any other way, just the aching hunger and never-ending need for blood. I held no bitterness towards what I was. But for the first time in my long life, I saw myself through someone else's eyes. I could understand her fear. She could have come across any other vampire and not be in the danger she was with me. I'd promised her she would be mine, heart, body and soul. I was already hers and she didn't know it. I'd do anything to protect her, but what if it was me she needed protection from?

Chapter 19

Quinn

My parents had asked me over to have my birthday lunch at home, but I wasn't ready for that yet. That would mean going through photo albums, talking about *her*, and probably standing in the bedroom that had once been hers. After Niamh had died, I laid in her old bed sobbing, hugging her pillow. I couldn't bear to be there. The front of their house looked over the beach, and I didn't want to listen to the waves crashing on the sand. The sea had taken my sister from me and had lost the calm it once had. I had suggested we go out instead.

They waited outside the restaurant for me.

"Kia ora!" Dad greeted me in Te Reo Māori.

Dad was a tall man, usually towering over most people. He was Māori with a lighter complexion, his brown eyes always full of kindness. His calming presence radiated from him. Around his neck hung a Pounamu pendant.

"*Tēnā koe*," I responded, giving him a quick hug.

Dad had made sure to teach both me and Niamh Te Reo Māori, and we'd spent a lot of time in New Zealand. My sister had resembled him more, while I was almost a mirror image to Mum. As soon as we pulled apart, I turned to face Mum. Her parents were Irish, but she'd been born in Australia. She had the same curly red hair and green eyes I did.

"Hi, sweetie," Mum smiled at me. "Happy birthday."

I wrapped my arms around her. "Hi, Mum. Thanks."

We walked inside and were seated quickly and handed menus.

Mum's eyes instantly lit up, not bothering to wait. "So, tell me about this man you're seeing. Matteo someone?"

I groaned inwardly, expecting this. "I'm not exactly seeing him."

"The photo at the gallery suggests otherwise." She pulled out her phone. "But this one from last night shows there is something between the two of you."

She showed me a photo that had been taken in the moment that Matteo had helped me to my feet. His look down at me was filled with such concern, and I had my hand on his arm. I'd been tagged in it by someone at the bar, and it wouldn't be long before that would be plastered all over the place.

"A drunk got a bit rough; he helped me to my feet," I explained.

She and Dad exchanged a knowing look.

"Okay, fine, he's taking me out for dinner tonight," I said.

Mum beamed at me. "Oh, that's great sweetie! Tell me about him."

I knew what she was wanting to hear. That I was head over heels for someone, so she could gush over the fact. I'd spent years with Steven, and she had never warmed to him, had always told me he wasn't right for me. I didn't know how she knew.

I sighed. "Well, he's Italian, so he's got that accent." Once I started, I couldn't hold back the words. "And as you know, he's an artist, plus owns that gallery. He walked into The Underground one night while I was singing." I paused, recalling that night. "There was a moment where it just felt like the two of us. I felt like I was singing to him."

We stopped talking when the waiter came to take our orders.

"How does he feel about your singing?" she asked once we were alone again.

Her question was aimed at the fact that Steven had wanted me to quit singing. He'd insisted it wasn't a real job and that I should stop dreaming.

"Well, apparently he came inside because he heard me sing. Said he was drawn to it. Whatever that means. I think he was just getting his flirt on."

Excitement flittered through both their faces. "That's great!" Mum exclaimed.

I lowered my eyes, wishing I could tell her everything. That I was attracted to a vampire. Or that what I was really afraid of was that it wasn't really his being a vampire, but my own intense feelings for such a creature. "I can't stop thinking about him," I admitted out loud. "But I'm scared."

121

Warmth welled behind my eyes.

She touched my hand. "I know you are, and that's understandable. Steven wasn't for you, and he hurt you. But maybe there's hope for the artist. You always did like the accents."

The waiter brought us our drinks. I reached for my wine, taking a sip. "Just don't try pushing me into it, Mum. Tonight is just one dinner. Let me get through that first. I'll see where things go." *I just need to survive this. Hopefully he doesn't tear my throat out.*

"Anything you say," she said. But the look on her face was as if I'd just declared love for him or something. Her eyes glimmered with hope and joy.

"I mean it!" I grumbled.

She nodded quickly and took a sip from her wine glass. Dad watched us both, deep in thought. Their marriage had been one I'd always envied. Sure, they had their share of disagreements, but they were always so committed to each other. In love. I could only hope to have a relationship as strong as theirs one day.

"Congratulations on your tour," Dad enthused. "Our little rock star. I'm proud of you."

Pride swelled in my chest. They'd both encouraged both my own and Niamh's singing from a young age, and I couldn't be more grateful. Mum used to sing professionally until she met Dad but was now a music teacher. Dad owned a security company, and after last night I wondered if I should ask him for security, especially when we went on tour.

"Thanks Dad." My smile was wide. "It all feels a bit surreal."

"Your sister would be just as proud," Mum assured me. "She always had hope that you'd achieve your dream. You've worked so hard, you deserve this."

I glanced out the window then, to find a woman watching me. She had long, dark hair and had a glint in her eyes that reminded me of Carlos. The way she watched me reminded me of every predator I'd seen on a nature show. Hungry.

When she caught me looking, her lips curved into a smile. The hairs on my arms raised.

"Do you know her?" Mum asked with a frown.

I shook my head. "No, I think maybe she's just a fan," I lied.

Amusement shone through her eyes then, as if she had heard me. I had no doubt that she had, and I started to wonder how many vampires were in Melbourne.

Chapter 20

Quinn

Whe night fell, I found myself excited to get ready to meet Matteo. Never able to resist dressing up, I pulled out a form-fitting dress, loving the deep emerald. It would bring out the colour of my eyes. I pulled my hair up, then changed my mind, instead letting my curly red hair sit around my shoulders. Exposing my throat like that to a vampire would only be asking for trouble.

"Why am I doing this?" I wondered for the millionth time.

I caught the lift and smiled as Dan entered.

"You look nice," he said, failing at hiding his disappointment. "Have a hot date with the gallery owner?"

So, he'd read the article, and he had probably seen the

photo of Matteo last night. I studied Dan, and for a moment, I doubted my decision. Dan was attractive and would be the safe decision. He'd pursued me for the past few months and would eagerly accept any invitation from me.

You don't want 'safe'. Unsure where the thought came from, I forced myself to smile.

"Thanks," I said, my voice light. "I do actually. Are we still on for our usual run in the morning?"

His eyes widened as if it was the last thing he expected from me. "You know it, I wouldn't miss it."

"Same. I look forward to it," I told him, meaning it.

He left in the car park, and I wondered again if holding him at bay was a poor decision on my part. The second before the lift door closed, I opened my mouth, ready to call him back. But my curiosity once again got the best of me.

I walked from the building and froze, finding a limo parked out front. Matteo stood in front of the open door, red rose in one hand, the other held out to me. People walking past were staring, and heat rose to my cheeks. The suit he wore looked expensive, and his hair was slicked back. A black woollen jacket sat over the suit. His mouth curved into a smile as his eyes met mine, and for a horrifying moment I wondered if he was listening to my racing heart.

"My fair maiden, the most beautiful in the city tonight," he said in his Italian accent.

My heart skipped. *Damn, I always knew my attraction to accents was going to get me in trouble.* People recognised me and took their phones out to take photos of the two of us. *If only you knew it was a vampire you were so eager to take a photo of.* I reached out a trembling hand, taking his. As he took my hand, calm rushed through me. He gave a deep bow and

125

brought my hand up to his lips, a glimmer of mischief in his eyes.

I hope you know what you're doing.

"Shall we give the city another photo opportunity for the front page?" he asked.

"I don't think—"

He pulled me to him and dipped me in one swift motion and I gasped, unprepared for that. I stopped, gazing up at him, my hand on his arm for balance. His dark eyes stared into mine, and I found myself hoping he would kiss me. Like he had on the balcony.

He lifted his eyes to those around us. "I think that should be enough to get the people of Melbourne excited."

I held back from telling him it would probably be all of Australia.

He guided me into the limo before following me in, and he pulled the door shut behind him.

The heat of his gaze intensified. "What changed your mind about meeting me?"

"My friends convinced me to meet you, and we'll be in public." I shrugged. "Plus, I guess I'm just curious."

"About?" He watched me from his seat.

"Why I drew a vampire's attention. You're pretty persistent. What really drew you to me? Is this a long game for a hunt? So, you can wine and dine me, and then dine on me?" I asked.

His eyes flashed red. Only for a moment, but long enough. I tensed again.

"I won't deny that I'd like that, but it was your voice that drew me into that bar, not your blood. I've never heard one like it. I was in mid-hunt when I heard you. And when I saw you on that stage, you looked alive, as if the music were a part of you. So, I decided right there that I would make you mine," he said

He'd said that last night, too.

"But I'm *not* yours," I told him. "You cannot lay some dark vampiric claim to someone you've only just met."

"Do you want to know what I think?" he asked.

I was curious. "What?"

"That you're as drawn to me as I am to you. And that not once since you set foot into the limo have you considered yourself in danger. I sense no fear in you." He leaned forward, towards me. "In fact, your gaze shifts between my eyes and my mouth, so if I were to kiss you right now, you wouldn't fight it." His hand lifted my hair from my neck, fingers brushing my throat. "I think you will offer me your throat willingly before the end of winter."

His voice was soft and hypnotic, and heat flooded through me, as he continued to stroke my neck. I couldn't move, and he leaned towards me, fangs descending. Arousal turned to fear, and I pulled away from him, pushing his fingers away. His red eyes narrowed.

"Don't move," he growled, and I froze as he did lean forward then, pressing his face to my neck and breathing in. This close, he smelled of cedarwood and sea, pulling at the painful twinge in my heart.

Is he smelling me? Terror flooded through me as it dawned on me that I was alone with a vampire, his fangs inches from biting into me. His tongue was unexpected, as if he were tasting my skin. He growled, a sound that spoke to a deep part of me, and I fought the urge to run. He'd told me not to move, and something in me trusted that that was the right thing to do.

127

"The scent of fear makes us give chase," he said at last, pulling away with what looked like difficulty. "It is intoxicating, so you must *never* run from a vampire, if you hope to live through an encounter with one."

"I believe you," I said simply, attempting to push down my fear. "I don't like where our conversation is going, though. I will not welcome your bite. I had hoped agreeing to join you for dinner would be an evening of civility. It seems I was wrong."

"Civility?" He drew his eyebrows together.

"Civil conversation. No vampire stunts. That you'd keep the fangs away."

The red in his eyes faded and he smiled, his teeth normal. "I can do that. Perhaps you have some questions?"

I had a lot of questions, but wanted to eat first, and maybe drink some wine to calm my nerves.

Chapter 21

Quinn

W e arrived at the restaurant and his mannerisms changed again as he left the limo, holding his hand out to me. He played the part of a human well. I took his hand, allowing him to pull me out. Then, tucking his arm around mine, he led me into the restaurant. I fought against the urge to pull my arm out of his. He was at least making an effort to be civil, so there was no reason for me not to be.

He spoke in Italian to the staff that greeted us, and we were led to a dark, candlelit booth in a corner. The tables around us were empty, though apart from that, the restaurant was busy. Matteo pulled the chair out for me, waiting for me to sit before sliding it forward.

"An authentic Italian restaurant," I marvelled.

"Of course. Your friend said you loved Italian," he reminded me, with a satisfied smile.

I resisted the urge to laugh.

"That amuses you?" He took a seat opposite me.

"Mia wasn't referring to food when she said that!" I shook my head, laughing.

He stared at me in confusion, then understanding glinted in his eyes and another small smile twitched at his lips. "She meant men. You like Italian men."

My cheeks flushed. "Italian, Irish, Spanish. It's not so much the men as it is the accents."

"You like accents?" He raised his eyebrows.

I shrugged. "They're irresistible. My weakness, I guess you could say."

"I'll keep that piece of information from Carlos," he chuckled.

"I don't think I like Carlos," I admitted. "He scares me more than you do." The other vampire's gaze was always so intense.

He laughed. "He likes it that way. I didn't like him when I first met him, either. He grows on you." He leaned forward on the table. "So, you agreeing to have dinner with me had nothing to do with me being a vampire, but because of my accent?"

I understood then why the tables around us were empty. We were going to have a very open conversation, and he didn't want people nearby to hear us. Had he compelled the staff, or paid them?

"Why do I feel like you're disappointed?" I asked.

"Not disappointed." His lips curved into that smile again. "Women are usually drawn to me because what's within me calls to them. The vampire draws in its prey. I'm not used to my accent being the attraction."

A waiter approached us then, speaking in Italian to Matteo. The only word I recognised was *vino*.

"I like red wine," I spoke up and the waiter stared at me.

Matteo said something I didn't understand, and the waiter hurried away.

"Did I say something wrong?" I watched the waiter.

"No, not at all. They're just not used to people outside the Italian community coming in," he explained.

I glanced at those in the restaurant. Were they all Italian? "But we're in Australia."

His shoulders shook. "Most Australians can't read the menu. Have you not noticed that people form their own communities? They don't exclude others, it just gives them a welcome feeling. A reminder of home, belonging."

I nodded. "Like Oakleigh, with the Greeks."

He smiled. "That's right."

"So, you consider yourself a part of the Italian community." The idea seemed strange.

"I do like the reminder of old Italy, but I have my own community," he clarified.

"You mean other…" I leaned forward, dropping my voice to a whisper. "Vampires?"

"Exactly," he confirmed. "We can be ourselves around other vampires."

The menus arrived, and we spent time in which Matteo explained what was on it. Listening to him speak in Italian, even if it was just off the menu, was strangely alluring.

"Can I just order spag bol?" I whispered.

"You can, just maybe don't call it that." He feigned offence, which made me laugh.

I focused on the menu again. "I don't know what to order," I admitted. "I would have been happy just going out for steak and chips. I've never eaten at a restaurant this fancy."

His smile faded. "Was this too much? When your friend said you love Italian, I thought this would be perfect."

"I don't think I'd expect anything less from a vampire," I admitted. "Sitting at a bar with someone so exotic does seem a bit plain." I skimmed over the menu, no idea what to order, afraid it would be something I wouldn't like. "Maybe you can order something for me that you think I'd like?"

"You're putting a lot of trust in me," he noted.

The waiter arrived with wine and poured our glasses. Matteo spoke in Italian to him again, and I wondered if I should attempt to learn his language.

"So, you can eat, then. Regular food?" I asked when the waiter left.

"I can. I love to eat regular food." He sipped wine and looked down at his glass. "I enjoy flavour. I just have a very particular taste in a different kind of wine. One that I hunger for, that I need to survive."

I didn't know what to say to that, so I took a sip of my drink. It was rich, oaky with an aroma of fruits. A good wine. Expensive.

"You said you were mid-hunt when you heard me sing…" I started. "Was it the woman you killed that night?"

"No. Unfortunately, I lost that one. She got away when I walked into the bar." He reached across, stroking my hand that I'd placed on the table.

I fought down my need to pull it back. He wasn't threatening me. "Lucky her."

His eyes grew serious. "We don't hurt them. We can...our bite injects venom into their system. The only thing they feel is pleasure from our bite. Afterwards, they don't remember that a vampire fed from them."

My curiosity had surpassed my fear. "How often do you... feed?" I asked, my focus once again on his mouth.

"I hunt every night," he admitted.

Every night? My thoughts spun. "Why aren't there more bodies showing up, then?"

His smile returned. "I see we've gone right from questions to interrogation."

"Sorry, I didn't mean that." I shifted in my seat.

"You have nothing to be sorry for. Vampires once killed openly, centuries ago, before my time. But there are laws in place now. Accords." He hung his head, ashamed. "Only, there are times when I lose control, like I did that night. Sometimes a feeding goes too far, or my hunger becomes too great. We chase humans who smell of fear; it's something we cannot resist easily."

His thumb stroked the back of my hand again.

I sat back in my chair, pulling my hand away, studying him. "Would you have killed me? When I saw you at the gallery... saw what you are?"

"If you had run from me, most likely. I wouldn't have been able to resist. But I managed to calm you before that happened." His soft tone was relaxing me.

"Are you using your influence over me now?" I asked. "To calm me?"

He sat back. "Yes, your fear spiked. Sorry."

133

I finished off my glass, and he poured another for me. My nervousness started to blur as I finished that one too.

"Maybe you should slow down," he said.

I ignored his comment. "If you're not hunting me or playing some vampire mind games, why are you so set on pursuing me?" I blurted. "You put on this front of a man for the public eye, one that even my friends fall for. But you're not human, so why bring me here?"

I reached for the bottle of wine.

"I'm a little old-fashioned," he said, moving the bottle out of my reach. "Taking a woman out for a nice meal is a very gentlemanly thing to do."

"Please let me have the wine." I reached for the bottle again, and he gave in, passing it to me. I filled my glass. "You picked me to invite to dinner when you could have chased anyone. Why me?"

I caught his expression as he gazed at me. One of pure desire, and I thought I saw hunger too, a burning need that scared me. A predatory look. I knew I was staring into the eyes of the vampire. "You are a beauty," he said. "One that I cannot stop thinking about. I see who you are, deep inside. A part of you that your friends might not even know. I intend to pursue you, to make you mine. I hope you can look past the vampire." He reached up to my face across the table. His hand covered one side of my cheek. It might have been the wine, but I leaned into it a little. "There is fire in you that calls to me, just as your voice did." His eyes met mine and I couldn't look away. "I feel the need for honesty. Quinn, the more you resist our dance, resist me, the more I will give chase, until you are mine. I'm afraid I am quite determined."

Our food arrived. I didn't know how to respond, or even

how I felt about his words, so I made myself busy eating.

Chapter 22

Quinn

Matteo took me back to my apartment building. He'd taken off his jacket, placing it around my shoulders.

"Aren't you cold?" I asked.

He pulled back his shirt sleeve, holding his arm out. I touched it, finding him warm this time. "I feel it. I'm not affected by it as you are. Blood keeps us warm," he explained.

That explained the tee-shirt then at the bar. I pulled my hand back.

His words sunk into me too slowly. "So you fed, before?"

He nodded. "I wanted you to relax, to have fun. Being hungry as I sat across from you might have shown. You might not have enjoyed yourself as much as you did."

"I did enjoy dinner," I admitted. "The wine. The atmosphere. Oh, and the company." I couldn't hold back my grin.

"Wow, quite an admission," he laughed.

We walked through the laneway that my apartment overlooked.

I let go of my worry slightly. "Despite you being a vampire, tonight was alright."

"See, I'm not always a monster. When I choose to, I can be quite the gentleman." He glanced up. "Perhaps you'll allow me to do this again. I, too, enjoy your company."

"You're trying to court me. You really are old-fashioned," I laughed. "Against my better judgement, I wouldn't mind spending time with you again."

He smiled and glanced up again. Confused, I looked up, too. "Why do you keep looking up?"

"I played the part of a human tonight in the hopes to put you at ease. But will you let me be me before I bid you goodnight?" he asked with a glint of mischief. "I promise no fangs. Just a little...fun."

Before I could answer, he lifted me into his arms as easily as if I weighed nothing. His body was a wall of muscle, as I'd imagined, and warm. I was hit by that scent of cedarwood and sea again.

"What are you doing?" I asked, starting to panic.

"Going up," he replied, and his muscles coiled before he launched us into the air.

I wrapped my arms around his neck and squeezed my eyes shut, pressing my head into his chest. "You *can* fly?" I gasped.

Laughter rumbled from him. "Do I look like a superhero to you? It's not flying, just jumping. You can open your eyes, you won't fall. I've got you."

I opened my eyes as we landed on a balcony, light shining around the closed blinds. His muscles tensed again, pushing us up a second time. "Oh my god, what if someone sees us?" I whispered.

"Who would believe them?" We paused on another balcony.

"The entire world, if they catch us on camera," I pointed out.

"Even if the world sees it, no one will believe it's real. Everyone will think it's fake. There are vampires who monitor such happenings, to keep us in the dark." He pushed up again.

This time I recognised my deck chair on the balcony. He lowered me to the floor and remained perched on the railing. "Why do you not lock your door?" he asked as I pushed my door open.

"I live on the twentieth floor. Up until now, I've never had to worry about a visitor landing on my balcony," I reminded him, with a grin.

"Don't go inside yet," He hopped from the railing. "Admire the view with me." He held a hand out to me.

I hesitated. But again, I didn't feel threatened.

"I can't say no to that, it is a beautiful view." I took his outstretched hand.

He pulled me to him, wrapping his arms around me from behind as we faced the cityscape. Glimmering lights of the buildings, emerging from the blanket of night. His warmth enveloped me, and I leaned into his embrace. Unsure why I felt so safe in his arms, I leaned my head back against his shoulder.

"Are you doing this?" I asked, my voice soft. "I feel so…at ease."

He turned me around to face him, tilting my chin up. "Is that what you believe?" he asked.

I was trapped in his gaze and saw nothing there but sincerity. "No," I admitted. "No, I don't believe that."

His attraction to me and attempts to woo me were getting to me. He *was* old-fashioned, and part of me liked that about him. I returned to leaning against him, looking over the city. My face was starting to go numb, and regardless of his jacket, the cold pressed in.

"You should go inside," he said. "Before you do, I'd like to kiss you."

My heart pounded. I turned my head, meeting his eyes. "But you said…"

"Not a vampire's kiss," he promised. "No fangs." His eyes dropped to my lips.

There was definite appeal to that. That first kiss had had an effect I couldn't deny. "Okay."

He spun me around, a firm hand pressed in against my lower back. His fingers grasped my chin, and he brought his lips down to meet mine. His kiss was tender at first but became more demanding, and I gave in to it completely. His tongue pushed past my lips, meeting mine without hesitance. Warmth burst in my chest and desire consumed me as all else faded but him. I had never felt such a way about a kiss and wanted it to go on forever.

He started to pull away, and I grasped the back of his neck to indicate I wasn't done. His hand on my back pulled me harder against him, and a deep shiver tore through me. I realised if he wanted to stop, he could probably have easily overpowered my attempt to hold on to him. Heat wrapped its way around my spine. A spark deep inside of me yearned for more. He pulled away — this time, with strength.

His eyes were red, and he was breathing hard, his fangs on display. He seemed as stunned as I was. "Sorry," he breathed. "I became overwhelmed. Your scent, your blood." A growl rumbled up that sounded more like a purr. "Your arousal."

I decided to let it go, trusting that he hadn't meant for the fangs to come out. But I was disappointed in the abrupt way the kiss had ended, leaving me wanting more. "Wow," I gasped, breathless. "So that's what it's like to kiss a vampire."

The shiver was not from the cold, and I wanted to kiss him again.

"My vampire's kiss can be just as pleasurable, if not more so," he whispered, his fingers brushing my throat. "But that was just a normal kiss. No vampire whatsoever. Until the end."

"There was nothing normal about that." I could still feel the softness of his lips. "You're a good kisser," I blurted and winced. *You're a good kisser?* The kiss mixed with wine had turned my brain to mush.

His smile was suggestive. "I've got six hundred years on you, my little *cantante*. I'd be doing something wrong if I didn't know how to seduce a woman by now." His fingers caressed my cheek. "I do want to taste you, with every fibre of my being. But until you are comfortable with what I am, I will keep my fangs to myself. I will not bite you until you ask me to. You do not have to be afraid of me, Quinn."

His words sent more shivers down my spine, and I had no idea what a *cantante* was. Despite everything, I was trying to resist my attraction to him and failing miserably.

Chapter 23

Quinn

I woke up to the sound of my intercom ringing. I stumbled into the lounge.

"What?" I snapped into the intercom.

"It's our spa day!" Mia reminded me, waving at the camera.

Oh shit. I'd forgotten. I'd also missed the gym with Dan.

"Come on up, I'll be in the shower," I offered.

I caught sight of a box on the balcony. "You've got to stop leaving me gifts on the balcony." I muttered and pulled it inside, placing it on my coffee table. It was a large box, with ribbon around it, and a note on the top.

Quinn, please do me the honour of wearing these at the Masquerade on the evening of the thirteenth next month.   -

Matteo.

An invite was attached to his note, with my name on it.

I lifted the lid carefully, afraid of what I'd find. Inside, in a nest of green fabric, was a beautiful black and gold Venetian mask, with feathers that held a green tint. As I was staring at it, Lilith and Mia walked in.

"Oh my god," Mia whispered. "We get an invite, she gets a mask and dress! Quinn, that's beautiful!"

"You got invites?" I asked.

"They were dropped off this morning," Lilith said, and her eyes fell on the painting I still hadn't hung on my wall. "He's really lavishing you with gifts!"

"How was dinner last night?" Mia gushed. "We want all the details."

Lilith pulled the mask from the box as I lifted the dress, tears forming in my eyes. It was a beautiful dress, green with a long satin skirt, the bodice of lace and off the shoulder.

"Oh hun, what's wrong?" Mia asked.

I shook my head. "This is too much. The painting, the mask, and this? I don't even know if I should go."

"If you have a gentleman wanting to shower gifts on you, he's deemed you worth the chase," Lilith said. "Why wouldn't you go?" She lifted a hand, pointing to her and Mia. "We are. An excuse to buy a nice dress and have a fancy night out? Yes, please!"

I couldn't look away from the dress. "You're going?"

She sighed. "Quinn, you have a man who wants to spoil you. Let him, even if it's just to see where it goes."

I nodded. "You said you got an invitation, too. Why did he invite you?"

"I think because we know you. Maybe he wanted to make

sure you didn't feel alone." Mia grinned. "He's so romantic."

Lilith helped me return the dress to its box. "Go, shower. We have time, we can have a coffee before we go to the spa."

I lay back with my eyes closed as a mud mask was painted onto my face, my nails being manicured.

"So, he kissed you?" Lilith asked beside me after I gave her and Mia all the details I could, omitting anything relating to vampires. "I could see, that first night, that he was into you. And that you felt the same, since you did miss the thing with my solo."

I groaned. "You're not going to let me live that down, are you?"

"Why would I? You missed the solo on account of gazing across the bar at a hot Italian artist-slash-gallery owner." Lilith said.

The beautician had finished my nails and started to massage my hands. I sighed with bliss, letting myself relax.

"This is the life," Mia murmured.

In that moment, I couldn't agree more. I smiled. "Maybe we should treat ourselves more often," I suggested.

"You two need to not spend all your money before we've made it," Lilith commented with amusement in her voice.

"Spoil sport," Mia grunted.

"We should go shopping for the two of you for new dresses," I said. "Unless Lil thinks that's excessive spending?"

"Of course it is," Lilith said. "But for such an event, I could make an exception."

"What is the reason for a masquerade ball, anyway?" Mia wondered out loud.

"I don't know, someone rich decided to host a fancy event?" Lilith replied. "Rich people and their extravagant lifestyles. They like to show off their money."

"When we're rich, we'll probably do the same," Mia daydreamed.

The massage on my hands stopped, and fingers pressed into my head. I'd thought I couldn't be any more relaxed, but that proved me wrong.

"Doubt it," Lilith's voice had a smile in it. "Quinn would still be going out for steak, or 'Death by Chocolate'. I'd still be getting more tattoos, and Mia…"

"Mia would fit into it, though," I laughed. "She has expensive taste, for everything."

The three of us laughed. Laughing easily pushed down the gloom that threatened to rise. That had been lurking since I'd woken up.

After we finished at the spa, we went shopping for dresses for the masquerade.

"I'm going to propose to Mia," Lilith whispered as we

waited for Mia to try on a dress. "At the Melbourne concert. On stage. I have ideas for how to pull it off, and I'll need your help."

Excitement burst through me. "Oh my god, of course! That's awesome!" I glanced towards the changing room. "I'm so happy for you both!"

She grinned. "Maybe Matteo can be your plus one at our wedding."

Matteo. The kiss from last night replayed itself.

"You're thinking of that kiss again, aren't you?" Lilith asked.

"How did you know?" I couldn't deny it.

"Because you have that wistful look on your face. Are you falling for him?" She joked.

Despite him being a vampire, he'd been such a gentleman. Apart from his moment in the limo, and fangs and red eyes at the end of the kiss, he had done his best to not terrify me. To put me at ease. He'd answered questions, and we'd had a decent evening. I didn't want to think of falling for a vampire, so instead, I focused on the part he'd played for our date. The man.

Usually men wanted one thing, but there was something else he wanted from me, and I wasn't sure this would end well. "I don't know, maybe?"

She gave me a smile. "Something's still holding you back, though."

"I'm just being cautious," I lied. "He's a mysterious guy, I guess it's too early to tell if this is anything serious."

Lilith smirked. "Do I have to warn him that if he hurts you, I'll hunt him down and kill him?"

I couldn't hold back the laughter at the image of Lilith

unknowingly threatening a vampire. "You wouldn't kill him."

"No, but I'd kick his ass. I've been trained in three different styles of martial arts, so you know I could." She stood, taking on a stance to prove her point.

Her family had forced her into lessons when we were kids, and I had no doubt anyone who tried to attack her would find themselves having a bad day rather quickly.

"I think I'm going with this one," Mia announced, stepping into view.

She wore a red and black dress, with a matching mask and black gloves. Lilith gazed at her, speechless. Mia stared back, the two of them not moving.

I loved these two and the devout adoration they held for each other. I hoped to have that and wondered if Matteo would be that guy. I let out a longing sigh.

"Is that sigh about a certain hot Italian art gallery owner, slash artist?" Mia asked. "Other than the extremely steamy kiss, did anything else happen? You're very vague on the details."

Maybe because he's a vampire and I'm coming to terms with that. It hit me hard, that I was coming to terms with the whole thing. There was no one I could talk to about it, but in the daylight hours, I was a lot calmer about him being a vampire than I had been last night. I couldn't deny that our kiss had definitely had an impact.

"The dinner was alright," I said. "I couldn't read the menu, so he had to help me."

Mia grinned wide. "So romantic." She narrowed her eyes. "If he hurts you, we'll just set Lil on him."

"Lil already made that threat." I wished I could tell them everything. But I needed to talk to someone about my fears, even if I couldn't reveal the whole thing. "What if there's a side to him that isn't, um…" I stopped. There was no way to say anything without sounding strange.

Lilith leaned forward. "Are we talking kink or a player?"

"You have to stay away from those cheaters." Mia narrowed her eyes. "One was bad enough."

"No, he's not…I mean…" I struggled to find words.

"So, he has a kink, then." Interest sparked in Lilith's eyes. "Tell me."

I had to make something up before the next word out of my mouth was 'blood.' I'd never lied to my friends before. "Biting," I said.

Lilith frowned. "You said he kissed you. He bit you?" Her eyes shifted, an unreadable expression on her face.

"No, but he may have a thing for it." Half the truth was better than a complete lie. "But he won't do it if I'm not comfortable with it."

"Good. I mean if you want him to, by all means, you might enjoy it, too." Lilith grinned across at Mia. "I know I was pleasantly surprised by what Mia was willing to do."

"I don't want him to," I admitted, probably a little too quickly.

"Then make that known," Lilith told me.

"I have," I affirmed.

Mia gripped my hand tighter. "Then there will be no problem. He's not Steven. If he's a monster, like Steven was, it will be known."

I forced the pain of Steven down. That man had broken me, and I'd almost lost a main part of me because of him. The manipulation, and the moment I'd learned he'd cheated on me.

147

"At least this one likes my voice," I brightened. "There's no way he'd make me quit." I forced a smile. "Your dress is beautiful, Mia. Time for Lil to try hers on."

Chapter 24

Matteo

Almost two weeks had passed since I'd taken her to dinner and then kissed her on her balcony. Every day I had left her a rose, stopping only to listen to her deep breathing and steady heartbeat, before leaving her my gift.

In the early hours of the morning, with a rose in my hand, I leapt to her balcony. I caught movement inside and found her walking through her living room, her back to me, completely naked. In the centre of her back was a tattoo of a rose with a music staff. As if sensing me, she turned around, and I dropped my gaze immediately. I only caught the briefest glance, but it was enough for me to memorise every curve, every inch of her body. There was a scurry of movement inside as she ran for clothes. I considered leaving and stared at the rose in my hand.

The door slid open. "Matteo? Um…" She stood there in a tee-shirt and pajama pants, at a loss for words.

I held the rose out. "I merely came to leave you a gift before the sun rose. I meant no intrusion." Finally, I lifted my eyes, meeting her gaze. "I did not expect to find you awake or so…exposed."

She stared at the rose in silence, then took it carefully. "Perhaps you should come inside, instead of skulking around on my balcony."

She turned around, putting my rose in a vase with the other three I'd left that week. Their floral fragrance combined with the lingering aroma of burning candles. I stepped inside, and she sat down cross-legged on the couch.

The scent of her lust clung to her. I breathed in deep. "That smell," I growled, my feral rising to the surface, but I fought it, resisted the need to strip her bare and plunge myself deep inside her, while I fed. "You're…" My eyes dropped to between her legs.

"Oh shit, you can smell that?" Blood rushed to her cheeks.

"I can hear your heartbeat, smell your body wash, and yes, I can smell your arousal." I smiled as the red of her blush deepened.

"Well if you must know then, I kind of had a … dream about you," she admitted.

I chuckled. "It must have been quite the dream. I wasn't aware I had that effect on you." No more than the effect she had on me. I'd awoken from dreams of her with an erection and fangs. I knew the moment I claimed her body, I'd taste

150

her blood too. But I wouldn't take either until she asked me for both.

"You can sit down," she changed the subject. "I won't bi-" Her eyes widened and she slapped a hand over her mouth. "Oh god."

I chuckled and took a seat next to her.

She turned around to face me, her eyes grazing over my face. "Maybe I should start closing my blinds. The thought never occurred to me that I'd have some peeping Tom on my balcony in the middle of the night."

"Peeping Tom? No, you mistake me." I turned around to face her, only to find her smiling.

"It's okay Matteo, I'm joking." Her body shook with laughter as she watched me again.

I couldn't keep my eyes off her. Our gazes locked, and the sound of her heart filled my head.

"What is it about you?" she wondered aloud. "I should be terrified, but I... your presence is strangely comforting. Like I know you. Had we met before? Did you compel me or something?" There was no accusation to her question.

I wanted to reach for her, caress her cheek, her throat. "I can assure you that the first time we met was at that bar." Her presence warmed me. "Although I saw you a few months ago outside a music studio when I met with a model."

Her eyes lit up. "Oh my god, yes. The blonde. I remember that now."

She lifted her hand towards my face and stopped. "I have a vampire in my apartment at some god-forsaken hour, and all I can think about is that kiss. Why am I not afraid of you?"

She should be afraid. She should be terrified. But I couldn't find the words to tell her such. I would never willingly hurt her. "I too think of that kiss."

Her hand slipped into my hair, the movement pleasant. I reached out, my fingers brushing her throat. The two of us leaned forward, but she stopped.

"I still need time," she whispered.

The yearning in her eyes told me exactly what she wanted. What we both wanted.

"Time?" My mind was foggy with need for her.

"To come to terms with what you are." Her gaze remained on my lips, hers parted, her breaths soft.

She was resisting what she wanted. "You desire me," I declared.

She licked her lips. "I'm not denying that. I need to see who you are as a man, to know you aren't just a monster trying to seduce me. For my blood, or for my body."

I sat back . "You know that I've killed. That scares you." Again, I hated the feral nature that set me apart from other vampires. If she could ever look past the vampire, she'd find that part of me, and it filled me with shame.

She pulled her lip through her teeth. "Someone was killed two nights ago. Puncture marks in their throat, blood missing. Just round the corner. I know you watch to make sure I get home safely, so you were here. Was it you?"

Her unexpected change of direction and question left me reeling. She'd pulled back. She was asking if I'd killed someone. "No." I told her. "I didn't kill." That would be impossible with Carlos on my trail at all times, but I refrained from telling her that. Maybe there was a blessing to the supervised feedings after all. I had followed her, as she said, but I left when my hunger became too great, calling for Carlos. Had the red haze risen before he arrived? I couldn't recall, and I hoped that was not the case.

"How many vampires are there in Melbourne?" she asked. "I saw one watching me, when I had lunch with my parents."

Someone was watching her. I wanted to growl, but it would only frighten her more. I needed to claim her soon, for all to see. The clan had to know she belonged to me, so they'd know they were forbidden to touch her.

"We have a clan here, we've been here for a year," I admitted. "I cannot speak of them."

"A year?" she frowned. "How have you been here this long, and we've never met? Oh my god, how do I know a vampire hasn't already fed on me?"

"None have." I grabbed her hand, bringing it to my lips. "Even if it had been years ago, I'd know." I kissed her hand. Her heart fluttered.

"Can you smell that, too?" Her discomfort over my picking up her scent of lust still embarrassed her. She averted her eyes.

"Humans who have been fed from do have a certain scent." I released her hand. "Do you want me to leave?"

"I want to say no." She sighed.

Admiration for this woman for her honesty rose. "I will give you what you need," I told her. "I will make you mine, Quinn. But not while you hesitate like this." I stood. "I know you will sing tomorrow. I'll be there. If you'll allow me to."

She beamed at me. "I'd like that." She climbed to her feet. "Thank you, Matteo. I appreciate that you're not being forceful with this."

I allowed a small smile. "It's not easy. But at least this time you're not just saying no. I do believe you're warming to me."

"Maybe." Her lips twitched. "Thank you for the roses, they're beautiful, but maybe limit the gifts you leave on my balcony."

"You don't like them?" I glanced at the vase.

She followed me to the balcony. "I do, it's touching, but it's a lot. I mean, *a lot!*"

I hesitated before leaving her and lowered my lips to her forehead. Her heart soared, and I wanted to pull her into my arms. Instead, I let myself drop the twenty floors and raised my eyes. She leaned on the railing, looking down at me.

"What have I gotten myself into?" she wondered aloud.

Chapter 25

Quinn

He'd seen me. Naked. Raw, unrestrained desire had reflected in his eyes and flooded through my entire body. To make matters worse, he'd smelled my lust, having caught me moments after a dirty dream. Of him. I watched him leap from my balcony, and stared down at him, relieved to find him not a bloody splatter on the ground below.

"What have I gotten myself into?" I asked myself again as he stared back up at me.

In a blur, he was gone.

I walked back into my apartment, moving towards the roses. I breathed in their sweet floral fragrance. I had a man who wanted me, spoiled me with gifts, and his attention was definitely lowering my guard. Not a man. A *vampire*. I paced my living room trying to clear my head. A deep ache pierced my heart. I yearned to call him back but needed to stand my ground.

I wanted to talk to someone about it all, to help make sense of everything. Mum had always told me I could talk to her about anything, no matter what, but did vampires fit into that? How would Lilith and Mia react to my insistence that vampires were real? Tears welled up as I thought of Niamh. She would have listened and offered advice. Even if she didn't quite believe me.

I grabbed my jacket, keys and phone, locking my door as I left. I could talk to Niamh. Just talking aloud might help. I took the lift to my car and drove towards her resting place. I hadn't visited her since the funeral, unable to bear the pain of losing her. But I needed her now, more than I thought possible. It was a quick drive, since the roads were empty.

I parked outside the gates just as the sun started to rise, and made my way up the rows of headstones. The cemetery was deathly quiet. I found hers easily.

Niamh Aroha Bailey, beloved daughter and sister. 1991-2023. Rest in peace.

I lay a dolphin figurine in front of her headstone.

"I miss you so much," I whispered. "There is a lot in the last year that I haven't been able to share with you." I bowed my head, closing my eyes, letting tears fall freely. They left warm trails down my cheeks. "I never take off your pendant, and it feels like you're always with me." I wrapped my fingers around the silver dolphin. "If there's ever a time I needed you, and your sisterly advice, it's now."

I let it all flow out. About meeting Matteo, and how drawn to him I had been from that first night. That I'd had dreams about him and that he left me gifts. I reached the part about finding him in mid-feed.

"Vampires are real, can you believe it?" I laughed, shaking my head. "There's another one that terrifies me, but I feel safe with Matteo. Until I remind myself he's a vampire, and he's actually killed people. I'm not sure he feels remorse over it, either." I could almost see the way she'd listen, giving me all her attention.

"If you care about him, and see yourself with him, what does it matter what he is?" Her voice was so clear, so real.

"It scares me, what he is," I confessed. "He's already admitted he wants to taste me."

"What is it you're really afraid of, Quinnie? That he's a vampire, or that he'll be like Steven was?" Again it struck me how she sounded as if she were really here.

I lifted my head, to find her standing next to her headstone in the clothes she'd died in. Her dark hair had been pulled into a braid, her brown eyes focused on me.

I stood, staring at her in shock. "Niamh?" My eyes welled up, pain pounding me in the chest, fighting against the sheer joy at seeing my sister again.

Her smile was full of warmth, as it always had been, her eyes and features so like Dad's. "Hey. It's about time you came to visit me." I stepped forward to hug her, but she held her hands up. "Don't bother, you won't be able to."

"How are you here?" I asked. "You've been dead a year."

"You caught a vampire in mid-feed, but you're struggling to realise there are more than just vampires out there?" Her laughter was light and happy. "Also, go you! Calling

157

a vampire? I've heard they make great lovers. Their bite is supposed to be really something."

I pushed my hands into the pockets of my jacket. While I had come to talk to her, this wasn't what I'd expected. "What do you mean I *called* a vampire?" I pushed down the thrill. Imagining myself in bed with Matteo made me clench at her words, 'great lovers.'

Her expression grew serious. "Oh, never mind. Poor choice of words. You came to me for advice." She walked away from her grave, sitting on a nearby wooden bench.

I followed, noticing her lie. She was always bad at covering things up, and I'd push her on it later.

"Well, I can't exactly talk to Lil and Mia about it. Or Mum and Dad. I came to try to make sense of everything. You used to listen to whatever I needed to talk about, and it would help, just talking out loud." I sat down next to her.

She said nothing for a while, her focus on the ground, eyes far away as she contemplated my words. Finally she lifted her head, looking straight at me. "I think you should do what you said you'd do. Give him a chance, see who he is. He might surprise you. Everything about him seems a perfect match for you."

I rolled my eyes. "You're talking about all this 'the one' thing again, aren't you?"

Pain flickered across her face. "Luke was the one for me. I've seen how my death destroyed him. I feel hollow without him, like I'm dying all over again." She forced a smile. "Matteo may very well be the one. Are you willing to lose that because you don't believe in it? To always regret not taking a chance on him, just because he's a vampire and it scared you?" She started to reach for my arm but stopped.

"So I ask you again. What is it you're really afraid of? There are terrible people, and Steven proved to be just that. I'm sorry I wasn't there to help you through that, by the way. But just because Steven was, doesn't mean Matteo is going to be."

I did cry then, heaving sobs, with hot tears that slid down my cheeks. All the loss and loneliness of the last year that I'd held in. Losing my sister, and a part of myself.

"Oh, Quinnie, I wish I could hug you," her voice broke. "I was here, I saw everything you went through."

"You were here?" I glanced at her. "Why did I never see you? Why didn't you show yourself?"

She hung her head. "Because it was you, who needed to seek me out. You only saw me because you admitted to yourself you needed me, and my sisterly advice." Her eyes filled with regret. "Listen, Matteo could very well be the one to help you heal. You need to trust yourself. He wouldn't be here if he wasn't worthy of your heart."

I wiped away tears. "What do you mean by that? And the 'calling' him thing, too. There's something you're not telling me."

Her eyes glazed over, her face blank. "You should talk to Mum."

I scoffed. "She's never going to believe me. Vampires? She'll drive me to the nearest institute."

Niamh's grin returned. "She knows a lot more than you give her credit for. Dad does too. Besides, who do you think told *me* about vampires?"

Chapter 26

Quinn

Niamh had given me a lot to think about. Part of me wondered if she was right. It was possible that my fear after what Steven had done was holding me back.

The following night, on my way to The Underground, I took a detour. I stopped at his gallery. There was no sign of Matteo, only the staff who worked there. *Probably off doing whatever it is vampires do.* I quickened my pace, heading towards The Underground. I was going to be late.

"You're late!" Lilith fumed. "Oh my god, Quinn, you weren't picking up. I called you six times! My next call would have been the police. There's a killer out there, I thought you'd been-" She cut her words off when Mia grabbed her hand.

The bar was packed. Posters of our tour lined the walls. Pete approached us.

"Tonight's your last night. I've been instructed to only let you sing three songs tonight, and I've had to increase the door fee," he said.

"Three songs?" I asked. "Will that cut into what you usually pay us?"

"That's why the door fee is higher," he shrugged. "I had to make money somehow."

"What do you mean our last night?" Mia demanded.

"This isn't what we agreed to, Pete." Lilith's eyes reflected her annoyance.

He glared. "You booked a tour. Your organisers want to make money out of it. Letting you continue to play at the local pub goes against that. Don't think I'm happy about this, you're my main attraction on Fridays."

Disappointed, I met Lilith's eyes. "The price of success, I guess," I muttered.

My income was going to be cut after this.

"Which songs?" Mia asked.

"Alone, Free to party, and City Beats," Lilith said. "Those will amp up the crowd."

"I've never seen it this busy." Mia stared around the bar in shock.

"Something to get used to, I guess." I picked up my guitar. "Ready?"

The music started, and again I couldn't hold back my joy.

I could have been imagining things, but I thought I could feel Matteo's eyes on me. Not wanting to miss Lilith's solo again, I avoided looking into the audience. But the memory of his kiss was harder to avoid, and out of nowhere, I felt hot under the lights. Mia must've seen something, as she caught my eyes, hers reflecting concern. I forced a smile.

My energy was buzzing, as was the bar when we reached our three songs.

"I'm sorry," I said into the mic at the end. "That's all we're allowed for now, but tickets go on sale in a couple of weeks for our Australia-wide tour."

Cheers rose from the crowd. Many regulars who watched us play every week grumbled their displeasure, and a few came to talk to us as we were packing up. I had my back to the bar, talking to Mia when her eyes darted away from me, and she smirked.

"Your groupie is here," she said in a singsong voice.

"Shhh!" Horrified, I glared.

"What?" She rolled her eyes. "It's not like he can hear me."

I took a deep breath to steady my nerves and turned, approaching him. Laughter sparked in those dark eyes.

"So, I'm a groupie now, am I?" he mused, his voice too low for Mia to hear over the noise of the bar.

"Something like that." I grinned.

Niamh's words played over in my mind. The ground had felt unsteady, but now it had corrected itself. I knew that I'd made my decision, but it still terrified me.

"Are you okay?" he asked. "Your heart is unusually fast." He breathed in deep. "And you smell like lust again. I'd like to hope it's me that has that effect on you." His mouth lowered to my ear. "That is a delicious aroma, I must say," he growled.

My body was reacting to his presence. I yearned for his touch, his lips. I wanted him. The image of him naked against

162

my body caught me by surprise.

"Um." I couldn't think of anything to say. "I'm glad you're here."

"You are?" He lifted my chin, to look into my eyes.

His smile warmed me.

"Yes," I said, taking a deep breath.

"I was thinking perhaps I should walk you home," he said. "Only this time, beside you."

I couldn't argue with that. "Sure, just no vampire stuff."

He smiled. "I promise to keep the fangs away, until you ask."

I studied him, satisfied that he seemed genuine. "Okay, just let me say bye to the girls."

He waited, his eyes never leaving me as I told Lilith and Mia I was heading out. Mia gave me a wicked grin. "That's my girl. It's about time you went out to get some D."

"Mia!" Despite my shock at her words, I shook my head as I left them to return to Matteo.

Before I could pull on my jacket, he draped his own over my shoulders, heavy and warm. Outside, he reached for my guitar case, taking the handle before I could do anything. Then he held his free arm up for me to take. As my hand connected with his arm, I took note of his warmth. He'd fed before coming here. I hoped they were still alive.

"You're strange," I commented. "This whole gentleman thing, carrying things for me, the men I know don't usually do this."

"Just because I am what I am, doesn't mean I can't maintain manners," he said as we walked.

I laughed. "So, chivalry isn't dead?"

He looked down at me. "Why should it be? Have you been

treated in such a way that you believe that?"

I froze, mid-step, avoiding his eyes. "I was involved with someone who...well let's just say he didn't respect me. Or my dreams. I lost a part of myself while we were together." The heartbreak was still there, but in Matteo's presence I felt less of it.

His fingers brought my chin up. "I'm sorry. I hope you find yourself again."

We walked in silence, and for the first time since discovering our world had vampires, I started to appreciate the situation. I didn't have to worry about any mugger, or some guy thinking he could hit on me. It dawned on me that walking beside a vampire made me feel safe from all the dangers that existed in the world of humans.

We were stopped by people who recognised me, asking for photos. An overly excited guy who introduced himself got a bit handsy, and Matteo very firmly intervened.

"This is like having my own personal bodyguard," I declared. "Maybe I should take you on tour with us."

"Is this normal for you? People recognise you a lot," he commented.

I pointed up to a poster featuring me, Lilith, and Mia, announcing our tour. "You came into my life at a very strange time," I admitted. "But it's what we've all been working towards for such a long time."

"This is your dream," he commented, his eyes on the poster.

"Yes. I always knew I would sing. I went to school with Lil and Mia, and they were my best friends, and they had their own passions for music, so we created our band. We were happy with everything, but the end goal was always to sing in a stadium." I glanced at him. "Was there anything you dreamed of? You know, before?"

He was silent for so long that I looked up at him, to find him looking at me thoughtfully.

"I wanted to paint, and show the world my art," he said. "As a human, I remember my family had…expectations for me and my brother to fulfil. Follow in our father's footsteps, of which painting was not. I was considered a dreamer. Only my brother cared about my art. He let me paint him once."

"Now you own a gallery." I couldn't help but wonder what he was like. "I still can't believe you've been around for over six hundred years." We continued walking. "You've seen so much history. You were around during the Renaissance. That's incredible." I could feel his eyes on me and glanced up, surprised to find him smiling again. "What?"

"You've quickly gone from being afraid of me, to being in awe of when I'm from." He gave my arm a slight squeeze. "There is something about you that's more relaxed. More comfortable in my presence."

"Well, I can't say I'm comfortable with the idea that you 'vant' to suck my blood." I put on a terrible movie accent, and he scoffed. "But I also can't deny you have your charm. I haven't had attention like this for a few years, and I think I find your methods hard to say no to."

"My methods?" I caught the amusement in his voice.

"You shower me with gifts, take me to expensive restaurants, and even walk me home. You certainly know a way to a girl's heart." I sighed. "It's a different type of attention than what I'm used to. In fact, my last boyfriend…" I stopped walking, my eyes widening. "I mean, um…" I froze up, my brain refusing to bring any words to undo what I'd just said.

"Boyfriend?" he asked in a low voice.

"Well, um, I don't know what else to call you, other than my persistent vampire stalker," I frowned. "I'm sorry, I guess I got too comfortable for a second there."

"Don't apologise for being comfortable," he gushed. "It pleases me that you're comfortable. If you'll use such words, perhaps you'll permit a more intimate touch?"

"Such as?" I prepared myself.

He shifted his arm, sliding it around my back to pull me closer to him. It was not what I expected, and I didn't hate it. Without thinking, I slid my arm around him.

"I don't think 'boyfriend' might quite be the correct term to use for what is clearly sparking between you and me, but I do like that you referred to me as 'your' vampire," he said. "I'm happy to see you more relaxed at my touch."

We arrived at my apartment building, and this time he walked me through the front door. It seemed strange to stand in the lift with him. We stopped at the car park level, and Dan got in.

"I saw posters of you and your friends," he said to me, giving sideways glances to Matteo. "I can say I knew you before you got famous."

I laughed. "I'm not famous."

"I don't know about that, you do have a lot of people take your photo," Matteo offered. His voice was light, but beside me, he'd tensed, his arm tightening around me. "You have an ever-growing fan club, from what I saw tonight."

"You're that gallery owner," Dan said.

"I am." There was no warmth in the way Matteo spoke to Dan.

"It seems you don't have a shortage of your own fans. Women in particular." Dan's tone changed, and I picked up jealousy.

Matteo narrowed his eyes. "I'm sorry, who are you?"

Dan stuck his hand out. "I'm Dan. Dan Wilson."

Matteo took his hand, shaking it, while pulling me closer with his other arm, if that was even possible. "Matteo Barone," he grunted, making it clear he didn't like Dan.

"Relax, champ, I'm a friend of Quinn's," Dan said.

As they pulled their hands apart, Dan flexed his as if in pain. I pushed down the urge to roll my eyes. Unsure if Matteo would get the meaning of being called champ, I turned my attention to the numbers. Nine. Ten. Eleven. *Why is the lift moving so slowly?*

The feeling in the lift had chilled, as Matteo and Dan eyed each other up. When he finally got out, Dan turned to force a smile before the door closed. "I'll see you in the morning, Quinn."

The door closed, and a growl rose from Matteo.

"Hey, don't do that," I said. "He's harmless. Nothing but a puppy."

"The affection and desire he feels for you suggest otherwise," he frowned. "What does he mean he'll see you in the morning?"

"He helps motivate me in the gym," I said. "Nothing you need to worry about. Please, Matteo, don't ruin what has otherwise been a peaceful night." We got to my floor, and I pulled away from his arm.

He followed me into my apartment and placed my guitar in the corner, before taking my hand. "I've displeased you," he said. "Please allow me to make it up to you."

"How?" I asked.

"You haven't eaten. Perhaps I can accompany you to dinner.

167

As you say these days, my shout."

I hesitated. I was hungry but wasn't sure a fancy restaurant was what I wanted.

"Would you let me do that? We can get your steak and chips. Anything you want. Then I want to show you something," he said

"Okay," I relented. "But no jealous, possessive shit."

"No jealous, possessive shit," he agreed.

Chapter 27

Quinn

After we had eaten, Matteo took me to his gallery, leading me to the little dark corner where his art was on display. Our footsteps echoed around the empty room. He hadn't turned all the lights on, so the low light made the empty gallery a little eerie. I stared at the painting of me.

"I'm curious, how did you paint this so fast?" I asked.

"I was struggling, and Carlos thought to bring me paints. Painting helps calm me. The only thing that I felt inspired enough to paint was this."

"Carlos said something that night. That it helped you, painting this." I was gentle with my question, hoping this wasn't too personal.

He kissed the back of my hand again, his warm lips sending shivers through me. "I faced punishment for my actions, for killing two people. We're not supposed to kill. It was not an easy punishment. Yes, painting you helped."

I wanted to ask what the punishment was.

"Starvation," he answered my unasked question. "Three days, chained to a wall, with no blood. Carlos sat with me through all of it. I hope you never see me like that."

I pointed to where it looked like there was a glow around me. "Am I glowing?"

"That's the fire I saw in you," he told me. "When I saw you singing, you looked so alive, so in tune with who you were, but there was a yearning in you."

"A yearning?" Those dark eyes were locked on to mine, and once again, I was trapped in his gaze. My heart thudded loudly in my ears, which I knew he could hear.

"You wanted more." His eyes dropped to my lips. "You called me into your life, Quinn, and I'm here to stay."

I held my breath, hopeful for a repeat of that last kiss. It felt like an eternity of us not moving, before one hand finally slid around me, pressing into my lower back, his other reaching up towards my face. His fingers were gentle, caressing my cheek, barely brushing me, but enough to make me shiver. Then he pulled me to him, his kiss intense, hungry. In that moment, all that mattered was that I was aching for him and craved more. So much more. My hands slid across his body, heat twisting through me.

"I want to taste you," he said when we pulled apart. I couldn't move as he leaned in again, this time towards my throat.

170

"Please, don't," I whispered, my fear returning.

He didn't react, only drew closer, his breath warm against the base of my throat, hand grasping the back of my neck. My stomach flipped. I knew I wasn't putting up enough resistance to him, and for a horrifying moment, I wondered if I wanted his 'vampire's kiss,' as he liked to call it. *Did I call you into my life? Why weren't you here earlier?* The urge to lift my head slightly, to expose my throat to him was unbearable, but I dared not move. I was playing with fire, and instead of that terrifying me as it should, a tiny voice inside me told me I should enjoy it.

"I'm not going to bite you," he asserted. "Not yet. You have to ask me for that, and you will. You'll be begging for it."

Instead, he licked my throat, starting at the base, ending just below my ear, sending a deep tremor through my entire body. I gasped. Satisfaction rumbled from him, reverberating through me. I clutched his arms, not entirely trusting that my legs wouldn't give out. As if he could sense the weakness in my knees, he lifted me in his arms.

I barely blinked, and we were in his office. He laid me on his couch. He lit some candles, a soft yellow glow filling the room. He turned to face me, and his eyes were shadowed in darkness. Flames cast an eerie glow over the planes of his face. Warm, I took off his jacket. His smooth movements reminded me of a jungle cat. He pinned my body under his on the couch and kissed my throat, his lips soft, moving up over my jaw.

"There's that lust again," he said, his voice husky. "Perhaps you want me to taste you down there."

He moved down, his fingers pressing against me through my jeans. I couldn't form the word to say 'no,' not that I wanted to. His hands stilled on my zipper, his eyes on my face, as if waiting. It took too long to realise he was waiting for my permission. I gave a slight nod, and his eyes flashed red as he gave me a wicked grin. He took his time to remove my jeans, eyes never leaving mine.

He lifted my shirt and placed soft kisses on my stomach, his hands grasping my waist. I squirmed, already wet, wanting his mouth on me. His kisses moved south painfully slowly, leaving my skin on fire. He took time to nuzzle my inner thighs and parted my legs. His eyes took me in before he finally moved to where I wanted his mouth. I moaned as he ran his tongue over my clit, swirling, moving it up and down, gazing at me the whole time.

'*How do you like it?*' his voice was inside my head.

"Harder," I whispered. "Faster."

He obliged my requests, and I couldn't look away from his face between my legs. Shivers of pleasure ran through me and I grasped the back of his head, lifting my hips slightly. His earlier comments of having six hundred years of experience seducing women ran through my mind.

Tiny spasms started to run through my body, and I gripped the couch, chasing the pleasure from the feel of his tongue. My back arched. Amusement shone through his eyes as I clenched my legs against his head. My breathing was somewhat ragged, and my orgasm hit me hard. My vision dimmed, and I wasn't completely sure I hadn't blacked out. I was still trembling when Matteo crawled up my body, pinning me to the couch. We lay still as I struggled to catch my breath, his hand brushing my face and hair. The contact helped ground me as I clutched him to me, trying to calm the deep shivers.

"I like hearing you scream my name," he whispered in my ear.

I scoffed. "Please. I'm not a screamer." Had I screamed?

His slow smile widened. "You weren't before, but you are now. Perhaps your human men haven't done it right."

His erection was pressing into me through his jeans, and I ground myself against him, unable to control myself. He moved in a way that revealed his own lust, shifting against me. He buried his face in my neck, and his mouth opened. I tensed, half-expecting him to bite me. A deep shudder passed through him, followed by a growl. I reached for his face, lifting it towards mine. I ran my hands over the rough stubble.

"Your turn," I whispered, reaching down for his jeans.

As he slid down his trousers, I moved from the couch. He sat down, his arms across the back. Kneeling before him, I licked the length of his shaft before drawing it into my mouth. With one hand on his hip, the other at the base, I swirled my tongue over his head. He groaned, leaning his head back. When he looked down at me again, his eyes were heated, red.

"Keep going," he groaned. "Take all of me."

I moved my hand from his base, and his hips' movement was subtle with my motion. He hit the back of my throat, and I fought against my gag reflexes.

His movements became more fluid as he chased his own pleasure. His hand reached forward, flexing through my hair. "That's it," he growled. "I'm close."

His breathing became ragged. I moaned around him, my own arousal spiking again as I watched him. Small twitches passed through his body as he held my gaze. His hand gripped the back of my head. He grunted, and warm liquid splashed the back of my throat. I swallowed. He pulled me up onto the couch again, pinning me beneath him. His lips crushed against mine, and he pulled back, pushing hair off my face.

I felt brave as I gazed into his eyes, then at his mouth.

"Show me," I said.

His fangs slid down, indenting his bottom lip. With a finger I pulled back his top lip, the canine longer than I remembered. He held very still, so I moved slowly, pressing my thumb against the fang. Shock sparked in his eyes. I pulled him down for another kiss, knowing that I had fallen hard and that there was not a damn thing I could do about it.

Chapter 28

Quinn

E very night for the rest of the month, Matteo either visited by appearing on my balcony, or he left gifts in his place. Usually roses, a bottle of wine, or chocolate. The days he visited, he would take me somewhere. Either dinner, or walking through the city, an arm wrapped around mine. He tried to take me to the beach once, but I pleaded with him not to. He'd been curious for the reason, but he didn't push me.

I'd gotten to the point that I looked forward to his visits. Most of the time, he was warm, and I appreciated that he never pushed to feed from me. Although I learned to recognise days when he was hungry. Not just the lack of warmth, but a glint in his eyes as he watched me.

That day was no different. The moment I got home, I looked out the door expectantly. There he was, perched on my railing like a gargoyle, not moving, his eyes on me.

"How long have you been out here?" I asked, opening the door. "It's freezing."

"An hour," he said with a shrug, and he climbed down from the railing.

An hour? I took my jacket off, throwing it on the chair. "Maybe you should come inside. You know I keep the door unlocked. If you need to sit while you wait for me, I wouldn't mind. I'm just going to grab something to eat."

Too tired for much else, I made Vegemite toast and Milo. I offered him some toast. "Hungry?" I asked, taking a bite.

He stared at me, then at the toast in my outstretched hand.

"What?" I spoke around a full mouth of toast.

"I'll pass on your Australian cuisine. Nothing about what you just put on your toast looks or smells appetising," he said.

I swallowed my mouthful and sniffed at the toast. "You don't like Vegemite?"

"Not in the slightest." He appeared appalled that I'd asked.

"That's it, get out!" I said, putting on my best serious tone, and I pointed at the door. "Leave. Now. You speak blasphemy! Not in my home!"

He didn't move, a shocked expression on his face, and opened his mouth to speak but couldn't seem to find the words.

I couldn't keep a straight face. "Matteo? I'm joking," I laughed. "Oh my god, your expression! If you're going to live in Australia, or appear at my balcony every night, maybe get used to our humour."

"That's humour?" he asked.

"It is — well, to *us*, it is." I finished my toast and downed it with Milo.

"I want to paint you," he declared.

"You already did that, from the night we met," I reminded him.

"You inspire me to paint." He smiled. "I want to paint you *again*."

"Um, okay. Do we go to your gallery for that?" I reached for my jacket.

"No, here is fine. Perhaps you could look over the city." He pointed to the balcony.

I smiled. "That sounds like fun."

"Make yourself comfortable. I'll return soon." And with that he was gone.

My intercom went off, the sudden sound jarring me. "That was fast." I muttered. "Now you want to come in the front door?"

I frowned at Mia and Lilith on the screen.

I pressed the button. "Hello?"

"Just us," Mia said.

Shit! "Um, did we have plans?"

"Rude! It's movie night!" Mia's fake-offended tone was enough to make me laugh.

I'd completely forgotten about movie night.

"It's open," I replied, pressing the button to unlock the door.

I wrote a note: 'M. *Don't come in, unexpected company. Sorry.* - Q' and tucked it into my chair on the balcony, hoping he'd see it. I closed the door and blind.

Mia and Lilith walked in, and I stood with my back to the door.

"What's with the look of guilt?" Lilith asked, eyeing me.

"More importantly, since when do you close the blind?" Mia grinned. "What are you hiding?"

I willed myself to relax. "Nobo...nothing," I said.

Lilith narrowed her eyes at me. "Why don't I believe you?"

There was a sound on the balcony and my heart skipped. *Crap!*

"What was that?" Lilith asked.

"Nothing." I widened my eyes trying to look innocent.

Mia pulled the blind to reveal Matteo with his easel and paints, as if he'd been there for ages. There was no expression of concern on his face, as if he wasn't worried about what they'd think.

"Um, have you been out there long?" Mia opened the door and glared at me. "Is that why you closed the blind? You shut him out on your balcony?! It's freezing." She rolled her eyes.

"What are you doing out there?" Lilith asked.

"Painting?" he phrased his answer as a question, as if it were obvious.

Lilith stared at the empty canvas.

"Excuse us!" Mia grabbed my arm and pulled me away, Lilith moving with us. "Please tell me you're not posing nude for him," she whispered.

Matteo made a strange sound, and we all turned to look, but he was focused on the easel. I knew he'd heard Mia's comment, and I resisted the urge to smile.

"Don't get Mia wrong. We're happy you're spending time with him. It's been awhile since we've seen you this happy. But this could be bad if it gets out. A nude painting? It's too early for bad press for any of us. I hope you know what you're doing, Quinn." Lilith frowned.

"I am not now, nor will I ever pose for anyone naked," I promised. "He just wants to paint me, with a view of the city. That's all."

"Stop trying to be secretive, then," Mia said. "I was really looking forward to tonight."

"Okay, sorry I couldn't join you tonight. How about we meet up tomorrow night?"

"Right, we'll call you." Lilith turned towards Matteo. "Have fun painting!" She winked at me.

I let them out, locking my door with a click, and turned to face Matteo.

"So, you won't pose nude?" he asked. "That's disappointing. I guess I should go."

"Wait, what?" I blinked. "You're kidding, right?"

Frustration surged through me as he picked up the easel.

"You're really leaving?" I asked in a small voice.

He was in front of me in an instant. "I thought I'd try your Australian humour. I guess I need to work on that." He lifted my chin. "I didn't mean to upset you."

"You were joking?" I asked, relief flooding in.

He gave me his smile. "That was for telling me to leave."

"Okay, alright, we're doing this, are we?" I laughed.

"Doing what?" he asked.

I shook my head. "Never mind. So where do you want me?"

He pulled me onto the balcony. "Just lean on the railing, looking out over the city." I did as directed, and he picked up a red rose. "Hold this."

As I took the rose, breathing in its floral fragrance, I was

179

too careless. A thorn dug in. My finger stung, and Matteo froze.

"You're bleeding." His eyes turned red.

"What?" I lifted my hand. "Oh yeah, I-oh." I frowned. "Um, I can go to the bathroom, and find something to wrap around it?"

"Now why would you do that?" he asked lightly, but he looked like he was holding himself very still. "Let me…" He reached a hand out to me.

I knew what he meant, and there was no need to play dumb. Giving him a taste of my blood scared me. "I don't know…"

"No biting," he promised. "See, no fangs."

Reluctantly, I lifted my hand to him, unsure that I should. He held my hand with such tenderness to his mouth, licking the trail that had run down my finger. A deep rumble echoed from him, and my stomach clenched. With my finger in his mouth, I couldn't deny I was a little turned on.

He released my hand. "You taste as delicious as I thought you would," he growled. "Perhaps be careful with the rose, though. The scent of your blood entices me. I might not be able to resist taking more next time."

I stood frozen in place, asking myself why I didn't just let him drink from me. He positioned me into a pose, brushing my hair back from the shoulder closest to where he'd be painting, so it all hung over the side. As his fingers touched my throat, I met his eyes. Hunger was there, and I wondered if tasting my blood had sparked it. He moved to stand directly behind me with his hands on my waist, gentle as he nudged me into position. He was warm, and I yearned to lean back, for his arms to wrap around me, to hold me to him.

"Look out with longing," he whispered in my ear, and his

180

fingers grasped my jaw, gentle as he turned my head to the angle he needed.

Longing. That won't be hard. His hands left my body, and I started to ache for his touch.

His figure was at the edge of my vision. He didn't talk, and it was hard not to look at him. Maintaining the pose started to become painful, and I wasn't sure how long we'd been there before I started to shake from exhaustion and the cold.

"If you need a break-" he offered.

"No," I replied, determined not to complain.

He was there again, behind me. "We've been at this for a while; you're allowed to take a break." His hands were insistent as he turned me around to face him, my eyes in line with his mouth. Something heavy wrapped around my shoulders. His jacket. "I'm sorry, I forgot that you'd feel the cold more than me. Let's get you inside to warm up."

"You really don't feel the cold," I marvelled as he nudged me through the door. "Lucky."

"I do. It just doesn't have the same effect on my body that it could on yours. You can get hypothermia; I can't," he told me.

I pulled his jacket around me and turned my heat pump on.

"Come here," he commanded, pulling me to him. His arms wrapped around me, his body warm. Drawn into the heat, I returned the embrace, leaning against him, my head against his chest. "I'm sorry," he murmured, as his hands rubbed my back as if to warm me.

"It's okay." My teeth chattered. "How are you so warm?"

"Blood," he reminded me.

I was aware of how strangely comfortable I had become

with his being a vampire. I'd asked him many questions and avoided asking one.

"Other than to survive, what else…?" I didn't quite know how to ask the question.

He didn't answer right away, and I wondered if my questioning had been too personal.

"To survive is above all else," he started. "The smell of human blood is hard to resist, but if I don't feed, it's harder to maintain control over what I am. Hunger has been known to drive vampires mad. I would cease to recognise any humans, and a very animalistic nature would emerge." He stopped. "But blood and sex can also come hand in hand. One hunger awakens another."

We'd had oral sex a few times, but he'd avoided penetration, and it made sense. To have penetrative sex would likely lead to feeding from me.

I stiffened. "So, you have sex with people you feed from?"

His laughter vibrated through me. "Sometimes. Not since I met you, though."

I closed my eyes, savouring his arms around me and the warmth from his body. "Is it difficult to be around me?" I asked. "To smell my blood?" *Oh god, what about when I had my period?* Humiliation swept through me.

"I put myself into temptation in your presence, but I feed before I see you. My hunger is sated, so you do not have to worry about me losing control."

"But you've said it yourself, you want to taste my blood," I said.

"And I *have* tasted it," he reminded me. "A gift granted to me by the rose." When I didn't respond, he continued. "It does have appeal, to claim you as mine, so that no others may touch you. To give you my 'vampire's kiss.' and to share my life with you, to show you the world. *My* world."

"To share your life with me?" I asked. I wanted to look him in the eye but didn't want to pull away from the warmth.

"I mean exactly what you think I mean," he confirmed.

"You mean you would have me become like you?" My peace was broken. "Become a vampire?" The room spun.

"You'd be with me, *forever.* You'd be mine, *forever.*" He sounded so sure of himself.

I did pull away from him then. "What if I don't want that?"

"Then I will wait until you do," he vowed.

I shook my head. "How can you think I would *ever* want this? Would you do that to me, knowing how I feel?"

"I will never force anything on you, Quinn. But your acceptance of me, and what I am, does show that you will change your mind in this."

"Is this what you saw at the end of your pursuit? To win me over for that?" I couldn't understand why he would chase me for something I didn't want. "Is that all it ever was?"

"I have displeased you." He reached towards me.

"You think?" I let out a sound of frustration. "Matteo, we will not agree on that. *Ever.*" A lump had formed in my throat and my stomach churned.

Pain glinted in his eyes, and he turned around. "I'm sorry," he said with regret in his voice. "If you want me to leave you alone, I will."

Don't let him leave. Despite my horror at his revelation, I wanted him to stay, to finish the painting. I wanted to attend the masquerade ball on his arm, to dance with him in the beautiful green dress he'd gifted me. I wanted his company, as his attention had made me feel special. *Wanted.*

183

"I *don't* want you to leave," I admitted. "I just don't want you to want this for me. Is it not enough that we just be as we are?" *Whatever this is.*

"What life can I give a human?" he asked. "There will be no children. You'll be fifty, and I'll still be as I am now. I'll always hunger for your blood and will have to leave you to feed from others. There is so much that both of us would deny ourselves."

He'd put thought into this.

"You assume I want children?" I asked.

"Is that not what all women want?"

I scoffed. "Your idea of what women want is a bit outdated."

"Then what do we have?" he asked.

I leaned against him, my head on his chest, arms wrapped around him, breathing in his smell of the cedarwood and sea. "*Now.* We have *now.*"

Chapter 29

Quinn

W e were in Brisbane, doing a tour of the concert venues. Two days before we'd been in Sydney, and we were due to fly to Perth the following day. Then Adelaide.

"This is incredible." Mia stared out at the stadium.

Overjoyed, I couldn't hold back my grin. "I can't believe it. There will be thousands of people here for us."

"Tickets are officially on sale," Lilith said, staring at her phone. "Our interview will air tonight, too."

"How is this happening right now?" I asked. "Only a few weeks ago…"

"Shhh, don't question the music gods," Lilith said. "It just *is."*

I wrapped an arm around each of them, hugging tightly. "May the music gods continue to bless us."

Mia let out a cheer. Lilith followed, then me. The photographer with us took photos.

"What's for lunch?" Lilith asked. "We've got a few hours before we have that radio interview."

"Oh, there's a new waterfront restaurant that just opened up!" Mia announced.

"How do you always know about places that just opened up?" I asked.

She shrugged. "I just know."

Lilith shook her head.

"Okay, fine, I saw it in the magazine on the flight." Mia grinned. "One of us has to know these things."

I closed my eyes, soaking in the warmth of the sun on my face. "It's so warm here for the middle of winter."

"Compared to the shit weather in Melbourne, you mean?" Lilith tilted her own face upwards.

Mia's phone beeped. "Woah! There's been another murder in Melbourne."

Lilith reached for the phone and frowned but said nothing.

"Is there any more info?" I was curious.

"Same as the other ones," Mia told me, reading over Lilith's shoulder. "Dark alleyway, what looks like bite marks in the neck."

"Give me a sec." Lilith pulled her own phone out and made a call, walking away from us.

I frowned at the article on Mia's phone. "How many is that now?"

"Four." She met my eyes. "You have to be careful in the

city, Quinn. Don't walk alone at night. There's some psycho out there. I worry about you."

No chance of that with a vampire escorting me everywhere. "I'll be careful," I promised.

I read the article again, curious. Matteo had mentioned a vampire community. *Did one of them kill someone?* The nudging thought made its way in, and I didn't want to think about it. I was scared that *he'd* done it, and what that would mean.

"Okay, let's go!" Lilith said, finishing her phone call. "I'm starving."

We looped arms and left the stadium, only to find a small group waiting for us.

They took photos. and I pulled my sunglasses over my eyes.

"Maybe we should've brought disguises or something?" Mia asked.

I smiled as our photos were taken, then our limo arrived. We climbed in and I breathed out a sigh of relief.

"That's intense!" I said. "That is going to take a lot to get used to."

"It got worse since our tour was announced," Lilith said. "Did you see the views on our videos last week?"

"And our albums!" I squealed with joy. "I had no idea we were this well- known. Are we sure this is what we wanted?"

The three of us sat in stunned silence.

"We'll get used to it," Mia reassured us. "It will be awhile, but we have each other. We can do this."

At the restaurant, we received the same amount of attention, until the manager and waitstaff worked to keep people from our table. Grateful for being able to eat in peace, I breathed in relief.

"We need to introduce your new song, Dark Eyes," Lilith said.

I wanted to sing it to Matteo before I made his song public.

"Well, we're recording the album next week, should we add it to that?" Mia asked.

"No, maybe the tour can be the intro for it," I said.

Lilith laughed. "You want to sing it to him first, don't you?"

"I do. I don't know how to bring it up with him. 'Excuse me, I wrote this song about you?'"

"Oh, what are we going to open with?" Mia asked.

"Shadows of the Heart," Lilith didn't hesitate. "It'll be a good way to get their energy high."

"You just like that one because of your solo," I laughed.

"Well, yeah." Lilith smirked.

The waiter brought over a bottle of wine. "Compliments

of the owner," he revealed, and he started to pour glasses for us. Mia held her phone up to the bottle and took a photo.

"You and your Instagram pics." I rolled my eyes when the waiter left.

"Actually, I wanted to look at the wine. Do you realise he's given us a five-hundred-dollar bottle?"

Lilith's eyes widened. "Is this our life now?"

"It seems so," I said. "Let's enjoy it."

I sipped the wine. "Good wine," I noted. "Mum would appreciate this."

"How is your mum?" Mia asked. "Is she coping okay since your sister—"

I didn't miss the look Lilith shot her, which silenced Mia.

"It's okay." I forced a smile. "I miss Niamh and can't keep pushing down what happened. It does feel like me and Mum have grown closer. I think she's afraid of losing me, too. She lost her eldest, and as much as I hurt, I can't imagine what the loss of a child would feel like."

"What about your dad?" Mia asked tentatively.

"I don't know. He prefers to not show emotion, so it's hard to say what's going on with him. He's always too busy being a rock for everyone else."

"I can't imagine losing my brother," Lilith said finally. "He's a real pain in the ass, but he's my brother."

"Appreciate the time you have with him," I told her. "The last time I saw Niamh, she was more interested in Luke, and wouldn't stop texting him. If I'd known it was the last time I'd see her, I would have put her phone in her glass of water so we could appreciate the moment."

Mia raised her glass. "Life is short; live it while we can."

I lifted mine, me and Lilith clinking our glasses against

Mia's. "Live your dreams." I quoted another of our songs. "Appreciate the now."

I smiled at Mia and Lilith. *Whatever life brings, I have them to see me through it.*

Chapter 30

Matteo

I waited for Quinn outside her building. She'd been travelling to other states to see the layout of concert venues, so tonight would be the first time I'd lay eyes on her in over a week. My recent feed warmed me, a necessity if I was to spend the entire evening with her. To have her so close, I needed to resist my own temptation. She'd made it clear she had no desire to turn. I hadn't let go of that want, but I wasn't yet willing to walk away from her. Carlos had finally brought me sunglasses enhanced by Luna, the Magic Wielder, offering to be there with me when I turned her.

As I waited, people stopped to stare, something I was becoming accustomed to again. A part of me that had never died, the enjoyment of public recognition from six hundred years ago, would always be there. But they recognised me as the man dating Quinn Bailey.

I recognised her heartbeat as she descended in the lift.

"Quinn, relax," she muttered to herself, and took a deep breath and exhaled. "Breathe. It's just a vampire wanting to take you to a masquerade ball. No biggie."

I smiled. This woman intrigued me, and I couldn't get enough of her presence.

She walked through the door, and I stopped breathing. She'd done her hair up, her bare throat on show, the mask in place, green eyes standing out. But the dress was what made my heart skip. It hugged her body in all the right places.

"You're staring," she noticed.

She wore perfume that had a slight hint of vanilla beneath the fruity scent.

"You're breathtaking." I reached for her hand, leaning forward to kiss it. "Absolutely exquisite." It was an effort keeping my gaze from her neck as I helped her into the limo. "All eyes will be on you tonight."

She cast a quick look over me. "You're not so bad yourself. You look like you were born to wear suits. I could *almost* forget you're a vampire."

"Almost." I murmured and leaned forward, breathing her in, brushing her throat lightly. "You wore your hair up. Is that tantalising neckline all for me?"

Colour rose to her cheeks as she lowered her eyes. Fear spiked, but not enough to be a danger to her. "I meant what I said," she murmured. "No talk of turning me. Let's just enjoy this evening."

I was not used to women so unafraid to make their wants

known, and I had to admit it only drew me to her more. I hadn't spent a lot of time in the human world, only on the edges of it, feeding and sex when I needed to. Modern women had become bold.

"Can I kiss you?" I asked.

Her eyes lit up as if she'd been hoping for a kiss. She nodded.

I shifted forward, until my body was over hers. This close to her, the scent of her blood tempted me. Our lips pressed together, rougher than usual, a kiss full of desire, and longing. Her lips were warm, and soft. Her mouth pressed hard to mine with urgency, her hand grasped the back of my neck. I pulled back, her eyes burning. Unable to resist, I caressed her throat, kissing it. I was tempting myself, and my canines ached. My lips touched her soft skin, and she went very still.

"I won't bite you," I murmured against her throat. "You'll have to ask me for that." Soon, she'd be begging. I was sure of it.

Her breaths revealed her hunger for me, for my 'vampire's kiss'. I could feel her weakening in her resolve to not let me bite her. I let my fangs emerge, almost touching the pulsing in her throat. *Say the word.* I willed her silently. *All you need to do is ask me.* It took everything in me not to bite, and I growled, driving her heartbeat faster, her scent of lust making me hard. Her reactions to my growls had intensified over the past few weeks. She'd developed a liking for them.

I rested one hand on her side, the other pulling her dress up. I touched her, finding that she wasn't wearing anything under the dress. I growled again. "You are tempting me, my little *cantante.*"

Her soft intake of breath brushed against my ear as my

193

fingers pushed inside her. I paused, watching her face. Her muscles pulsed tight around my fingers, and she pushed up ever so slightly to indicate for me to keep going. I pulled them out, gently stroking her in a circular motion, teasing. Her grip on my arm tightened as I moved my fingers through her wetness.

I breathed in the scent of her lust, fighting my own desire for her. With one hand stroking her, I had her pinned beneath me. I could have her if I wanted, and she wouldn't fight me. Her hips rose, her hand pressing down on mine through the dress, and she threw her head back, a moan escaping from her.

I couldn't look away from her throat. It took everything to continue working her with my fingers instead of unzipping my trousers and driving into her, hard. But if I did that, I would need to feed, to bite into her throat and taste her blood. I'd resisted that urge and — truthfully — I wasn't sure how much longer I could.

"Don't...stop..." She panted, her back arching up. "Oh god, Matteo..." Her words died in her throat as she breathed hard, grinding herself against my fingers.

Her lips parted, her eyes focused on my mouth, my fangs. Desire flared in their depths, and for a moment I thought she was going to ask me what she'd insisted she never would.

Desperate for her to ask me to bite, I licked her throat. I wanted all of her, and it *hurt*. With my lips to her throat, her desire beating against me, I was on the edge of giving in. Of taking what I wanted. She came, her entire body spasmed, arching up, her trying not to scream. I almost did the same just watching her climax.

Her heart thundered in my ears, fine tremors passed

through her body.

Ask me to bite you. I willed her silently. She'd probably orgasm again if I did.

"Matteo." her voice was rough, as if she had trouble speaking.

"Mmm," I groaned against her throat, hopeful.

"We've stopped. We're there," she whispered.

I growled in frustration but didn't make a move as she caught her breath.

"I need to clean up before we go out there," she murmured. "Do you have anything?"

Finally, I lifted my head, moving away from her throat, with a deep chuckle. "No, but I can assist with that."

She held still as I shifted, lifting her dress over my head. With deliberate, easy movements, I lapped up her juices from between her thighs. She squirmed and let out a gasp. "Matteo, you're going to make me come again!"

"We can't have that," I said, my mouth above her heat.

"Please, stop," she pleaded, unconvincingly.

I finished cleaning her and moved out from under her dress, pressing my mouth to hers. I knew she could taste herself, but her hand slid over the back of my neck, holding me there.

When we tore ourselves apart from each other, her cheeks were flushed, her eyes glinting. "You should probably put your fangs away," she said, her voice low. "Did you just mess up my lipstick?"

I smiled down at her. "It looks fine, but I'll let you compose yourself if you wish."

I climbed out and held a hand out, waiting. After a minute, she took my hand and I pulled her from the limo, pulling her arm through mine.

"Are you ready?" I asked.

"Give me a minute," she requested, taking a deep breath. "I can't believe you did that. The driver…"

I held a hand up. "Won't remember a thing by the end of the night." I'd compelled myself a limo driver, all for Quinn. The driver would wake up in the morning with no memory of me or where he'd been this evening.

She was as affected as I was that we'd both come close to giving in. To our desire, to each other. I appreciated her needing to take her time; it gave me a chance to push down the feral part of myself. I needed to move like a man. To play the part acceptable to humans, not frighten them with my burning hunger for the woman on my arm.

Quinn laughed nervously, pushing her forehead into my shoulder. "You're-" she cut herself off and took another deep breath, letting it out slowly. "Okay, I think I'm ready."

Chapter 31

Matteo

I escorted her into the ballroom. Chandeliers hung from the ceiling, lit with candles. The entire room looked as it would have in my time. Violin notes hung in the air. There were many beautiful women here tonight in expensive dresses, but none more beautiful than the one at my side. Masks of all colours covered faces. I had compelled invitations out of the organisers for Quinn and her friends. Her presence drew attention from the moment she arrived

"This is incredible," she whispered, her eyes searching the room in awe.

"Dance with me," I requested. "Please?"

"Okay." She let me guide her to the dance floor. I placed

one hand on her back and led her into the waltz. She had clearly never danced this way before, but with my guidance, she caught on quickly.

"You said you used to attend events like this when you were human," she reminded me. "Tell me about them."

I cast a quick glance around the room, catching the familiar vampire scent. I pulled her to me so I could speak into her ear.

"You want to know about me as a human?" I asked. "I was boring."

"That's impossible," she replied without hesitating.

"I was an artist but lived in privilege. My father was a man of importance; we always held balls where he brushed elbows with very well-known elites. There was no one in Venice who didn't know my family."

I stopped, catching sight of Gabriela. Her brown eyes dropped to Quinn before meeting mine with a slight smile. Behind her, Carlos glanced in my direction and took in the sight of Quinn.

'*She smells tantalising,*' he whispered through our bond. '*You've already given her pleasure tonight, that scent. I do believe you'll have her tonight. Body and blood. She desires you, Matteo. They can only hold out for so long.*'

I turned my back on him and focused on dancing with Quinn. His words gave me hope, but I couldn't hold on to expectation.

The room was full of vampires; at least half the clan were there. Events like this were a draw to my kind, so it was no surprise they were there. I decided against telling her how many vampires were in the room. She would likely entice them with her fear.

"Tell me about Venice," Quinn murmured. "What were you like?"

"Venice was my whole world," I said. "I never dreamed of leaving; it was all I knew. I found it peaceful to sit at the front of our home and watch the gondolas go past. I'd sit there and paint. Couples would often ask me to paint them." Just talking to her about my life in Venice reminded me how much I missed it. I stopped talking as the memories washed over me.

We danced close, our faces inches apart, and again her want washed over me. My mouth hovered over hers, but I waited. Her lips parted, and I kissed her. My heart burst; hers skipped. Everything around us seemed to fade. All I could smell was her. Her blood, her perfume. Her scent. My hearing only focused on her heartbeat. Her presence had become my entire existence, and she clutched at me as if afraid of being torn from me. I pitied anyone who tried — I'd tear them apart.

We separated and she rested her head on my shoulder.

"I hope to see Venice one day," she mentioned. "It sounds beautiful. The only place I've been to outside of Australia is New Zealand. My Dad's from there, and we visited his family a lot."

Her heartbeat was still racing, but not with fear.

"Maybe I'll take you there." I couldn't hold the words back. I hadn't returned to Venice for a long time, and the thought of taking her there brought me joy.

"Don't tell me, you have a private jet." I could hear the smile in her voice.

"No, but I do like to fly first class," I boasted.

"Of course you do." She laughed.

We danced in silence for a time. Me with my hand on her back, Quinn with her head on my shoulder. I caught her friends watching her with smiles on their faces. I listened to their conversation.

The taller, blonde one met my eye, and gave a brief nod. "It's been a long time since I've seen her that happy," she noted.

"Steven really did a number on her. I didn't think she'd ever look at another man ever again." The other girl said.

"Your friends are talking about you," I told her.

"Nothing bitchy, I hope," she joked, not lifting her head.

"No, they're happy for you," I said.

She scoffed. "If only they knew I was in the arms of a vampire."

I stiffened. "This isn't one of those things you'll discuss with them, is it? Not all humans accept my kind." *Especially not hunters.* I knew hunters were in Melbourne, had seen some patrolling the streets in the last few weeks, probably looking for me.

She did pull away then, to look up at me. "I won't betray your secret."

"I know you won't, *mi amore*." I stroked her cheek, and a new song started. "Do you want a rest? I think there's food if you're hungry."

"That would be nice," she said. "I should say hello to Lil and Mia."

As we left the dance floor Gabriela approached. "Matteo." She brushed my arm. "You look ravishing. Please do introduce me to your friend."

Quinn locked her arms around mine and she moved to stand partially behind me. She'd deduced that Gabriela was like me and did a good effort of reining in her fear. Gabriela didn't miss anything.

"She knows what you are. That's not like you at all." She turned her gaze to Quinn.

"I saw you," Quinn said with a shaky voice. "You were watching me. At the restaurant."

She'd mentioned it once. I hadn't realised she'd been talking about Gabriela.

"You're watching her?" I growled.

"When a member of my clan is seen in very public settings with a human, I tend to take notice." She glared at me. "All these years, and you don't know what sticking to the shadows means?" She smiled at Quinn. "I suppose you love that you've snagged yourself a vampire, don't you. You like the danger. Or is it the pleasure from his 'vampire's kiss'?" Gabriela's smile was hungry, and I bit back a growl.

"He hasn't fed from me," Quinn countered.

Gabriela's eyes darted to mine in shock. "What are you doing, Matteo?"

"Gabriela, go and find your human and worry about him. Leave mine alone."

"Yours? I see." She gave Quinn a hungry smile. "Welcome to la Primera Familia, little human."

Before I could say anything, I caught the whiff of blood. Gabriela half-turned as if she'd caught the scent, too. "Smells like Carlos has started early. I think I'll join him." She narrowed her eyes at me. "There are more bodies that you and I will talk about."

Her smile grew cold as I pushed past her and led Quinn towards her friends.

"Who was that?" Quinn asked.

201

"She's the head of our clan. I've known her for a long time. She's very old." I didn't like that Quinn was now on Gabriela's radar. "She's what you would consider a queen in my world."

We reached the edge of the dance floor, and she led me to her friends, introducing us.

"What was all that about?" Lilith asked, nodding towards Gabriela.

"Nothing." Quinn said quickly. "Have you two danced yet? Isn't this amazing?"

Lilith's eyes remained on me as Quinn and Mia spoke, before focusing behind me, which I could only assume was on Gabriela.

Mia grasped Lilith's arm. "Let's go dance!"

A ping went off, and Lilith pulled out her phone, frowning.

"That looks serious," Quinn said. "What is it?"

"There was another murder earlier tonight, on Bourke Street," Mia read over her shoulder. "A woman was found down an alleyway."

I feigned interest. "Down Bourke Street?" The location was not far from Quinn's apartment, and where I'd fed earlier. I struggled to remember if I had lost control. All I remembered was the feeding, before returning to my limo. *Did I slip up again? Gabriela will no doubt have words about that, too. Will she starve me again or cage me?*

Quinn's hand tightened around my arm. I could feel the change in her, as she gazed at me. I gave her a quick shake of the head but wished I could be sure I hadn't killed.

"So, your brother is on that case then? Like the other ones?" Quinn asked.

"Yeah, he is," Lilith said.

"On the case?" I asked.

"Her brother's a cop; he usually gets the strange cases. He got the pair from the alley a couple of months ago, and the others last week."

Lilith's eyes met mine, and a spark of suspicion shone from within their depths as she turned her attention to Quinn with a frown.

Chapter 32

Quinn

The night was magical. That's the only word I could think of to describe it. I'd been spending time with Matteo enough to recognise other vampires. It wasn't just the way they moved, or the hunger in their eyes, but something inside them sent warning bells off in my head. Other than Gabriela, I figured out three others were there. I spotted Carlos.

Matteo had told me enough about Carlos for me to know he was a lot older than him. Not one I wanted to be near, though. Even at the distance between us, the hungry look he gave me, everything about him screamed, 'Stay away; avoid at all costs.' Just as it had the first time I met him.

"He would like to join us," Matteo whispered in my ear. "If you want to?"

He hadn't spoken much of Gabriela, and I had the feeling he didn't like her all that much. But Carlos was important to him.

"I'm not sure," I admitted, aware Carlos would hear me at this distance. "Gabriela was enough for one night."

His lips moved, as he said something that Matteo no doubt heard clearly across the room. Matteo chuckled. "He says he promises not to bite."

I gave in. Surely Matteo would keep me safe. I nodded, and Carlos started to move towards us.

Matteo's hands slid around my waist, pulling me against him. "You're okay," he reassured me.

Carlos was lean, he didn't look as if he had the muscle definition Matteo did, but I figured that meant nothing. He'd be just as strong as, if not stronger than Matteo.

"Good to see you again," Carlos said, and before I could move he'd grabbed my hand, bringing it to his lips in the same way Matteo did. "A true beauty. Has he tasted you yet?"

I shook my head, unable to speak; and as his eyes lifted to mine, I couldn't look away. The intensity of his gaze was hypnotic, and I half-wondered if he was compelling me. But somehow I didn't care. I leaned against Matteo, his firm body against mine, arms holding me up. Carlos dropped my hand.

"It's a pleasure to meet a human with such a power over Matteo," he declared and finally looked away, releasing me. His intense blue eyes lifted to Matteo's. "I do hope you'll allow me to dance with her. I want to get to know her. Find out what kind of dance partner she is."

I pressed myself further into Matteo's body. I did not want to be alone with Carlos.

"I don't think she's ready for that yet," Matteo moved his arms, wrapping around me entirely.

His voice was light, but there was a tone of warning to it. I wondered if there was something else they were saying in their words.

"She looks like she'd suit a faster dance, more daring, like the Flamenco. The Waltz is so boring." There was mischief in Carlos's eyes.

"But she's comfortable with the Waltz," Matteo said. "Until she wants otherwise, that's what we're sticking to."

Again, I had the feeling they were talking about something else. Their conversation switched to Italian, only adding to my curiosity as to what they were talking about. Matteo's voice took on the possessive tone that I'd heard with Dan. Carlos backed off.

"Pity," Carlos said, and shifted his eyes back to me.

Again I was pulled in by his intensity. *What is it with the gaze of a vampire that I can't escape?* He smiled and bowed. "A pleasure, again," he said. "I'll see you soon."

"Did he really just bow?" I asked. "What was that?"

Matteo turned me around to face him. "He wants me to share you," he said. "Uh, in bed."

Oh. While I appreciated Matteo's honesty, that was not what I expected. "I get the feeling you're not the sharing kind."

"Especially not when I haven't yet had you myself," he attempted a smile, but I felt like something bothered him.

I put my hand to his chest. "It's okay," I murmured. "You don't have to share me. I don't want anyone else, I want

206

you." I put meaning into my words, hoping he knew what I meant. "Just you." I glanced around the room, watching Carlos, annoyed that he'd bothered Matteo so much. "Can we leave?" I asked. "I'd like to have you all to myself for the rest of the night."

The intensity of his eyes almost matched that of Carlos. An almost feral look rose. "I can do that," he said and with effort, he led me from the dance floor.

I waved to Mia and Lilith as we left. The two of them were wrapped up in each other, but managed to give me a smile. I knew what they were thinking about my early exit. They'd be asking questions the following day.

Matteo guided me to the limo and helped me in, the interior warm. Sitting opposite him, I couldn't help but look him over.

"I have a surprise," he told me after a few minutes of driving. "I'd like a chance to enjoy the peace and quiet before we go back to the city." The limo stopped. "It's going to be cold, though, so you might want to put that on." He pointed to his winter jacket that I'd noticed on the seat when we'd ridden to the masquerade.

I pulled it on, loving its heaviness and warmth. As Matteo opened the door and climbed out, he held out his hand to me. I reached for him before the crashing of waves on a beach made me freeze. Not realising, his fingers closed around mine and he pulled me to him.

"You brought me to the beach," I could barely speak.

He stilled. "You don't like the beach? The full moon's reflection on the water is beautiful, I thought you'd appreciate it."

"No, please take me home," I pleaded, closing my eyes. "I

207

told you last time. I can't be here." Tears threatened to spill over, and I grasped the dolphin pendant.

His arms tightened around me. "What happened?" His voice was gentle, full of concern.

I opened my eyes to find Niamh watching me. "My sister…" I choked on words. "She drowned, and her body washed up not far from here."

He pulled me out of his arms to meet my eyes. "You avoid the beach because of her?" I nodded, tears welling up, stinging. "That's the pain you carry." Once again I was in his embrace. "I'm sorry," he murmured. "We can leave."

"Quinn," Niamh whispered. "You don't have to fear the ocean. Find the calm it once gave you. Let Matteo help you. He smells like that for a reason."

I burrowed my face into his chest, breathing in his scent. I choked back a laugh. Trust me to fall for someone with that scent while trying to avoid the sea.

"I'm okay, Quinn," Niamh reassured me. "I can't move on until Luke joins me. But you need me, too. I have to guide you to let go of your fear. You'll find your happiness with him. Just as I found mine with Luke. Don't let go of him."

"Let me take you home," Matteo said into my hair. "I thought to be romantic, not to cause you pain."

Niamh smiled at me and walked towards the sound of waves crashing on the beach. I forced myself to listen to the sound of the waves.

"No." My voice trembled, vibrating into his chest. "I can't avoid this my whole life."

"Do you want to walk on the beach?" he asked.

"Not yet." I pressed into his embrace more. "Just stand here."

We didn't move, and silent tears fell from my eyes. His presence helped steady me somewhat.

"Do you want to tell me about her?" I jumped as his voice broke the silence.

"No," I replied. "Not yet. Sorry I'm being so emotional." I was ruining the night. Maybe it was time to face the music. Or go home.

"Take all the time you need," his warm breath tickled my ear. "We'll stand here all night if you need."

Chapter 33

Matteo

The night passed quickly, and Quinn had spent much of the night in my arms on the dance floor. Her presence had become irresistible. The limo was parked up near the beach, and my driver slept as I leaned on the bonnet with Quinn, my jacket around her shoulders. Bringing her out here was meant to be romantic, and I had uncovered a deep wound instead. After half an hour of holding her, she'd worked up the courage to face the sea.

She remained silent as she stared into the dark, in the direction of the waves, her head on my chest.

"This is nice," she murmured. "Thank you for being patient. I should have done this months ago."

"Death affects everyone differently. You deal with it in your own way," I knew loss all too well.

She lifted her head to look at me. "Who did you lose?"

Her question threw me. I hadn't thought of my family in many lifetimes. "I lost my wife," I admitted. "And with her, a part of my soul. But I'd already died, and in a way I mourned my own death, too. Everything I lost when I became a vampire."

"So you died to become a vampire?" she asked.

I nodded. "When a human is given enough vampire blood, it overwhelms and shuts down their system, causing a mortal death as the change takes place. Only, they're not really dead. They go into a slumber, ready to be awakened by their maker."

"How did it happen?" There was curiosity in her eyes. We'd not discussed my turning, so for her to ask me was a step forward for her.

"Is this too personal of a question?" she asked when I didn't answer right away.

"No, it's not too personal." I pulled her tighter, letting the memory of my last days as a human wash over me.

I left my villa to make the short walk to my art studio. My daughter was asleep. The night was a warm one, and I enjoyed the walk.

I didn't know what hit me. One minute I was walking, the next I was on my back staring up at bright red eyes and fangs. I fought to get away, and made it to my feet, but barely got far when a hand wrapped around my throat and once again, I fought to escape. Teeth pierced my throat, and I still fought, until I passed out.

When I awoke, I was in a bed I didn't know and felt lightheaded.

I sat up, and she was there again. A woman with red eyes; and somehow, I knew my life was over.

"I have a wife and child," I begged her. "Let me live so that I might see them again."

"You'll see them again," she said.

While she fed from me, I never stopped fighting to escape. She laughed at my failed attempts to get free, telling me how weak I was but that she could make me strong. I pleaded with her and tried to bargain, but it was hopeless. I thought the torment would never end. She forced me to drink her blood. I was desperate for more; hunger I'd never known became a new torment. She told me that if I wanted more of her blood, I needed to show her I was worthy of it. I was locked in a room with a woman, bleeding and begging me not to hurt her. I fell on her, not understanding why I needed her blood. The vampire blood, combined with the act of feeding on a human, was enough to trigger a change in me. I lost consciousness.

When I awoke, I knew nothing of my life, only her. She locked many in the room with me to feed from. With my memories restored, I escaped, returning home.

I managed a day before my hunger showed itself. My wife caught me feeding.

"What are you?" she asked. "Monster!"

Her fear was too much. She ran from me, and I gave chase, catching her easily. She didn't scream, just pleaded with me not to kill her. I couldn't stop, couldn't hold back what I'd become. What Bianca had turned me into. I bit into her, and she did scream then, struggling to free herself. But my strength was too great, as was my hunger. I fed deeply to satisfy my hunger. The red haze only cleared when her heart stopped. I looked down at her, at what I'd done, my heart breaking.

"My love," I whispered. "I'm sorry." I caressed her face, closed her lifeless eyes. Anguish rose in me, and I let out a roar, unable to contain my grief.

"Father?" My daughter stood over me staring at her dead mother. At me. "Father, what did you do?"

Quinn's voice pulled me back. "You had a family," she said. She'd pulled away, her eyes on my face. "I'm so sorry, Matteo." Her hand pressed against my chest as if to sooth the deep pain that had embedded itself there. "What happened to your daughter?"

The horror in Quinn's eyes hurt. She was afraid I'd killed my daughter.

"I told her to go to her uncle, and never return. That she would be safe with my brother. He would protect her." I could barely speak the words. "My brother took her in, and her descendants, my descendants still live there today. Along with those of my brother."

"Did you ever see Bianca again?" she asked.

"I did. She summoned me through a link that had been created with the exchange of blood. It's called a blood bond. I had no choice but to return. I was furious at what I had done. What *she* had done. So I killed her." I growled at the memory. The very thing that had left me half-feral.

Quinn's hand slipped around my arm again. "I'm sorry you experienced that," she said. "But Bianca got what she deserved."

"Perhaps," I said, trying to push away the storm of emotions threatening to overwhelm me. It was best that I didn't think of the past. "It's *very* rare for a vampire to kill the one who turned them," I said, brushing her cheek. "Do you mind if we change the subject?"

213

"Of course. I'm sorry if I caused you pain..." she spoke in earnest.

"Only if we continue to talk about it." I flashed her a smile. "I prefer to think about the beautiful woman with me now. You're alone with a vampire, and your heartbeat is steady. I'm impressed."

She stared out at the ocean. "You said people don't feel pain, when you..." she stopped, unable to finish.

"You really do have a lot of questions, don't you," I laughed. She hadn't asked this question before, had in fact avoided the subject altogether. I was hopeful that this was a sign of her considering letting me drink from her. "It can. It can be excruciating. But we can choose to release a venom when we bite, that will put the humans into a state of pleasure and desire."

Despite her uncertainty, she was intrigued. I brushed my fingers over her neck again.

Her breath hitched and I smiled. She would ask me to bite her that night, I was sure of it.

"The man that would have hurt me...did he..." once again, she couldn't finish.

Her question surprised me. Another topic she'd avoided. "He screamed," I told her. "After what he would have done to you, I wanted him to suffer. Unfortunately, he stabbed me. Repeatedly. So I tore out his throat. I had already made up my mind to kill him, even though that broke the accords. At that moment, I didn't care." I stopped. "Is this disturbing you?"

"No...well, yes," she confessed. "I still don't like the idea that you killed. But I can't say that guy didn't deserve it. You knew what he was going to do. I'd probably be dead if it weren't for you."

"I could smell the desire on him," I told her. "It was of dark urges and intentions."

"Oh, that's right: You can see into our minds." She looked off into the distance. "I'm glad you didn't make me forget. This is definitely an experience I hope to remember."

'And so you shall.' I still wasn't certain how I could talk to her as if we were bonded, but I liked it.

She pressed her fingers over my mouth. "How is it that you speak to me without talking?" Her curiosity was making her bold with her questions, less unsure of herself.

'It's something I've only been able to do with Carlos. Because we have a blood bond. Never with a human,' I told her.

"Can you hear what I'm thinking now?" she asked.

Not only could I hear her thoughts, but I could smell them on her. I lifted her chin and leaned in for a kiss.

Chapter 34

Quinn

The kiss was deep, searing, and my heart soared. I wanted it to go on forever, and for the first time since seeing his red eyes and fangs, I let go. Of my fear, my worry, and my mistrust. I was alone in the dark with a vampire, listening to the ocean, and for the first time, I wasn't afraid of what he was. As we pulled apart, I struggled to focus my thoughts.

"Wow," I murmured.

He took in a deep breath, and I somehow knew he was breathing me in. My heart skipped again. He'd told me what his bite did, and curiosity got the best of me.

"So your bite really doesn't hurt?" I asked.

His fingers brushed my throat. "It really doesn't hurt," he promised.

I could tell what he wanted. We'd been very close earlier in the limo, and I had been about to ask him.

"I want to," I admitted. "Even if it's just once."

He responded by pulling in for another kiss, this one ravenous where I could actually feel his hunger for me. The interior light of the limo reflected on his face, and I could see his eyes were red.

"Quinn." His voice changed, as if he were struggling to speak. "What you're asking…"

"I know. I told you I'd never ask for that. But I'm asking for it now."

He lifted my hand. "I won't bite your throat. The way I'm feeling, that is likely to lead to other things."

Other things. I hadn't had proper sex in months, so I certainly wouldn't complain about that. I also didn't want him to lose control while his teeth were buried in my throat. But I nodded. His eyes locked on mine as he turned my hand over and brought my wrist to his mouth.

He paused. "Don't tense." He slid his tongue over my wrist.

I forced myself to relax as his fangs pierced my wrist. It only hurt for a second before I was engulfed by sheer pleasure. It swept through me, and my entire body went limp. My eyes rolled back. Heat swelled within me, and I let out a moan before I could stop it.

Then it was over. His fangs withdrew and I opened my eyes. He was holding me up.

"Um." I breathed out. "Wow."

His teeth flashed, fangs still extended. "My thoughts exactly."

I reached a hand up to his mouth in wonder. "That was intense."

Waves of warmth still flooded through me.

"Do you want to go home?" he asked.

"Now? I…" I stopped blurting out what I really wanted. "Sure."

"Give me a minute, I'll wake up the driver." He moved to the driver's door. It dawned on me then that he hadn't hired the limo like I'd initially thought. With the ability to compel people, he'd likely taken the driver and car in an attempt to impress me. He was from a time where money created the kind of impression he was accustomed to. But it was not any idea of money that had drawn me to him. It was him.

I stepped away from the limo, the sounds of the ocean loud, filling me with calm energy as it always had. I had avoided it too long, and all it took was for Matteo to bring me out here. I started to sing a few notes. It took me a while to realise I was singing a song I'd written a year ago. It came out of me quietly at first. As if I was hesitant. Then the words and power flowed through me, through my voice. A farewell to Niamh. I felt like the sea was listening as I finished. She stood beside me staring in wonder.

"I've missed hearing you sing," she whispered. "You wrote a song for me." Tears slid down her face. Then she was gone.

Matteo's hand barely touched me. Comforting. "Your voice really is something," he said. "But that was haunting. Beautiful."

"I should have sung that at her funeral." I wiped my eyes. "Bringing me here tonight was the best thing you could have done. Thank you."

I kissed his cheek, and he held one arm out. "Should I get

you home now?"

I took his arm, and he led me back to the limo.

He sat close to me the entire ride back, not that I was complaining. The effects of his fangs had only opened up how much I wanted this man, and I hoped he wouldn't just leave when we arrived back at my building. I leaned against him, head on his chest, his arm around me, holding me close.

As we arrived, he released the driver. Much to my delight, he walked me inside. As I opened my door, I turned to face him, finding his eyes on me in wonder. I knew what another kiss had the potential to lead to. For the both of us. I knew I wanted his kiss. His 'vampire's kiss'. I reached up, both hands on either side of his face, and brought his lips down to mine.

Somehow we made it through the door, and he nudged it closed without breaking our kiss. His arms were gentle as he wrapped them around me. I wanted more, and desire swelled again. I reached for his pants, and he stopped, pulling back.

"Don't stop now," I said, shrugging his jacket from my shoulders.

His eyes glinted with hunger and desire. He pulled his suit jacket off, removing his shirt. I ran my hands over his bare chest and down to his abs, muscles beneath my hands defined. I reached for his trousers again and heard a ripping sound. My dress fell from my body.

"Wasn't that expensive?" I asked against his mouth.

"It would have taken too long to get you out of it," he replied. "I am not a patient man. I can always sell a painting and buy you a new one, or a hundred."

I chuckled as I undid his belt. He quickly discarded his

219

trousers and lifted me in his arms. In a split second we went from my front door to my bedroom. He threw me on the bed and followed, a wicked gleam in his eye as he crawled up the length of my body, a deep growl in his chest.

His lips brushed my navel, moving up as his hands caressed me. My entire body was on fire from his touch. I reached for Matteo, wanting my hands on him, wanting him.

"Oh my god," I gasped. "I want you inside me, now!"

He lifted his head from my stomach long enough to smile before moving towards my breasts. His tongue flicked over my left nipple, teeth adding to the pleasure that he'd lit within me. Every nerve felt exposed, and I let out a moan, sensitive to his touch. My fingers dug into his back while I squirmed under him, aching and eager. I whimpered, breathing with need, his movements painfully slow.

"Please, Matteo," I groaned. "I can't take it anymore, I..."

My words cut off when a deep growl resonated from Matteo. He moved up again, lips brushing against my throat and jaw before finding my mouth. I clutched at him, every part of my being quivering with need. The sounds he made reverberated through me.

Finally, he pushed into me, thrusting deep. His hips rolled forward, my muscles pulsing around him. As he slid in and out, his body against mine, I lifted my hips to meet his rhythm.

His eyes turned bright red, raw hunger shining through. There was no shock or fear at the sight of his vampiric nature anymore. Only a deep yearning. I'd already experienced the effects of his venom earlier that night. I craved his bite as much as he hungered for me. My blood and my body. With one hand I cupped his cheek, pressing my thumb to his canine. His fangs lengthened, long and sharp, drawing blood from my thumb. He froze.

"It's okay," I whispered, smearing my blood on his lips. "I want you to."

His gaze became fervent, and he licked his lips, a rumble vibrating from him. The sound and action lit a new fire. One that threatened to engulf me.

"Are you saying what I think you're saying?" he asked with a hard thrust that sent a deep wave of pleasure through me.

I nodded. "I want your bite," I breathed. "I'm asking you, just as you said I would. I'll beg for it, if it'll help."

For once I didn't want him to wait, to be the gentleman. I tilted my head, baring my throat, pulling him down. He dragged his tongue over my neck, and I braced myself. His lips brushed against flesh, soft, barely touching but scorching. Then with a growl that made my muscles tighten, he bit down. I gasped. Warmth and euphoria spread across me and sent me soaring. His tongue slid over my throat, tasting me, drinking me.

A shudder passed through him. His grunt of pleasure vibrated against me.

"You taste of desire and music," he murmured and bit again, deeper.

Light-headedness swept over me. A sliver of panic was drowned out by the waves of bliss that carried me higher. A scream broke free and my orgasm hit hard, leaving me breathless and trembling as he fed from me.

Chapter 35

Matteo

I lifted my head, blood dripping from my mouth, wrenching myself from the red haze.

"Quinn." I felt drunk, as if I'd overfed. Something was *wrong*. "Are you alright? Did I hurt you?" The heavy scent of blood threatened to pull me under again. I pulled out and lifted myself up, straddling her.

Her eyes half-opened, and she smiled before closing them. But her heartbeat was erratic. I caught sight of her throat. I'd bitten too deep, torn it a little, and she was too far under the effects of my venom to feel pain. I pressed my hand against her throat, trying to stop the bleeding. Memories of my wife dying in my arms flooded through me.

Merda!

"Quinn," I mumbled. I frowned, and my own heart skipped. *I took too much. I've hurt her.* I shook her shoulder. "Quinn, open your eyes."

Barely conscious, she managed to open her eyes, and she reached for me.

"Quinn, I took too much," I emphasised, my voice rising in panic. "I bit you deeply. Too deeply."

'Am I going to die?' Her thought was loud, and not yet as concerned as she should be.

She would most certainly die. Drowning in dread, darkness engulfed me. Carlos would know what to do. But I hesitated to reach out to him. He'd only tell me to turn her. There was only one solution, and it was still risky.

I didn't try to lie to her. "Yes, you will. I *have* to give you my blood. Otherwise, you'll be *dead* in minutes. You're going to bleed out."

Her eyes became panicked then, as she focused on my fangs. *'I don't want to be a vampire.'*

"You won't be," I promised. "But it will make you hungry for a few days until my blood leaves your system. If you do feed off human blood, you will become like me. Remember what I told you?" She would also change if she died, or if she drank too much of my blood, but I wouldn't allow that to happen. I would do as I had promised her.

She said nothing, yet her heart said plenty. If she didn't drink my blood right then, she would die. Her eyes closed again.

"Quinn, I won't force you to drink from me, but if you don't, you'll *die*." I fought against rising panic. "Open your eyes!"

223

The seconds of silence ticked by. Her heart filled the silence. Finally, she opened her eyes, and I caught determination and anger. "Don't let me die," she whispered.

A tear slid down the side of her face, and I wiped it away with my thumb.

"I won't. Will you drink from me?" Her heart continued to race, trying to compensate for the loss of blood.

She could only nod. I tore into my wrist, pressing it to her mouth. I had *never* shared my blood with a human before. Many times over the centuries I had wondered what my life would have been, had I shared my blood with Marisa. My wife, my first beloved. Had I done that, she would still be at my side, and I would not have met Quinn. I had taken Marisa's life from her, and I did *not* want history to repeat itself with Quinn. I wouldn't, I *couldn't* let her die, too.

At first nothing happened, except for her eyes closing, and I held my breath, waiting, one hand pressed against her throat to slow the bleeding. Then her tongue flickered against my wrist, into the tear I'd made. She shuddered, groaning. I remembered that feeling, the first taste of vampire blood. It had been like fire, unlike anything I'd tasted before. And I recalled the hunger that came with it.

"Keep drinking," I whispered.

But she didn't need telling. Her mouth clamped on to my wrist, and I heard her swallow. Vampire blood was irresistible to humans, and she'd be hungry for more. I was creating a bond between us. It would fade in time, but she might find it overwhelming. I would need strength for the both of us to endure what would soon follow. I knew all too well what she was to face in the coming days. While I wanted more than anything to have her by my side for eternity, I would *not* take that choice from her as it was taken from me. She would ask me to turn her, *without* the influence of my blood persuading her to give in as I had.

Her hands came up, holding on to my arm as she drank. I smiled with relief. "That's it," I urged.

Her eyes opened then, bright red. It was a shocking difference from their usual green, but normal. Her mind slipped into mine as the connection of a blood bond opened between us.

'I can hear you.' Her thoughts were of wonder and surprise.

"You're bonded to me because we've exchanged blood. You'll have my hunger, and my senses," I told her. She would likely hear the heartbeats of everyone in this building.

'You said my eyes were red.' Through the bond, her voice trembled.

The wound in her throat closed under my hand.

"This will all fade in a few days. That's enough." I started to pull my arm away.

Her hands tightened, and she growled against my wrist, biting down, instinctually. Frustration surged through her. I lowered myself over her, kissing her forehead. Her heartbeat stabilised, becoming strong again.

"That's enough." I told her again. "Stop."

She released my arm. The sight of my blood on her mouth and chin was enough to make me hard again. It would be all too easy to get drawn into the vampiric frenzy that came with exchanging blood for my kind. To exchange more blood, and to fuck while under a haze of bloodlust. At the sight of my blood on her mouth and chin, I fought back the rising need to give in to my urges that were normal among vampires.

'That's my blood on his lips; I've never been so turned on.' She

was already heavily under my blood's aphrodisiac effects, but her human self surged from within. Confusion and disgust, at her own lust, led to fear.

I had done this to her. I'd wanted to taste her, and the moment she trusted me enough to offer me her throat, I'd almost killed her. I was not accustomed to the remorse that flickered through me and almost didn't recognise it. A human emotion that I had let go of long ago, as all vampires did over time. A necessity. Now, as I sought to comfort her, it all flooded back.

"I'm sorry, *mi amore*," I whispered, hoping she'd believe me.

Her gaze locked onto mine. "You lost control." There was sympathy in her voice, as if I were the one needing it. This woman was truly remarkable.

I nodded. "I did." I couldn't explain to her how, either. I'd thought she'd be safe. I'd fed earlier that night, so it wasn't hunger that caused this. Something about being inside her had overwhelmed me. The moment I entered her, I'd felt complete, and all self-restraint had given way to the need to *claim* her, by marking her. "I'm sorry," I said again. I had no other words to offer her.

She clung to me, a desperate embrace of someone coming to terms with her near-death. "I'm okay." Her whispered words were for both our sakes. She cradled my face, looking into my eyes. "I'm alright, Matteo."

I turned my head, kissing the palm of her hand.

Relieved that she was no longer in danger, I relaxed. "You're going to find you'll feel an increase in arousal, alongside hunger for blood," I told her. "It's normal, all a part of my venom's effect, and having my blood in you." I stroked her hair.

She scoffed. "I can't deny, there is a definite increase in arousal," she said. "Or that I want you to bite me again."

Desire for her flared. "You do?"

"I do." She exposed her throat to me, without fear.

"I already took too much," I told her. "If I do that this time and kill you, you will return a vampire." I knew what else this could lead to, had seen it before.

"Then don't take too much," she said as if it was as simple as that.

I couldn't look away from her throat, though, my fangs aching to bite into it.

"Do it," she whispered.

I hesitated. She would soon get caught up in our heat and want more of mine in return. She shared my bloodlust, and I would need to monitor her to keep her from biting down on the wrong throat.

Her hand slipped to the back of my head, and she lowered it to her throat. I growled, deep in my chest and opened my mouth, my fangs piercing her flesh once again.

Her moan almost made me come then and there, and she ground herself against me. I eased my cock back into her as I fed from her. The taste of her blood had changed; the added fire of vampire blood surged through me as I drank. This time I stopped myself from going too far again, and I lifted my head. Warm blood trickled down my chin, and she rose to kiss me again. The exchange of blood was increasing both our drives.

Her muscles pulsed around me as I slid in and out. Our bodies pressed together, eyes locked. Her small moans as I sunk myself deep into her drove through me. I felt her hunger, her wordless need as her eyes focused on my throat.

Lifting one hand, I used my own fingernail to slice into my neck. Her eyes fell to the small cut, and she didn't hesitate as she lifted her head. I lowered my neck to her mouth. With her lips against my flesh, her tongue licking the cut, I sped up, driving hard into her, unable to hold back.

The pleasure was never-ending, her skin against mine as we moved, not getting enough of each other. Her pleasure flowed through me, through our bond. We chased orgasm after orgasm, exchanging blood through the night. I had never known bliss as I did then, our bond deepening. I had never felt this close to a human in all my years as a vampire, and I didn't want it to end. Finally, as the sun started to rise, we finished, sated and exhausted. She lay on her back, breathing heavily.

"This is incredible," she said. "Normal sex is never going to be the same again. I've never…" She laughed and turned her head towards me. My stomach flipped again at her red eyes. "This gives a new meaning to mind-blowing sex. I don't want to stop, but I can barely move."

Her words were enough to make me want her again, but I held back. We'd already been at it all night. Instead, I turned on my side, resting my head on my hand. Her mouth and chin were covered in my blood, and at that moment, pleasure still shone through her eyes. I kissed her again. "Hold still," I instructed.

I licked her chin, and her eyes widened. I continued, cleaning my own blood from her face. It had been a long time since I had shared my blood, and I had yet to experience this with a human. She closed her eyes as my tongue ran over her face. I pulled back and caressed her cheek. "You're beautiful," I declared, unable to hold back. "And you're mine."

"Heart, body and soul?" she smiled, her eyes on my mouth. "Why do my teeth hurt?"

"Heart, body, and soul," I reassured her. I grasped her chin, probing into her mouth. Her canine incisors were longer, more pointed. Not quite fangs, but the difference was significant to that which was normal for a human.

"Another side effect. You have baby fangs. They will return to normal when all this has passed," I informed her.

Her baby fangs were quite a sight.

Why do I have the sudden urge to lick him clean? Her thoughts tumbled into my mind.

"It's normal for us, too," I told her. "I won't stop you."

Her tongue dragged across my chin, hesitant at first. *Not as satisfying as his.* I closed my eyes as she licked her own blood from my face.

She'd make a great vampire.

She froze, my runaway thought clearly caught.

"I'm sorry, I cannot help my thoughts," I murmured.

"You still want to turn me?" she asked.

She was deep in the effects of my blood, and had I requested it, she would have allowed me to turn her.

"Yes," I admitted. "But I will only turn you if that's what *you* want. That's *not* a decision you should be making now."

"Why not?"

"My blood is in your system; so, what you're feeling, you can't see past any of it to think clearly." Bitterness crept through me: my own change had been in that haze, and I would never willingly do that to another. At that moment, if I had asked her, she would have allowed it. But I wouldn't do that to her in this state. "Go to sleep," I urged. "It's been a long night."

Chapter 36

Quinn

I t was hunger that awoke me. Burning through every fibre of my body. Matteo was no longer in bed, but I could sense his presence nearby. The night washed over me. I'd let him feed from me, and the moment his fangs pierced my throat everything had changed.

Something had gone wrong. He'd fed too deeply, tearing into me, and I'd awoken to him urging me to drink from him. What followed was the most pleasure I'd ever experienced. He'd once told me sex and blood go hand in hand. But that was beyond anything I could have imagined.

"Matteo?" I called out.

He was there in an instant. "I'm here. How do you feel?"

His eyes were dark, focusing on mine, concern shining through.

"I'm hungry…or thirsty," I said. But the word was wrong. *Ravenous.*

"That's your hunger for blood," he said.

I groaned, the need almost painful.

He knelt by the bed, his fingers brushing my cheek. "You'll be okay, as long as you don't give in to that urge to feed. It's going to be overwhelming. I'm sorry."

I sat up. "How long before this passes?"

"Usually, I'd say three days," he said.

"Usually?" I didn't like the sound of that.

"Well, you took *a lot* of my blood last night, so in this case it might take longer." He winced. "I'm sorry, I didn't mean to share so much of my blood with you. Once we were bonded, I couldn't help myself." I could see the remorse in his eyes. He knew he'd let me down, he knew he hadn't kept his many promises to me.

"How long?" I asked again.

"A week?" He frowned.

"You don't seem sure about that." I froze. A noise started, like a thousand drums, pounding against my head, followed by a roar. "What is that sound?"

He tilted his head as if listening. "Human heartbeats," he told me. "And traffic."

"Oh my god," I put my hands against my ears. "Can you hear this all the time? How do you bear it?"

He gave me a sympathetic smile. "I've had a few centuries to learn to tune that sound out."

"How do I do that?" It wasn't just a sound, but the scent. I could smell blood, people.

231

He grabbed my hand, holding it to his chest. I felt his heart. "Focus on mine. The rest will fade."

I tried as he said. "Why is yours slower?" I asked.

"Because it is not human. *I'm not human,*" he reminded me. "Keep focusing on it."

With great effort, I let his heartbeat surround me and the rest faded. "My teeth hurt." I said.

He lifted my chin, finger pulling back my top lip. "You have baby fangs, they want to bite into something."

I pictured it then, biting into an exposed throat, letting the blood wash into my mouth. The vision was so strong I could almost taste it. "Can I bite you?" I asked, hoping for relief from the hunger and need.

Unmistakable desire flared in his eyes, turning them red, and he gave me a small smile. "As much as that appeals, I can't let you do that," he confessed. "The more you drink from me, the longer this will take to go away. There will be a point when your system will be overwhelmed with vampire blood, and it will start to turn you. If it's not already doing so."

"Oh." I bit at nothing, trying to get rid of the feeling of needing to bite someone.

He grabbed my jaw. "Don't do that, you'll only hurt your teeth." His eyes focused on my baby fangs again, and I could feel his attraction.

"You like my baby fangs," I laughed.

"They are a beautiful addition to your lovely mouth," he said. "But they will disappear when the rest of this does."

I climbed out of bed, still naked. Somehow, I knew the sight of me aroused him. "I need to go to practise with Lil and Mia."

His face hardened. "No. You are not leaving this apartment."

"Excuse me?" I growled. "One night of sex does not give you control over my life."

"While you're like this it does." He was firm.

"Get out of my way." I pushed him and he hit the wall. Surprise flickered in his eyes. *She shouldn't be that strong.* He moved forward too fast for me to see, and he wrapped his arms around me —not an embrace, but holding me. I couldn't move. "Let me go," I demanded.

"Quinn, while you're hungry like this, you *cannot* be around humans *at all.* Their blood will be hard to resist. You will give in to it, and you will feed. Your body will do everything it can to satisfy that hunger. That will trigger the change, and there will be no turning back. Your human body will shut down while that happens, and you'll awaken a vampire. Being around your friends isn't an option. I've already told them that you're sick."

The fight left me. "How do I get rid of this hunger?" I asked. "If I can't leave my apartment, and I can't bite you, I'll go mad."

"You have to ride it out." He turned me around in his arms, his gaze softening. "I'll be here the whole time. I've called Gabriela to come and have a look at you."

"Gabriela?" I did not want other vampires in my home.

"She won't hurt you. She's older than me and knows more about this." He tried to reassure me.

Doubtful, I nodded anyway.

"She's just going to check over you to make sure there isn't too much vampire blood in you," he said.

I panicked. "What if there is?"

"Let's not worry about that right now." He cupped my cheek with his hand.

I frowned. "But you were worried enough to call her." Again, a surge of jealousy. I wasn't the jealous type, so it confused me.

His mouth found mine, silencing my words, and I didn't resist him. There was a connection between us that hadn't been there yesterday, and all the energy I'd spent fighting my attraction to him was gone. My body wanted him, wanted more of what we'd done last night. If only he didn't have clothes on.

His laughter rumbled through my mind. "Relax, my little *cantante.* Once Gabriela has left, we can return to bed. We have the next few days for that." He lifted a robe from the floor. "Put this on for now, and come with me. I made you something."

He led me into the lounge. "Why is my blind closed?" I asked.

"Because you will have my sensitivity to the sunlight. It's not lethal, just unpleasant. Especially when you're not used to it." He moved towards the kitchen. "Sit down."

I sat in my favourite chair. When he came back, my mouth watered. The smell of warm chocolate greeted me, icing lathered over it, with ice cream on the side.

"You made a chocolate cake?" I perked up.

"I've noticed you have a sweet tooth, in particular for chocolate." He held the slice towards me.

I glanced at him. "Is this a distraction?"

He placed the cake on the coffee table in front of me. "Am I that transparent?"

I reached for the cake. "I'm not complaining."

The flavour of the cake overwhelmed me, a rich tang that filled my mouth.

"What did you make this with?" I asked with a full mouth. "It's delicious."

"Nothing not already in your kitchen. Everything is going to taste, smell, and sound more vivid than you're familiar with. Enjoy it." He sat on the couch, watching me.

He wasn't wrong. The very scent of him surrounded me. His smell of cedarwood and sea was stronger now, filling the room and reminding me again of the beach on a hot day.

"You smell nice, too," he said. "Chocolate and coffee."

"Can you hear all my thoughts?" I asked.

"Yours right now are rather loud while we're connected like this. We have a blood bond that opens us both up to each other's thoughts and emotions." He grinned. "It makes things interesting in bed, to feel each other's pleasure. That's why we were able to go on for a long time last night."

Heartbeats started to close in again, so I took a deep breath, focusing on his. I moved from my chair to the couch, leaning against him. "Why do you have a heartbeat?" I asked. "Are you not dead?"

His hand brushed my arm, the contact lighting a fire within me. "You really shouldn't base your expectations about real life upon what you've seen in movies. Finish your cake."

There was a knock on the door then. I rose to my feet, suddenly nervous as Matteo opened it.

Chapter 37

Quinn

Gabriela walked in, her eyes on Matteo, and the door barely made a sound as she closed it.

He knelt before her. "Thank you, my Queen."

She had a scent similar to Matteo's. I wondered if it was the vampire I could smell. It wasn't human, and I wasn't sure how I even knew that. A musk that made me think of predators. Her heart beat slowly, like his, while my own raced like a jackhammer.

"I was happy to hear from you. I can't say I enjoyed your rudeness last night," she said. "Remember your place, Matteo. After that, now you come to me for help." She was enjoying this, flaunting her power over him. "Get up, I don't have all day. Carlos is displeased with me, and I need to address his defiance."

Matteo had told me she was a Queen in his clan. Something in me recognised that, but she wasn't *my* Queen, and a growl burst from my throat. Her eyes turned red as she faced me.

"Be careful," she warned me. "Know who you're growling at, little human."

But I didn't care. The deep need to make it known to her that she was in *my* territory overcame me. I growled again.

"She doesn't like my presence at all," she commented to Matteo, amusement curving her lips.

It annoyed me that Gabriela was talking about me as if I weren't right there. She raised her eyes to me again. "What is he to you?" she asked me and trailed her hand across his chest.

"Gabriela," Matteo pleaded. "Please don't."

"Mine." I didn't understand why I said that. Nor the growl coming from me.

The woman shook her head. "I can already tell a lot of your blood is in her. Let me guess, you gave her your blood for some reason, and the two of you fell into a pleasure-induced bloodlust feeding off each other well into the night."

"Something like that," was his reply.

"You *lost control,* didn't you?" she asked. "Bit too deep?"

He said nothing, his eyes on me.

"I see. I'd like to know why you wouldn't just let her turn. You've denied yourself a companion for centuries. Why would you give her your blood if not for that? She must be something special to you. Maybe I can have a taste, see what all the fuss is about." She flashed fangs at him.

His eyes turned red, and his growl rumbled, a low sound that almost echoed as he turned all his attention to Gabriela. I felt a protectiveness in him, mixed with rage. "She's *mine!*" he growled, his fangs visible.

Laughter burst from her. "You're a perfect match, just as bad as each other." She held her hands up. "Okay, I won't touch her, but you need to let me look at her. Will you calm down enough to do that? I can't have you attack me when I'm here to help you."

It took him a while, but slowly his mind relaxed, and his fangs retracted. "Look at her," he said.

She stepped towards me. I stepped back. She sighed, lifting her glare to Matteo. "I need you to calm her down, too. She's likely to try to take my fingers."

Matteo was in front of me then, his eyes filling my whole vision. "Quinn, she's not here to hurt you. She's just going to look over you, like a check-up you'd get at the doctor."

His words took a hold of me. Somehow, I knew he was using his vampire ability to calm me, but it wasn't to force me to do anything I didn't want to do. He only wanted me to become calm. I let his sway wash over me and nodded.

She was there then, her fingers gripping my chin. "Open your mouth," she commanded.

I opened my mouth, and her fingers pulled back my lip. "Baby fangs. Matteo, how much blood did you give her? She's practically one of us already, just *one more* drink away from it being *permanent*." She glanced over at him. *"Either yours or human blood, she is on the cusp here."* She leaned in, breathing in deep. "She still has a human scent, though, so there *might* be enough of her left to remain as such."

Her head turned towards my door, examining the blinds,

and my own gaze dropped to her throat. I wanted to bite down and drink deep, hunger making me dizzy. I started to lean forward. Her hand wrapped around my throat. "No!" she spoke to me as if speaking to a child. "I am not for biting. Not if you want to hold on to your humanity. My blood is old and will complete the change already tearing through your body."

"So, she is turning?" Matteo asked. "Is it too late to stop it?"

"Open the blinds," she told him.

He was next to me one second, by the window the next, and harsh sunlight poured through the door. I pulled back, throwing a hand up, whimpering. It hurt. Not in a way that burned me, as I had seen in movies, but it hurt my eyes. The blinds dropped, and I was relieved to be plunged into cool darkness again.

Gabriela gripped my chin again, looking deep into my eyes. "How do you feel?" she asked me.

"Hungry," I responded without thought.

"Describe your hunger," she said.

That one I *did* have to think about. "It's deep within, with a pain I never thought I could feel over being hungry. I keep visualising blood gushing, as I bite..." I stopped. "The people in this building smell delicious. My teeth hurt." I met her eyes. "Matteo won't let me leave, I just want one bite. Please, tell him I need to go."

Her hand left my chin.

"Do you realise what you've done?" she asked Matteo in a low voice.

"I didn't mean to. Is there any hope?" His voice was pleading.

"She obviously has some hold over you. You don't resent what you are, why don't you want her to be as you are?"

"Because she doesn't want it," he said.

She looked at me. "Clearly, she does. I don't feel any resistance to what's happening to her. With her line of work, it's not as if she'd be short of groupies to feed from."

"Damnit, no! She made it clear, before I gave her my blood, that it's *not* what she wanted."

"Then it must be the blood, is that it?" She smirked.

"Yes! You know it is!" he boomed.

She shook her head sadly. "What you're seeing is not because of your blood or her hunger Matteo. There is a deep yearning that she was probably unwilling to admit to, a morbid fascination maybe. Perhaps she wasn't fulfilled in her life. It was there before you bit her. If you let her turn now, she will not resent you for it. She's already animalistic, and has laid claim to you, so I think she'd be a natural. She might have a hunger that rivals yours."

"Does she have a chance?" he asked.

"Yes. A *small* one. You'll need to stay with her until she's back to her old, boring self." She actually looked disappointed.

"How many days?" he pulled me towards him as a pang of hunger hit me.

I pressed my face into his chest, breathing him in.

Gabriela sighed. "A week, maybe two? You understand what you're doing, don't you? There is no leaving her alone. She will take *any* chance she can get to feed. There will be no hunting for you. In that time, you could easily lose control again. This time she will die or turn."

"That won't happen." His hands rubbed up and down my

240

back.

I pulled away, suddenly restless.

Her eyes met mine again. "That's a shame. I like her." She smiled. "This will certainly damage your reputation. The great Matteo, finally tamed by a human woman. You really are something, child. Appreciate that."

She was gone, leaving me reeling. "What did she mean, 'tamed'?" I asked.

He shook his head. "Nothing. Come on, let's go back to bed."

The idea of it appealed to me. I followed him to my bedroom.

"Get into bed," he said, and I didn't fight the command. Then he knelt beside the bed, running his hand through my hair. "Quinn, I need you to go to sleep."

I fought his command then, with difficulty. "Won't you come to bed with me?"

He smiled. "I will. There's something I need to do first. I'll be back."

I sat up. "You're leaving? She told you not to."

"Not for long. It's best that you sleep while I'm away." He caught my eye again. "Sleep, Quinn."

This time his voice broke through, and I closed my eyes.

Chapter 38

Quinn

Rivers of blood. A figure in the dark, with blue eyes. I'd seen him before, knew his curly hair, his olive skin. He approached me with a smile filled with hunger.

"Carlos." I tried to back away.

"Feed," he whispered. "You'll feel much better."

He towered over me, his eyes pulling me in. I couldn't look away.

"I know you think you don't want this," he said. "But there is already a hunger in you, a longing. This is what you've been waiting for. Feed. Complete the change, be with Matteo, forever."

Matteo.

I woke up alone, the hunger worse, a deep pain growing.

"Matteo?" I called out.

My apartment was silent, but those around me weren't. I pulled the blanket over me, hoping to go back to sleep in the warmth of my bed. The whole experience was confusing and painful, and I just wanted it to be over. I didn't feel like myself, everything was dreamlike, and the constant beating of hearts hurt my head. I wanted to feed one minute, and remembered I didn't want to be a vampire the next. The moments of wanting to feed were increasing.

I heard a beep and sat up. *My phone!* Climbing out of bed I soon found it in the kitchen. There were messages of 'Feel better' from Lilith and Mia.

I opened one from Dan. *<Sorry I missed you at the gym today. I hope you're okay.>*

"No, I'm not okay, I'm hungry," I grumbled. Then I smiled. If I asked him to come over, he wouldn't hesitate. I sent him a quick reply and waited.

His response was as eager as I knew it would be. *<On my way.>* Something in me, a small voice told me I shouldn't be doing this. I shrugged it off as I waited for Dan.

His knock sounded and I almost flew at the door. Forcing myself to slow down, I let him in and smiled.

"Dan, I'm happy to see you," I caught his scent, breathing it in deep. "Oh, you smell so good." He was so close, him and his blood.

His eyes widened. "What's wrong with your eyes? They're red."

Damn, I'd forgotten about that. His heart pounded, and

the spike of fear enticed me forward.

"Why are you here?" Matteo demanded from behind him.

"It's Dan," I said, beaming at Matteo.

"You shouldn't be here, Dan," my vampire grumbled.

Whatever this bond was between us, I could feel Matteo dip into my mind.

"This human thinks he can lay claim to you?" He growled and pushed Dan into the room, closing the door behind him. "She's mine."

I couldn't see anything beyond the red haze, Dan, and the smell of fear. I drew forward, hoping Matteo would let me feed.

"Why did you invite him here, Quinn? You *cannot* be around humans, especially those you know." Matteo's tone rang with anger.

"You were gone," I complained. "I'm hungry."

He grabbed my chin, lifting it. "It's worse, isn't it?" Deep regret glinted through his eyes. "I'm sorry, *mi amore*."

"What's going on?" Dan asked. "Is she okay? She looks high. Why are her eyes like that?"

"You know I cannot allow you to do this," Matteo told me, his eyes red. "As much as I want to, I gave you my word."

The fear emanating from Dan made my teeth hurt, and Matteo reacted. Instead of telling him not to move as he'd told me, he said one word. "Run."

Dan knew he'd walked into something he shouldn't have, and he *did* run. But he had nowhere to go. Matteo stalked him, no longer resembling anything human in his movements. I followed, drawn in by instinct.

Dan faced Matteo from the far end of the room. "Please, don't hurt me," he begged.

His heart pounded, and I was sure he'd peed himself a little.

It sunk in that Dan was about to die because of me. I vaguely acknowledged the thought that he wouldn't be there if I wasn't so desperate to put a stop to my hunger. But I said nothing as Matteo sped across the room, pressing Dan into the wall. I hadn't seen him hunt before and was fascinated. He held a hand around Dan's throat and leaned in.

"The idea of sharing him with you is tantalising," Matteo said. "But his desire for you is enough to make me want to rip him apart. It's best you stay where you are."

"Quinn, help me," Dan managed to say, before Matteo struck.

His action was smooth, everything about him predatory. The scent of blood filled the room, and I stepped forward involuntarily.

"He did nothing to me," I said finally. "He's here because of me, but he never touched me. He has no claim to me, and he knows it."

It felt like forever before Matteo responded. "You brought him here. Because you were hungry. You didn't want anything else from him?"

Dan fell to the floor as Matteo turned to face me, fresh blood on his chin.

"I saw him as a way to escape the pain," I said.

Matteo lifted Dan. "She's just saved your life, but she's more of a danger to you than you realise. Go. Forget you were here." His arms were around me, holding me as I tried to get to Dan.

"Why does it hurt so much?" I cried, unable to tear my gaze from Dan as he stumbled past.

"This is what hunger is. It's what it becomes for us if we

don't feed," he said, gently.

"You feed every day. To avoid this." I shook my head. "I can't take this anymore. Can't I just sleep until this is over?" I clung to him.

He smiled. "Come on, we'll go to bed."

I let him pull me towards my bedroom and stopped at the door. "Don't leave me alone again."

"Don't worry, I won't, not this time. I was stupid to leave you the first time," he admitted.

In bed, he wrapped me in an embrace. "This is how vampires get their reputation," he said. "To sleep all day. Close your eyes. I'll be here when you wake up."

"I just want to look at you," I said. "My very own vampire."

He smiled. "You said something when Gabriela was here. Do you remember what you said?"

I remembered. "That you were mine."

"Do you know what that means in our world?" His eyes shone.

I sighed. "Why would I know? I was just annoyed that she was there, and she had her hands on you."

"You laid claim to me," he murmured, his fingers brushing back my hair.

I could tell that it delighted him, but it only confused me more. "I still don't know what that means."

"It means I belong to you," he declared.

Chapter 39

Matteo

I watched Quinn fight her craving. We lay in bed, mostly sleeping, with her clinging to me as the worst pangs took her. They came in waves, and I felt her pain. I'd known that hunger for centuries but couldn't do anything for her. She buried her face in my chest, whimpering, clinging to me. Reminded of my own madness when I'd been in the same position, I pulled her tight to me, comforting her. Her lack of appetite for human food worried me. I'd made her something to eat, but she'd refused it.

Thunder rumbled outside.

"Please," she cried. "Let me feed, Matteo. It's what you want, anyway."

I wanted so much to let her, it would end her pain, and I did want her to turn. But she'd made it clear she didn't want that. Yet.

"You know I won't do that. I gave you my word," I told her.

Her whimpers turned to growls and she started to fight me, trying to pull out of my embrace. "Let me go."

I held tighter. She lifted her head and tried to bite into my throat.

"Stop," I commanded, using the blood bond to make her obey.

I didn't want to use our bond that way, but it was necessary. I focused on helping her to avoid my own hunger. It wouldn't be long before that became impossible to ignore.

"I feel your hunger," she said. "You should feed."

"I won't leave you," I promised.

"But you need to feed." She stroked my face. "Don't you have a vampire Uber Eats or something?"

"And bring a human here for you to feed on?" *A vampire Uber Eats?* I tried not to laugh.

Tears streamed down her face. "I only wanted sex," she blurted. "It was really good sex, but I didn't think any of this would happen."

Really good sex. Her words spread warmth within me.

"I just want to lie here," she said. "But you need to feed."

She was more herself again. The thought of leaving for just a minute crossed my mind. I could find my way into any apartment in this building. But she would probably call the human again. Finding him in her apartment had been unpleasant. I'd felt the control slip as my feral nature wanted to kill him.

"I'll be okay," I lied. My hunger was already starting to

weave its way through my body, and I needed blood, soon. Or someone would die.

Her eyes met mine. "Feed, Matteo, please." She tilted her head.

It was hard not to look at her throat when she was right there, so close. I leaned forward without meaning to, fangs lengthening. "If we do this, I'll need to feed from you every day until this passes from you," I said.

She didn't say anything, just pulled my head to her throat.

I had never fought what I was, never resisted the call of blood, and always taken my fill. But in her arms, it took everything to only drink enough to take the edge off my hunger. As I pulled away, she closed her eyes with a smile on her face.

"It almost makes me forget how much I'm hurting," she whispered. "Your 'vampire's kiss' really is something."

I licked my lips. "So is your blood," She said nothing, and I thought she'd fallen asleep. I kissed her forehead. "You're really something," I murmured.

Her mouth widened into a grin that exposed her baby fangs, and her red eyes stared into mine. Once again, the sight of them made me wonder if I should just let her turn. She really would be a beautiful vampire, impressive with her green eyes and voice. She'd be irresistible. *I've lived so long without a hunting partner.* The craving for her companionship gripped me. I quickly pushed it down before she could sense my thoughts through our blood bond.

"So are you," she said aloud. "Without all the vampire stuff, you're quite alluring. Even with the vampire stuff, you're hard to stay away from."

I wanted to take her, but instead, I pressed my mouth

against hers, and she moaned, suddenly rough in her kiss. We pulled apart, but she pressed forward, licking my lips.

I laughed, realising what she was doing. "Your own blood isn't what your body wants." It wasn't what would be needed to turn her.

She let out a frustrated sigh, closing her eyes again. This time she fell asleep. I watched her face and could feel her start to dream. Curious, I let my mind into hers.

Inside, I found her on the ground, sitting in a corner, shaking in fear. "Quinn?" I ran to her.

She didn't react to me but looked up at something behind me. I turned, to see another version of her, red eyes, fangs. I rose, standing in front of Quinn defensively.

"I know you want her to be me," Vampire Quinn said. "You're in the way of what you want, and what she wants."

I couldn't deny the sight of her as a vampire was an attraction hard to resist. I looked down at the terrified human part of her. "She doesn't want it," I said.

"But *you* do. I've felt it in your thoughts more than once. You seek a hunting partner. Let me feed, Matteo. You wouldn't have to worry about hurting me or losing control with me." Her eyes focused behind me, and I saw dream versions of myself and Quinn in a feeding frenzy. "Experience my first hunt with me," Vampire Quinn whispered in my ear. "Teach me to hunt." The dream versions rose up from their meal, red eyes, blood dripping from their faces. My apparition kissed Quinn before licking the blood from her chin. "Kill with me. I want to be your hunting partner as much as you want it. You wanted to claim me as yours, where else did you think that would lead?"

I wanted it. The sight of Quinn feeding, the idea of hunting with her, I yearned for it. I could let her feed and neither of us would look back. She'd be forever connected with me.

"I *do* want that," I admitted. "More than anything, and I have since the first day I saw you."

Vampire Quinn grinned. I looked down at the last of Quinn's mortal self, holding on, terrified of her vampire self. I could kill it, and Quinn's struggle would be over; she would embrace her new life.

"Please, Matteo. I *don't* want that. You said you'd *never* force anything on me," the human Quinn said.

I took a knee in front of her, reaching a hand out, pushing back her hair. Green eyes met mine, pleading.

"I claim you as mine," I told her. "You've claimed me. There is no other way for us. It is the way of vampires to claim one another, to turn the humans we claim."

She shook her head, tears spilling over. *"Please* don't. *Don't* take that choice from me."

I backed out of the dream and removed her arms from around me, climbing out of bed. She remained asleep.

"Matteo." Gabriela's voice called to me from the balcony, Carlos's presence with her.

I walked out onto the balcony. Night had fallen. Gabriela sat on the railing, with Carlos leaning against it, watching me over his shoulder.

"Pictures of you and a human woman have many asking questions. We're supposed to stay out of the public eye. I was happy to accept your little art gallery, but being with her isn't staying out of the public eye. If she dies, you're the first one the police pull in for questioning," she said.

"She won't die." I replied.

"I hope not," she glanced towards the window of the bedroom. "She's more vampire than human right now. You're really not going to take the opportunity that's presented itself to you?"

"Turn her," Carlos instructed, his hand on my shoulder. "I know you want to."

I groaned. "Not you, too."

"She will be one of us," Carlos said. "From what I hear, you've claimed her, and she claimed you. You cannot protect her from what will be."

Again, I wavered. He was right, and I had already made preparations for her to join me.

Gabriela twisted around leaning towards me, her red eyes on my chin where I knew Quinn's blood remained. Slowly, with a glint in her eye, she licked at the blood. "She has a sweet tooth; I can taste the chocolate." I pulled out of her reach. "Oh, Matteo. You used to like when I did that."

Movement inside caught all of our attention. Gabriela smiled and leapt off the balcony. From below, her voice reached me. "Let her turn. It will be less painful for the both of you."

"If you're not careful, this isn't going to end well," Carlos warned, and he followed Gabriela.

I turned around as Quinn stood in the doorway. "Go back inside," I told her.

"No, I've been cooped up inside for two days, at least let me stand on my balcony."

It was not a good place for her to be, and I knew it. I could hear the same thing she could. The heartbeats. The delicious scent of blood. But I agreed anyway.

"I want to ask a question, but I'm almost afraid of the answer," she said.

252

"Ask anyway." I suspected it was about Gabriela. I detected a whiff of jealousy.

"I know what you said, but —" She hesitated, facing the city. "How do you know her?"

"She found me and pulled me from a dark place." I explained. "I was feral after killing my maker. Severing the blood bond between vampires like that has an impact, and I was lost. I had no one to guide me in my new life, to teach me to control my hunger, how to feed without drawing attention. I fell into a blood-drunk feeding frenzy, and hunters probably would have killed me if it weren't for Gabriela." She wouldn't meet my eyes, pangs of jealousy still within her. "You don't have to be jealous," I said. "She is my Queen. She was never my lover." The very idea was laughable. "She spent years trying to pair me with others, but I never took her to my bed."

She relaxed, and breathed in deep, joy on her face. "It's so good to be outside," she said.

My chest squeezed. "Quinn, perhaps you should go inside."

She frowned. "That smell…"

"That's why you should go inside," I said.

I moved towards the door, reaching for her hand, but she jumped from the balcony before I could stop her.

253

Chapter 40

Quinn

I was falling. Wind pushed at me, and the ground rushed up. Arms wrapped around me tight, and Matteo's eyes bored into mine, fury blazing in them. He tucked my head against his chest and hit the ground. He'd landed on his back, protecting me from the fall by wrapping his arms around my body. The impact was jarring, leaving me winded. I blacked out momentarily, and when I came to, Matteo hadn't moved, his eyes closed.

"Matteo?" I asked.

He grunted, but his eyes remained closed. The smell of humans was everywhere, heartbeats deafening, but I couldn't move with his arms caging me to him.

"Matteo?" I started to panic.

"Why did you do that?" he demanded.

I had reacted to the smell of blood and leapt from my balcony without thinking. I'd seen him do it so often, yet I couldn't believe I'd done so. But I remained silent, waiting for him to open his eyes.

"You're *not* a vampire, Quinn. You would have *died*." Finally, he opened his eyes and let out a groan. "That *hurt*." He half-sat up, waves of pain emanating from him.

"Aren't you supposed to land on your feet or something?" I asked.

He glared.

"If I hadn't been diving to catch you, I would have landed better." His hand grabbed my wrist. "Quinn, someone's coming. I need you to forget your hunger, listen to my voice and my heartbeat. Can you do that?"

I nodded as he released me and climbed to his feet. Pain passed through the connection between us again. He leaned on me heavily. Footsteps approached.

"You're hurt," I said. "I'm sorry." It was my fault.

"Hey, are you okay?" A voice behind me made me freeze.

Matteo met my eyes. "It's okay, I need him to come here. Bring him here. He can help me."

I turned around. "Please, he's hurt," I said.

The man didn't move. "What's wrong with him? What was that noise? It sounded like something fell."

I tried to ignore his heartbeat. *Focus.*

I didn't know what else to say. "He fell," I said. "He's hurt."

The man approached us then, watching Matteo. "How high up was he? Were you down here already?"

"Come to me," Matteo commanded, their eyes locked. "Help me. Do not be afraid."

The man walked towards him. "I'm not afraid," he murmured.

Matteo rushed past me. I barely saw him move, but he hit the man with the full force of his body, and they landed hard. Then the scent of blood hit me, and my hunger soared. I was standing over them before I realised I'd moved.

"Let me have some," I whispered.

Matteo said nothing, but I could hear him drinking, his hand clasped over the man's mouth.

"Are you going to kill him?" I asked.

My question seemed to bring him out of feeding as he raised his head, looking at me. "I fell twenty stories and landed on my back, to save you. That is a necessity, I need his blood. What I need is more than he can give and walk away from. Yes, I'm going to kill him. Because of you."

He lowered his mouth to the throat again. A strangled choke escaped from me as I took a step away from them. My vision blurred and I realised I was crying. Matteo's anger at me hurt above all.

His hand touched my shoulder. "I'm sorry, I shouldn't have said that. What you're feeling is our blood bond. Come on, let's go back to your apartment."

I shook my head. "It's too much. There's too much temptation. I can smell them and hear their heartbeats. I want to feed, and it's only getting worse. Just let me feed so we can be done with this."

"You *can't* make this decision right now," he said.

"Then what do I do? How long before I leap off my balcony again, or walk into one of my neighbours' apartments?" I demanded.

He nodded thoughtfully. "You're right, this is not going to work. I have an idea. I need my phone."

"What's your idea?" I stared at the dead body.

"Well, I won't call for a vampire Uber Eats." He pulled me to him. "Come on, you'll need to grab some clothes. I'll have my car dropped off."

"Where are we going?" I let him pick me up in his arms, leaning against his warm chest.

"My house. It's far from any temptations. All you'll hear is the sea." He paused. "Do you think you'll be okay?"

I nodded.

He jumped, taking us back to my apartment. I packed some clothes into a bag and heard him sending a message.

"Your friends are calling," he said.

"Can I talk to them?" I asked.

"I don't see why not. Just *don't* invite them here," he said.

He passed me my phone. I answered the call and put it on speaker.

"Quinn?" Mia's voice was filled with worry. "Are you alright? Are you feeling better?"

"I feel like crap," I admitted.

Lilith's voice came through the phone. "Did something happen the other night? You were fine when we saw you. Is this about Matteo? Did he…" She cut her own words off and I frowned.

"Did he what?" I pushed.

She sighed through the phone. "I just hope you know what you're doing, Quinn."

Matteo hit the mute button. "Just tell her you weren't feeling very well, and I've been taking care of you."

257

I grinned. "Taking care of me? Is that what you call it?"

Instead of answering, he took the phone off mute. I repeated his words to Lilith, but her silence worried me.

"I want to hear all about that kiss," Mia said. "I want all the details."

Matteo smirked.

"I'll call you when I feel better," I promised. "I'm going back to bed." I ended the call. "I hate lying to them."

"I know. Come on, let's go." He took my bag from me.

I moved towards the balcony.

He grabbed me by the wrist. "No, we're going out the front door this time. My car is out the front, waiting."

"Past the people?" I panicked.

"I'll have a good grip on you. Just focus on my heartbeat the whole time. Breathe in my scent." With my keys in hand, he led me out, locking my door.

The descent was the longest I had ever experienced. A couple were in the lift with us, and it took everything to hold on to Matteo. I buried my face in his chest, letting his scent override theirs. *Is this what he feels every day? This hunger? How did he not feed from me earlier?*

'I learned control. Mostly.' His voice in my mind was strange. But I was getting used to it.

The couple got out on one of the parking levels. I was relieved that there was no sign of Dan.

We reached the front door, and people were crowded around on the street looking straight at Matteo and me. There were no cameras, so it wasn't fans trying to catch a glimpse of either of us. It was too late at night for that.

"Don't move," he whispered. "Let them see you. Don't be scared."

"Who are they?" I asked, frozen in place.

"Vampires. They want to see the woman I claimed. Gabriela's obviously been talking."

There had to be close to thirty vampires there, all watching us, not moving. Then Carlos stood in front of us. I remembered my dreams.

He lifted my hand, lowering his head to kiss my fingers as Matteo did. "It is a pleasure to see you again."

Instinct screamed to run. His very presence filled me with dread.

He leaned in, breathing deep. "You have claimed him."

I felt a mental nudging from Matteo to answer.

"I have," I said.

All eyes shifted to Matteo. His eyes turned red, and he bared his fangs. "She is mine," he said to them. "I have claimed her as such. I have tasted her blood. None shall harm her. I ask that if I cannot, you will protect her."

The words echoed in my mind, taking a hold of my heart, and burying themselves deep within my soul.

"Bare your throat to him," Matteo encouraged. "It's a way to recognise his status."

I did as he asked, confused as to why I was supposed to recognise his status. "I thought Gabriela was in charge?" I asked.

Carlos laughed against my throat, a low chuckle. "She is," he rumbled. "I am her second. She will accept you when she's ready."

Accept me? All questions flew from my mind as Carlos's lips touched my throat, fangs pressing against flesh. I whimpered, leaning against Matteo for comfort, grabbing his arm against my chest. He tightened his embrace, and lowered his head, licking my neck below my ear, and kissed me. I found the action calming. I didn't understand what was happening or why Carlos had his fangs on my throat.

Afraid that Carlos would bite, I stayed as still as I could. He nuzzled me, rubbing his cheek against mine.

When he finally stepped back and met my gaze, his voice whispered in my mind, an echo from the dream. 'Feed.'

Just like that, they were all gone.

"What was that?" I asked.

"They came to recognise you," he said, leading me to a black car with tinted windows.

"What does that mean? Why did Carlos do that?" I climbed in as he held the door open for me.

The inside of the car was warm, with a clean smell.

"By acknowledging my claim, they accept that you are mine. Vampires are forbidden to harm you. If you're ever alone and they see you, they'll protect you as one of their own. You probably won't know they're there, though. None can taste your blood, any who do will be punished." He smiled. "It is our way. Whether you become a vampire or not, you are part of our world now."

Chapter 41

Quinn

Matteo's house in Portsea was not what I expected. It had large glass doors looking out to the sea, with a modern kitchen, and a flat-screen TV and bookshelves full of books.

"You expected a castle?" he asked as I stared. "Or something more like a dungeon for a vampire's lair?"

"I don't know if it was quite that much, but it wasn't this," I said.

I bit at nothing again, another pang of hunger driving through me.

He squeezed my hand. "Don't do that."

I groaned. I sympathised with Matteo more, understanding the hunger he endured. For six hundred years, and I was struggling after a couple of days.

"It wasn't always easy," he whispered in my ear. "Having such a feral nature only made it more difficult. You will be yourself in a few days."

Through our bond, even though he tried to hide it, I could feel his disappointment. He wanted me with him, like him. I wasn't sure I could deal with hunger like this with no escape.

"Let me show you something." He led me down a long hallway and opened a door at the end.

The room inside was huge. He'd led me into an art studio, filled with paintings.

"Woah, this must be everything you've ever painted." I walked around, admiring each one individually. His method of painting had changed over the years. "You modernised," I marvelled.

"I have a storage room under the house with more. Unfortunately, I don't have anything I painted as a human. I did find some in a museum once. It was very exciting. My brother likely had involvement with that. But I've had centuries, and this was what helped calm my feral self." He cast a look around the studio, pride evident on his face.

I noted many were of Venice. "You miss your home," I commented, pointing.

He nodded. "I once terrorised the streets of Venice, a half-mad creature — and for that, Gabriela forbid me from returning. But Venice is a beautiful city and I dream of it often. It will always be my home." His eyes filled with pain as he stared at a painting. I realised they were all of night scapes.

I tried to imagine being banished from Melbourne, the city

I'd called home my entire life. "I'm sorry." I gave his hand a squeeze. "I hope she lets you return one day; no one should be exiled from their home."

I stopped at a painting of the Colosseum.

"Matteo, some of this could rival the best of them," I said in awe.

His smile widened; then his smouldering eyes darted over me.

"I want to paint you," he said.

"You already did." I laughed. "Twice."

"No." He brushed locks of hair from my face, a look of hunger in his eyes. "I want to paint *you*. For my own...private collection."

The tone he used on the word 'private' made me suspicious. "Why do I feel like you're asking me to pose naked?" I asked.

His eyes skimmed down the length of my body with longing. "Because I am," he said.

My heart skipped. "What if someone sees it?"

"No one will see it. Just you and me," he promised.

I hesitated. "Can I think about it?"

His fingers brushed my neck. "Take all the time you need."

I appreciated that he wasn't pushing me into anything, but I felt excited by the idea as he led me from the studio.

We moved to a deck overlooking the beach, and he wrapped a blanket around us. The waves were soothing, as they always had been. Only a twinge of pain pulled at me, the loss of Niamh would never go away. That she'd returned in ghost form couldn't change the fact that she was dead. I wondered if I should talk to mum and dad about her.

"Do you ever just sit out here and listen to the waves?" I asked. "I could get lost in that sound."

"All the time." He pulled me to sit on a wooden seat beside him. "I paint out here, too."

I leaned against him, listening to his steady heartbeat.

"Do you like what you are?" I asked him.

He took a while to answer. "I've been a vampire too long to think of anything else. I was only a human for thirty years...I think it was thirty years. I never fought my nature or felt bitterness for being what I am." He paused. "What I didn't like is that it was *forced* on me. I was minding my own business, and my entire life was taken from me. I wouldn't have made this choice for myself had I been thinking clearly." He paused again, and I caught a deep despair, thoughts of his wife in his mind. "Or that by killing the one who did this, I'd become so feral."

He hated the word, I could feel it through my heart. He hated that his lack of control and darker nature separated him from other vampires. I touched his chest, wishing I could ease his self-loathing. Through our bond I felt a twinge of something else. His existence across time had not diminished the love of his wife, and regret that he had not been able to see his daughter grow up.

He twisted in his seat, intensity burning in his eyes. "Do you hate what I am?"

His question took me by surprise. "I did," I admitted. "You terrified me. To learn that vampires are real was not something I ever would have imagined possible."

He lifted my chin, gently. "Do I still scare you?"

"No," I admitted. "I suppose I saw past the vampire. I see the man. I see you."

"And?" He didn't move, his gaze holding me captive again. "What do you see in that man?"

264

Feelings flooded in, and an understanding that there would be no other. My heart ached. For him. Only him. His touch set me on fire, his presence all-consuming. I sought the words to tell him. "I see a man I feel like I've known my entire life," I whispered. "I don't care that you're a vampire, I want no one else. My heart is yours."

His fingers brushed my cheek.

"I once loved a woman who gave me a child, and she will always have a place in my heart. But you have my whole heart, and had I died an old man, I would never have known you. Now that I've found you, I'm not letting go," he asserted.

The longing in his eyes set off a blaze, hunger and need bursting within my chest. I wanted him more than I'd wanted any man before. As if he heard my desire, he picked me up and put me on his lap, the blanket falling from our shoulders. One hand holding the back of my head, his other pressed to my lower back. He pulled me in, his kiss rough, yet I could tell he was somewhat restraining himself. He struggled against the need to let go, afraid to break me, our bond wide open.

Straddling him, I cupped his face in my hands, just as ferocious.

His hand slid under my shirt and cupped my breast. His lips moved, trailing fire from my mouth across my jaw, his need telling me what he wanted. I tilted my head slightly, inviting him to bite me, and his fangs pierced my throat. I could feel him drinking, and his contentment at having me in his arms. A deep protectiveness enveloped me, coming from him, and a feeling of belonging, and growing satisfaction from my blood. I thought I could feel the blood bond winding its way around us, tighter. Floating on euphoria, I was disappointed when he withdrew, returning to kissing me again.

I wanted my hands on him, but his tee-shirt was in the way. He pulled back, yanking it off in one smooth movement before pulling mine from me. He rose from the bench, and I locked my legs around his waist.

"Wait," he said. "Give me a moment."

I let him dislodge from me and watched as he lowered the blanket to the ground, before disappearing. When he returned, he had pillows and added them to the blanket. He lowered himself, grasping my hand and pulling me with him. "Lie down," he whispered. "Let me look at you. At what I have claimed for mine."

I lay on my back. He pulled my skirt away, kneeling over me. I tried not to shiver in the cold.

"Are you real?" he asked in wonder, his hands on my body. "How did I chance to lay eyes on such a goddess?"

He nuzzled my breasts, his searing lips trailing down towards my navel. I ran my fingers through his silky hair, barely able to believe he was real either. He lifted his head, fangs glinting. "I'm going to bite you somewhere else," he said.

I closed my eyes, and his breath warmed my inner thigh a moment before his fangs sunk in. I gasped, a shudder tearing its way through me. The sound I made was loud and agonising as a wave of desire and elation hit me, replacing my hunger. He shifted slightly, and his mouth pressed against my heat, hands on my waist. He licked, sucked and nibbled, sending waves of pleasure through me. His tongue was persistent, unrelenting, only to stop when his lips pressed down, soft and teasing. I groaned, desperate for the stroke of his tongue. He rewarded me, pushing me towards ecstasy, his eyes never leaving mine.

His fangs scraped my flesh, and I wondered if he was going to bite me again.

'Do you want me to?' His voice was in my head.

I nodded, unable to speak, and a second later, I felt his canines sink in again. My entire body tensed, core clenching, and my hips rocked. *More!* I ground myself hard against his mouth, hands on the back of his head, holding him there. The feel of his tongue as he licked drove shudders through me. Wrapped in pleasure, heat curled around my spine. My back arched, and I tilted my head back, screaming as my orgasm hit me. Then his mouth was against mine again, tender at first, then hungry. I clung to him as my body was racked by deep shivers.

"Oh fuck," I gasped. "That was…" I couldn't finish the sentence as he thrust deep and fast, entering me with a possessiveness. Still shaking, I dug my nails into his back as he drove into me with a roughness I had never experienced before. His name fell from my lips as I wrapped my legs around his waist. His fangs pierced my throat, and I let his hair run through my fingers as he drank from me and drove me towards another orgasm.

Chapter 42

Quinn

W e'd lain in bed all day, and I couldn't have been happier. I just wanted to look at him, have his arms around me.

"How's your hunger?" His voice burst through my calm state.

I grunted, not wanting to talk or think about it.

"Is it worsening or improving?" He probed his fingers between my lips, examining my teeth.

"How do you live like this?" I asked for probably the hundredth time. I'd dreamed of blood again, the need deeper than it had been to find a release from the pain of hunger.

He removed his fingers, drawing me to him, in a tight

embrace. "I'm sorry I did this to you. Is it any easier without the sound of heartbeats surrounding you?"

"Don't blame yourself," I breathed in, his scent a comfort. "It *is* a little easier without so many heartbeats, and their smell. Plus, you distract me from it," I admitted. "Your bite, the sex, it's enough to overpower everything for a short time. Even hunger." I slid my hands over his bare chest. "I've never spent this long naked." Not that I was complaining.

Overcome by the urge to, I leaned in, pressing soft kisses across his throat. He shivered.

"I do like having your lips there," he murmured. "But be careful that it's not hunger driving you for that." My stomach rumbled, and he laughed. "Looks like your appetite has kicked in again. Good, I was wondering when that would happen."

"What do you mean?" I asked.

He moved away, climbing out of bed. "When was the last time you ate food? Human food?"

My mind went blank. "Um."

His eyes sparkled with amusement. "Chocolate cake, a couple of days ago. You should probably eat."

I sat up. It felt like a lifetime ago. Had I really gone that long without eating food? I hadn't been hungry until now. "Do you have food here?" I asked.

"A fully stocked kitchen. Cook to your heart's content," he said. "I'm going to be painting." He winked at me. "I'm feeling inspired."

"Does that mean I have to put clothes on?" I half-joked, climbing out of bed.

"Now that's an image I'm going to take with me to the studio." His eyes raked down my body slowly, the glint of desire there. "Not if you don't want to. But do you really want to be in the kitchen naked?"

I dressed, then made my way to the kitchen. I'd brought my laptop, so I opened it up to play music while I cooked. It was a recording I'd made the year before with Lilith and Mia. Before Niamh's death, and I had not yet known the grief I did only weeks later when her body was found.

Unable to contain myself, I sang along, dancing around the kitchen. Bursting with joy, I let my voice go, belting out the words, glad to not have neighbours close enough to worry about. I had a vampire who adored me, and for whatever reason, I had brought him to me; I wanted to hold on to him as long as I could. The idea that I had any power over a vampire almost made me laugh. I wanted to tell him he could paint me naked. I hoped he'd come in so I could.

Matteo appeared at the door, his expression similar to that of the one he wore the day we met. He moved towards me, stopping just in front of me. Frozen in place, he stared, unblinking.

I stopped singing. "What? Did I do something wrong?"

He didn't move.

"Matteo?" I stopped the music. "What are you doing?"

His stillness sent a chill down my spine.

"Matteo," I whispered. "Stop that, you're scaring me." I pushed at him, willing for him to respond to me.

He came out of his trance, blinking. He turned, looking around the kitchen as if unsure how he'd got there.

"Are you alright?" I asked.

"I-" He frowned. "Did you call me?"

His confusion reached me through our bond. "No? Are you taking the piss?"

His face went blank. "Taking the piss?"

I tried not to laugh. "Mucking around? Joking?" I put a hand on his arm. "What happened, Matteo?"

He glanced around the kitchen again, and the paintbrush in his hand. "I don't know. I was in the studio, then I wasn't. I heard you, just as I had the first night we met. Only this time, it felt almost forceful." The confusion in his eyes changed to a look I didn't understand. Fear?

"Are you drunk?" I asked, trying to lighten the mood. "Have you been breathing in too much of those paint fumes?"

"We only get intoxicated on blood, and I haven't had enough for that," he clarified.

Uneasy, I sought to change the subject. "So, I'm okay if you want to paint me," I said. "Naked."

His eyes flashed red. "Then after you've eaten, join me in the studio," he instructed, and he was gone.

After breakfast, I found my way to his studio, nervous. "Matteo?"

"Come in," he called out. "I'm getting a new canvas ready."

I walked in to find that he'd set up a leather seat in the

middle of the room. Candles were burning, spread around to create romantic lighting.

"I have wine to calm your nerves," he said. "Or I can calm you myself."

I reached for the wine and turned to face Matteo, to find him stark naked.

"Um," I stared. "You're…"

"Naked? Of course, you can't expect I'd be the only one to have fun during this, did you? I thought I'd give you something to look at." He gave me his mischievous grin. "Take your clothes off when you're ready."

I unbuttoned my shirt and let it drop to the ground before removing my jeans and panties. Last, I removed my bra. He guided me to the seat.

"Sit down," he said, and moved my body until he was happy with the pose. "Are you comfortable?" he asked. "Are you warm enough?"

"I'm okay." I felt a little awkward. "It's not cold in here."

"Good. I have one more thing." He moved towards the corner of the room before returning with a mic. "Hold this, my little *cantante*."

He handed the mic to me.

"What does that mean?" I asked. "You keep calling me that, I hope it's nothing bad."

He smiled. "My little singer."

Every now and again, he stopped painting to ensure I was comfortable. I remained still, with my eyes locked on his, trying not to look at his cock. If I'd done that, I would have wanted him. When his eyes turned red, I knew he was painting my throat.

"Perhaps you'd like a drink," I said, feeling brave.

In a blur, he was in front of me and leaned over. "Is that what you want?" he asked in my ear. "You're awfully brave, offering your throat to a vampire." He let out a deep growl, and I found myself wanting him to bite me.

"You're aroused," he said, flashing fangs as he leaned in close to my throat, taking in a deep breath. "Oh, Quinn, you smell divine." He lowered his finger to my clit, circling it, before pushing two inside of me. "So wet, for me." His voice had become guttural, and I clenched around his fingers. I moaned, opening myself up to him. All I needed now was to have his mouth on my throat. Feel his fangs pierce me. "You desire my bite now." His voice made my stomach flip.

I was in a position where one hand was on the microphone, the other behind me, my whole body open to him, so I had no way to stop him if I wanted to. I shivered as he licked my throat, and I moaned with need. I held myself still, waiting.

"Ask me to bite you," he ordered, his fingers still sending waves of pleasure through me. "Beg me for it."

"Please." I met his eyes.

"How much do you need my bite?" he asked, a glimmer of hunger shifting over his face.

"I need it," I gasped. "Matteo, you're driving me mad. Please."

"I told you you'd be begging," he growled.

I waited, holding my breath, hopeful he'd stop tormenting me.

His lips touched my throat, and I whimpered, dropping the mic to hold the back of his head. As his fangs sunk in, warmth spread across my chest and another moan escaped.

I sighed with relief, letting the effects of his bite take me flying.

'*Your excitement for my 'vampire's kiss' warms me,*' he whispered in my mind. '*I do like hearing you beg. It's as intoxicating as your blood.*'

He shifted me around and pinned me under his body, his fingers gone from me, leaving me empty.

"I can't get enough of you," he said, licking my wetness from his fingers. "Over six hundred years and I've never wanted anything more."

His words left me speechless. I ached to have him inside me, and he responded to my voiceless desire. I clung to him as he entered me slowly. His thrusts started relaxed, and he held my gaze. He seemed to sense when I needed him to go faster and quickened his rhythm. It was just the two of us, our bodies slamming against each other; and in that moment, there was nothing else I wanted.

He filled me, his movements hitting pleasure with each thrust. I bit his shoulder to try to hold back the scream, my body shaking as my climax surged through me. He came, tensing, his eyes rolling back. The groan that he let out pierced me to my core. He pulled out and simply held me, soft kisses blazing over my cheeks, eyes, and lips. Drowsy, I closed my eyes and felt him lift me into his arms.

"What are you doing?" I could barely form words.

"I've worn you out. We can finish the painting later." His voice sounded far away.

He lay me on the soft satin sheets in his bed, pulling his doona over me.

"Don't go," I pleaded, reaching out for him, my eyes still closed.

His body pressed in against mine as he climbed in. "I'm not going anywhere, *mi amore*. Rest, you need it."

I lay my head on his chest, and his hand rested on my back. I let sleep pull me under.

Chapter 43

Quinn

'*Quinn.*' A voice pulled me from my dream of blood.

I opened one eye to find Matteo's face right in front of mine, his breath cool. I groaned, pulling the doona over my head. I recalled my dream. Carlos had been there again, telling me to stop fighting. To give in to the hunger.

Matteo laughed. "I'm sensing you're not a morning person."

"Not when someone wakes me up," I grumbled. "What time is it?"

"Five thirty," he said.

"In the morning?" I asked, my tone rising.

"In the morning," he confirmed.

"Why are you waking me at this hour?" I demanded. "This is inhuman."

"I need to hunt." His voice was quiet.

His words were enough to completely wake me up. I pulled the doona back, sitting up. "Hunt? You want to chase me or something?" I asked.

Laughter rumbled from him. "No. I've not been feeding enough the last few days, and I need more than I should take from you."

"You're leaving me?" I grabbed his arm, trying to stop him from going.

"Not alone. Carlos is here." He pulled away.

"Carlos?" My voice came out high-pitched.

"Yes, don't worry, I trust him. He won't hurt you." He half-turned, and Carlos stood in the doorway, arms folded across his chest.

Carlos didn't seem happy. "You should not be hunting alone."

"I cannot leave her alone in this state. Right now, she's my priority. Just keep an eye on her; I won't be long," Matteo replied.

Carlos glared. "And you're *my* priority. Chances are, it will probably be me that has to drag you in the *next* time you kill."

I lay down again, pulling the doona back over me, and I tried to ignore their conversation. I was tired of the hunger and didn't know what I wanted anymore. I had told him I didn't want to be a vampire, but a week connected with him and feeling the way I did, I started to question myself. The dreams of Carlos weren't helping.

"Quinn." Matteo's voice pulled at me again.

I grunted.

"I'll be back soon," he said. "Don't do anything to her," he warned Carlos.

Matteo's absence bothered me, and I became curious. I threw the doona back and stared at Carlos, standing in the doorway with his arms still across his chest, watching me.

"That was you in my dreams, wasn't it?" I asked.

He took a step away from the doorway, towards me. "It was." He appeared next to the bed in an instant. I recoiled, which he noticed with a small smile. "I don't know why Matteo won't turn you. It would be easier on both of you. I know he wants to."

"I don't want to be turned," I told him.

"I'm not sure even you believe that right now." He flashed me a cold smile, showing fangs. "Just say the word, I can bring you a human and we can be done with this."

Hunger surged at the thought. He leaned towards me, and everything about him terrified me.

"That's your instinct you're feeling," he said. "Trust it." Seeing Matteo as a vampire for the first time had been nothing compared to what I felt with Carlos. "I haven't been human for a very long time; I forget how to pass for one." His eyes met mine, and I shuddered. "Matteo has his gallery and studio, but I have no desire to live in the human world or pass for one of you. Human instincts tell you to run because you should. If I kill, it's not a mistake or out of anger, like your lover. It's because I want to."

The urge to run overwhelmed me. He was the very monster I was afraid of when I had first seen Matteo for what he was. I crawled backwards on the bed instinctively, needing to get away from him as he crawled towards me. His eyes turned red, and he breathed in as Matteo often did.

"I do love that scent of fear." He smiled. "Run."

The word took hold, and I was moving before I could stop myself. Choking back tears I didn't understand why Matteo had left me with Carlos. I ran through the lounge and straight out the back door that led on to the beach, only for the bright sunlight to hurt my eyes.

I collapsed, shielding my eyes, and curled up instinctively, whimpering. Something dark was thrown over my head, and arms lifted me, pressing me against a warm body. The smell was wrong, I knew it wasn't Matteo. Leather and cinnamon.

"I'm sorry," Carlos said, taking me back inside. "I got carried away. You shouldn't have done that."

"You told me to run," I muttered. "I thought you were going to kill me."

A low chuckle rose from him. "I was having fun."

"It wasn't fun for me," I protested.

He pulled his jacket from my head. "You're all right," he told me. "I didn't think you'd run outside. You may have our hunger and all, but you don't have our instincts. We tend to avoid the harsh rays of the day. They do hurt without our sunglasses."

He laid me back on the bed, his gentleness surprising.

"Why did you do that?" I demanded, irritation making me bold.

I knelt on the bed, my face inches from his, my anger overwhelming.

"I was having fun," he repeated. Amusement glinted through his eyes.

My temper flared. "Yeah, you said. Matteo told me *you*

279

wouldn't hurt me."

"In all fairness, I didn't." His smile only added to my annoyance. "You ran into the sunlight, not me. It hurt me more than you when I had to follow you. You're welcome."

"You're an ass," I snapped.

He burst out laughing and snapped his teeth at me. "You're a brave one, aren't you, young one? Matteo's different since he met you, and I'm starting to see why." Finally, he moved away from me, and I felt like I could breathe again. "My offer is still there, though. I can feel your hunger. All you need is to ask me. I will have a human here in less than a minute."

I opened my mouth, not sure what was about to come out. The front door opened, and disappointment passed over Carlos's face. Matteo walked into the bedroom, signs of a feeding on his face, sunglasses in place.

"You've been up to something, I can feel it," Matteo said to him.

"Just getting to know your beloved." Carlos shot me a look and winked. "I like her."

Chapter 44

Quinn

s we were walking on the beach, the bliss I'd been in for a week melted away, replaced by crushing guilt. I pressed my hand to my chest, letting out a small cry. I felt like I'd just woken up from a dream, where the monsters followed me out. In this case, *I* was the monster in how I had behaved. Trying to feed from Dan, and Matteo killing the bystander because of me.

I couldn't walk, gasping in panic. I didn't know what was worse. The crushing guilt, or the absence of my connection with Matteo.

"Quinn, you're okay." Matteo's voice seemed far away.

I couldn't speak as tears streamed down my face. He lifted

my chin, looking into my eyes.

"The blood bond is severed. My blood is gone from your system." He sounded as disappointed as I felt by our bond being broken.

"I killed him." My voice was barely audible.

"No, you didn't. *I* did." He wiped tears away with his thumbs. "I shouldn't have said what I did. I killed him."

"Because of me." I shook my head. "I must bear this burden for the rest of my life."

His fingers continued to caress my face. "You do not need to carry that weight."

"Who will, then?" I knew I was getting hysterical, but I didn't care. "You? Somehow I doubt you'll give him much thought. Do you value human life at all?" My words stung him; I didn't need a blood bond to see their impact. "Even I gave him no thought afterwards. I was so lost in what we had that nothing else seemed to matter." That hurt more than my responsibility in the man's death. I had lost myself in Matteo, and in doing so, I had lost sight of my morals. "A man is dead," I whispered. "Because of me." I had crossed a line, and there was no return from that.

"Be calm," he murmured. His mind brushed against mine, and a calm washed over me, which only pissed me off.

"Don't do that! You can't take this away. Wipe it away just because you feel nothing? I'm not like that. I'm not like you!" My world spun, and in that moment, I needed to be away from him. "Take me home."

Hurt flickered in his eyes. I may as well have punched him. "You want to go home?"

I started to walk back to his house. "I wanted to be like you. I dreamed it every night. Carlos told me to feed, and I almost gave in. When he offered to bring someone to me, I almost said yes. I would *never* want that."

He caught up to me easily, but had no words, his silence hurting me as I knew I'd hurt him. We walked back to the house in silence.

In his bedroom, I pulled everything together, and he led me to his car. The ride to the city was silent. My actions over the last week burned through me.

"Stop the car," I told him. "I think I'm going to be sick."

He pulled over and I barely got out before I vomited. Matteo's hands on me, pulling my hair back didn't help, and I couldn't look at him. I climbed back in the car and stared ahead. He didn't drive, and I could tell he was looking at me.

"Quinn." His voice was soft. "*Mi amore,* look at me, please."

I turned away from him, staring out the side window. "Please, Matteo, I just want to go home."

"Please look at me," he urged again.

I knew if I did, I would melt into his eyes and want his arms around me. "I can't," I said at last. "Just take me home."

The absence of his presence, of the blood bond was hurting me. I missed him and pushed it off.

We finally pulled up outside my building, and I hesitated. Everything in me screamed not to get out of the car, and that I was making a decision that would hurt the both of us. I opened the door.

"Quinn," he whispered.

I paused.

He reached for me. "Please, *mi amore.*"

Tears slid down my face, my heart shattering. I climbed out and closed the door, drowning. I turned to gaze at him through the window. "I need you to give me space until I

283

work out how I'm going to deal with this. Do not appear on my balcony; no gifts, nor visits within my dreams. That includes Carlos, too."

Another expression of hurt passed over his features, and I turned away before I could change my mind. I needed my friends, even if I couldn't tell them everything, their presence would be the company I needed.

As I returned to my apartment a sense of relief washed over me to be home. I turned on the lights and called Mia.

"Quinn?" Lilith answered the phone. "Are you feeling better?"

"I need you here," I said as I walked into the lounge. "Both of you," my voice shook.

"We're on our way," Lilith said. "I'll bring chocolate, and wine."

I gasped, Matteo was standing on my balcony watching me through the glass.

"Are you alright?" Lilith asked.

"Just get here," I pleaded and hung up.

"Let me in," Matteo said.

"No. I meant what I said Matteo. Please leave me alone," speaking the words hurt. I took a deep breath and let it out. My heart squeezed, and tears stung.

His eyes darted to the door handle, and I moved quickly to lock the door.

"Quinn, I've claimed you," he reminded me. "That cannot be broken."

I'd claimed him too, while under the strange influence of his blood. His eyes wouldn't leave mine, so I pulled down the blind and turned up my music so I could drown out any words through the door.

Niamh stood in front of me, sympathy in her eyes. "Oh, Quinn."

Chapter 45

Matteo

She'd locked me out and closed the blind. Music blared through the door. I stood on her balcony not moving, hoping she'd open the door again. Her heaving sobs pierced my heart. I considered breaking my way in but didn't want to frighten her more. After what may have been an hour, other heartbeats entered her apartment. Her friends spoke softly, comforting her.

"I'm sorry Quinn, I was really hoping you'd find happiness with him," her friend Mia said.

"Will you tell us what happened?" Lilith asked.

Her hurt and guilt battered against me like waves. Her anguish weighed on my own heart, and I could do nothing to ease her suffering.

"I...." she paused. "I can't talk about it."

Her words from the beach echoed in my mind. *'I'm not like you.'* Like me. A feral. I wasn't a good man by human standards. It had never bothered me until that moment. Because of her.

"Did he hurt you?" Lilith asked. "You have to tell me if he hurt you."

"No, he didn't." Her voice tore through me.

I let myself drop from her balcony. I'd heard enough. A part of her still rested in my heart, and I wandered the streets, her presence still wrapped around me. I had enjoyed her companionship while she was blood bonded with me, and I had forgotten that the human consciousness couldn't take the weight of guilt. I had been caught up in my own desire to have a hunting partner. An end to my solitude.

Footsteps approached, and I caught Carlos's scent.

"She'll return to your arms soon enough," he said.

"Perhaps this is what I deserve after what I did," I replied.

My chest hurt, as if Quinn had shoved a knife into my heart, and I no longer wanted to feel this pain.

"You'd both be happier right now if you'd just turned her," Carlos grumbled.

"I couldn't do that to her," I muttered.

"You've let her humanity affect you," he said. "I thought you wanted her."

"I do." I stopped, turning to him. "I want her to want this, to want me as I am. But how can she? How could a human filled with such light ever love a feral?"

His eyes softened. "She does. I could see it clear as day. Don't give up on her yet. You gained her trust once, you can do it again."

"All she sees is that I've killed people." I glared at him.

He laughed. "Why does that bother you now?"

"It doesn't. But it bothers her." I was getting irritated by his presence. I wanted to be free of him, to hunt. I quickened my step.

"What will you do then?" He kept pace with me. "Your feral nature is pushing through. Go home, Matteo. Before you do something you're going to regret."

He was right about my feral nature rising up, and I had no desire to fight it. I wanted to give in, feed until I couldn't see straight. So I didn't have to feel whatever this was. As I embraced that part of myself, the noise of remorse and pain faded away. I would bury myself in the bliss of the red haze.

The city beckoned. Hunger soared in me. "I'll do what I do best," I said, flashing my fangs at Carlos. "Feed."

Something dangerous glinted in his eye. "Don't do anything stupid. You know there are hunters in this town. Too many humans have died already, and it's drawn their attention. I'm not letting you get yourself killed. By them or Gabriela."

I laughed, unconcerned by his worries. "Hunters can barely take on a new vampire. I'm six hundred years old. What can they do against me? And Gabriela has not caged me yet. All she does is for show."

I focused on the humans around me, trying to find one worthy of the hunt. I picked up a sweet scent and followed it.

Carlos grabbed my arm. "Don't do this, I'm begging you," he urged.

I growled, pulling my arm from his grip. "Either join me

or fuck off."

His gaze hardened. "If you break the accords, the hunters will have the right to kill you. Remember what they did to Lucrezia."

"To hell with the accords, and the hunters." I left him, tracking my prey. He let me go, but not before his sorrow flooded through our bond. And his fear. I shut myself off from him, and buried the last of my resistance to my true nature.

As I hunted, the sight of a red-haired woman filled my head. Her baby fangs, then the sight of my blood dripping from her chin. I forced it all down, focusing on the hunt. I'd allowed her to make me want to be a man worthy of her, momentarily forgetting about the vampire that I was.

I caught up to my prey, a young woman in her mid-twenties. She had black hair and brown eyes. I could have pulled her under my sway, instead choosing to show her what I was. I wanted fear. I wanted to give chase, to make her scream. I reached for her arm, pulling her to me.

She saw my fangs and my eyes, her heart raced, and the fear spiked, but not enough. I needed more fear, I needed her to scream before I fed on her.

"I'm going to give you a fighting chance," I told her. "I'll give you a head start before I chase you." I leaned in, whispering in her ear. "This is a race for your life. You must stay outside, though. No running into restaurants or bars."

She whimpered, shaking her head.

"Run," I whispered with a smile.

She turned and ran. I waited, letting my hunger build as the aroma of fear sang to me, along with her heartbeat and the scent of her blood.

289

"Time's up," I murmured and gave in to the bloodlust. I stalked her through the streets, taking my time. The longer the chase, the more delicious her fear-spiced blood would be.

She started to gain hope that she had lost me once she reached Alexandra Gardens. I slammed into her, taking us both to the ground. "I'm sorry," I whispered in her ear. "Your fear…It's exhilarating…" I lowered my head, breathing her in. "It's delicious. Scream for me."

She did. And as I bit into her throat, I released no venom. It hurt her, screams of fear turning to pain.

I picked up a heartbeat approaching. Someone was interrupting my meal. I lifted my head with a hiss, the warmth of blood on my chin.

"Hey, what's going on? What are you doing to that poor woman?" A human stood over me, anger in his voice.

This was going to be a fun night.

"W-what are you?" he asked.

I rose from the ground. "What does it look like?" I stalked towards the human, and he took steps back. The scent of fear pulled at me, and I gave in to bloodlust completely.

I was well overfed and intoxicated on the scent of fear and blood I'd taken when I found my way to my art gallery. My assistant, still working, was startled at my arrival.

"Oh, I'm sorry, I thought I was alone," she said behind me as I stared at a painting of a red-haired singer on a stage.

I turned, knowing my appearance to be horrifying to humans, revelling in the quickening of her heartbeat. The lower half of my face was covered in blood, my eyes bright red, with sharp fangs on display. She took a step away from me, her chin quivering. That scent of fear was tantalising.

"Aren't you going to scream?" I asked her. "Your worst nightmare has been right before your eyes this whole time."

She did scream for me, and she ran, the sound music to my senses. I moved through the gallery, nothing but a shadow as she found me in front of her every time she ran from me.

"Please don't kill me," she begged, tears streaming down her eyes. She was refusing to look directly at my face.

I grabbed her chin, forcing her to look at me, to see the creature that stood before her. "Beg for your life." I laughed. "Scream for me."

She surprised me by falling to her knees.

"Please. Let me go." Raw fear sounded in her trembling voice. "Don't hurt me."

"Hurt you?" I laughed. "I'm going to kill you."

"Please," she begged, and whispered the word over and over again.

"Did you know, vampires can smell fear? We're drawn to it." I crouched down in front of her, my face inches from hers. "It is irresistible and makes drinking your blood a truly pleasurable encounter. It adds a kick to it that I find intoxicating." Her words became sobs. I moved to whisper in her ear. "There can be pleasure, or pain in a vampire's kiss. What do you want? Pleasure will spare you from experiencing how slow and painful your death can be."

Her eyes closed.

"Open your eyes." I pushed on her will, bringing her into mine. "I want you to see everything."

Her eyes met mine. She couldn't look away.

"Answer my question. Will you have pleasure, or pain? If you choose pleasure, you'll enjoy your own death as much as I'll enjoy your blood."

"Pleasure," she whispered.

I sunk my fangs into her throat, and let her blood spill into my mouth, giving her what she wanted. I guided her to the floor, aroused by her moan. She clutched at me, pressing hard into my erection. I withdrew my fangs. "When I said you could have pleasure, I didn't mean *that*, my poor, weeping assistant."

I left her on the floor, under the effects of my venom, writhing in pleasure. I'd return to her soon enough. I was blood drunk, immersed in the red haze, and all I knew was bliss.

I found myself once again staring at the red-haired singer on a stage. Green eyes flashed in my mind, and a hesitant smile as she looked up at me.

"Matteo." Her voice was real enough to be there, whispered in a moment of desire.

A long and enraged roar burst from me. I moved away, studying my other paintings. Painted by a creature longing for his equal, for an end to his isolation as he saw an eternity alone, there was a separation between me and him.

"Fool," I muttered.

This gallery had been a dream from long ago, and I wanted to destroy it. To forget all that had occurred, and to leave this city. There were plenty of cities, anywhere in the world, that I could make into my hunting ground. This one suffocated me, and I had to make sure there would be no reason to return. I would somehow break free of the Queen's hold and find a city with no clan. In my office I found a lighter and moved around the gallery, setting fire to anything that would burn. Canvases, curtains, frames, and paints.

I watched the paintings burn, everything going up in

smoke. The fire spread faster than I anticipated, cutting off my exit from the front. Smoke filled the air, pungent and thick. Heat surrounded me, and I attempted to get through the flames. Pain engulfed me until finally I escaped through my office, only to find myself face to face with three vampires: Gabriela, Lorenzo, and Carlos.

"You let people see you," Gabriela said. "You made them aware of us. Lorenzo and Carlos have been cleaning up your mess all night."

"I'm sorry, Matteo," Carlos added. "I cannot help you this time." He appeared truly regretful and reached for me through our blood bond. I forced him out, unwilling to have him bring me to my knees.

"Get out of my way," I growled.

"We can't do that. You've risked too much tonight. This will bring the hunters down on all of us," Carlos said

I laughed. "What, you're going to cage me?"

Lorenzo rushed at me, and I stopped him with a punch to the chest. He went down hard.

A moan came from inside the gallery, followed by a cough. Gabriela and Carlos turned to the sound.

"What will it be?" I chuckled. "Take me down, or save the human from the flames?"

"Go," Gabriela ordered Carlos. "Get her out."

Carlos stepped into the burning building, only to return moments later carrying my assistant. One side of his face was burned, but the burn soon faded.

"You destroyed your own gallery." He shook his head in disbelief. "Matteo, you had a chance that you wouldn't lose her. You've razed your own life to ashes."

Gabriela turned her eyes to me, and I knew what was

coming. The rest of the clan stepped from the shadows.

"Kneel," she commanded.

I fell to my knees.

Chapter 46

Quinn

"You want to tell me why you keep closing your blind?" Lilith asked.

Instead of answering, I sat down on the couch, wine glass in hand. Lilith moved towards the door, pulling open the blind. My heart pounded, but relief surged through me that Matteo wasn't still there. Glad he'd left, I took a sip of wine. The dry flavour with a touch of fruit washed down my throat. A flash of Matteo feeding me his blood made me shudder.

Mia poured more wine for herself in the kitchen, sticking another slice of pizza into her mouth.

The aroma of hot cheese made my mouth water. "Bring

me some," I called out.

"I need you to tell me what's going on," Lilith said, her tone worried. "You're sick for a week, but now you come back after a breakup, and you look traumatised." She sat sideways on the couch, facing me.

"Nothing," I lied and turned my head to avoid looking at her.

Out of the corner of my eyes, she continued to watch me and stood up.

"What the fuck is that?" She towered over me and grabbed my chin.

I pulled out of her grasp. "Ow. What are you doing?"

She put her hand to her hip. "Quinn, I know a vampire bite when I see one. This explains a lot. Is it Matteo?"

Her question floored me. *How does she know about vampires?*

"What are you talking about?" I tried to laugh. "Vampires? You've been watching too many movies."

"You know I hate vampire movies." She glared.

"Vampires?" Mia asked, her eyes darting between the two of us.

"It seems Quinn has been letting one feed off her." Lilith gave me the side-eye.

Mia's eyes widened. "It's definitely Matteo. He looks like he could be a vampire. He's got that whole dark and mysterious thing going for him."

Instead of answering, I finished my glass of wine. Mia's lack of surprise told me that however Lilith knew, Mia did too.

"That woman he spoke to at the masquerade, I knew something was up when you were scared of her. She's one too, isn't she?" Lilith said. "Quinn, please don't lie to us."

I looked between the two of them and relented. "She is. He is." I said finally, relieved to not have to lie to my friends anymore.

"Did he turn you? Is that why you were sick?" Lilith's eyes narrowed, and she drew a wooden weapon, taking a step from me.

"Don't be ridiculous," I grumbled. "Is that a stake?"

"You need to tell me right now what happened between you two. Quinn, vampires are dangerous. They have no remorse and just kill whoever they want. You're lucky you weren't killed."

"Matteo wouldn't hurt me," I said.

"But *he did*. Clearly, he did something that upset you. Was he feeding off you this whole time?" Lilith's anger shone through her eyes, with disgust. "You let a vampire feed off you?!" She glanced at Mia. "I'm not sure we can trust her. They have a way to make people do whatever they want. He could have turned her, and she would have let him without a fight."

"He didn't turn me," I said again.

"Did he make you do something?" Mia asked in a gentle tone.

I burst into tears. They both wrapped their arms around me.

"You need to tell me everything," Lilith said. "I have to call my family in."

"Your family? What do they have to do with anything?" I sniffed, rubbing at my eyes.

"Please, Quinn," Mia urged. "She knows about vampires. If you're in trouble, she can help you. Her family can help you."

297

"My family hunts vampires," Lilith explained. "Please Quinn, you need to tell us everything."

Stunned, I stared at one of my closest friends. I'd known her my entire life. "You hunt vampires?" I'd thought I knew everything about her.

She stared back "And apparently, you date one. Or dated. Who would've thought?" She touched my arm. "I'm still me, Quinn. Your best friend. Please, tell us what happened."

Reluctantly, I told them everything. Lilith listened with narrowed eyes, Mia with a frown.

"Why didn't you tell us?" Mia asked at the end. "Why did you feel the need to keep this from us?"

"You really ask me now about keeping secrets when you both held one yourself?" I snapped.

"Telling Mia what my family did was one thing; it was a little hard to hide from her when she stumbled across my weapons collection. I had to get clearance to tell her. It's not something I could figure out how to talk to you about," Lilith told me.

"So, you've killed vampires, then?" I asked her.

Despite my hurt over Matteo, I didn't want him to die. The blood bond was gone, but I still felt a connection to him. I still cared about him and couldn't help but wonder if I'd made a mistake sending him away. I'd hoped we would talk after what had happened, I just wasn't ready to face him after the fact that someone was dead because of me. I took a bite of the pizza Mia had left on the table for me, the cheese greasy on my fingers.

"Actually, no. Never faced one yet." She waved the stake at me. "The vampires usually adhere to the accords, so we haven't had to." Lilith shrugged. "Although lately, we've been trying to find which vampire broke them."

Surprised by the relief that flooded through me, I said nothing. She got up to speak on the phone in private, likely with her family. She went onto the balcony, the cold air blasting in through the door.

"I still can't get over the fact that you posed for him naked," Mia giggled. "You said you wouldn't."

I hadn't seen the painting yet; he'd planned to show it to me when he gifted it to me. "It seemed kind of sexy," I admitted. A tear slid down my cheek and I brushed it away.

"Oh Quinn, I'm sorry hun. I could see you were really into him, even that night he showed up in the bar." Mia hugged me.

The pain in my chest was suffocating. I glanced over at Lilith, lowering my voice to Mia. "Being bonded to him really changed how I saw vampires, and him. That hunger was nothing I could have imagined. He wouldn't turn me while I was like that, but there were times where I wanted it. I wanted him to turn me."

She let me go. "I'm glad he didn't."

I sighed. "It hurts, Mia. Everything happened so quickly, his gifts, and determination to pursue me, I was so flattered by the attention."

She glanced towards where Lilith was talking. "She suspected something strange was going on when you reacted the way you did to that woman, Gabriela. She thought she saw a couple of vampires there, one of which apparently spoke to you and Matteo for a while."

Carlos. He'd wanted to share me. I was grateful that Matteo hadn't agreed to that.

"He scared me," I admitted. "A lot."

"She was hurt that you wouldn't tell her." Mia sighed.

"Yet she held this from us for years," I muttered, bitter.

An awkward silence passed between us.

"Quinn, Mia, look at this." Lilith called us out to the balcony

Flames from a nearby building blazed.

"Should we call triple zero?" Mia grabbed her phone from my coffee table, returning to stare. "What if someone's hurt?"

Sirens screamed through the streets. The fire truck's lights passed by my building.

Dread pressed across my chest. "Oh my god, that's his gallery."

"Wait, are you sure?" Lilith asked.

I nodded. "He showed me once where it was, from this balcony. I'm sure of it."

As we watched, the flames engulfed the entire building, the smell in the air strong of smoke.

I turned to Lilith. "What did your dad say?"

She kept her eyes on the fire. "There've been bodies showing up all over town, vampire feedings. My brother is working tonight and was called into the first crime scene. Two bodies at Alexandra Gardens. They're on high alert."

"Bodies?" I asked. "You're sure it's a vampire?" I didn't want to believe it, but somehow I felt like Matteo was involved.

"Bite marks on their throats are a dead giveaway that some vampire has gone on a killing spree." Lilith said.

She wouldn't meet my eye. She was hiding something from me.

I sunk into the chair. "Did I do this, too?" I asked. "Is this my fault?" I wasn't sure how much more guilt I could take.

Every breath became more painful, anxiety sinking in. Tears welled up.

"No!" Lilith put her hand on my arm. "You are not responsible for anything he's done. If this is him, he's going to find that twenty hunters will be seeking him out. We *will* find him."

"You're going, too?" I panicked. I didn't want her to face any vampire. But I also didn't want Matteo to face her. I wasn't sure what would happen if they came face to face. "Please don't. Lil."

"I have to go." she said. "We've all been called in." She turned to Mia. "Babe, stay with her. If he comes back…" She crouched down in front of me, eyes full of worry. "Quinn, if this is Matteo, and he comes back, it's likely he will try to hurt you. Even *turn* you. If he's been killing people all night, he is under the effects of bloodlust, probably drunk. In that state, they're more dangerous than ever."

He would never hurt me. "Okay."

"Why does that make them more dangerous?" Mia asked.

"They're more animal than human, and beyond reason," Lilith said, darkly. She looked around. "Maybe you should come inside and lock the door."

Again, I didn't argue.

"Okay, well, wish me luck?" She kissed Mia and left.

It was just the two of us. Mia frowned. "I hope she's okay."

"Do you want some more pizza?" I asked her, unsure what else to say.

She shook her head. "I don't think I can eat while she's out there hunting vampires."

We went back inside. Mia locked the door and pulled down the blind.

I turned on the TV. "How long have you known about this? About vampires?" I asked.

She hesitated. "A year."

I'd only known Matteo for a few months. She'd hidden this from me for a year. Lilith had hidden it for as long as I'd known her. I couldn't deny that it hurt. "I still can't believe she's a vampire hunter. Although now the martial arts makes sense."

On TV, the fire at the gallery was being reported on. My phone rang.

"Who's calling you at this time of the night?" Mia asked. "If that's Matteo, you can't answer that. What if he can hypnotise you through the phone?"

I didn't recognise the phone number, so I accepted the call. "Hello?"

A male voice came through the line. "Hello, I'm Detective Green, is this Quinn Bailey?"

"It is," I frowned at Mia and put the phone on speaker.

"I'm calling you about a fire at Matteo Barone's art gallery."

"What's wrong?" I asked, my stomach clenching. "Is he okay?"

He paused before answering. "We actually don't know. We can't reach him. I was hoping you'd know his whereabouts."

"I'm sorry, no, I haven't seen him all night. He dropped me off at my apartment and left." A feeling of dread filled me. *Something's happened. He shouldn't just be missing.* "Wait, is he in the gallery?"

"Until the fire's out, we won't know," the detective's voice softened. "We did find a woman who said she was inside before the fire. She can't remember how she got outside, but thinks she might have seen Matteo. We're doing everything we can to get the flames under control."

"He was inside?" My voice shook. *Matteo...*The pain that pierced my heart overwhelmed me. *Please don't let him be dead.*

Chapter 47

Quinn

Matteo was missing. People were dead. I needed a distraction. I needed to think, so with Mia asleep on my couch and Lilith still out hunting vampires, I headed to the gym. When I found Dan there, baring twin scars on his throat, I winced.

"Hey, Dan," I smiled, hoping guilt wasn't written all over my face.

"Hey, mate, I figured you'd still be away with that artist bloke of yours, so I started a couple of minutes without you," he replied.

"Sweet as, guess I have to catch up." I set the treadmill to a comfortable pace.

We ran in silence for twenty minutes before he stopped, out of breath.

"Stopping already?" I asked, focusing ahead of me. "You okay?"

He heaved out a loud exhalation. "Yeah, I've been lacking energy for the last week. I don't know why."

I glanced over at him. My eyes were drawn to the puncture marks on his throat again. He had no memory of what had happened. Matteo had taken care of that. "Do you want to stop? Or keep going?" I grinned at him.

"Oh, challenge accepted!" he laughed, taking to a slow jog again.

He stopped another five minutes later. "Yeah, nah I think I'm done. Don't let me slow you down though, you're in good form. You bring me to shame."

I stopped the treadmill, eyeing Dan. I'd once told myself he was the safe option, and there was attraction between us. I needed to get past my feelings for Matteo. There had been no update from the police on if he'd been found yet, and I couldn't shake the feeling that something had happened.

"How about breakfast?" I asked before I could think about what I was doing.

My response took him by surprise. "Breakfast? Really?"

"Yeah, why not? I do like a big breakfast after my run."

His jaw dropped, but he recovered and gave me a wide smile. "Uhh, sure, come on then. How do you like your coffee?"

He led the way to his apartment on the eighteenth floor.

I glanced around in admiration. He had bookshelves full of books, comics, and DVDs.

"I'm out of bacon," he said from the fridge. "What about

pancakes?"

"Dan, you spent all this time trying to get me in bed, do you really think I came here for breakfast?" Before I could talk myself out of it, I pulled my tank top over my head and threw it at him.

My top hit him in the back of his head and he turned around, his eyes wide as he took in my bare stomach. "Uhhh…"

"Why don't you show me the way to that bed?" I murmured.

He walked to his bedroom without a word, then turned to face me. "Are we really doing this?" His entire face was lit up with hope.

Only then did I feel awkward and ask myself what I was doing. *This isn't me.* But I had committed and was already half-naked. I moved to take his tee-shirt from him, and he didn't hesitate to discard his shorts. He pulled me in for a kiss, his tongue pressing past my lips. My hands moved over his firm abs and up to his chest. He pulled at my leggings and then we were naked, pressed against each other.

"Lie back," I whispered.

He didn't hesitate, watching me with interest from the bed. I crawled towards him, kissing his torso. He sucked in a breath, his hands on my head. As I trailed my way up, he groaned. I pressed my lips to his collarbone, brushing them over his neck, his breathing ragged, and his hard-on pressed against me. I reached the puncture wounds Matteo had left.

This sight of Matteo emerged before me, fangs on display, eyes red and his anger at finding Dan in my apartment. I pulled back, staring at Dan in horror. As he smiled back at me, his head tilted as I had done to Matteo.

"What are you doing?" I asked.

He frowned. "I… don't really know. Don't stop."

It was too late though, I couldn't get Matteo out of my head. Missing or not, I couldn't do this to him. He'd claimed me, and it was everything to him that I'd claimed him in return.

I pulled away. "I can't," I admitted. "This was a mistake."

He didn't answer, and I realised he'd fallen asleep.

"Well, you really know how to flatter a girl," I muttered and pulled myself from his bed. I'd been about to do something I couldn't undo, and my heart had not released Matteo yet. "Sorry Dan, I don't think this was supposed to happen." I still didn't understand what had possessed me to do this in the first place. Was I that hurt, that I would climb into another's bed?

I pulled on my leggings and retrieved my tank top from where it had landed in his kitchen.

Without glancing back, I closed his door behind me and headed towards the twentieth floor.

When I reached my apartment, I heard Mia's panicked voice, followed by Lilith's trying to calm her. "I don't know where she is! She clearly left while I was asleep!" She lowered her voice. "Do you think she went looking for him?"

I sighed and opened the door. "Nope, I'm right here!"

Mia gasped. "Oh my god! Where were you?!"

"I went to the gym," I said. "I needed to clear my head."

Lilith scanned my face. "Is that all?"

I glared. "What do you mean is that all? I went for a run." She didn't turn her gaze from me, her eyes concerned. "Alright, fine. I was at Dan's," I relented.

Mia squealed and burst out laughing. "I always knew you'd

307

get down and dirty with him. How was he? You weren't gone long." She gasped. "Oh, no, was he that fast?"

"Nothing happened," I admitted. "I couldn't do it, but he kind of fell asleep." I turned my attention to Lilith. "So? Miss vampire hunter. What's the story?"

Her shoulders stiffened. "I know you're only asking because you're worried about Matteo. But no, we didn't kill any vampires. In fact, there is not a single vampire on the streets right now. It's like they've all gone into hiding."

Relief flooded through me.

"None?" Mia asked. "Where are they? Quinn herself said that there are at least thirty here."

Lilith shrugged. "I don't know. After those people died, and the gallery burned down, I'd say they're aware that we're looking for them."

I let the two of them talk while my mind wandered. Maybe if I tried to find him, I'd have better luck. Or Carlos might know how to find him. Maybe I should try his house.

Lilith's eyes were on me, hard and cold. "I know what you're planning. I want to show you something."

She held her phone up to me, and a drawing of what was clearly Matteo was on her screen. "He was what they called 'the *vampiro Veneziano*' from more than six hundred years ago. Over the space of three years, he killed hundreds of people before they sought out hunters, my ancestors, to help them. Unfortunately, he vanished before they could eliminate him." She put her phone away. "He's among the worst of them, Quinn. There are killing sprees all across Italy that we link to sightings of him. Until about two hundred years ago, when he left Italy, and the same pattern started showing up in other countries. Switzerland, Austria, France, Germany."

I couldn't find words.

"Wait, if you had a drawing of him, why didn't you recognise Matteo?" Mia asked.

"Because it wasn't until his killing spree that Dad felt the need to dig through hunter records and find it. No one in the family thought that such a cold-blooded vampire from Italy would be here."

I knew then that it would be hard to get away from Lilith and Mia. I wanted to find Matteo, but if I sought him out, I'd bring her entire family down on him.

Chapter 48

Quinn

Our tickets had sold out, so we went out for dinner to celebrate. This time Lilith was the one to keep us waiting. She showed up looking distressed.

"Are you okay?" Mia and I asked in unison.

Lilith hesitated. "Dad caught a vampire last night; it took down three of my cousins. Two of them are in hospital with broken ribs." She pressed her lips together, looking down at the table. I wondered if that meant the third cousin had died.

My heart skipped a beat. "Is it…?"

"No, they're starving it now to find out where he is." Lilith frowned at me. "You can't protect him, Quinn. I can only hope that when we *do* kill him, you'll be free from the sway he has over you."

I bit back on responding, hurting at where our friendship was. She seemed resentful at me for getting involved with a vampire. The strain had only escalated.

Mia put her hand over Lilith's. "I'm sorry about your cousins."

Now that she could be open about her family's secret, everything was about vampire hunting.

"Why are you in a band?" I asked. "It's clear that your entire life is hunting vampires. So why bother?"

Her eyes met mine. "We all had to follow an interest that gave us some light in the dark world we live in. Richie chose to help people, and he can do that as a police officer. My mum loves history, so she took a position at the history museum. Me, I love music."

"But your future is in hunting?" I asked.

She lowered her eyes then. "If I had to choose, yes."

Mia gasped. "What? You never told me that! You'd walk away from the band?"

"Then why the hell have you been with us all this time?" I demanded. "You know what our end goal was; what was all this for if you would have just walked away?"

"What about if you became a vampire?" She slammed her hand on the table. "I didn't say I would quit or anything. I want the tour as much as both of you. We've all worked hard towards this. But if it came down to it, and I had to choose, it would be to hunt. My ancestors have been hunting vampires for centuries. Ever since the vampire war. In fact, I believe that woman Gabriela may have been there. Likely Carlos, too. If they're Gabriela Ramirez and Carlos Rivera, they're worse than Matteo."

With what I had felt in Carlos's presence, it didn't surprise me.

Mia sighed. "We're here to celebrate. Maybe we can keep our conversation music-related. I'm kind of sick of hearing about vampires."

"Yes!" I said. "No more vampires. This is about music. Even if you'd leave it all behind."

"I'll stick to band and tour talk," Lilith agreed. "I'm sorry I said what I did. It won't come to that, I promise."

A cold dread trickled down my spine. I needed to run, get out of this restaurant. Something was wrong. I shivered, glancing around.

"Are you okay?" Mia asked.

"I don't know." I frowned. "I just feel uneasy all of a sudden. Like I need to get out of here."

Our food was brought to our table, and I stared at the steak and chips, no longer hungry.

"Shit." Lilith said. We both looked at her, waiting for her to explain. "You were blood bonded with a vampire."

"Damnit, Lil!" Mia rarely showed anger, but she did now. "We just agreed."

"No, I know, but we should listen to Quinn's instinct."

The entire restaurant went silent, heightening my feeling of foreboding. Lilith paled, her eyes on something behind me. I caught a flicker of fear within them. "Lil, what is it??"

"I'd like to join those lovely ladies in the corner," A deep, accented voice said behind me. I knew that voice. My heart pounded, my mouth dry. We needed to leave, but I couldn't move.

"Certainly, sir, right this way." The waitress sounded off,

and I couldn't help but wonder if he'd compelled her.

"Thank you, beautiful," he said to the waitress.

The waitress giggled.

"We need to leave, right now." Lilith started to rise. "Get up and move."

"Don't get up on my account; stay." His voice turned my heart to ice.

He was too close for comfort. I still couldn't move. I gasped. I turned around slowly, finding Carlos right behind me. He smiled, as he sat at the empty chair, closest to me, Lilith also within his reach. But he ignored her, watching me.

"Um, what are you doing here?" I asked, unable to hide the tremor in my voice. "This is a private dinner." I tried to keep a smile on my face to hide my fear from Lilith and Mia.

"You're brave; I knew there was a reason I liked you." He placed his cold hand over mine. I tried to move it, but his grip was too strong. "You still belong to Matteo," he said. "Even through his hunger, when all of him is screaming to feed, his thoughts are still focused on you."

My heart skipped. He smiled as if he had heard it. *Of course he heard it.* He leaned over, helping himself to a chip from my plate and putting it into his mouth.

"Vampire, you have not been invited here." Lilith said in a low voice, and stood, her chair scraping and drawing the attention of everyone in the restaurant. "Leave, now. This is a violation."

I panicked; her manner would not go down well with him. "It's Carlos," I whispered in warning.

Her eyes widened, but she stood her ground.

He didn't react, and he actually looked bored as he took

313

another chip. "These are good," he stated. "I hope you don't mind, I'm a little hungry."

"Take all my food, why don't you?" I muttered, annoyed at him eating from my plate.

He laughed. "I would, but your steak smells a little too well done for my liking."

"You need to leave," Lilith demanded. "You are not welcome here."

He barely glanced at her, watching me the whole time. "Sit down, Hunter, you wouldn't even have time to reach for your weapon before I snapped your neck." I'd never seen anyone make such a threat while so calm. So matter-of-fact. "Here," he said to me. "I'm sure you're hungry, have one. They're good." He held a chip out to me.

I shook my head.

"What do you want?" Lilith demanded, sitting down, her body tense.

"Tell your Hunter friend to address me with respect. I won't be spoken to that way by a human." He leaned forward. "Come on, we're friends now; you don't have to be afraid of me. Eat, young singer. You shouldn't deny your appetite; it's unnatural."

Friends?

I suspected it wasn't the food he was talking about, but the appetite I'd had for blood. I had no choice but to open my mouth, letting him push the chip in. He pulled his hand back, licking his fingers. I chewed on the chip. It was covered with chicken salt, hot and soft. It did nothing for my appetite.

"Where's Matteo?" I asked. "Is he okay?"

"He dreams of you." He lowered his voice. "I know you still yearn for him as much as he does for you."

I hated that he was right but wouldn't give him the satisfaction to admit that.

"Excuse me?" Mia called out to our waitress. "Can you ask this man to leave? He's not welcome here."

He leaned in towards her. "Little girl, hold your tongue, or I'll rip it from your head." Again, no change in his manner, which only made it more chilling. I didn't understand why he was threatening my friends, but trying to show me a softer approach.

The look of sheer terror in Mia's eyes worried me. I put my hand to her arm, to comfort her. Lilith had turned red, fury shining through her eyes.

"Please don't threaten my friends," I said, surprised at the steadiness of my voice. "This is a special night for us that you're interrupting."

His gaze shifted to my face. "I'm continuously impressed by your courage. You're terrified; I can smell your fear." He flashed a smile at Mia. "Not as much as hers. A most pleasurable smell." His eyes returned to me, his thumb stroking my hand. "You know what fear does to us. You'll need that courage. I hope you survive what's ahead of you, young one, I really do. I do like you. You would have been good for Matteo."

He stood up, grabbed my hand, and lifted it, lowering his head at the same time. His lips brushed the back of my hand, and I shuddered. "It's been a pleasure to see you again, young singer. I will see you soon." He smiled at us all as if he hadn't just threatened us. "Ladies."

With that he walked out, glancing back at me once. The ability to breathe returned.

Lilith sent a message, probably to her family. "I still

can't believe we have Matteo, Gabriela *and* Carlos here. La Primera Familia, here? This is a lot. *Too much.*"

I stared. "What do you mean?"

"Gabriela and Carlos were part of the first clan ever formed. We have three of the deadliest vampires all here in Melbourne. This might be too much for my family; we need to call others in."

"He was at the Masquerade," Mia said with a small voice. I wondered if she was going into shock. "I remember because I saw him kissing a different woman to the one he arrived with-" She gasped. "He was feeding, wasn't he?"

"Probably," Lilith said, and looked at me. "Are you okay?"

I clenched my jaw as I searched the restaurant. There was no sign of Carlos, and I couldn't help but wonder what he meant. No matter how much I convinced myself I was done with the vampire world, it wasn't done with me.

Chapter 49

Quinn

We left the restaurant, laughing over some joke Mia said about Dan. I had missed the happier moments. We turned down an alleyway to cut through to the next street. The shadows stretched out, plunging us into darkness.

A cold tingle of fear crawled up my spine. "Stop," I cautioned. "Something's wrong."

Mia's grip on my arm tightened, and Lilith pulled out a weapon.

"What are you doing?" I whispered. I didn't know why I was whispering.

"You're reacting to vampires again. We should take you

out on a hunt; you'd be useful for finding them. I'm trusting your instincts." She lifted her stake, moving ahead of us.

We took a cautious step forward.

"Hello, little human," a familiar voice said.

I froze, unable to see her. "Gabriela." *I've got to learn to stay away from alleyways.*

"You're looking well. Delicious as ever." She stepped forward from the darkest part of the alley.

Lilith stood next to me, calm, tightening her hand around the stake.

Gabriela smiled, advancing on us. "Child, put that away before you hurt yourself."

"What do you want?" I demanded.

"A vampire claimed you. One of *my* vampires. That makes you *mine*." She took another step towards me.

I took a step back. "Please leave me alone." I'd somehow been able to control my fear with Carlos, but Gabriela spoke to a deep part of me, and I fought against the urge to run. Matteo had once told me *never* to run from a vampire.

She stopped in front of Lilith. "Move," she commanded. "Or I'll move you. Forcefully, in which you might break something."

Lilith moved aside, exposing me to Gabriela. Shadows moved in the dark, and I numbly realised others were with her.

"You're still his." Gabriela reached out towards me, not quite making contact. "Do you know what happens when a vampire claims a human?"

"The human is turned," Lilith said quietly.

Gabriela laughed. "The Hunter gets it. Clearly, you're well educated in our ways. Pity you're so unprepared," Her eyes returned to my face, her smile gone. "Time to go."

I scoffed. "I'm not going anywhere with you."

Other vampires stepped out of the shadows, familiar faces. We were surrounded by at least twenty. Mia whimpered.

"Mia, they can smell fear," I whispered. "Try to stay calm."

"This one refuses me. Can someone speak to what is expected of her," Gabriela said.

"She must be turned," Carlos said from the shadows. "We witnessed Matteo claim her, and she claimed him in return."

They started to close in. My heart raced. "You're forbidden to hurt me." I said.

"No one here is going to hurt you. The protection *isn't* extended to your friends, though." The hungry glint in Gabriela's eyes was clear. She would kill Mia and Lilith.

Lilith spoke into her phone. "This is hunter Lilith De Micheli. Need immediate support. Multiple fangs. I'm on Bourke St, near -"

Carlos moved too fast to see, and before she could finish speaking, he grabbed her phone and crushed it in his hand, throwing it on the ground. A snarl tore from him as he wrapped his fingers around her throat. "Fucking Hunters."

I moved forward. "Please don't hurt her," I pleaded, putting my shaking hand on his arm.

Mia hadn't let go of me. Carlos released Lilith, holding his hand out to me. "It's time to go," he beckoned.

"I don't want to be a vampire." I pulled Lilith behind me, not sure why. "I never wanted that. I told him."

Carlos laughed. "You will. Once you turn, you won't care. You'll be a vampire; nothing else will matter. Only blood."

Gabriela sighed. "Kill them. Bring her."

"You're breaking the accords." Lilith said. "You cannot

take a human life."

"Why don't we bring them?" Carlos asked. "She'll be hungry when she wakes up. There's something ironic about them being her first feeds. Especially the hunter, and all her aggravating talk about the accords." He growled at Lilith. "I was there; I know about the accords. I lost many people in that war. Friends. Don't speak to me of the accords, Hunter. I have not broken them."

Other vampires reached for Lilith and Mia.

"No, please." I met Carlos's eyes. "Please, don't hurt them. Let them go." I glanced over at Lilith and Mia. They were as close as sisters to me; I couldn't be the reason anything happened to them. Tears streamed down my face. Mia's eyes were wide, Lilith's narrow.

Gabriela studied me with dark amusement twisting her features. "Carlos, you've had some deliciously wicked ideas before, but this might be my favourite."

"No." I stepped away from Lilith and Mia, lifting my arm, ready to take Carlos's outstretched hand. "Not them. Let them go, I will go with you. Without a fight."

Gabriela and Carlos laughed, as did the rest of the vampires.

"What?" Lilith's anger rose in her voice. "Quinn, you're not serious."

I faced them both. "I can't be the reason you die." Despite my words, I didn't feel all that sure of myself. I was agreeing to become a vampire for the sake of my friends, and it terrified me.

Vampires surrounded me, forcing Mia and Lilith back, separating me from my lifelines.

"Little human, you won't care who it is you feed from,"

Gabriela murmured, running her fingers up my arm. "All you'll know is hunger, and the need for blood."

"But I care now." I muttered. I stared around the vampires at Mia and Lilith. "I'm sorry," I said, a lump in my throat. "Looks like we won't make that tour after all."

"No," Lilith shook her head. "We'll find you, Quinn. My family will find you."

"Oh lovely, a dinner party!" Gabriela's laughter echoed around us. "Hurry up, say your goodbyes, before I change my mind and kill them here and now."

Two vampires stepped aside, allowing me to hug Mia, then Lilith. "If you find me, and I'm turned, kill me," I whispered to Lilith. "I'm sorry."

Lilith grabbed me. "I can't let you do this. I won't." Her eyes were hard. "My family will be here soon."

"Take her." Gabriela commanded.

Carlos grabbed at me, pulling me away from my friends.

"Where are you taking me?" I demanded.

"To Matteo," he replied, lifting me into his arms as Matteo had done so often.

My chest squeezed, and a shiver ran through me. "Why?" I wanted to see him, and I wondered if he would turn me. He'd made promises; would he break them again?

"It must be him to turn you; you belong with him." Carlos explained.

I risked a glance over my shoulder. Mia was staring after us in shock, and Lilith was on Mia's phone.

"Don't worry, you'll see them again." Gabriela smiled down at me. "You made the right choice, little human, I'll be glad to have you in my clan."

"I don't want to be in your clan. I just want to live my life."

I struggled against Carlos's grip. "Let me go, I'm capable of walking."

I wanted to scream, and cry. My life had become a nightmare, and I had willingly given myself to it in order to save my friends. The idea that I would soon be a vampire made me want to vomit.

Gabriela stopped and turned to face me. "We're going to take a faster way."

Carlos's arms tightened, and Gabriela's eyes bored into mine. "Don't struggle. Just relax." All tension left my body, and I leaned into Carlos, away from Gabriela. "Go to sleep," she said, and everything went dark.

Chapter 50

Matteo

H unger burned, my fangs hurt, longing to bite into flesh, to let blood gush down my throat. I had lost track of how many days had passed since Gabriela had shut me into a prison made to keep vampires. Chains hung from the ceiling, wrapping around my arms and neck. The invisible restraints of a magic wielder's power blazed across my chest, pulled around me tight. Even the reinforced steel cage was sealed with magic. The only way I was getting out would be if Gabriela released me.

What I had done plagued me as all I had were my thoughts. I'd lost my gallery, including the painting of Quinn. I'd given in to bloodlust, and shame burned through me as I thought of how much I'd let her down.

I was too weak to move and stood motionless, head bowed. We were in the cells that Gabriela had built when we arrived in Melbourne. I'd never thought I would find myself caged. I would probably never leave. Footsteps approached, but I remained as I was, wondering how long she'd starve me. It took me a while to realise Gabriela was standing on the other side of the bars.

"Have you come to torment me again?" I asked, not bothering to lift my head. She had been doing this constantly, and I was tired of it.

"Look at me," her voice was filled with ice.

I kept my head bowed, a deliberate attempt to disobey her. She'd caged me, I wasn't about to make it pleasant for her. "What do you want?" I asked instead.

"I have something for you." She unlocked my cage, stepping into it. "I think you'll like this. I know you want it." There was amusement in her voice.

"What do you know about what I want?" I snarled.

She tore my shirt open, still bloodstained from my feeding frenzy, her hands on my chest, trailing down to my abdomen. "Matteo, don't you remember? Once Carlos taught you how to hunt, you were magnificent." She brought her face close to mine. "Mmmm, I think he remembers, I see a stirring in your eyes."

I snapped at her, my teeth clanking, biting nothing but air as she pulled from my reach. Once again hunger swelled, and I fell into the red haze.

"There he is!" Gabriela's glee shone from her face. "I thought we'd lost you for a moment there. The feral in you isn't happy about being caged."

"What are you trying to achieve?" I asked.

"I want to know why you let a human you claimed go. She made demands of you. You! That's not our way, they do not have sway over us! We take what we want. Either their blood or their bodies, and when we claim one, we turn them."

"What is it that really bothers you?" I demanded. "Was it because she's human, or the fact that a human made me feel a way that no vampire you paired with me did?"

"You still belong to me," her attempt to sound amused failed. I'd gotten under her skin.

"Not by choice. I may not have been in a cage, but you've still held me prisoner for six hundred years." I wasn't sure why I was baiting her. She could use her power over me to make me suffer. As the clan's Queen, she had power over us all, and no one could resist her command. I wished I could leave, as did many others. "Let me go, and we'll see what happens."

"Do you really hate me that much?" She grabbed my hair and yanked my head back to expose my throat before she bit into it without warning.

The release of her venom hit my system, stronger than that of other vampires. I moaned, unable to control myself as warm pleasure rolled through my body. A growl rumbled from me. She slid one hand around my back, holding me in place as I rubbed myself against her, hard and full of desire. When she was done, she stepped back, watching me. I took a minute to snap out of what she'd done to me, and I bared my fangs, hissing. The chains held me back as I struggled to wrap my hands around her neck. The desire induced by her venom wore off, leaving me shaking with rage. She smiled as she watched me, a cold glint in her eyes, one of victory.

My blood dripped from her mouth.

Blood trickled from where she'd bitten me, down my throat. She'd sunk her fangs in deep. Hunger flared in me, worse than it had been before.

"Carlos," she said in a low voice, licking her lips.

Carlos walked into the cavern with a human in his grip. The rush of blood sang to me; a red haze rose up. Savage hunger tore through me, and I pulled at my chains, trying to break free. Just one drop of blood would make me go mad, but I wanted every last drop. Growls sounded from my throat.

Gabriela grabbed my jaw. "Stop," she put command into her voice and my fight left me.

"You torment me only to taunt me with food?" I demanded.

"I bring you a gift." She moved away from me, leaving my cage open. "Look at what I brought you."

I shifted my gaze, catching green eyes. *I know those eyes.* I managed to push through the haze of my hunger, through the feral part of my mind. Red hair, and a face I yearned to hold. Currently staring straight ahead as if she saw nothing. Clearly an effect of Gabriela's influence. It hurt to see her under the sway of another. I couldn't protect her, couldn't even reach her while she was like this. Her presence here was dangerous while I was in such a state of hunger.

"Remove his chains," Gabriela commanded her guards.

"What are you doing?" I asked. I meant my question for Carlos.

'I'm sorry,' he spoke through our bond. *'You know I cannot disobey our Queen.'* His tone on the word Queen was filled with bitterness.

The chains were removed, but I held myself perfectly still,

using every ounce I could to stay where I was. My body trembled with the effort.

"So, will you kill her or turn her?" she laughed.

Her words hit me hard, an arrow straight through my heart. "What?"

"Did you think caging you meant you would escape punishment?" All amusement disappeared. "You have us hiding like rats after what you did. Every hunter is scouring the streets for us." Waves of anger pounded against me. "It all started with her, so it'll end with her."

She prowled towards Quinn, standing behind her, fangs on display and leaned forward, breathing in deeply. She brushed fingers over Quinn's throat, a movement that mesmerised me. "Bite her," she ordered Carlos.

He leaned over her, my most savage growl echoing from me.

I took a step forward without meaning to. "Get away from her. She is claimed. To harm her is forbidden."

Carlos stopped, eyes wide that I'd growled at him. '*Matteo, calm yourself, I won't hurt her. She is compelled, she won't feel a thing.*' He bit Quinn, and she didn't react, unable to.

"Get away from her," I repeated. "She is mine!" I wanted to tear them both apart.

Carlos lifted his head, the smell of her blood almost enough to floor me.

Gabriela lifted Quinn's chin, pulling her into her power again. "Tell him."

Quinn's eyes moved, meeting mine, empty. Her mind was buried deep beneath the fog and darkness that was Gabriela's control.

"I am yours," Quinn murmured. "Drink from me, give me

327

your blood. I'll be with you, forever." Her voice was flat, forced by Gabriela.

My fangs ached. All I wanted was to bite into her soft throat. "Stop," I told Gabriela. "Release her."

"Walk to him, little human," she commanded.

Under Gabriela's order, Quinn walked forward. She stopped just beyond my reach. Not trusting myself, I took a step back. Her heartbeat, and very scent of her pounded against me, my hunger begging me to feed. But there was another scent on her. Fainter. The human she had almost fed from, one whose desire had risen off him in waves the first time I saw him. It was like she'd punched me in the chest.

Gabriela's impatient growl was soft. "Close her in with him."

While Gabriela's back was turned, I made an attempt for freedom. My run took me past Quinn, and I pushed down the temptation of her blood. I ran straight into an invisible barrier, thrown back. I got up, growling at Gabriela's laughter.

"The Bloodking has ordered me to kill you," she revealed. "I'll need a replacement for my clan."

I sensed alarm in Quinn, as if she were slowly becoming aware of what was happening. My need for her blood rose. It had been days, maybe a week since I'd fed. If they locked her in here with me, I wouldn't last long before I gave in.

The door to my prison closed with a loud thud, and Gabriela led everyone from the cavern.

Quinn blinked. "Matteo?" She looked around. "Where are we?" She kept her distance, wary of me. "*Please* don't turn me." The tremor in her voice tore at me.

I turned away from her again, wrapping my hands around the bars, to prevent wrapping my hands around her. "You're going to die in here if I don't." I clenched my jaw. "I haven't fed in days, and all my control is about to break. You're locked in a cage with a starving, half-mad vampire, and neither of us can prevent what is about to happen."

The tantalising scent of her fear wafted towards me. "Why does she want me so much? Why is she so determined for you to turn me?"

"It's about punishing me," I grunted. *"Mi amore*, I'm so sorry."

I couldn't resist my hunger any longer. All I could hear was her heartbeat and the rush of her blood, her scent calling to me. She took a step back.

"No, please don't. You promised," she pleaded.

"I promised you I wouldn't turn you. I will keep my word. Unfortunately, to satisfy the hunger, I need more blood than you can give. Just know that I fought this." I felt my control slipping.

"What good will that fact be when I'm *dead?!*" Tears welled up in her eyes, the scent of salt mixed with her fear. "Matteo, please don't—"

I could no longer hold back and moved towards her, pulling her into an embrace as I bit down. Her blood tasted sweet, and I groaned against her throat, sinking into darkness.

Chapter 51

Quinn

Matteo had the decency to not let me hurt as his fangs sunk in. His arms around me were cold, his embrace tender. I was about to die, but at least it wouldn't hurt. As I tilted my head back, the familiar haze of pleasure enveloped me. One hand shifted, holding the back of my head as we sunk to the ground. This was the man I'd seen, one who had cared. Perhaps Lilith was wrong about who he was.

When he growled, I knew I'd lost him. I turned my head to try to catch a glimpse of his eyes. Pure hunger shone through; he was no longer recognisable. I reached for his face, and he growled again, a savage sound that reverberated through my body. A tear fell as I closed my eyes. There was no point fighting him or pleading with him. There was nothing left of him to plead with. He was lost in his own bloodlust.

"You never got to hear your song," I whispered.

Of all I regretted, that's what gave me the most grief. He'd helped me heal from my sister's death, shown me that Steven hadn't completely destroyed my spirit. I yearned to sing to him, to somehow reach him. Light-headed, I focused on the words I'd written. For him.

"Tonight the room dissolved except for you and I." My voice shook at first, but I called upon as much as I could to sing. "I skipped a beat as my reply."

I put everything into the song, what I had felt when I wrote the lyrics, and the days I had spent with him. "And from the stage all I could hear was one refrain. The need to see you again"

I sunk into drowsiness, unsure if he could even hear me.

Strong warm arms held me; breath caressed my cheek.

"I'm sorry, Quinn," there was a devastation in the voice, deep pain that tugged at my heart. "Please wake up."

I groaned, opening my eyes. "How am I...Please tell me you didn't..." Everything was fuzzy. "Did you turn me?" Despite my question, I didn't feel the hunger.

His eyes were still red, but he was no longer the animal. "You *did* something to me." His eyes shifted to focus behind me. "To *all* of us."

I followed his gaze to find five vampires standing at the door to the cage, their eyes red, watching us, including Carlos.

"How am I not dead?" I muttered. "What happened?"

"*Your voice saved you.* There really is something extraordinary about it. I would even say *supernatural.*" He stared at me in wonder.

"Supernatural?" I tried to get out of his grip but lacked the strength to move.

"You started singing. I was deep under my hunger, and yet, I heard you." His thumb stroked my cheek. "I heard you," he whispered in wonder. "Somehow, you pulled me from deep within my bloodlust with your voice. Once I'm that deep in, I had thought that nothing could pull me out."

Carlos took a step forward. "We heard you as if you were calling to us. *We couldn't resist that call.*"

"But I'm not a vampire. How is that possible?" None of this made any sense.

I finally let myself see Matteo since I locked him out on my balcony. His shirt had been torn, the front of it soaked in blood. The entire bottom half of his face showed results of his feeding, with my blood adding to it. His fangs were on display, and his eyes bright red.

Tired, the exhaustion that washed through me was one I had never experienced. I wondered if I was going to pass out.

"Lilith told me what you did," I said. "Is that my fault?"

He caressed my face. "No, it is not your fault. Do not ever blame yourself, *mi amore*."

"They're hunting you," I said. "Her family are vampire hunters, and they want you." Surprise flickered in his eyes. "I'm not entirely sure I can blame them. What you did…"

"Ask the hunters what they do when they capture a vampire," Carlos said with anger. "Ask what they did to Rowan." He glanced over his shoulder to one of the other vampires. "Josef, his maker, felt everything before he died. Ask them. They call *us* monsters."

I closed my eyes.

Matteo's fingers pushed my hair from my face. "I took a lot of blood. You might need a blood transfusion." He kissed my forehead, and I opened my eyes again. "Carlos can take you to the hospital." His eyes hardened in Carlos's direction. "Hurry, before she comes back."

I was passed into Carlos's arms, not the threatening vampire he had appeared earlier, but almost gentle.

"Go, live your life, mi amore. Be happy." Matteo smiled at me.

"She's not going anywhere." Gabriela had returned.

I didn't hear what she said next over Matteo's growls. He moved forward, putting himself between me and her.

Wooziness had set in, and I struggled to stay awake. Unable to hold my head up, I leaned it against Carlos's chest. He wasn't the wall of muscle Matteo was, but still solid, warmth soaking into me. I had no strength to fight him.

333

"I want to go home," I murmured to Carlos, not sure if I was forming words.

Gabriela's eyes lit up with laughter. "There is no going home for you, little human. You may as well accept that."

She took a step towards me, towards the cage, and fear flooded through me. Instinctively, I appealed to Matteo. "Please...Don't let her." *Please protect me.*

A series of multiple growls echoed Matteo's. The male vampires who had been drawn in by my voice stood protectively in front of the cage, blocking Gabriela from getting to me. Carlos tightened his arms around me, growling, a low, deep sound that should have filled me with fear. Instead, I stared at his face in wonder. I could feel his presence, and Matteo's and the other vampires.

She folded her arms. "Get out of my way. Now."

No one moved.

"I said move." There was an expectation in her voice, as if she knew her command would force them to move. They all shuddered but remained.

"What did you do to them?" she demanded, eyes on me. "I can feel that your presence is in the way of my command. How do you hold sway over them?"

I lost consciousness.

Chapter 52

Quinn

I woke up in hospital to the sounds of machines beeping, and the strong, bitter smell of disinfectant.

"Ava, look, she's awake," Dad said from next to me.

"Dad?" I turned towards the voice.

He gave my shoulder a gentle squeeze. "Good to see you awake, Rock Star."

"Sweetie, we were so worried," Mum said, her eyes full of concern. "Your friends are out in the waiting room, and an officer. They're waiting to talk to you."

I couldn't talk. Their presence made me realise that if I had died in that cell, they would never have known what happened to me. If Matteo had turned me, they very well could have been my first victims. Despair overwhelmed me, and I let out a sob.

"Shhhh, hey, you're all right." Mum ran her fingers through my hair, humming.

The sound was a comfort to me, and I relaxed. "What happened?" I murmured, trying to remember how I'd ended up in hospital.

"We got a call saying that someone had dropped you in Emergency, insisting that you needed a blood transfusion," Dad said.

"The doctor said you had lost a lot of blood, but there were no injuries, so she couldn't understand it."

Carlos. Grateful that he'd done as Matteo asked, I would have to thank him if I ever saw him again. I didn't know how much time passed, Mum holding my hand, Dad just standing there with his arms crossed.

"Are you going to tell me why you're letting vampires feed off you?" Mum asked.

There were way too many people in my life who knew about vampires, while I'd been oblivious.

"I didn't let them do anything," I grumbled, not bothering to deny anything. "I got locked in a cage with a starving vampire."

Mum pressed her lips together. "Yet you survived. How?"

I shook my head. "I don't know. I really don't. One minute his fangs were in my throat, the next…" I struggled to remember. There had been a conversation, or had I imagined it? "I don't know," I said again. "I thought I was about to die."

"How the hell did you get yourself involved with vampires?" Dad asked.

I didn't know how to answer that question.

"Why don't we let her talk to her friends?" Mum said. "Liam, she looks like she's been through a lot. Be gentle."

He relented. "Right. Let them in, I have to go back to work, anyway." Despite his stern voice, he cast me another worried look as he walked out.

I rolled my eyes at Mum. "He thinks I'm still twelve."

She frowned. "Today has been hard for both of us, my songbird. I hope we never receive a call like we did today. We already lost one daughter; we thought we were about to lose another."

"I'm sorry," I said in a small voice.

"It's okay, just whatever it is you're doing, be careful." She smiled. "I'll go tell Mia and Lilith they can come in." She quickly left.

I had wires attached to me, with a sharp pinch of a needle in my arm. The machine beeping next to my bed made me grit my teeth.

"Quinn?" Mia's voice shook as she stood in the doorway. "Oh my god!" She ran to me, hugging me, before slapping my shoulder. "I was so scared for you!"

Lilith stood behind her. "So, you got a blood transfusion," she said. "I thought for sure when they took you that we'd never see you as a human again."

"Lil, we don't have to talk about that now!" Mia said, squeezing my hand.

"Actually, we do. Sorry, Quinn; Richie has some questions." Lilith moved aside as her older brother entered.

As always, her brother's resemblance to Lilith was uncanny. The same white-blonde hair and blue eyes.

"Hi Richie," I said. "I suppose this is Hunter business."

He smiled at my forwardness. "That's right. Your association with vampires is a concern, but I'm relieved that I didn't have to kill my little sister's best friend."

I flinched. He'd always been brutally honest, and that day was no different.

"So, what happened?" Lilith asked. "Did you see Matteo?"

I didn't want to talk about it. I was tired of thinking about the whole ordeal. "Gabriela shut me in with him in the hopes to make him turn me. Or kill me, I don't know which."

"So, why didn't he?" Lilith's brother asked, eyes on my throat. "Clearly, he fed on you. Vampires aren't known for their control. They're animals who look like us, and they spread their plague, so why are you in a hospital bed right now, after a blood transfusion, instead of another one joining their ranks?"

"Why the hell are you blaming me for this?" I demanded, my temper flaring. "I'm the one who was taken and fed on. I almost died, but this is my fault?" I glared at Lilith. "I gave myself up to protect the two of you. She would have killed you."

Lilith's face softened.

"Richie, go easy on her," Lilith said.

"It's Richard," he grumbled.

"Right now, it's Dick," she replied.

I snorted. Mia's eyes lit up as she tried to suppress laughter.

Lilith sat in the chair Mum had been in. "Quinn, is there anything you can tell us about where they took you? Richie thinks they have a den somewhere, and we can take them all out at once."

Take them all out at once. She really hated vampires enough to kill them all. She was so different from the best friend I'd grown up with. I didn't understand her hatred of vampires. Matteo had never denied what he was, and he had shown me he was capable of remorse. Of tenderness.

"I'm sorry," I said to Lilith's brother. "I don't even remember how they took me there. They took me away from Lil and Mia in the alley, then suddenly I was in the cell with Matteo."

"Cell?" Richie's interest piqued and he stepped forward.

"He's locked up after what he did. I don't think Gabriela was very happy with him," I explained.

Richie pulled his phone out of his pocket.

"Dad, it's me. Matteo Barone is subdued. That's why no one has seen him." He listened. "Do you think that will work?" His eyes darted to Lilith, and she rose, moving towards him.

"What's he saying?" she asked.

He shushed her. "How do we go about doing that? Right. Are you sure she will agree to this? Well, it can't hurt, I guess, unless we all die." He hung up.

"What was that about?" Lilith demanded.

Richie grabbed her by the arm and dragged her from the room.

"I guess we don't get to hear," Mia said. "Even though she told me everything, she's still so secretive." There was hurt in Mia's eyes.

"I'm sure she just wants to keep you safe," I said. I shifted around in the bed, trying to get comfortable. "Can you pass me some water?"

"Quinn?" Mia passed me a glass of water from the side table.

"Yeah." I gulped back the water, cool liquid a relief, refreshing.

339

"I was really scared for you. We have our tour in a few months, and I was scared you'd never get to see your dream come true." She touched my shoulder. "Our dream. Lilith went looking for you, and I didn't sleep at all last night. I was so worried. For both of you."

I touched her arm. "I was, too," I admitted. "I wasn't really thinking about the concert at the time, but I actually thought I would die." Guilt washed over me then. In the moment I thought I was dying, my last thought hadn't been about my friends or family, but about Matteo, and his damn song.

"The tour," Lilith muttered at the door. "I'd almost forgotten about it."

"This vampire thing has taken over our entire lives," Mia said. "I miss our old life, before a sexy Italian vampire tried to make Quinn his queen."

I scoffed. "What?"

"His queen?" Laughter danced in Lilith's eyes.

"I don't know, isn't that what they do?" Mia shrugged.

The tension that had been between me and Lilith lately partially melted as we burst out laughing.

"Mia, no more of your dark romance books," Lilith shook her head. "Especially the vampire ones."

Mia gave a sly smile "I don't hear you complaining when I get frisky because of my books."

"I guess now we know why you hate vampire movies," I said.

"I grew up knowing about the real thing. I never understood why people were so obsessed over them. Why they were romanticised." Lilith grabbed my hand. "I'm glad you're okay. We tried to find you, but we didn't know where to start."

Carlos's words echoed in my mind. It was on the tip of my tongue to ask her about Rowan.

"I'm okay," I reassured them both. "I just hope Matteo is."

"Hopefully soon, we won't have to worry about him," Lilith promised. "Ever again."

"Why? What did your brother say?" Mia asked.

"They're going to try to get Gabriela's attention by offering to take Matteo off her hands." Lilith's eyes were on me as she said it. "He thinks her anger at Matteo might be enough for her to give him up." She met my eyes. "So we can kill him, as our ancestors were hired to do."

Chapter 53

Quinn

A scream pierced the dark. It took me a while to realise it was mine. Lights switched on, Mia and Lilith ran into my bedroom. With their arms around me, I struggled to let go of my panic. I caught a whiff of cinnamon and vanilla alongside candles and honey.

"Shhh, you're alright," Lilith's voice soothed, rubbing my back.

I cried as they hugged me. "Why is this happening to me?" I sobbed.

I was exhausted. Unable to get a decent night's sleep, every night was filled with red-eyed figures, their fangs dripping. And Matteo. Lots of blood.

"You almost died at the hands of a vampire," Lilith said. "More than once. It's normal that you react to such a trauma."

"Am I ever going to be free of this?" I wondered, irritated. "We have other things to deal with. I need to sleep. We have our photo shoot tomorrow. I'm going to look like shit." I didn't like the idea of photos with me showing shadows under my eyes.

"I can give you sleeping pills," Lilith said. "It's a natural remedy my Mum makes."

I hesitated to take anything to help me sleep. "No, I'm going to try to sleep again. Just, stay with me?"

I lay back down, pulling the doona over me, and closed my eyes. I knew I wouldn't sleep. After what felt like ages, I heard Mia and Lilith whispering. I kept my eyes closed, breathing deep.

"Richie and Dad found one, told it to get their message to Gabriela," Lilith said. "We're all going. After one taking three of my cousins out, another hunter family is lending us extra hands. They're coming down from Sydney."

"When?" Mia's arms were around me as she spoke to Lilith.

"In two nights. If she accepts our meeting." Her voice darkened. "It's just a waiting game now. I have to admit, it makes me nervous."

Mia's warm breath skimmed across my forehead. "Please be careful, Lil. I'm really worried about both of you."

There was movement, and I imagined Lilith tucking a hair back over Mia's ear as she normally did in their tender moments. "I will be. If all goes well, we'll be rid of him soon. I want her to have her life back, she's worked so hard for us. We booked that tour because of her voice. I hate what they're doing to her," a sigh. "I want to kill the lot of them, but short

343

of another war with them, we need to keep the peace."

War? I frowned.

"Quinn, are you awake?" Mia asked in a normal voice. "Are you listening to us?"

I opened my eyes. "It's hard to sleep with the two of you yammering on the way you are." I cracked a smile. "I'm glad you're here, though."

"Go back to sleep. Sorry we woke you," Lilith said.

I sat up. "I need to pee, anyway. What time is it?"

The light of a phone lit up Mia's face. "Three am."

"We can watch a movie?" I asked.

"Sure, I'll go find one," Mia said, heading towards my living room.

"No fucking vampire shit!" Lilith said, following her.

When I came out of the bathroom, I found Mia and Lilith facing the door to my balcony. Lilith had her weapon drawn, positioned in front of Mia in a protective stance.

"What's going on?" I asked and froze.

Carlos was perched on the railing of my balcony, his hair and clothes plastered to him from the rain. As soon as I entered the lounge, he stepped off, reaching for the door.

"Oh, for fuck's sake!" I said. "Why do you keep coming back? Can't you leave me alone?" Carlos opened the door, allowing in the roar of the city below. "You're soaked, please don't be dripping rain all over my floor." I pleaded.

To my surprise, Carlos remained at the door. "You do not have to fear me," he said, eyes on me softening. "Did I not take you to the hospital?"

The intimidation from Matteo's, and the restaurant was gone, with a gentler side shining through that I didn't trust. His change in character confused me. What game was he playing?

"You also threatened them," I snapped. I'd faced death too many times in such a short time and managed to push past my fear of Carlos.

"I will not hurt you. Your voice still echoes in my mind, I'm not quite sure what you did." He stared at me in wonder. "You have a *power* in you. Gabriela has lost command of those of us who heard you, and she's furious."

"What do you want?" I demanded, ignoring his claims of me having power. I had no idea what he was talking about.

"You're cranky. Maybe get more sleep." he smiled, showing fangs. "This is not an hour humans are usually awake."

"If you lot leave me the fuck alone and stop haunting my dreams, I will," I grumbled. "I'm awake because of you. Because of her." I glared at him. "It's not an hour we're usually awake, so, you're just hanging out on my balcony for the fun of it?"

"That is not our doing. If you're having nightmares, it's your own doing." He paused, watchful.

"I doubt you came here for chitchat," Lilith said. "Why do you continue to torment her?"

"Actually, I'm here for you, Hunter." He turned his attention to her. "Your family wanted to get a message to Gabriela. She accepts your invitation. Name the time and location. Neutral territory, of course."

Lilith gave him the details, and he turned to me. "He has never known remorse, but he feels it now. You have changed him." He glared at Lilith. "I hope what your Hunter friend has planned doesn't come to fruition. I think even you would feel the effects of that."

His eyes pulled me in.

345

"Please don't." I braced myself.

"Don't what?" Lilith asked, her face swimming before me. "What are you doing to her, vampire? Have you not done enough to her?"

Consciousness was slipping away, so I didn't hear his response. He stepped forward, and I fought against his compulsion. Trying to stay awake. "No, stop." I pleaded.

I fell, aware that Carlos, wet and cold, caught me before darkness pulled me under.

Instead of unconsciousness, I found myself surrounded by nothing, Carlos standing in front of me.

"What are you doing now?" I asked with dread.

"Sleep," he replied. "I will protect you from your night-mares."

He reached a hand towards me, but I stepped out of his reach.

"Why?" I asked. "You have no obligation to me."

He flashed me a smile. "I've had an obligation to Matteo for a long time. I know him well enough to know that his last thoughts will be of you. To know that you're safe."

A weight pressed against my chest. "Why are you talking as if he's about to die?"

He lost his smile. "The Hunters have a dark fate planned for him. I saw it in your friend's mind. If they're successful, this is going to hurt the both of us. But you need to sleep. I'll watch over you."

My sleep after that was dreamless.

Chapter 54

Matteo

I'd never known such excruciating hunger. I bit my own tongue just to taste blood, the scent of it driving me into a frenzy. I snarled at shadows that weren't there, voices of the past emerging from the depths of my own mind. The blood of my last feed had long since left my body, her scent and voice only a memory.

Engulfed by thirst for blood, I caught the whiff of people moving around me. Two. Not human. They'd fed recently, warmth rising from them like an inferno while I seeped in cold. Deep rumbles vibrated from inside me in warning. I held still, my head moving as they approached, my fangs bared.

'*Matteo,*' the silent voice called out, and I jerked my head around, trying to find its source.

Matteo. I knew that name.

"He's gone truly feral," another voice then, a whisper. "Is there any pulling him back? He was always halfway there, anyway." The words were familiar, yet meaningless.

I snapped my teeth at the owner of the blue eyes in front of me. Strong fingers gripped my jaw. "He's still there, I can feel him under the hunger. Matteo, it's me, I brought you something."

I bring you a gift. The Queen had said earlier. Days? Months? And she'd presented me with a human woman. The woman's face flashed before me. The scent of blood tore all control from me. Chains rattled as I pulled on them, launching myself at the man who dared touch me.

'*Matteo, stop. Drink.*' The silent voice commanded me, speaking deep within, and I had no choice but to obey. The command of a maker.

Something was held to my lips, liquid flowing into my mouth. I groaned, immediately wanting more, pressing forward and I choked, spilling it. Laughter boomed in my ears, and again, blood poured down my throat. I tried to reach for the vessel, my chained arms held immobile.

"Take the chains off him," the person feeding me said.

"Will they come off?" came the response as I guzzled more blood.

As I swallowed, my hunger only heightened, strength returning to me. My mind started to clear, the voices and words more familiar.

"Luna didn't take much convincing. He still can't leave the cage without Gabriela's say-so, but you'll be able to remove the chains." The owner of the voice had a tight grip on my arm. The chains pulled free, and he held me up. *'Keep drinking, get your strength back.'*

The blood wasn't as fresh as I would have liked, but somehow, it was still warm.

"Josef. It's almost empty; get another one," the one feeding me said.

The room came into focus, with more blood forced into me. Carlos, Josef. My clan. I stopped drinking and turned my focus to the door. I'd been locked in here to starve. One shaky step was all I got before Carlos stopped me. "Matteo, no."

Matteo. Me?

The thermos was pushed at me again, and I took it from him, my starvation far from sated. Blood enticed me and I gulped it back, my hunger waning.

"Do you know me yet?" the one in front of me asked

I ignored him. My fangs ached to bite into flesh, I wanted fresh blood, accompanied by screams.

Laughter echoed around me. "There he is. He's slowly coming back. I'm sorry, *amico*, I could not bring you a human. A pity, for your last meal to be from a thermos."

I groaned again, taking the last of the blood. "More."

Movement to my left had me hissing.

"Josef, stop. He's slipping in and out; he doesn't quite recognise us yet." Blue eyes met mine. "I have one more. It won't be enough to satisfy you, though; she starved you for too long, but at least you'll have your mind back."

He gave me another thermos, and I held it to my lips, wishing again I could have a human feeding me their blood, fresh from a soft throat.

349

"He still looks feral," the other one said. "Maybe you should have left him buried under his bloodlust. The less he feels, the less you'll feel. Maybe."

The words settled into me, and I stopped drinking to look at Josef. Their heartbeats were slow, steady. But my teeth ached. I moved, and Carlos stopped me.

"His blood, or mine, won't help you, Matteo." He pulled me to face him. "Do you know me yet?"

Matteo. Me. "Carlos," I said, shifting my attention away from Josef. "You're Carlos." Our bond pulled me back, everything in focus. "What are you doing?"

"I brought you blood," he said. "You were hungry."

I swayed on my feet, feeling a little intoxicated. How much had I drunk? "Why?"

Carlos smiled "Welcome back! Feeling better, I see. Why don't you finish your drink?"

I finished off the blood he'd given me. "You didn't answer my question," I said.

He reached for me. "Because you'll need it for what you're about to face." Fingers traced over my cheek, and I caught sadness deep in his eyes. Pain.

"What are you talking about?" My voice felt raw.

He had never looked so serious as he did then. As torn. "Gabriela's giving you to the hunters."

Dread crushed me, and I almost fell to my knees. "Why?" Fear spread through my chest, suffocating.

"They sought her out to offer her a deal. They'd leave her, and us alone. But they wanted you." He gripped my shoulder as if to steady me.

My madness threatened to bury me again, but I held on to the bond with Carlos.

'I can't protect you.' His voice in my mind was filled with pain. *'I'm sorry.'*

This time I did fall to my knees.

'We can leave, start a new clan,' I urged, staring up at him. *'I would recognise your power.'*

'Matteo, stop.' The raw emotion in his voice hurt my own heart. *'It's bad enough I will feel your death. Don't do this.'*

"She'll be here soon." Josef said.

'Quinn freed us from Gabriela's sway.' I wanted him to accept my pledge. *'I know you feel it. I am no longer part of her clan. I feel a connection to Quinn, instead, and I know you do too. She has a powerful voice.'*

He frowned, meeting my eyes. *'Those who heard her voice would agree. It does not change anything. She is human. She's not one of us.'*

His eyes were red, a deep emotion glinting within.

"She doesn't have to be," I pleaded with him. "I'll not leave without her." I bowed my head. "I swear myself and my loyalty to you."

"I reject your pledge. I cannot fight for you, Matteo. That would put the whole clan at risk. Gabriela has already given you up." Carlos crouched and pressed his hand to my chest. "You cannot ask this of me."

His rejection hurt. But I pushed it aside. "They will torture me. You'll feel it. You'll feel my death."

Josef knelt beside Carlos, eyes on me. "They tortured Rowan before they killed him. If you can find a way to escape, take that chance."

Carlos glanced at him and then back to me. "If you do, you cannot come back to us." My thoughts turned to Quinn. Carlos chuckled. "Your singer is okay. She had nightmares, but I calmed her mind. If you escape, do what you must with her, but leave Melbourne immediately."

We both knew there would be no escape. Gabriela would hunt me down. I couldn't put Quinn in danger like that. I wished I knew what to do.

"When I die, protect her," I said. "Promise me, Carlos. Let no other vampire claim her." The idea of anyone trying to lay claim to her hurt, and the feral within threatened to emerge again.

Gabriela entered the cell. I hadn't even heard her approach.

"Again with that damn human." Gabriela's impatience had turned to anger. "Carlos, enough. On your feet. Now."

Any other day, he would have had no choice. Her order would have had him on his feet immediately. But she could no longer command Carlos.

Instead, he touched his forehead to mine. *'Be brave in your death, Matteo. I will be with you. I will talk to you until I can no longer. I will do everything in my power to keep your beloved safe.'*

His words were enough, and I climbed to my feet, standing face to face with Gabriela.

'I would have followed you.' I hoped my final words to Carlos would have a lasting impact. *'It has been an honour to be bonded with you.'*

'The honour is mine,' he said, and rose to his feet, standing next to me.

Chains rattled as she held up shackles.

"You're going for a walk," she said.

Chapter 55

Quinn

I gripped the steering wheel, staring at the house. His house. Next to me, Mia was uncharacteristically quiet.

"I must admit, I'm impressed that you stayed at a beachfront house without panicking. That he was able to provide that comfort for you," Mia noted.

I'd told her about how he took me to the beach the night of the masquerade, and just held me as I tried to control my panic. Lilith was unable to see past her hatred of the monsters she'd been brought up to hunt. Despite all that happened, I couldn't bring myself to hate Matteo. Mia was quietly seeing what he had done for me, helping me heal.

"Okay, ready?" I asked.

She took a deep breath, letting it out slowly. "Ready to go into the home of a vampire in the middle of the night, while my girlfriend and her family prepare to kill him?" She choked back a laugh. "Sure. Why not."

"He's not here." My attempt to reassure her felt like I was trying to convince myself to go inside.

"So, should we count to three and open the doors?" she asked. "Or are you just going to stare at the house? Maybe ease up on the tight grip; that can't be good for your fingers."

I relaxed my hands, pulling them away from the steering wheel. "Okay, let's go." I pulled my beanie over my head, then opened the door.

A cold wind pulled at my clothes as I climbed out, and the smell of the ocean swept over me. I turned on the light of my mobile phone, aiming it at the ground.

"How are we supposed to get inside?" Mia whispered.

"He never locks his back door." I hesitated before leading her around to the beach.

"Of course he doesn't," she muttered. "I mean, who would be stupid enough to break into a vampire's house? Aside from us."

"This was your idea," I reminded her, my voice equally hushed. "You're the one who said I should take the painting before someone else finds it."

Her footsteps behind me and gasping breaths filled the silence. Despite us both knowing Matteo wasn't there, she was scared. I reached the beach-facing part of his house and turned towards the sea. Waves crashed in the dark.

"I shouldn't have left him," I admitted, overcome by regret. "I've never regretted anything in my life as much as walking away from him. If I had stayed, things would have been different."

"Maybe it was a mistake bringing you here," Mia said right next to my ear. "He's a vampire, remember? He wanted to turn you into one."

Memories emerged from the dark. His soft kisses. His gentle touch. That while he had wanted to turn me, he'd helped me through intense hunger for blood, ensuring that I didn't feed. The feeling of the bond that had connected us now left me empty. Alone.

"I swear, I still feel him," I said.

It had to be my imagination. That familiar presence, though faint, still whispered inside my mind. As if he had left a part of himself behind.

Mia put her hand on my arm. "Quinn. It's cold, and pitch black, can we just do what we came here to do? Maybe Lil was right, and you can sense vampires. I'd rather not be standing out here in the dark when one shows up."

I walked up the steps towards his door, wood creaking beneath us. On the deck, I stared at the seat we'd sat on.

"I don't hate him," I admitted. "I can't. I know Lil wants me to, but you two didn't see how he was. He wasn't a complete monster. There is a gentle side to him."

"I know you don't." Mia sighed. "I'm sorry, Quinn. I wish it could have ended another way. It's too late to change anything now."

The door slid open easily, and I shone the light around as I entered. His house looked the same as it had been the last time I'd been there. Our coffee cups sat on the bench next to his espresso machine.

"We danced in here." I pointed. "I played music on my laptop that he'd never heard, and he still managed to find a

355

way to dance to it."

"I hope ghosts aren't real, 'cause he's haunting you and he's not even dead yet. Which way to the studio?"

Suffocating grief pressed against my chest. I led the way down the long hallway, pausing at his bedroom.

"Please don't reminisce over all the sex you had with him in here and how he drank your blood." Mia sighed. "Quinn, I know you fell for him, and I don't hate vampires the way Lil does, either, but I don't want to think about what he did to you. Please."

"Well I wasn't thinking about that until you brought it up," I joked. Outside his studio, I pushed, and the door swung open, creaking slightly. The smell of paints filled the room, and I switched the light on.

In the centre was the leather seat I'd sat on, where Matteo had drunk from me, and claimed my body.

"Is that it?" Mia pointed, an easel and canvas remained still covered.

"I think so."

"Are you going to look at it?"

I frowned. "Not while you're here. I love you both to pieces, but not enough for you to see a nude painting of me. No one can see this."

A heavy footstep made us both freeze, staring at each other in shock. A second one, closer. Inside. "It can't be a vampire, they don't have heavy footsteps," I whispered to Mia.

Chilling laughter reached us. "Unless we want to announce our presence, of course." An unfamiliar male voice echoed through the empty house.

I couldn't breathe. Mia gripped my arm tight, nails digging in, gasping in my ear.

"Why don't you come out?" his voice softened. "I'm not here to hurt you, or your friend."

Mia shook her head at me, eyes wide, lips quivering. I couldn't move. My heart beat so fast that my chest hurt.

The vampire sighed. "While I have more control than Matteo does in the presence of fear, it's still irresistible. Please, get a handle on that. If I was here to hurt you, you'd already be drained and broken on the floor you stand on. Now, come out. I don't want to have to come in there and get you."

I forced my feet forward, pushing my fear down with a deep, shaky breath. Mia followed. We moved towards the lounge, surprised to find the light on. In the middle of the room stood one of the vampires from the cell. He had shoulder-length blonde hair and grey eyes, and his height had him towering over Matteo's. His long beard was fine, trimmed, and I realised all the others had been either clean-shaven, or had slight stubble. He looked to be in his mid-or late thirties. His mind brushed against mine.

He smiled. "Vampires don't grow facial hair. Nothing changes about us from the moment we die. Many got rid of theirs in the modern times, but I'm hesitant to. Even as a human, I was rather vain with my hair." His eyes shifted to Mia. "She's still afraid. I can calm her, if that helps."

"Mia?" I whispered. "He won't hurt us." I hoped he was telling the truth, but I didn't relax.

She nodded but remained clinging to me. He moved too quickly to see and stood before us. Her grip tightened. His eyes had turned red, and he breathed in deeply.

"Ahhh, that smell really is delicious. But I need you to calm down. Take a deep breath, and as you let it out, release your

357

fear with it," he instructed.

Mia did as was told, and he stepped back.

"Quinn," he said, shifting those grey eyes to me. "I'm happy to finally meet you. I'm Erik."

I realised his accent was different from those of Matteo and Carlos. "You're not Italian," I blurted.

He laughed. "No, I'm from Norway. From when you call the Viking Age."

"You and the others, you protected me from her," I said. "I'm grateful for that. Will she come after me?"

The laughter died from his eyes. "I think she might. She reacts badly when she doesn't get her way."

I stepped away from Mia, to face him. "So why are you part of her clan? Matteo clearly dislikes her. I see that same dislike in you. Why stay with a Queen you can't stand?"

He watched me. "Carlos was right: You have courage." He glanced over at Mia. "How are you doing? Feeling better?" She nodded, and he smiled. "Good."

"Did you follow me here?" I asked.

He smirked, stroking his beard. "I've been following you since you left the hospital. A favour Carlos asked of me. For Matteo's sake." He glanced around the room. "I'm surprised you'd come back here, though. I heard you speaking of art. From singer to art thief. Interesting."

My cheeks heated, and I averted my eyes.

A low chuckle rumbled from him. "I see. I won't stop you from taking it." He paused. "Back to your question. Many of us chose to join Gabriela's clan. She was a strong warrior, turned by one of the original vampires. The Bloodking himself. I fought alongside Carlos in the war, and he didn't hesitate to follow her when it was decreed that we form clans.

She was an easy choice. So we became the first clan that formed: *La Primera Familia.* But power was a heavy burden on our Queen. One that she should never have accepted. She soon abused that power and denied any of us the chance to leave. We had no choice but to do as she said. Until you."

"Me?" I really didn't understand what I had to do with any of this.

"Those of us who heard you sing noticed that Gabriela has lost her hold over us. So for that, we will always protect you. I've been following you to make sure Gabriela doesn't try to hurt you. You, and your friends, need to be careful." He scowled. "Even the Hunter."

I studied him. "You're not as intimidating as I thought. Not like Carlos."

He scoffed. "Carlos likes to be intimidating. He's been a vampire for a long time and lives for it. Once you get to know him, and he gets to know you, he's a big softie. He's very protective of the clan." He glanced towards the art studio. "Now, would you like my help with the nude painting, or can you manage it yourself?"

His strength and eyesight would make it easier to carry in the dark. "Help would be appreciated," I admitted.

Mia gasped. "You're letting a vampire help?" she whispered next to my ear.

Erik chuckled. "We can be useful, at times."

He followed us back to the studio, and before I could stop him, he lifted the cover, dropping it quickly. "One of Matteo's best works yet," he said, his eyes red as he cast a look over me. I noticed the flash of fangs. "I do hope you appreciate what he's done. A true masterpiece." He lifted the canvas, careful to keep it covered. "Lead the way, dame."

359

Chapter 56

Matteo

Gabriela moved to shackle me. Luna's cold energy closed around my wrists when the metal did. There would be no escape while I had these on. The silver bracelet on her wrist meant I was tied to her. I wouldn't be able to run far if I tried.

"You made a deal with Hunters," I said, seeing no point in pretending I didn't already know.

She glared at Carlos. "Your bond with him was so you could keep him in check, not to disobey me."

He dropped to his knee before her. "I'm sorry, I could not bear the pain he was in."

She lowered her hand, caressing her fingers through his

hair. "You've been with me for a long time, Carlos; we've seen a great deal. If you continue to vex me, you'll join him."

He lifted his chin, baring his throat. It angered me to see him submit to her.

'You should be a King of your own clan,' I told him through our bond. *'Instead you kneel to a power-hungry Queen who can no longer command you.'*

He didn't answer me, his eyes on Gabriela. She turned her back on him.

"Move." She pushed me, and I had no choice but to walk. "They heard that you were caged and offered to leave us alone if I gave you to them. Looks like your human did have her uses, after all." She walked out ahead of me and glanced over her shoulder once.

Quinn. I still felt the effects of whatever it was that had happened when she sang. It was as if I could still hear her; an echo of her voice remained. Carlos had said the same thing after he returned from taking her to the hospital. That his connection to the clan felt off, and he could sense her.

"You're giving me to Hunters?" I stated in disbelief. "Knowing what they do to our kind?"

"You're a gift," she said. "It keeps them off my back."

We reached the door of her den, and I hesitated. It had been a number of weeks since I'd breathed in fresh air. The cool night against my skin felt good. But this wasn't freedom. For only the second time in six hundred years, fear pierced my heart. "You would willingly give me to them? After what they did to Lucrezia." She'd died because of me. Hunters had tracked us down a century ago, because of me.

She glared at me. "Keep walking."

I forced myself to fall into step beside her. The power of

her command had no impact on me, but I wasn't about to let her know that yet.

"Good to see that whatever she did has worn off." Gabriela commented. "Which makes me wonder if she's actually human after all. Listening to vampires talk about her voice, it's evident that she clearly did something. I've known a few beings who had abilities with their voices, I might have to visit her to see what she is."

I fought against my possessive nature, wanting to rip out Gabriela's throat. The idea that she would hurt Quinn was enough for me to growl.

"Stop." Gabriela laughed. "Even if you weren't in chains, you wouldn't have it in you to rise up against me. I'd tear your heart from your chest without hesitation." She turned around, facing me. "Maybe I'd have Carlos deliver it to her."

I resisted the urge to look at Carlos. I could feel him behind me.

'I would not,' he whispered. *'Know that even after your death, I would never do anything to hurt you. That includes hurting her.'*

'You do hurt me by staying a part of Gabriela's clan.' I accused, and waves of his pain battered against me.

"Hurry up." Gabriela said. "The Hunters are waiting."

As I followed her, I sunk into regret. She had sought me out centuries before and saved me from Hunters, only to be giving me to them now. They were known to make their punishment great before they killed. I'd had the chance to turn down her offer, to send her away, but I had welcomed the companionship of her clan.

Footsteps surrounded me; half the clan were with us. Despite making a deal with the Hunters, she still would not trust them enough for her to show up alone.

We walked for what felt like an hour; the strong scent of a forest hit me before I caught sight of the trees. Hunters were there, waiting for us, at least fifty. One of them was Quinn's friend. Gabriela approached one who was clearly the leader.

"I agree to your terms," she told him. "We follow the accords, but this one has always caused trouble. For the sake of peace, I give him to you as a show of good faith."

"Richard, Lilith. Take him to the truck," the leader instructed.

"You might want to be careful with him, he's hungry," Gabriela said, watching Lilith. "Good to see you again, child. How's the little singer?"

"Don't talk to me, filthy bloodsucker." Lilith walked towards me, beside a man who was likely her brother. Her hatred was clear, rolling off her. I had never seen this side of her in the interactions I'd had with her before.

"How is she?" I asked softly.

"Recovering from what you put her through, having nightmares. Now shut up and move." Despite her hard tone, worry for her friend sounded in her voice.

"You'll want this." Gabriela held out the silver bracelet. "Whoever wears it, he cannot get far from them while you're travelling. It's likely he'll try to escape."

The male Hunter grabbed it and put it on his wrist, and I became bound to him. Even if I tried to run, I would be pulled back to the Hunter. They held crossbows on me, pushing me away.

Carlos met my eyes as I passed by him, a glint of regret in them. I stopped.

"Goodbye, Matteo," he said, his voice full of pain. "I'm

sorry."

I tried to turn, for one last look at the man who had been like a maker to me for six hundred years. But with crossbows lifted, Hunters forced me to keep walking. These Hunters were taking no chances. If I so much as sneezed, they'd likely put an arrow in my heart.

They led me to a prison truck.

"Get in," Lilith told me.

I climbed into the back of the truck, and they secured new restraints to me, sitting in the back with me. They kept their fear controlled, but the beating of their hearts reawakened my hunger. Carlos had fed me, but nowhere near enough.

"Are you sure you want to do that?" I asked. "Gabriela has been starving me." I smirked at Lilith when she glared at me. "I am rather hungry, and you both smell delicious." I showed my fangs to emphasise my point. I would not make this easy for them.

Carlos's presence surrounded me. I leaned into it, determined not to show the Hunters my own fear. Letting his strength in. It was a comfort to know that I wouldn't die alone.

'I'm with you.' His words were warm, yet full of pain.

"Richie, can I just fucking kill him now?" Lilith grumbled as the engine started, the truck moving away.

They were taking me away from the other vampires, from my clan. I clung to Carlos, our minds quiet, not needing to speak yet.

"You know we can't do that, Lil." He glared at me. "As much as I would like to."

"Ah, yes, you'd rather torture me first." I forced a smile. "Show the humans how much you protect them, by torturing a man on his knees."

"You're not a man," Lilith's eyes glinted dangerously at me, her fingers on the crossbow twitched. "Can we muzzle him, then?"

"Agreed." Richie smiled coldly at me. "How your friend fell in with the likes of a vampire is beyond me. But to let it feed from her, to use her that way. Then she bonded with it." His lip curled up in disgust.

I hated their continual use of the word it, and his talk of Quinn filled me with rage. They forced a muzzle on me, and I fumed, showing them my red eyes, letting out a threatening growl, lunging forward.

Richie laughed. "Calm down, vampire, it will be over for you soon enough. It won't be easy, though. The last one screamed, begging for us to end it."

I had never hated humans, merely taken my fill from them when I needed to. I knew I had nothing in common with them, any more than a human would with a cow or sheep. But the Hunters had a hatred of us that had lasted generations, and I had been lucky to escape their wrath up until then.

Lilith kept the crossbow aimed at my chest. The truck was too small for me to move far; if she fired, there would be a point at which an arrow would hit home.

I glared at Richie. *I'll kill you first.* Hunger mixed with fury, and I smiled at the thought of tearing him apart.

"Maybe you shouldn't antagonise him," Lilith said, her eyes on me. "We did have trouble trying to bring the last one down. He's so much bigger."

Both of them kept their eyes and their weapons on me the entire time. Finally, the truck stopped, and doors opened.

365

Surrounded by silent Hunters, I was pushed towards a concrete bunker. Footsteps of the Hunters echoed in the hollow cell. The scent of vampire blood hit me. *Rowan.* Red splattered the walls. They secured me using chains and removed the shackles with which Gabriela had restrained me. No longer bound by Luna's magic, I started to seek a way to escape. *Stupid Hunters.*

I caught the eye of one who was foolish enough to meet my gaze. He didn't move, couldn't as I drew him deeper into my mind.

'Let me free.' I urged him. The second he moved forward to do so, the rest pulled him away. *Damn.*

The leader of the Hunters arrived, staring at me through the door to the cell.

"We've got him," he said to his family.

Cheers rose from those around him, their joy.

"He's evaded our ancestors for six centuries. The vampire of Venice will be executed. Tomorrow. Make sure he suffers first, though."

'Carlos...' I'd heard Lucrezia's screams as we tried to free her. We all knew the cruelty of Hunters. I was about to experience it first-hand. Alone.

'I'm here, Matteo. You're not alone.' His voice was far away.

The leader of the Hunters opened the door, and I glared as they entered, crowding around me with their crossbows raised. The drummer wasn't there. The leader shot me in the chest, deliberately missing my heart. I roared in pain, pulling on the chains. Other arrows pierced my throat and torso. Filled with agony, I couldn't fight any of them as more arrows were fired at me.

The torment for which the Hunters were so well-known

had begun.

Chapter 57

Quinn

For the first time in a year, I went to my parents' house. Niamh had told me to speak to Mum, and I'd put it off. But after what happened in the cell, I needed to know. They had a house in St Kilda near the beach with spacious rooms and large windows with a large backyard.

Dad opened the door to my knock, surprise on his face. "Quinn, come in." He stepped aside, letting me inside. "Good to see you." A large smile broke out. "Really good to see you."

I gave him a quick hug and removed my jacket before following him into the lounge room where Mum was sitting with coffee and Tim Tams. Several photos hung from the walls of Dad's parents, my two uncles, and cousins, along with a framed rugby jersey from the team Dad had played for in New Zealand. Mum's were framed together on a bookshelf: my uncle, three aunts, and cousins. In the corner of the room was a baby grand piano, decorated with photos of Niamh and myself, along with awards we'd won in music and singing competitions. As I walked past the piano I played a few keys, and I glanced at a photo of us at the beach when I was ten.

"Quinn, what a surprise to see you, is everything okay?" Mum stood up, wrapping her arms around me. We pulled apart, and she turned to Dad. "Why don't you get a hot cuppa for her?" She held her hand out to the couch. "Please, sit down." Dad headed to the kitchen.

I took a seat, sitting forward. "Mum, I need to ask you something. Um, it might sound strange. Niamh told me I needed to talk to you, and I get the feeling it's related."

"Niamh visited you? You saw her?" she glanced towards the door. "Love, Niamh paid Quinn a visit."

"You knew she would," came the reply, followed by the sound of water as he filled the jug.

Her reaction wasn't what I expected. "Yeah, why are you not surprised?" I asked.

"Sweetie, it's okay. We can talk about that. First, what did you want to ask?"

Now I had more questions. I took a deep breath and let it out slowly. *Here goes.* "Am I…human?" The words tumbled out. "Something's strange about me. I need to know if…" I left the sentence hanging and shrugged.

Mum squeezed my hand. "We do have a lot to talk about, don't we?" Her focus was drawn to the back door. "Is someone with you? Did someone follow you?" She rose

369

from the couch.

"No?" I glanced at the door. "Why?" A shiver went down my spine. I knew that feeling. "Oh no." I had been followed, alright.

Dad walked in, carrying a mug of coffee for me, and he laid it on the table. "Ava, what's wrong?"

"Why don't you come in, vampire?" she said in a soft voice.

The door opened, and Carlos walked through. His usual smirk was gone, his eyes red, fangs showing.

Dad glared. "How about you put all that away in my house," he grumbled. "Why are you following my daughter?"

Their lack of fear surprised both Carlos, and myself.

"How did you know he was there?" I asked.

"I think while I'm in unfamiliar territory, I'll stick to this," Carlos said, wary. "How do you know about vampires?"

Mum smiled at me, and she cast a stern look at Carlos. "We can sense vampires, and most other paranormals. Their mind tricks don't always work on us, either. If any have ever tried to compel you, you were probably aware of it at the time." She pointed to the chair furthest away from us. "If you're going to follow Quinn, at least sit down. I've known about your kind for years. Also, I'd appreciate it if you stopped trying to get into my mind."

My parents' lack of fear of him worried me.

"What are you doing here?" I asked him.

"Keeping a promise to Matteo to keep you safe," he met my gaze. "You asked your mother an interesting question. One to which I, too, would very much like to learn the answer." His gaze shifted. "Please, explain yourself," he instructed Mum.

Mum's cheeks reddened in anger. "You do not instruct

me in my own home." She glared. "I do not need to explain myself to you."

I needed to keep the peace. "Mum, please, how about we finish our conversation?" I shot an apologetic look at Carlos.

"What is with your family?" he asked me. "All of you speak with such boldness and blatant disrespect."

Mum pointed to the chair. "Sit, now," she ordered, using a tone I knew all too well. Her 'Mum voice'. "There is no place here for your vampire arrogance. If you want to challenge me, I'll be all too happy to show you why that is a very bad idea."

"Mum!" I couldn't believe how she was talking to him.

Carlos didn't move.

A humming rose from her. I knew the sound, one of comfort. Only, it came from within her. Her eyes glowed green. Carlos fell to his knees, hands covering his ears, groaning in pain.

"Mum, stop, what are you doing?" I asked, shaken.

"How about we all sit down, put away the fangs and Siren Song, and be civil?" Dad said, always the peacekeeper.

Mum's humming stopped, and she returned to her place on the couch. Dad sat on the other side of her, his hand on her leg as if to comfort or calm her.

Siren Song? "What does he mean, Siren Song?" I asked.

"You're sirens." Carlos climbed to his feet. "I've met a few of your kind. They never hid what they were, though, and they didn't smell human, as you do." He took his seat.

Mum raised her eyebrows. "You must be very old to have known sirens as they were centuries ago."

"I thought they had died out," he said, leaning forward.

"We're their descendants, and we never lost our voices, nor

our love of the sea." She glanced back at me. "Unfortunately, your sister's call to the sea was too much for her."

"Maybe you should start at the beginning," I said, grabbing a Tim Tam from the coffee table.

Mum sat back. "You're right. Well to start with, to answer your question, yes, you are human." She sipped her drink. "You're also a siren."

Siren. Love of the sea. She'd told me stories of sirens when I was younger. "Wait, you mean mermaids? I'm descended from fucking mermaids?" I stared at her in disbelief. "No, I'm pretty sure I would have noticed if I had a fishtail."

Both my parents burst out laughing. Carlos's intense stare bored into me.

Mum's shoulders shook with laughter. "Mermaids aren't real, sweetie. That part of the myth was created from the minds of men. I never did understand it."

I had no words, so I waited for her to continue.

"We were women of the sea who sang to find the one our heart desired. Unfortunately, our voice still affected all who heard it, drawing them to us. We became hunted, so we left the sea. Unfortunately, we never returned."

"Why are you just telling me this now?" Stunned, I stared at both of them. "Why did you keep this from me? Is this not something I should have known, been prepared for?"

Mum hung her head. "Niamh reacted the same way when she found out."

I put my Tim Tam on the coffee table next to my coffee and started to pace the room.

"In the cell," Carlos spoke up then, addressing me. "Matteo should have killed you, but you dragged him out of his bloodlust. I believe your voice might be what allowed those of us who heard you to break free of Gabriela."

"Our voice does hold sway over men, and sometimes other women," Mum said, showing a little concern at Carlos's words. "It's how you were able to gain such a following with your music. But only one is worthy of your voice and your heart. One who you Called to you."

"What do you mean, worthy of my voice?" I sat down again. She'd given me a lot of information, and more questions.

"Our songs drew many men. But we sang to Call the one our heart desired. The one worthy of our song. We inherited that." She smiled at Dad, grabbing his hand. "I found mine. Niamh found hers. I believe you found yours." She laughed. "A vampire, of all people. That's a little surprising. I can't say any siren has Called a vampire before."

I frowned across at Carlos. "I drew in 'the one.' With my voice? Matteo?"

Mum nodded. "I know you've never believed in anything like that, but yes. I was starting to give up on you Calling yours. I was worried that Steven had ruined that, that he'd broken you."

"Why didn't you tell me?" I asked again, my voice rising with the hurt surging through me.

"You had to find it on your own, just as I did." She paused. "It was on me to guide your sister, just as she was supposed to be the one to guide you. Hence her visit."

I absorbed it all in a stunned silence. It was a lot to take in, that 'the one' was real. Despite that not being something I'd believed, everything about Matteo and the way we'd been drawn together made sense. Why I'd been able to accept him being a vampire. I grabbed the Tim Tam again and bit into the opposite ends, dipping it into coffee.

"Uh, what are you doing?" Carlos asked, his eyebrows knitted together, staring at me.

I finished my mouthful of gooey chocolatey goodness. "Tim Tam slam," I said, as if it were the most obvious answer.

He frowned. "And what is a Tim Tam slam?"

Dad chuckled. "Be careful what you ask, she'll be teaching you."

I offered a Tim Tam to Carlos. He took one and sniffed it before licking it and stuffing it into his mouth.

"Why is he here, and not the one who you Called?" Mum asked.

"The one she Called has been handed to vampire hunters, and from what I believe, they will execute him tomorrow morning," Carlos told her.

Mum's face fell. "Execute?"

Carlos leaned forward in his seat again, his intense stare on Mum. "What happens to either the siren or the one she Calls, if one dies?"

Mum had paled, her eyes filled with horror. "The survivor will never recover. They'll always feel the loss and will become unrecognisable." She grabbed my hand. "You saw what happened to Luke after Niamh died. He lost a part of his heart and will be that way until the day he dies. You Called a vampire. In doing so, you sealed your fate that you will *become* a vampire. If you don't, he would suffer, were you to die. But if he were to die, as your friend says, you will always feel incomplete. There is no other for you. Only Matteo."

Chapter 58

Quinn

The car was quiet, with Carlos next to me. I couldn't believe I was giving a ride to a vampire.

"They're torturing him," he murmured. "If they kill him, we'll both feel it."

"You feel it, don't you?" I asked.

He didn't say anything, staring out the window in silence. Our joint concern for Matteo allowed me to put aside my fear of him for the time being. I concentrated on the road. We'd talked for hours through the night, Mum and Dad filling me in. I learned about Niamh's death, that her draw to the sea had become too much on a night she shouldn't have been in the water. I realised that I needed to figure out how to prevent Matteo's death. She'd told me that I needed to learn what my voice could do, and it would take practice. Niamh would help me. But what Mum had said about my fate to become a vampire scared me the most. Everything I'd been through and it was all leading to that.

"How do I stop this?" I asked. "Carlos, please you have to help me." Tears welled up in my eyes. If Matteo died, my fate would be worse than death. "I can't lose him. I know you don't want to, either."

"He's not letting me track where he is, so I don't know how to find him," he said, his voice low. "I don't know how to get him out without starting a war with the Hunters."

The Hunters. Lilith. "I need to convince Lil to tell me. She's my friend, she'll—"

"Don't bother," he growled. "Your friend is a Hunter. They've been taught to hate us. Generation after generation, for hundreds of years. Hunters will never let go of that hate enough to listen to reason. Even if it means hurting you. They look at us and see monsters, and that will never change. They believe themselves to be the righteous protectors of humanity. We're enemies, and they don't take too kindly to humans who try to help us."

"Then I can talk to Mia." My voice was tinged with urgency. "She knows what Matteo did for me; she'll listen. If I tell her I'm a siren..." I choked on a sob. "She'll listen," I said again.

Finally he turned his gaze on me. "One thing I've learned about humans is that they can't handle anything different from them. You reveal that to your friend, she may not see you the same. Then she'll need to tell the Hunter. You're not quite human, Quinn, and that is a secret you will need to keep. Even from your friends. Someone, somewhere will find a reason to declare you and your mother dangerous. You saw what your mother can do. Your voice is a weapon, as well as enchanting."

I gripped my steering wheel. My friends would never betray me. "You don't like humans very much, do you?" I asked.

He scoffed. "Humans don't like me. So I return that sentiment. I've been a vampire for nine hundred years and have seen the worst of humanity, especially when it comes to my kind. I don't usually sit down to converse with my food. You and your parents may well be the first I've spoken to in such a meaningful way. That you're not completely human makes me understand why I softened to your presence."

"Call Mia," I said in a clear voice. My phone started to ring through the car speaker. Carlos let out a low growl beside me. "Relax, I'm not telling her. I'm hoping she'll tell me where Lil is."

"Quinn?" Mia answered right away. "It's four o'clock in the morning. Are you okay?"

"Where's Lilith?" I asked.

"She's at the farm, why are you calling me if you want to, oh shit." she stopped, realising her slip of the tongue. "You're looking for Matteo, aren't you?"

I met Carlos's eyes. "We are," I admitted.

She let out a sigh. "I had a feeling you would. Wait, what do you mean, 'we'?"

I took the exit off the highway. "I'm with Carlos."

Her silence stretched out.

"Mia?" I pressed.

"In terms of how vampires go, he is one scary guy. At least Matteo never scared me the way he does. Be careful, Quinn.

377

I know you love the guy, but he did almost kill you. Twice!"

"I know. I'll see you tomorrow." I said.

"See you tomorrow," she agreed, and hung up.

I took the turn that I needed to take me to the farm. "This is going to be a two-hour drive," I told Carlos. "Maybe an hour and a half with no traffic."

"Park the car," he instructed me.

"What? Here?" I frowned.

"Park the damn car!" he boomed.

I pulled over.

"Now get out," he opened the door and climbed out. "Lock your door."

I un-clipped my seat belt and did as he asked. "What are you planning to do?" I asked. "Run all the way?" I realised I'd forgotten my jacket.

He grinned. "Exactly." He reached for me, lifting me into his arms. "You have to show me the way. Let me into your mind, Quinn." His voice was soft, the brush of his mind pressing against mine. I relaxed. He took what he needed. "Now hold on."

I wrapped my arms around his neck, and he started to run at a speed no human could.

"Why *are* you helping me?" I asked, as the streets blurred by.

"You're good for him. I've seen him fight against his feral side for centuries. Your presence calms that side of him." He smiled, and it wasn't the cold or smug smile I was accustomed to seeing on him. There was warmth in his eyes. "I think I have a soft spot for you," he laughed.

Stunned, I leaned my head on his chest. "Thank you," I said.

Our conversation halted. But it wasn't long before I started to shiver, and Carlos noticed.

"Why are you shaking?" he asked.

"I left my jacket at Mum's," I said. "It's the middle of winter."

He stopped running and lowered me to my feet. "Put this on and wait here." He peeled off his leather jacket, handed it to me, then was gone.

I stood in the street alone for ten minutes, his jacket around me. He returned without a word and lifted me in his arms again. I noticed he was warmer.

"You stopped to feed?" I asked.

"It'll help keep you warm. I can't have you freezing to death on your way to rescue Matteo," he said.

Silence returned, and I struggled to keep my eyes open.

"I heard what your mother said. Your fate is to become a vampire," he reiterated. "It's what Matteo's wanted for you from the beginning."

I didn't want to think about that, so I closed my eyes, overcome by lack of sleep.

"We're here." His voice pulled me from a dream of Matteo, and he lowered me to my feet again.

"Okay, now what?" I couldn't see very far in the dark.

"I can sense him. He's in there." He pointed and scanned our surroundings. "There are a lot of Hunters here. I'm going to draw them away; you go in and try to help him."

A roar filled the air. Matteo's. Agony tore through my heart.

Carlos winced in pain and growled. "I'm going to tear all of them apart."

"What are they doing to him?" I stared into the darkness.

"They've shot him with arrows, deliberately missing his

379

heart. I can feel his pain, and he's hungry." He reached a hand towards me, lifting my chin. "You're a brave woman, Quinn, I need you to be so now. Run."

He was gone. Voices immediately rose from the darkness. I moved forward, hoping I was going in the right direction. People ran past me, shouting about vampires.

I found where Carlos had pointed to. A bunker, brightly lit around it. Inside it was just as bright and I ran forward, hoping it was empty. I ran past cells but stopped at one, somehow knowing he was inside.

Peering through the door, my chest ached. Tears spilled over. Matteo was chained to a wall, with arrows sticking out of him, and a muzzle on his face. A smaller arrow was embedded in his throat. His head was bowed, and his stillness was almost unnatural. It was the first time I'd seen him since he'd almost killed me, but seeing him like that caused a pain to pierce me deep within my chest. I gasped, unable to look away.

He moved, slowly raising his head, and meeting my eyes. I reached a hand towards the bar on the window without thinking. A tear slid down his cheek as he continued to stare at me, pain in his eyes tearing through me. He tried to say something, but it was muffled by the muzzle. Hands grabbed me, pulling me back.

"Not vampire, human," Richie said. "Quinn? What are you doing here?"

"What are you doing to him?" I asked Richie.

"Get her out of here," he said. "Before he makes her free him or something stupid." He glared at me. "How did you get here? Are you here with the other vampire?"

I was led away, and tears streamed down my face, and I

turned around as if to get a glimpse of Matteo one last time.

'Quinn, mi amore, I'm sorry.' I could hear his voice in my head, and it broke my heart. He knew he was going to die, and his sorrow and regret flooded through me. *'I would do it all over again to have the time I had with you, as short-lived as it was.'* His feelings flooded through me, an affection and tenderness. I was powerless to do anything to help him. *'I'm sorry,'* he said again.

"So am I," my voice was low, but I knew he'd hear me. I wished things could have been different. That we could leave, travel far from here. Surrounded by people I'd known my whole life, their cruelty hurt. That Lilith would be a part of this, hurt. "Carlos is here with me," I whispered.

Unfortunately, those escorting me out heard my words to him. "She's trying to communicate with him."

Lilith arrived. "What are you doing, Quinn? Everything you've gone through, and you'd let yourself fall into his sway again?"

"I'm not doing anything." I glared at her. "Is this really what you want to be? They tortured him!"

"They're monsters," Richie snapped. "Your sympathy with such a creature is unnatural."

"Monsters?" I scoffed at Richie. "You need to review your definition of what a monster is. He has an arrow in his throat. How is this humane? Is this what you did to Rowan? They grieved the loss of their own, just as we would. His death hurt them." I turned back to Lilith. "Lil, do you condone this? Does Mia know that this side of you exists?"

Matteo's presence surrounded me, as it had when we were bonded. He was doing it on purpose, reaching into my mind.

'I tried,' I thought to him, hoping he'd hear. *'I'm sorry,*

Matteo. I love you.' The need to say the words became important. If I were about to lose him, at least I'd have told him that.

His mind pulled back.

There was a loud noise and curses. "He's trying to escape," someone called out.

Lilith pushed at me. "Go into the house, Quinn. You'll be safe in the house."

I ran outside and stopped. Animal growls and screams came from inside the bunker. People were yelling, and then he stumbled from the bunker, tearing arrows from his body, removing the muzzle. His eyes found mine before Hunters surrounded him. He fought against them. Even wounded, he seemed to have no trouble, punching one and sinking his teeth into another.

"Get the spear!" a shout came, and I thought it was Lilith's Dad.

"Richie's down," Lilith screamed, running from the bunker with a crossbow. "He killed Richie." Her voice was heavy with emotion, and I felt for her. I knew the loss of a sibling all too well.

Her words had an affect on her dad. "Kill him!" he yelled. "I don't care how you do it. Take him down *now*. He cannot be allowed to leave here." His voice was filled with anguish and fury.

The moment his words were said, Matteo's body was filled with arrows again. He dropped to his knees and pulled them out, a deep growl rising from him.

"Lilith, hold him. I'll get the spear," Lilith's dad instructed.

I didn't know what the spear was, but it didn't sound good.

Matteo struggled to his feet, hunger flaring in his eyes as he attacked Hunters. He wrapped his hands around the throat of one, lifting him off the ground and throwing him against the concrete bunker. Another arrow pierced him, and he let out a roar, before sinking his teeth into the exposed throat of another. The Hunter screamed. It was a side of Matteo that I hadn't seen. His strength, rage, and hunger were on full display. Every time he took down a Hunter, his eyes sought me out.

"Carlos, where are you?" I asked in the dark. "We need you."

Lilith lifted the crossbow and let off an arrow, which pierced Matteo's arm. He turned to face her. All the other Hunters that surrounded him were dead or too wounded to move. I could tell by his stance that he was ready to kill her. She aimed for him.

My heart pounded as I realised, I was about to watch Matteo die. Or Lilith. Our friendship would never be the same. I wasn't sure she trusted me anymore, nor I her. That hurt more than anything. I turned my gaze to Matteo. If he died, I would feel that death for the rest of my life.

"Stop!" I shouted. "Matteo, please, don't kill her. I'm yours. I've always been yours," I sobbed. Realisation hit me that Mum was right. The weight of what I was about to agree to pressed against my chest. What I was giving up. My closest friend. My career. I took a deep breath. Tears were falling down my cheeks, and I whimpered. He was there in an instant, his arms around me. "I want to go with you," I clung to him. "Leave here. I'll go with you. Just please, I can't watch you die. You are my world. If that means I have to join yours, I will." He wasn't moving. "Matteo?"

"I'm hungry," he replied. "And wounded. I need blood

before we can leave. A lot of it. If you don't want to watch this, close your eyes, and cover your ears."

"Just not Lil, please Matteo," I begged.

Before he could respond, I caught sight of Lilith aiming an arrow at his back. The sight of Luke flashed before me. My sister's soulmate. Her death had *ruined* him. I couldn't let Lil kill my Matteo. My feral vampire who'd been so tender with me, keeping me from becoming a vampire even though that was what he wanted.

I made the decision in a split-second and moved around Matteo to beg her not to kill him. She nonetheless fired the arrow.

Chapter 59

Quinn

The arrow struck me in the chest, and a sharp, burning sensation made me gasp. A dull ache followed, and I struggled to breathe. Screams pierced the air. My name. Horror filled Lilith's eyes. I fell. Matteo rushed at Lilith before she could fire again, and the two of them fought.

I'm going to die.

"Matteo," I managed to ground out. He could help me. "Matteo," I called out again. I willed him not to hurt her.

There was a crack, followed by a scream of pain and anger. Lilith fell to the ground holding her wrist, crying out.

"Quinn, why did you do that?" He was there, lifting me in

his arms. I leaned my head against his bare chest, his cold seeping into me. My Matteo. I had missed his presence. There was a rush of wind, and when he stopped, we were surrounded by trees.

"Please, take it out," I gasped, reaching for the arrow. "It hurts." Tears streamed down my face, the pain beyond anything I'd experienced before.

"Shh." His hand grabbed mine to stop me. I reached my other to his face as tears spilled over, down his cheek. "Quinn, *mi amore*."

Carlos appeared beside him, his white tee-shirt ripped and covered in blood. "What happened?"

"The Hunter aimed for me," Matteo said, his eyes not leaving mine.

Don't let me die. I couldn't speak, my chest tightening. *Did he not hear what I said before I took the damn arrow for him?*

"I heard," Matteo said, hearing my thoughts. Hope reflected in his eyes.

All I saw was his face. "Please," I begged.

"She's going to die," Carlos said. "I've learned her death will have consequences on you. Turn her, Matteo."

"What are you talking about?" Matteo asked.

"She's not entirely human. And you two were meant to be. You'll feel her death, and I don't know what that will do to you. Just hurry up!" Carlos growled.

Matteo's fangs came out. His eyes, those red eyes that had once terrified me, filled my entire vision. He moved me and something jolted in my chest, the pain agonising, and tearing a scream from me. He'd pulled the arrow out, and warmth spread out as I started to bleed. His and Carlos's hands lifted me. Matteo brought the tip of the arrow to his own neck, slicing deep. Blood welled up, and he pulled me towards him, guiding my mouth to his throat.

"Drink, *vita mia*," he whispered. "Drink. You will need a lot more than last time, so drink."

I knew his blood, and already yearned for it. I opened my mouth, and latched on, letting his blood flow into me, and I closed my eyes.

"You need to create the bond," Carlos told him.

"I know." Matteo lifted my arm, and his fangs sunk into my wrist. The pleasure burst through me, easing my body into euphoria. A distraction from the pain. His mind opened to mine as the blood bond connected us. I let out a sigh against his throat.

'Keep drinking.' His hand stroked the back of my head, soothing me. *'Let go. No more pain, no more fear. Just the two of us. Forever.'*

I clung to him, as I took his blood. *Forever.* He was my forever. The cut in his throat healed, and I instinctively bit down.

"Let me," he whispered and pulled me back, cutting his throat again with the arrow, bringing me back to drink. "*Mi amore*, my blood is healing you. Remember what I said happens. It will overwhelm your system and begin to change you. It won't be as last time. You're going to experience a mortal death. You're going to sleep as your body changes. I'll be here when you wake up."

Mortal death. My fear of death kicked in, and I fought against him, panic rising. *I don't want to die.* I growled.

'Shh, Quinn. Remember, you're not really dying, only going to sleep. Keep drinking, you need to keep drinking.' A feeling radiated from him that surrounded me. Protectiveness. A

tenderness and warmth, followed by relief. *'I'll have her by my side forever.'* His thoughts brought tears to my eyes.

Memories washed over me. His memories. The moment he woke up a vampire with overwhelming hunger. His wife's death. Sending his daughter to his brother, where he knew she'd be safe. The moment he killed Bianca. His bond with Carlos. Gabriela's control over him, and over her clan. The moment he'd heard my voice and seen me at the bar. That first kiss on the balcony. Dancing, our faces inches from each other. What my voice did for him in the cell, pulling him out of bloodlust and breaking Gabriela's sway over him.

I felt myself fading as his blood flowed through me. I could almost feel it changing me, starting with the hunger, and I listened to his heartbeat. He pulled me away from his throat, his eyes burning into mine, shining with love. He stroked my cheek with such tenderness. Matteo's and Carlos's hands lowered me to the ground, the leather jacket still around me. I wanted to say something, to tell him I had Called him, but I couldn't form words.

"I can hear Hunters looking for us. We should leave," Carlos's voice was low.

'Quinn Ti amo. Sleep. I will wake you from your slumber.' Matteo whispered into my mind.

I slipped into darkness, taking his words with me.

Chapter 60

Quinn

My death didn't hurt, not like the arrow that punctured my heart. I still fought to hold onto life. As my human body died, an endless night closed in. An echo, a spark remained, but it faded as a new fire that burned deep emerged.

"Quinn," a voice called to me from the dark, commanding. "It's time to wake up."

I opened my eyes. He lay on the bed beside me, caressing my face. Matteo. I knew him, the strength of our blood bond wrapping around my heart and mind. His presence surrounded me. Hunger burned through me, an inferno.

"Quinn," his voice was both out loud and in my head, and

he smiled. "Welcome back to the living."

"I'm hungry." I pressed my tongue to a fang.

"I know. We'll hunt. I'll be with you, guiding you." He smiled down at me.

I sat up taking in my surroundings. "Where are we?" The room looked vaguely familiar.

"My house. I couldn't exactly take you to your apartment; the sounds of the city, and the humans in your building would be unbearable for you. More so than last time. Plus, the Hunters are waiting for you." His eyes never left mine.

His mention of Hunters brought a memory of pain. I rubbed at my chest.

"Yes, she shot you, but it's healed. You died as a human; now you're a vampire. Like me." He stroked my face, a light in his eyes. "Just as beautiful as ever, a goddess. Mine."

"She killed me?" I didn't understand the hurt at those words.

"She did. I will deal with her and what remains of her family afterwards." A glimpse of his anger showed. A burning fury born from his protectiveness of me.

I didn't want to think about Hunters or anything else. I only wanted to feed.

He rose from the bed, holding his hand out to me. "I have something special waiting for you."

I grabbed his outstretched hand, letting him pull me off the bed. A faint whiff drew my attention. Hunger flared.

"There's a human here," I said. "More than one?"

He chuckled. "That's you, from when you were human. Your scent lingered. It's stronger in my studio. A delectable fragrance. You were here recently, and your friend. You took my painting." He nuzzled my cheek. "The other is the one we'll be hunting."

The urge to kiss him overwhelmed me. I reached up to touch his face, need aching in me. He turned my hand over, his lips brushing my fingers. Everything in my mind was foggy, and I couldn't remember anything. But I knew him. He'd answered a Call, and he'd awakened something in me. I frowned, not knowing what that meant.

A heartbeat nearby drew both our attention. I growled, my canines aching.

"What's she doing here?" he grumbled.

I moved towards the scent, hungry, eager to feed. Matteo stopped me. "No, not that one. You won't like it."

"But she's human." I pushed at Matteo, but he wouldn't let me go. I growled, confused as to why he wasn't letting me feed.

"Stay here," he commanded, and his voice took hold. "I will send her away."

"Why?" I asked.

"After you've fed, when everything is clearer, you'd be ashamed of feeding from her. Please, Quinn, stay here. We will hunt," he promised.

He left me in the room, and his heartbeat and footsteps moved away, towards the door. I paced the room.

"What are you doing here?" he asked.

The human's heartbeat thundered in my ears. I could almost taste her blood, but Matteo had told me to stay.

"Where is she?" There was something familiar about the voice, but I couldn't place it.

"You really shouldn't be here, Mia," he told her.

"She's my friend." Her voice shook.

He let out a frustrated sound. "Not at the moment, she's

not. Right now, she's hungry and needs blood, and it's yours she wants." He hissed. "This is what your friend is now."

"She won't hurt me." The heart skipped, and a slight scent of fear hit me.

I growled again.

Matteo breathed in deep. "You're right to be afraid. She won't recognise you. All she'll see is her first feed. I can feel her growing bloodlust from here. She can smell your fear. It will take a few days, maybe even a few weeks before her human memories will emerge again. Right now, all she has is the basic vampire instinct, and you're nothing but temptation to her. I need to take her hunting. Then I will bring her to you, if that's what she wants when she's herself again. Your Hunter friend, on the other hand…" A growl rumbled from him.

"I know what Lil… what her family did. To you. I'm sorry you endured that." There was sympathy in her voice. "It wasn't Lil, though, she wasn't involved in that. She told me she couldn't stomach the idea of torturing someone."

"She killed Quinn." His voice had changed, taking on a deeper, more guttural tone. "You really should leave."

"Quinn!" the human called out. "Quinn, it's me, Mia."

"Please," I murmured to Matteo, knowing he could hear me. "Let me feed."

"Leave," he growled. "Before it's too late for you."

"Quinn, she's coming for you both. Lilith is after revenge over the death of her brother."

Something shifted in Matteo, his alert sharpening. "Did you bring a Hunter here?" There was fury in his voice.

The restraints that wrapped around me, tying me to the room, snapped and I lurched forward.

"Quinn, stop!" He tried to stop me, but I didn't care. My hunger was too great.

The scent of blood and fear called to me, and I answered. I pushed him and he hit the wall; a crack sounded as he did. But I didn't stop, hurling myself at the human woman, taking us both to the ground. I bit deep, tearing into the throat, relishing in the blood that filled my mouth. A scream split the air, and I put my hand over her mouth. I pulled back, to breathe in the fear. Terrified eyes met mine, and she struggled against my grip. Warm blood trickled down my chin. I pressed my nose against her, breathing in before I struck again, sinking my fangs into her throat, and latching on. Her fear drove me deeper into bloodlust.

Bliss. My entire being soared as I drank, the fire of my hunger nowhere near sated, but starting to lessen. My only need was blood, and a deep appreciation flooded me for the human below me. Hands pulled at me, and I growled in warning, refusing to be separated from what I needed. I was lost in the taste of her blood, her heartbeat, and waves on the beach.

"Quinn, stop." He tried to use the blood bond between us to pull me away. "Let her go, now."

No! My hunger was stronger than the pull he had over me. I closed my eyes, pleased at my first feeding, annoyed that Matteo wasn't sharing that pride with me. He wrapped an arm around my waist.

'Quinn, release her,' his voice was hard to disobey that time, speaking to a deep part of me. I immediately let go and he turned me to face him. His eyes darted across my face. "Do you know what you've just done?" he demanded.

His anger confused and hurt me. I had expected him to

be pleased. Perhaps I was supposed to share her with him. I wiped at my face, smearing the blood over his mouth. I smiled as hunger filled his eyes, and unable to resist, pressed myself against him, kissing hard.

His hunger rolled through him, both for the blood and for me. He shuddered, and his arms were around me. He turned, pushing my back against the wall, and a growl rose from his chest. We pulled back and I delighted at seeing his eyes red, fangs sharp, glistening in his mouth.

A deep satisfaction rose from him as he stared at me with amusement, and snapped at my jaw with his teeth playfully.

I glanced down at the woman, her heartbeat too fast to be normal. Matteo knelt over her. "I think you've taken more than I can do anything about. You bit deep. If I gave her blood, I'd have to give her too much for her to remain human. I have no intention of doing that."

Unsure why it mattered, I didn't care. I wanted Matteo to take me in his arms, for the two of us to be together and not worry about anything else. I glanced at the wall, realising I'd pushed him hard enough to make a hole. He laughed. "Yes, you'll need to get used to your strength, among other things." He moved towards me, his hands on my hips, pressing me against the wall gazing down at me with a look that made my heart swell. "Now that I no longer have to be gentle with you, the things I'm going to do to you, my beautiful siren." He cupped a cheek with his hand, and I leaned into his touch. "But I've arranged a hunt for us. He's waiting."

"What have you done?" a voice called, seething.

I turned towards the door, and hissed at the human facing us. At the crossbow in her hand.

"Hunter. You really shouldn't be here. You're on my

territory now. I will defend myself, and her." He looked down at me with a smile on his face. "Not that she needs it, she's quite capable."

This was my territory, too. I let out a growl in warning.

The woman had her arm in a sling, and pain came off her in waves. Her eyes fell to the body of the woman I'd fed from, then lifted to my face.

"*You killed Mia!*" A different kind of pain then, one not of any injuries, from deeper, from inside her. Not just pain, but dark fury that burned in her eyes.

Her blood called to me; my hunger surged. Before I could move, Matteo grabbed my arm, holding me back.

"She will feel the pain from this," he said to the Hunter.

"You did this," she said. "I'll kill you for all you've taken from me." Her eyes darted to me again, tears sliding down her face. "Quinn, this can't be what you wanted."

Matteo laughed. "What do you hope to do against two vampires with that? I've been around for six hundred years, Hunter. Even if your wrist weren't broken, you wouldn't be a match for Quinn. If I let her go, she'd be on you in an instant. You would not be able to fight her off. You were foolish to come alone."

"Quinn," the Hunter said, turning her anger back towards me. "How could you kill Mia?" Her voice broke.

"I was hungry," I replied as if it were obvious. *Stupid question.*

Matteo scoffed at my thought. The Hunter let out a cry of rage and ran at him.

He moved with speed, knocking the crossbow from her hand, and turned her around, pressing his body against her back, so she was facing Mia. "Don't be stupid," he hissed into her ear. "I will tear out your throat, and you will die next to her."

She didn't fight him, and he released her. As she turned to face me, there was nothing but pure hatred for me. "You chose a vampire over your friends."

I frowned. *'What's she talking about?'* I asked Matteo through our blood bond. *'I chose a vampire? I am a vampire. Are you going to let me feed from her or not?'*

'No. I have another planned. Let me get rid of her, and we'll hunt. This is a meal I intend to share with you.' Desire sparked in his eyes. "I've been waiting to hunt with you for a long time."

The promise of another helped me relax.

"You should leave," he said again. "She wants to feed from you, I'm not sure you'll survive her hunger. She's ravenous." Pride did sound in his voice then, and my own joy surged in response.

"You've broken the accords." Her eyes met mine. "From this moment forward, consider me your enemy," she declared. She addressed Matteo. "Can I at least take her body?"

"The longer you stay here, the more likely you will die," he told her. "I'll bring her body to you after Quinn has hunted. Now go. Before I break something other than your wrist."

The Hunter left.

"Finally." Matteo flashed his fangs at me. "Are you ready?" he asked. "Now we hunt."

Chapter 61

Matteo

I took Quinn to the beach. There was a light wind, the waves crashing on the shore sending salt spray in our direction. Her presence was captivating, and I couldn't keep my eyes off her.

The changes in her were apparent, from human to vampire. Her movements were those of the predator she was now. In the state she was in, she would not pass for human. I'd have to teach her to hide her vampirism, to move the way a human would. From her new vampire visage, blood on her chin, and the hunger in her eyes, she would be enough to send any human running. But to me, she was perfect.

I'd fallen for a human, and she'd finally chosen to be a part of my world, accepting the feral. My chest ached with the sudden emotion that flooded through me. *Love.* More than what I'd had with Marisa. A man and a siren, separated by centuries and brought together by fate.

"You fed from Mia before I could teach you the basics," I told her, delighting in being here to teach her. "But you can make them enjoy it, instead of screaming in pain."

"How?" she asked.

I tilted her chin up, pushing her lip back, pressing my thumb against a fang. "There is venom in your bite. All you need is to release it. Intend for them to feel pleasure at your bite." I grinned. "I do like them screaming, but it calls too much attention these days."

The human had gone further than I'd anticipated because of our visitors. My senses were more tuned than Quinn's, and I could hear his heartbeat, and the slight hint of absolute terror wafted through the air. But with Quinn beside me, I was able to resist giving chase.

I could tell when she'd picked it up, as her mind shifted, becoming more alert.

'That's right. That's the one we're hunting.' I told her. *'We can take our time, or we can make it quick. I do like to take my time, to savour the hunt, but you might have a different preference.'*

I could feel her hunger, as she gazed up at me. *'Savouring the hunt sounds like more fun.'*

'A woman after my own heart.' I held my hand over my chest, before resting it on hers. I couldn't look away from her. The yearning I held for Quinn had surged when she awoke, in a way I had never experienced before. Her fangs were a beautiful sight that I couldn't resist. I drew her into a kiss, sharing the affection I felt through our bond. To have

her with me, a vampire, filled me with a deep satisfaction. A wave of warmth hit me as her own feelings flooded through us both. She wasn't quite herself, but her feelings were still there.

"Are you ready?" I asked out loud.

I monitored Quinn, pleased that she was moving in tune with me. We stalked the human for an hour, deliberately drawing it out. She barely left a print in the sand, instincts for the hunt as natural as breathing. I'd wanted this from the moment I laid eyes on her.

Finally, the human became aware that he was being hunted. He caught glimpses of us, only to find no one there when he looked again.

'Time to eat,' I said, encouraging her to feed first.

The human turned to find himself face to face with Quinn. In reaction, he stepped back to find me behind him.

"Quinn?" the human's voice shook and his fear enticed me. Delicious.

She tilted her head. "You know me?" Her eyes shifted to me. *'Who is he?'* she asked silently.

I struggled to think of his name. She'd told me once, but I hadn't cared enough to remember it. "He's Dan." His desire for her had annoyed me, and I saw no better way to be rid of him.

'Remember, you don't want him to scream. Release venom into your bite,' I told her, and she struck.

Unable to hold back, I moved in, biting the other side of his throat. His struggles stopped, and he gave in to our venom. All he was to her now was nothing more than a meal, and I took great pleasure in sharing him with her.

"Quinn," he moaned, his hands on her.

A growl rose up from me, and I released his throat only to bite down again. This time harder, ripping into flesh, blood gushing into my mouth. Quinn responded by doing the same. My hand pressed to the back of her head, holding her to his throat. As she buried herself deeper into him, a happy rumble rose from her, like a purr.

He groaned again. "Quinn, you're hurting me. Stop."

'Don't stop,' I told her, the red haze rising up. I didn't try to hold it back.

I tore deeper, blood gushing as I ripped out a chunk of him. The only regret I felt as he fell was that I'd wasted blood in my possessiveness of her.

I kicked him. *Call me Champ, stronzo.*

I pulled Quinn to me, our kiss rough, the taste of blood on her lips only adding to the fire between us.

"You're mine," I whispered when we separated.

I took a look at Quinn. My heart, my love. Her mind would clear, and she would be more like herself after a couple more feedings, and my overwhelming need to protect her would likely clear, too.

I laughed at the blood over her face. I leaned in, waiting to see her reaction, and I lapped the blood from her face. It was a mixture of Mia's and Dan's. She closed her eyes, a rumbling of satisfaction deep within her chest. When I finished, she leaned forward, and her tongue on my face made me hard. I wanted to take her. But I wanted her in my bed. The sun would be rising soon, and while not lethal, it would be unpleasant for her. For both of us.

"Let's go home; it's been a long night." I kissed her again. "I want to get you out of those clothes and spend the day making you scream."

400

Chapter 62

Quinn

I knew nothing of my life before awakening as a vampire, only Matteo, as if I'd always known him.

"That's the blood bond," he said as he carried me in his arms back to his house. I loved the strength of his arms, his warm body against me. He'd insisted on carrying me, and I couldn't deny that I enjoyed it. "It binds us together. Your vampire instincts tie you to me as you adjust to your new self. Your mind is in shock after your mortal death, so it shuts down. You'll get yourself back in a few days." His lips brushed my forehead. "It might be a painful transition when you do, but I'll help you through it."

I could listen to that accent all day.

He shook as laughter boomed from him. "You're still you in every way." He carried me into his bedroom.

I stood before him, unable to take my eyes from his. Yearning washed over me with an intensity that left me breathless. He didn't move, watching me as if waiting. Raw desire smouldered in his eyes, along with pure love that shone through. I reached for his face, overcome with my own need and love. I needed to claim him, and for him to claim me.

"Mine," I said, and joy lit up his eyes.

"Yes, *mi amore*, I'm yours." He still didn't move.

I dropped my hand from his face, pressing it to his chest. '*What do you want, mi cantante?*' His hand lifted to push hair back from my face.

"I want you," I replied. "I want you naked, and I want your hands on me."

Matteo removed his tee-shirt. I brushed both hands across his wide chest to his abs. His fingers closed around my wrists before moving up my arms. I undid his jeans, and he discarded them. He took his time to unbutton my bloodied shirt, pulling it from me. We caressed each other, captivated. I wanted nothing else but his touch, and to touch him. He left a blazing trail of kisses across my collarbone to my jaw.

He lowered me to the bed, pinning my body beneath his. I reached up to cradle his face, and his eyes closed. When he opened them again, they were red.

"Are you still hungry?" I asked.

He breathed in. "Only for you." He kissed my neck, moving across to my shoulder and down my arm, his lips leaving me wanting more.

I tilted my head, exposing my throat to him, unsure if

he could drink from me. If vampires could feed from each other.

He kissed my palm, his lips stretched into a smile. "We can. At least this time I don't have to worry about taking too much or what my blood will do to you. I got a little carried away last time. Blood-sharing with you is something I long for. It is very intimate for our kind."

His fingers brushed my neck, and he sunk his fangs in. I held him to me, feeling like I was floating. Warmth and pleasure flooded through my entire body. He lifted his head, gazing into my eyes. Moving down my body, he bit into my breast before letting go and pulling my wrist to his mouth.

Buzzing with energy, I moaned. He released my wrist and moved down again, his fangs sinking into my inner thigh.

As he withdrew again, I groaned in frustration. He moved to whisper in my ear.

"I told you that you would be mine, heart, body and soul," he said.

I had no memory of that, yet I wanted him to claim me. My heart, my body and my soul.

"I am yours," I whispered. "My heart is yours. My body is yours. My soul is yours. All you need to do is claim me."

His cheek brushed against mine.

"I claim you," he said, his breath caressing my ear. "I claim your heart." His hand rested over my chest, and he moved down, his lips brushing the space over my heart. "I claim your body." His hand slid down, against my stomach and ribs. "And I claim your soul." Then we were kissing, and I was complete.

Matteo rolled us over, so he was beneath me, his hands on my hips. "Drink from me, Quinn," he murmured. "Claim me." He tilted his head to the side, baring his throat to me.

His blood was different from the humans'. There was more fire. There was no nourishment in it, but I soared.

"I claim you," I whispered, moving to the other side of his throat. His hand grasped the back of my head, and a low grumble rose from him. I lifted my head and kissed his chest. His heartbeat was slow, pulsing beneath my lips. "I claim your heart." I ran my hands over his abs. "I claim your body."

Sparks erupted as our lips met again. His need and desire and deep longing joined mine, our minds fused as the blood bond wrapped tighter around us, hearts beating as one. "I claim your soul."

Matteo rolled us over a second time, and he trailed kisses down, stopping at my breasts. I shifted my fingers through his hair as he used teeth and sucked, eliciting gasps from me. He continued moving down my body until his face rested between my legs. His mouth was warm, and he licked, bit, and swirled his tongue, and heat built in my core. I clenched, my hands grasping sheets as Matteo's tightened on my hips.

'*Scream,*' his voice in my head was heavy with lust, and he met my eyes with a wicked glint. '*Scream for me, Quinn.*'

"Faster," I begged. "Harder."

He did as I asked, the pressure of his tongue increasing. Pleasure and heat coiled within, and my hips bucked. I grasped the back of his head, holding him hard against me. Arching my back, I let waves carry me to the height of my orgasm, screaming his name as I surged with pure pleasure. Satisfaction flared from him. Fine spasms ran through me as he kissed my clit before crawling his way up to my mouth. I clutched him, still trembling, my body on fire.

His tongue was forceful against mine, and I ground myself

against his hardness, aching for him to be inside me. Matteo lifted his head to look me in the eyes.

"I like hearing you scream my name," he said. "I'm going to make you do it again. But first, my little *cantante,* you're going to beg for it."

He nudged his erection to my opening but paused, waiting. I pushed up and he pulled back.

"I said *beg.* Tell me how much you want me inside you," he commanded.

"Please," I murmured with a groan, feeling like if he continued doing this, I would combust. "I need you."

His eyes gleamed. "Tell me what you need."

I growled in frustration. "Matteo, please. I need you inside me."

His smile was one of triumph. "Will you scream for me if I give you what you want?"

He kissed my neck, fangs pressed against skin.

My body was on fire, and I wanted both his cock and his fangs. "Yes," I whispered. "Just please, Matteo…"

I didn't finish my sentence before he drove into me roughly, biting my throat as he did. My muscles pulsed around him as he entered, stretching me. A wave of euphoria crashed over me, and I dug my nails into his back. His thrusts were aggressive, but I wanted more. My hips rose up in time to meet him with each movement, and I wrapped my legs around him. The sensation of our bodies against each other, and him sliding through me, jolted me with waves of pleasure.

Our breaths came out in gasps, Matteo letting out little grunts. I bit into his shoulder, his lips still latched onto my throat, and our minds connected. A deep love emanated from him merging with me. I soared as ripples pulled me closer to coming, and I pulled on his hair. A loud moan escaped my lips against his shoulder. He tensed, and he lifted his head, our gazes locked in the heat of ecstasy.

He heaved against me, his breathing ragged, and he kissed me again.

"You're mine," he said. "And I'm yours. Forever."

Chapter 63

Quinn

"**B**reaking news. Bassist of Roses and Thorns, Mia Wallace has been found dead, while singer Quinn Bailey is missing, her car found abandoned. We are live now with remaining member Lilith De Micheli."

Lilith appeared on screen, in deep emotion, shadows under her eyes. "I am aware that there have been killings recently, and my brother's life was taken in the attempt to bring this monster to justice. But to lose my best friends, too, has been devastating."

"So, you think Quinn is dead too?" the reporter asked.

Lilith looked straight at the camera, and I knew she was talking to me. "I do," she said. "I hope they find the monster that did this, but I think it's too late for Quinn."

"Roses and Thorns was most well-known for their songs Alone and Feeling the Music, but If One of Us Hurts, We All Hurt was a favourite of fans. Singer Quinn recently had a steamy relationship with art gallery owner Matteo Barone before he too disappeared following a fire in his gallery."

A picture of the three of us flashed on screen from a photo shoot. So happy, and human. It was replaced by one of me and Matteo in masks, moments before a kiss.

"Roses and Thorns was due to go on tour around Australia in January, the three musicians making their mark in Melbourne."

I hit the mute button.

"She's dead," I said, numb. "I killed my best friend. How did I not know her?"

Matteo pulled me into his arms, and I sobbed into his chest. For the life I had lost. My dream was gone. I'd known what I was giving up when I'd asked Matteo to turn me, but it still hurt. One best friend was dead, at my hands. My other had declared me an enemy. She had not responded to any texts or phone calls from mine or Matteo's phones, and eventually calls just went straight to her voicemail, and texts remained unseen.

I caught sight of my parents on TV.

"With no body, Mum will never believe I'm dead." I watched them speaking to the camera. "With all we spoke about before Carlos and I went to find you, I feel like she'll know exactly what happened. She'll know I'm a vampire. I'm surprised she hasn't called." When she'd told me I was fated to become a vampire for Calling Matteo, she'd been so matter-of-fact about it. *How does she feel, knowing her daughter was a vampire?*

"You should call them," he said. "Quinn, I'm sorry, I know this will be a burden on you. Adjusting as you let go of your human life to make way for being a vampire."

I moved my face into his touch, closing my eyes. He lifted his other hand, pushing hair back from my face, and he leaned down, kissing my forehead. Tenderness flowed through our blood bond, a warmth and deep affection that made my heart swell.

"I live for you," he murmured. "Only you. Why did it take me so long to find you?"

"You have me now," I said. "My heart, my body, and my soul. I am yours. Forever."

His small smile lit up his eyes, and he brought his lips down to mine. Fire blazed through me, the bond opening our minds to each other. In him, a wonder to have me in his arms, and a deep loneliness that finally melted. *I found her.* He leaned his forehead against mine, and we remained motionless for what could have been minutes or hours.

"Are you hungry?" he asked at last.

I shook my head. "Not yet, but I know I will be. I can feel it, always beneath the surface. It's more manageable than it was when I awoke, though."

"You did well with your last feed; you pulled yourself out of the blood haze." He winced. "Something I was never good at. I've been controlled by my hunger; I was never able to break through it. I don't want the same for you. I will do what I can to guide you." I let him pull me into another kiss.

A slow heartbeat approached from the beach, fast. Someone moving with vampire speed.

"Who's that?" I asked.

His eyes lit up. "It's Carlos. He wanted to give us space when you awoke, to let me and you hunt together for the first time. He's eager to see vampire you."

Carlos stood at the door. He didn't knock, just waited for us to answer. His eyes passed over me, and a slow smile spread over his face, full of joy.

"Look at you!" He held a hand out in a way that reminded me of the first time he had done so. I'd been afraid of him then. Now, I took his hand without hesitation. The feeling of fear and dread that I'd always experienced with him was gone. Now that I was like him, I had no reason to fear him.

He spun me around. "You look good! Like someone destined to become a vampire."

I laughed.

"How do you feel?" he asked. "How are you adjusting to your new life?"

"There's a lot to get used to," I said honestly. "I died. That's pretty big. Unfortunately I killed my friend when I awoke."

"The Hunter?" he asked, glancing at Matteo.

I shook my head.

He squeezed my hand in sympathy. "We've all been there. I'm sure you know what Matteo went through when he awoke."

The Carlos that stood before me was completely different, and I had to admit I liked this side of him. Warmth and a genuine interest in my adjustment as a vampire.

'He's been a vampire for a while; it's all he is. He enjoys how he makes humans feel. Although he has admitted how he softened towards you, despite you still being human at the time, now you are seeing who Carlos really is when humans aren't around.' Matteo told me through our bond. *'He cares about his people.'*

His people. I was among his people, now.

"Tell me what else you've been adjusting to," Carlos continued the conversation.

"Seeing in the dark is fucking awesome." I hadn't been outside in direct sunlight yet, as my preference for sleeping during the day still hadn't worn off. Especially with Matteo's arms around me, his naked body against mine. But my vision in the dark had me gleeful. "Oh, and my strength. I knew you guys were strong, but nothing could have prepared me for just how strong."

Matteo grinned. "She pushed me through the wall when she first woke up."

Carlos laughed. "Yes, you'll learn how to take it easy with that. You might break a few things while you adjust." He winked at me. "Maybe even the bed."

"What did you break?" I asked.

"Humans," he said, but didn't offer more. "How was the hunting? Your first hunt together must have been quite the experience."

Matteo's pride flooded through me. "It was. She didn't need much guidance. I may have gotten a little out of control, though, and let my possessive nature get the best of me when he put his hands on her."

Carlos turned his attention to Matteo. "That's no surprise whatsoever. Am I to assume it was someone she knew, then?"

Memory of the hunt on the beach washed over me. The thrill of it, leaning into the bond with Matteo, and the scent of fear. I remembered the dark joy in feeding from Dan, how his blood had tasted, and wanting to please Matteo, wanting him to be proud of me. I'd torn into the flesh of Dan's throat when Matteo did. When we were done, his throat had been open, gaping. Torn open from our fangs.

His body had washed up a few days later. I'd killed two people and wasn't sure how I felt about it. It hurt to think of Mia's death, but I struggled to find remorse over Dan's. Which only shocked me more. Matteo had explained it was normal, that I saw humans as food now, and that I wouldn't feel what I would have before I'd died. He reminded me that I was no longer human, and that my constitution as a vampire would be very different. Emotions such as remorse would be dulled.

"Just someone from my apartment building," I told him with a shrug.

"When can I join you both for a hunt?" he asked Matteo. "I want to see your little siren in action."

"No time like the present," I said. "Matteo's teaching me how to not kill, to control my hunger. Something about the accords. Not like I haven't already broken them."

Someone else was approaching. Multiple someones. The strong scent of vampires was in the air. Matteo had warned me about this, that Gabriela would make an official summons for me to join her clan or leave her city.

"Gabriela?" Matteo asked.

Carlos shook his head.

Three men emerged from the darkness, standing at Matteo's door. Vampires. One of them was Erik. Carlos and Matteo were in front of me, growling in warning.

"What are you doing here?" Matteo asked.

One of the men stepped forward. He had dark hair and bright blue eyes. "We're here for her."

"She's not going to join Gabriela's clan." Matteo said. "I am no longer bound to her, either. I plan to seek a new clan."

"You've been freed, as we have," Erik spoke up then. His grey eyes were on me. "*She* did that. We haven't come to take her to Gabriela."

I stepped past Matteo and Carlos. "Why are you here then, if not for her?"

The third man with shoulder-length brown hair stepped forward and took a knee before me. He bowed his head. "We are here to swear ourselves to *you*," he said.

Something swept through me, and I could feel their minds. I took a step back as the others knelt beside him. "Me? Why?" I asked, dumbfounded.

"Since we heard your voice, we realised Gabriela has no power over us anymore. Once you were turned, we decided to join your clan," Erik said.

"Can we trust you?" Matteo asked.

"It's Carlos you should be questioning," the brown-haired one said. "She's his maker; they have been hunting together for a long time. Since before the war."

"You think to question me?" Carlos demanded, his eyes hardening.

"You are her second," the brown-haired one said. "You're loyal to Gabriela. You'd never leave her clan."

"You forget, Andreas, I too heard her sing." Carlos approached Andreas.

"Am I to believe you'd leave your maker?" Andreas scoffed.

"He snuck in to feed Matteo," The dark-haired one spoke up then. "I trust him."

I reached for Matteo for help as they argued. *'What do I do?'* I didn't know what any of this meant.

'They are choosing to join a new clan and have picked you to lead them because your voice holds power over them. You need

413

to either accept or reject their pledge,' he informed me through our bond.

'You heard me sing, and Carlos, does my voice hold sway over you?' I asked.

He laughed then. *'Mi amore, your voice held power over me since the day we met.'* He nodded towards Carlos. *'You don't have to accept their pledge, Quinn. In fact, I'm hoping you'll join me in kneeling to Carlos and swearing to follow him.'*

I turned my gaze to Carlos, who was glaring at Andreas. *'I thought he rejected you.'*

'He did, but things have changed now. Power has shifted because of you. Others may leave, too.' He turned his head towards the beach. Another set of footsteps approached. "I think we have another ready to swear to you."

"It's Lorenzo," Carlos said.

'What do you want to do?' Matteo asked me.

'I've been a vampire for all of five minutes. I know nothing about leading a clan or being a Queen. I will follow Carlos.' I agreed.

Relief crossed his features. *'Good, because Gabriela would have challenged you, and I'm not sure I would have liked that very much. I'm going to kneel to Carlos. You need to thank them for considering you, but state that you choose to follow another. They will either leave or kneel beside you.'*

Lorenzo stood at the door, taking in the sight of all of us before his eyes landed on me. He stepped forward.

"Stop," I said. "While I appreciate your gratitude for whatever ways my voice helped you, I am no leader. Thank you all for considering me, but I choose to follow another."

Carlos chuckled. "Did you tell her what to say, Matteo?"

His laughter died when Matteo knelt in front of him.

"I renounce Gabriela. I no longer recognise her as my Queen. I have relinquished my place in her clan. Instead, I swear myself and my loyalty to Carlos Rivera. I ask that you accept me into your clan," Matteo declared.

I knelt down beside Matteo. "I swear myself, and my loyalty to Carlos Rivera. I ask that you accept me into your clan." I repeated Matteo's words.

Erik, Lorenzo, and the others didn't move or speak, and silence stretched out as Carlos stared down at us. Then, as if they reached agreement at once, the rest of them knelt down beside me, repeating Matteo's words.

Carlos showed his fangs, eyes red. "I accept," he said at last. He held his hand out to me, pulling me to my feet. Matteo rose, then the rest of them. "Bare your throats to me," Carlos commanded us.

He moved to the others first, feeding from them.

"I name you as my second," Carlos said to Matteo. "We have a new vampire among us. She is new to our ways. I will accept her but will not drink from her without your approval. You must drink with me."

Matteo stood over me, his eyes red. *'Do not fight him,'* his voice whispered in my mind.

Carlos pressed in behind me, and they both struck as one. Having two drink from me was intoxicating, as their venom flooded me. I bit my lip trying to hold back a moan.

Instinct took over and I reached up behind me, grasping the back of Carlos's head, holding him to me, while my other hand slid around Matteo's back. A rumble of satisfaction rose up from me, and I closed my eyes. To have the two of them drinking from me was definitely a turn on, but there was also a sense of power in this. I could feel the act was

415

his acceptance of me into his clan: A faint link opened up, connecting me to Carlos and the others.

They released me at the same time and Matteo bit into Carlos, the older vampire raising his head high. Unsure about what to do, I watched, desire flaring in me.

"Drink from him, young one," Carlos said.

His words had a power on me, and I twisted around, my fangs ready and I bit down. Matteo's growl reverberated through me as he lifted his head from Carlos's throat and pulled me to him and into a deep kiss.

"We are a new clan: La Voz, The Voice," Carlos officially declared. "You shall protect me, and each other. In return, I shall protect you." He frowned. "However, we are in territory already claimed by another. She will challenge me. I think it's best we leave."

"I do miss Italy," Lorenzo hinted. The others murmured in agreement.

"I want to go home," Longing filled Matteo and flowed through our bond. "Venice. We could take my family home for our den. There are villas all across Venice that any remaining descendants can take. Gabriela prevented me from going back. I want to show Quinn my home."

"Well, I believe Rome was claimed by another clan when we left." Carlos nodded. "Venice it is," he smiled. "I must admit, I never went there."

The others closed in around me, breathing in my scent.

"Quinn is one of us now. She is part of our clan. Accept her," Carlos commanded. "This will be our den until we leave."

They reached out, touching my face and my hair. Erik nuzzled my cheek, followed by the others, before they all huddled together on the floor. I frowned at Matteo.

'It's alright. This is just strengthening the bond of our new clan. No different from wild animals huddling together for protection. We often do this as a new clan, or arriving in new territory.' Matteo comforted me and lowered himself to the floor.

Unsure what to do, I followed Matteo, curling into him. Erik huddled into my back. He rubbed his face against the back of my neck before licking it. His hand reached across, resting on my stomach. Lorenzo and the other two joined our huddle. One lay across my feet. I stared at Matteo in confusion, yet enjoying the contact, as if it were a natural occurrence. There was comfort in this. Safety.

'It's okay, they're all welcoming you into the clan.' Matteo reassured me.

Then another vampire entered. A blonde-haired woman. Carlos spun around, hissing.

"I follow who Lorenzo follows," she explained. "I cannot be separated from my maker." She knelt before Carlos, baring her throat. "I ask to be accepted into your clan, and I accept you as King," she said.

He fed from her for a short time. "Join your clan, Annika."

She lay behind Matteo, her eyes on me. "Welcome to our clan, Quinn," she murmured.

She already knew my name. I smiled back at her. Carlos lowered himself to the ground, joining us.

The feeling of the eight of us huddled together gave me a sense of belonging, that I would protect them, and that they would do the same for me. As a human, this would have been alarming, but I found it strangely comforting. I closed my eyes, and sleep pulled me under.

Chapter 64

Matteo

For the first time in days, it was just Quinn and myself. We lay in bed, her in my arms, our bodies warm from feeding just hours before. We'd hunted with Carlos, and I was impressed with her acceptance of his presence with us. Now that she was a vampire, there was an amusing banter between the two of them, a growing friendship replacing the fear she'd once had of him.

"We had another join us, Celeste. Which makes Carlos very happy." I kissed the back of her neck. "I'm pleased to see you and Carlos are connecting."

"He's not so bad," she had a smile in her voice.

The two most important people in my life were bonding.

"You have a fondness for him?"

She turned over to face me. "I do feel an attraction. Not like what's between you and me, but there's something there."

"I'm sure Carlos would appreciate that. He's fond of you, too," I gave her a soft kiss. "Carlos is known for his unique cravings."

She frowned. "Unique cravings?"

"I don't think I have the right word. Um, he takes both men and women to his bed," I explained.

"You mean he's bisexual?" Her eyes lit up with amusement. "That's not unique. Lilith's bi. Even I experimented in uni."

"No, I know he's bisexual." I tried to find the words. "I mean, he has a fondness for multiple lovers. Equally. He may take one to his bed on one night, then someone else the next. He has a closeness with Celeste, as well as Lorenzo and Annika."

Quinn's laughter burst from her. "I think the word you're looking for, my sweet vampire, is polyamorous. How have you lived this long and not known the word?"

"Polyamorous," I repeated. "I'm sure he'd find amusement that there is a word for it now." I gave her a gentle squeeze. "Are you okay?"

"Yeah. Are you?" she returned.

"You've gone through a substantial change in your life." I kissed her forehead "You gave up your entire life for me; don't think that has no meaning. I'm sorry for everything that you've lost. Do you want to talk about it?"

She chuckled. "You speak as if either of us had a choice," she gazed into my eyes. "I Called you with my magical Siren Song, binding us together, and sealing my fate into becoming a vampire."

419

"Do you have regrets?" I asked.

"Only Mia's death." Her eyes shifted across my face. "I knew exactly what I was giving up. Besides, I can still sing. I probably just have to be more careful when I do, now. Siren vampire and all."

The day I'd painted her naked, her voice had done something to me, and in the cell she'd pulled me out of a feeding frenzy by singing. She'd also broken Gabriela's hold over all those who'd heard her. We suspected that sharing my blood with her had enhanced that power in her voice. Her abilities as simultaneously a siren and as a vampire would be something she'd need to learn herself, as she was the first of her kind.

She pressed her lips against mine in a soft kiss that quickly became ferocious.

I tightened my arms around her, growling as I rolled us over, pinning her beneath me. When I pulled away, she gazed up at me, her eyes red. I laughed. "That's something you'll need to learn to control," I said. Confusion crossed her face, so I lifted my hand, indicating my eyes. "Hunger and arousal tend to change your eye colour. Anger can too. You can't be out in public flashing red eyes at humans."

She grinned. "That's fine, I'll just stay in here with you." Lifting her head, she licked my neck as I'd done to her so many times. I let out a deep rumble of contentment, and I lowered myself to give her easier access to my throat. She struck fast, without hesitation, biting deep. I couldn't hold back the moan as her venom flooded through from her bite.

She smiled up at me, showing her fangs. The sight of them sent a thrill through me.

"*Mi amore*," she murmured. I tried not to flinch at her poor attempt at the words. We could work on her pronunciation; we had plenty of time. That she'd tried was everything.

I trailed kisses from her jaw, stopping at her throat. I didn't move, lips pressed against flesh. Frustration surged through her. *'Beg me to bite you.'* I commanded.

Before she could, the presence of another approached and I lifted my head, hissing in warning.

Carlos stopped in the doorway shirtless, showing a wolf tattoo on his chest, one eye blue, the other red, and a flaming sword down his right arm. "She is yours." He didn't move, waiting. "But you and her are both mine."

It wasn't unusual for a vampire King or Queen to stake claim over underlings within the clan. Nor was it a surprise that Carlos might claim many in our clan. He was a man generous regarding with whom he shared his bed and affections.

Quinn caressed my face. *'It's okay with me if he wants to claim the two of us.'* When I still didn't relax, she smiled. *'Matteo, the two of you have a bond, are you really surprised that he wants to claim you?'*

She did make a good point. I could not deny our new King. "Mine," I reminded him.

"Yours," he agreed, and pointed to the both of us. "Mine."

Quinn reached out to him, but he waited for me. "We are yours," I said, and held my hand out to him. He unclothed completely and joined us on the bed as I bit into Quinn's throat, and he took the other side. The animalistic sounds that came from her pierced through me. I growled in response and moved to kiss her hard. She moaned against my lips, squirming under me. Carlos lifted his head, and I moved back to let him in.

421

I couldn't deny the sight of the two of them kissing did things to me. I found it captivating.

'K*nife?*' Carlos asked.

I knew why he was asking. This was normal for him. I'd seen such play, but I never took part in it myself. Without a word he was gone, only to return three seconds later with a knife from my kitchen. He pressed the blade against my chest, and I lay back. Quinn's eyes widened. As he sliced, it stung briefly, and blood seeped from the wound. He guided her to drink. She ran her tongue across the cut slowly. I shivered, my growl of pleasure low as I held her to me.

When the cut in my chest closed, Carlos handed the knife to her, pointing to his own chest. She glanced at me, hesitating.

"Go on," I whispered in her ear, reassuring. "It's okay." I drew a line down my chest with my finger. "Cut down here, where he did. Draw blood."

She sliced deep and started to lean forward. I tensed, but Carlos was firm before I could react. He pushed at her shoulder to stop her.

"Not you, young one. You can *never* drink from me. *Only* Matteo can. Guide him to my chest."

My blood was still on her lips as she pressed them to mine, before nudging me towards Carlos. His hand grasped the back of my head.

Then it was her turn, and I licked a line down her abdomen before slicing. I gave Carlos's chin a lick before pushing him towards Quinn. She squirmed under his tongue, and I moved down, kissing her inner thigh before biting her. She whimpered, her hand clamping down on the back of my head. I licked, eliciting a deep shudder from her. Carlos kissed her again as I moved my tongue through her centre, knowing exactly how to draw the most pleasure from her. I licked her, swirling my tongue and pulling her clit between my teeth.

I knew she was close to climax when her back arched, pressing herself against my mouth, her moans getting louder. Carlos simply watched, stroking himself.

She screamed her way through her orgasm.

Carlos laughed in my head. *'You have a screamer. She really is suited for you.'*

'No, I made her a screamer,' I boasted with pride.

I pressed myself against her body, deep tremors still ripping through her. She moaned into my mouth as I kissed her again. I rolled us over onto our sides, pulling her leg over mine. Carlos embraced her from behind and reached down, his hand sliding through her, before smearing her own juices over his cock.

I entered Quinn with a rough thrust, driving into her as we moved as one. Carlos spoke to her in Spanish, as he eased into her ass. Her eyes rolled back as we both drove into her. We found a rhythm that she seemed to enjoy. She clung to me, tensing as her second orgasm neared. I pressed our lips together, speeding up to push her closer, almost on the verge myself. I moaned at the feel of her muscles pulsing around my cock.

Pleasure spread through her, and she threw back her head, as she tried not to scream. Her throat was exposed, so I bit her as I came, and Carlos clamped onto her shoulder in his own orgasm.

The three of us lay there, breathing hard. None of us moved, just holding on, hearts racing.

Chapter 65

Quinn

We were due to leave that night. I'd been a vampire for less than a month, and I was leaving my family, my home. I missed that I couldn't talk to my best friends about all that had changed. That I had lost them both hurt, but I could only blame myself for that. They had always been there, but I had gained a clan who had accepted me without question.

Carlos ordered all vampires to leave the den for a few hours to ensure I felt comfortable about my parents being there. I made sure I was well fed, which led to both me and Matteo cleaning the blood from one another's faces before giving in to our desire for each other. Carlos had his own house to pack up and promised to be back later. Matteo had advised Carlos to have an escort like Erik or Josef in case Gabriela challenged him. But Carlos had declined the suggestion.

Mum and Dad would arrive soon. They had emptied my apartment, and alerted us that Hunters were still watching it. Movers had taken everything, also leaving the den empty. Every piece of art, furniture, and all that we owned was on its way to Venice.

"The others, where do they stay?" I asked.

"We each have homes of our own, but we often still end up sheltering together." Matteo told me. "It's called a den. We'll have one in Venice. We're a small clan, so I think Carlos will want us all together, rather than spread out."

A smashing sound came from the back of the house, glass raining down. We ran to find Carlos on the ground, the door gone. On the other side was Gabriela.

"You made a vampire on my territory, while part of my clan, but you think you can join another?" she demanded, fury darkening her eyes.

"I stopped being a part of your clan when you gave me up to the Hunters," Matteo growled.

Carlos wasn't looking good; She'd torn into his throat. Blood flowed freely from the gaping wound. He'd need blood. A lot of it. My need to protect him overwhelmed me as I growled. Matteo pushed me behind him.

"I challenged him, and he lost; you have no choice but to re-join me." Gabriela's eyes were red, and she bared her fangs.

"If he dies, then I succeed him as his second," Matteo said.

"He was *my* second!" she roared. "I made him what he is." She kicked Carlos. "Viper."

425

Carlos opened his eyes and made a choking sound. Relief surged through me. He tried to push himself up from the floor, but she forced him down with a foot on his back.

"I'm going to make you suffer for your betrayal, little killer," she said down to him. "Nine hundred years and you dare turn on me now? Did you not have everything you hungered for?" Gone was the woman amused by everything; her fury crashed against me in waves.

Matteo took a step forward, but Carlos shook his head.

"My loyalty and high regard for you ended when you started to abuse your power," Carlos revealed. "You used your command against us, made slaves of us for your own purposes. I've wanted to leave you for the past hundred years, but was unable to, until now."

"You took Matteo, too? He's mine!"

Carlos growled and tried to get up again. "Maybe it's time Matteo knows the truth about why you brought him to us in the first place."

Gabriela punched her hand towards his back, fingers outstretched.

Matteo left my side, moving fast as he let out a menacing growl, slamming into Gabriela, the momentum propelling them forward, away from Carlos. The wall shook as they hit it.

Savage growls came from Matteo and Gabriela. I knelt over Carlos. The sound of a car sent panic through me. *Mum and Dad*.

"Go," Carlos choked out.

I didn't get far before something hit me hard, knocking the air from my lungs. Gabriela slammed me into a wall, and her hand closed around my throat. Behind her, Matteo was on the ground, Carlos still where I'd left him.

"I'm going to rip your throat out, right in front of your maker," she hissed.

Everything stopped. Gabriela was on her knees, hands pressed against her ears, screaming in pain. Mum stood at the end of the hallway, entering the lounge with Dad behind her. She was humming, but it seemed to come from inside her. Her eyes glowed green, as they had when she took down Carlos.

"I'm glad I'm not on the receiving end of that this time." Carlos grunted.

"Siren," Gabriela choked. "I thought your kind had died out." Her eyes darted between Mum and me, realisation passing over her face.

"You know of us, then you know what we can do," Mum said. "I suggest you keep that in mind if you come near my daughter or her clan again."

She released Gabriela, who took the opportunity to leave. Fast.

"Mum, you're a badass," I marvelled. "How do I do that?"

She laughed. "Niamh will teach you. Your voice can draw people to you, but it can also be a weapon. You'll be able to bring people under your command, and bring enemies to their knees. Like I just did with whoever she was."

She stepped aside, and Niamh stood there. "Holy shit, you look so good as a vampire!" My sister grinned at me. "I'm so excited, I get to teach you siren stuff. Just no kinky vampire shit in my presence, I don't need to see any of that."

I laughed and glanced at Matteo, who was climbing to his feet. "Make sure you knock or something, then, before you drop in. We tend to bite and get it on whenever the need

427

takes us."

She rolled her eyes, then looked down at Carlos. "He doesn't look so good. Are Mum and Dad safe?"

Carlos growled from the other side of the room. His red eyes darted towards my parents. The wound in his throat had closed, but his hunger was at a dangerous point for Mum and Dad.

"You should probably leave," Matteo said to my parents. "He's going to need blood."

"We can help," Mum said, and moved towards Carlos without fear.

"Mum, stay back," I warned.

She ignored me, though, and crouched down in front of Carlos, Dad right beside her.

"Let us help you," Mum told him.

Torn between protecting my parents, and the loyalty I felt for Carlos, I took a step forward.

'*No,*' Matteo said.

"Please," I pleaded. "Don't let him hurt them."

Matteo moved towards them, ready to act if needed. He helped Carlos sit up. Mum held her wrist to his mouth, and I flinched when he bit her. The scent of her blood made my own fangs descend.

"Are you okay?" Niamh asked me.

I nodded. "Yeah, still getting used to some stuff. Matteo says it's normal, though."

Mum sat down, hard and started to hum. It was her happy humming, and I joined in, unable to help myself.

Niamh smiled at me, encouraging. "That's it. Mum's been humming to us our whole lives, it just takes a little while to work out how to control your intentions."

Matteo froze, his eyes on mine. Carlos released Mum's wrist, and Dad held his out. It didn't take long before Carlos pulled back, and with Matteo's help, rose to his feet.

"Thank you," Carlos told my parents. "Although, you shouldn't have risked yourselves for me; I could have hurt you. I would rather not have killed Quinn's family."

"Not while I was humming, you couldn't have." Mum revealed; and as she climbed to her feet, she swayed.

I was across the room in an instant, grabbing her elbow. "Mum?"

"It's okay, I'm just a little woozy, maybe I should sit down." She saw the broken door for the first time. "You'll need to replace your door." Then she passed out in my arms.

Matteo took her from me and carried her outside, laying her down on the only piece of furniture that remained, a permanent fixture of the deck.

"I think I'll stay here for a bit," Dad said from inside.

"Is she okay?" I asked.

Carlos stood behind me. "She will be. She probably just needs to take it easy for a while. I didn't take enough to do any real harm, but more than I usually do. From both of them."

Matteo frowned at Carlos. "You let Gabriela challenge you without your clan? What were you thinking? I told you to take someone with you."

"She was on me before I could react," Carlos grumbled.

"You're still hungry. You need to feed," Matteo said.

"You're a bossy second, aren't you?" Carlos laughed but became sombre quickly. "You should know, most of the deaths haven't been at your hands. I realised a century ago what she was doing, but she commanded me to keep my

429

silence. She's used your lack of control to hide those she kills. Naturally, everyone would believe it was you, and that worked in her favour. That's why she never caged you. You also didn't kill anyone the night you were caged."

"Why?" I asked.

Carlos frowned. "She despised the accords. Bringing a vampire with the feral nature that Matteo has to us, meant that she could kill freely. She knew she'd eventually have to kill him but planned to replicate what made Matteo as he was. It's why she was so adamant that you be turned."

Ice gripped my heart. "She would have killed him, leaving me unbonded. And feral."

Carlos cupped my face. "I'm glad that didn't happen." He lifted his gaze to Matteo. "I'm sorry I never told you. I couldn't. I tried many times."

Matteo's eyes hardened. "That makes sense. I never understood why she kept me around. Ferals were outlawed, and the Elders would have killed me."

Mum opened her eyes and took in all of us. "I passed out, didn't I?"

Matteo crouched in front of her. "You'll need to drink plenty of water. Can you sit up?"

He helped her, and I took a seat next to her.

"Liam?" she called out to Dad.

"I'm okay, just staying right here," Dad replied. "I'm a little light-headed. Plus, that venom is uh…" He left the sentence unfinished, much to my relief.

"Don't you have a plane to catch?" Mum asked.

"She's right." Matteo said to me. "Do you want time alone with your family?"

"Don't be ridiculous, my daughter Called you, you're

family," Dad said, finally on his feet.

"You are certainly members of our clan," Carlos said. "You will always be protected in Venice. Thank you, Ava, and Liam."

It sounded strange to hear Carlos using my parents' names.

Niamh leaned towards me. "He's hot," she whispered. "If I wasn't already connected to Luke…and dead…damn, I'd let him bite me any day."

I said nothing, glad Carlos couldn't hear or see her.

Dad pulled me into a tight hug. "I'll miss you, my little Rock Star," he whispered in my ear.

Mum pulled me into her arms next. "I have to stand before all of Australia tomorrow to show grief for the loss of a child I know is alive."

"I'm sorry you have to do that," I told her.

She nodded. "It will give the public closure. I don't think you've seen how upset people have been. Tributes have come in from across the whole country. Lilith came by; I can tell she's not sleeping."

I had avoided watching the news since the announcement of Mia's death.

"I love you, my little songbird. Be happy. Never stop singing," she said.

I let her go. It was time to leave, and we had one more stop on the way to the airport.

Chapter 66

Quinn

We parked outside the cemetery, and I opened the door.

Matteo grabbed my arm. "Be careful," he warned. I caught the scent and heartbeat of a human. "It's Lilith. She's alone, but be careful. I'll be watching."

He waited in his car as I walked through the cemetery, looking for the newest grave.

'*Mia Wallace, beloved daughter, and sister. Gone too soon. 1995-2024*'

A bass guitar was engraved in the plaque.

I lay a daffodil at the foot of the headstone. "I'm sorry. Mia," I murmured. "You didn't deserve that." I shook my head. "Life certainly took a strange turn, didn't it?"

It was only a number of months since Matteo had come into my life, and yet it felt forever ago that I'd sat with Mia and Lilith over coffee, laughing. They'd helped me through the worst times of my life, losing Niamh, and pulling myself together again after Steven. Vampires hadn't existed, and neither had sirens.

"I'm sorry you lost her, Quinnie," Niamh said from beside me.

"I killed her," I said. "She shouldn't have been there; this shouldn't have happened."

"Oh, Quinn," my sister's voice was filled with sympathy.

Footsteps approached from behind me.

"I was wondering when you'd show up," Lilith said.

I spun around, and she held her hands up, one arm still in a sling.

"I'll take this as a cue to leave you two," Niamh said. "I'm going to watch over Luke for a while. I'll see you in Venice." She disappeared.

"I came alone. No weapons," Lilith said. "Two people grieving over the same person. A temporary truce. I won't fight you over her grave."

I didn't quite relax, watching her carefully. She pointed to a nearby seat, and we sat down. Minutes of silence passed. Her heartbeat pounded in my ears as she stared at the ground.

"I'm sorry," I said again. "I really am. I'd just woken up, I had nothing but my hunger and vampire instinct. I didn't know who she was."

I could feel Matteo focusing on me, paying attention, ready to step in if he needed to. *'I'm okay.'* I told him.

'I'll be watching,' he repeated. *'We have to go soon. You have*

433

five minutes.'

"You seem more like yourself," she said finally.

"Mostly," I said. "But I'm not really me anymore. A lot has changed."

"There's a memorial for you tomorrow. Everyone thinks you're dead." Her eyes narrowed.

"I know, I heard. Your press conference certainly didn't help," I grumbled.

It would probably make leaving the country difficult. Matteo was already prepared to compel the airport staff. Carlos had requested a passport made up for me, for which I'd worn a black wig. Andreas apparently was skilled in technology and creating fake passports.

"How could you do this to your Mum and Dad? After Niamh?" Lilith accused.

I sighed. "They know."

She stared at her feet again.

"I'm leaving," I told her. "We're leaving. We're going to find a new home."

She met my eyes. "I think it's best that you do go. You can't stay here. I would hate to have to kill you. But you did kill the love of my life."

"You killed me first," I reminded her.

Tears welled up in her eyes. "Damnit Quinn, I know, and I have to live with that for the rest of my life. That I'm the reason you're a goddamn vampire. Every time I close my eyes, I see that arrow hitting you in the chest."

"Are you expecting anger from me? Or hurt?" I asked. "I am what I am and have accepted my new existence. Your guilt cannot change what happened. Not that I'd want to. I chose this. I asked him to turn me, even before the arrow."

"The Quinn I know would never want that." She passed a photo across to me. One of me, her and Mia, arm in arm. We were in the Brisbane stadium, cheering at the top of our lungs, wild joy in our faces. "When you chose him, this is what you gave up. You destroyed your own dream, and mine, and you took Mia's from her."

I knew she was deliberately trying to hurt me. In a way, her words did sink in, but I had forever to find my dream again.

"The Quinn you know is dead." I stood. "I'm glad I got to say goodbye to you. All I ask is that you don't come after us." I left the photo on the seat.

I returned to the car, feeling her eyes on me. Matteo kissed my forehead.

"That went better than I thought it would," I said as he drove towards the airport. "I'm going to miss them both."

I stared out the window, mentally farewelling Melbourne. "Is Carlos okay?" I asked.

"His pride is wounded." Matteo confirmed. "She caught him by surprise, and as a new King, he knows he should have been more prepared. It will be on me as his second to ensure he follows my advice next time. There may be those who challenge him. I haven't returned to Venice since I left with Gabriela. For all we know, it may be territory already claimed. I can only hope that isn't the case, for we will fight to claim it if we have to."

Chapter 67

Quinn

It was a long flight, and I was acutely aware of the roar of the engines, and the cabin full of humans, separated from first class where we were seated. Heartbeats, snoring and screaming children as clear as if they were right next to me. Their scent of blood reminded me how hungry I was. My fangs lengthened. I forced them to retract, determined to display the same control that everyone else seemed capable of. My fangs disappeared, to my relief.

"We're landing soon," Matteo announced. "I forgot to give you something with all that happened." He handed me a pair of sunglasses. "You'll need these," he said. "It's daylight."

They looked the same as the ones I'd seen him wear the

first time we met. I slipped them on. "Woah! These are really dark."

He smiled. "Magically enhanced, specially made for vampires. I had a pair made up for you."

I lifted up the sunglasses, meeting his eyes. "When did you have a chance to do this?"

A mischievous grin spread across his face. "I asked Carlos to order them after we had dinner for the first time."

He'd known enough to have sunglasses made for me, that I'd need them. That I'd be a vampire. "You really knew, even then?"

He stroked my cheek with his thumb. "Even then. Your insistence that you wouldn't want it only made me more determined I would have you. That I would turn you." He kissed my forehead. "You were so adamant that you'd never allow me to bite you. Look how quickly that changed. Now, you beg me for it."

I wanted to straddle him while he bit me, and he sensed it through our blood bond, his eyes turning red. "Oh, please do. I've sat here for hours, that's all I could think about." I glanced around at the rest of the clan and Matteo laughed. "They won't mind. Vampires aren't as concerned about sex as many humans are. I've known of some clans to..."

An image of multiple naked bodies squirming against each other shimmered through our connection and I gasped, surprised at my body's reaction to it. Pure lust, and I knew my eyes were red. "Vampire orgy?" My core muscles tightened. "Why am I so turned on by that?"

His hand came down, pressing against my crotch, before moving under my skirt. "Because while Carlos calls us bringers of death, we are also very much creatures of lust and desire. You'd be surprised what makes you wet now. We have plenty of time to explore that."

He continued moving his fingers against me and I shifted, grinding myself against them, my breath already ragged. I closed my eyes, listening to Matteo's breathing. His own lust spiked, and I could feel him watching me. I let out a soft groan as he pressed harder. I reached across, finding he already had an erection, and palmed him as he continued stroking me.

His warm breath against my neck only added to the sparks running through my body. I turned my head, my lips parting. His kisses had always been full of hunger, but this was insatiable, and I fell into the feral part of his mind. Surrounded by that nature, I couldn't hold back the growl, primal as a red haze rose up. I wanted him, and I struggled to hold myself still. I yearned to rip his tee-shirt to reveal his firm body and run my hands over his muscles. To sit on him, rocking slowly while his cock hit all the right places.

'Quinn, you make me feral.' His voice was a deep growl in my mind. *'Lean your head back. I want to bite you, to mark you.'* His need flooded me, a storm of want and savageness that threatened to undo me.

I leaned my head back against the seat, a delicious shiver passing through me when his fangs pierced my throat. His fingers were insistent, and I chased my pleasure, holding his hand down, feeling myself racing towards that moment I fell apart. My pressure on his groin didn't let up.

Bright stars exploded behind my closed lids as an intense orgasm hit me, fangs lengthening again.

I did move then, with tremors still jolting through me, sitting in his lap, my head back against his shoulder, pressing myself against him. His arms slid over me, one hand firm against my stomach, the other stroking my breasts. I rubbed myself against his crotch, moaning. He bit me again.

"That was a pleasure to watch," Carlos said from the other side of the aisle, his voice throaty. "Perhaps invite me next time."

I froze, returning to my seat. I'd been so wrapped up in my desire for Matteo, I'd forgotten we were on the plane, surrounded by the rest of the clan.

Still coming down from the high of what we'd just done, I glanced over to find a flight attendant kneeling in front of Carlos, her arm held out, which he pressed to his mouth. The tang of blood in the air reminded me of my hunger. I sat up, pressing my tongue to a fang.

"Should he be doing that?" I whispered to Matteo.

Carlos pulled her arm away and gave her wrist a lick, smiling over at me. He spoke to the stewardess in Italian, and she walked around to our aisle. Her eyes were empty as she knelt at our row, holding her arm out to me. "From your King," she said in a flat voice. "A gift."

"It's alright," Matteo told me. "It's how we're able to fly long distances. This cabin is closed off from the humans, and she won't remember a thing. We can go hunting when we land if you prefer."

Intrigued, I reached for her outstretched arm and cast a look at Carlos again.

"Young siren, you don't need my permission, but it is rude to turn away such a gift," he said, laughter in his eyes.

I bit into her wrist. Her blood hit my tongue, and the next thing I knew, Matteo and Carlos were pulling me from her. Matteo dug his fingers on either side of my jaw until I let go.

"Um." I didn't know what to say.

"It's okay. I shouldn't have done that," Carlos said. "Why didn't you say how hungry you were?"

"No one else seemed to be," I said.

Carlos grabbed my chin as Josef led the flight attendant away to sit down. He pulled my face, so I was looking in his eyes. "You're a new vampire, Quinn. You're still learning about your hunger and limits. You need to tell us. It's been a couple hundred years since we've had a new one with us, so we forget what it was like."

"If anyone knows about losing control, it's me," Matteo confessed. "I'll make sure to monitor you more closely."

The plane started its descent, the sound of the engines changing.

We'd spent the day in a villa, huddled together. I strangely enjoyed having the whole clan around me and was getting used to their presence. After hunting, Matteo led me to a boat, and I stood the entire ride, staring at Venice as we raced towards it.

Finally, we docked. Matteo helped me from the boat. As

I set foot on the floating city, I could barely contain my excitement. His arms wrapped around me from behind, his lips brushed the back of my neck.

"Welcome home," he exclaimed.

Bonus Chapter

Lilith

I 'd lost my brother, and I'd shot my best friend while trying to take down one of the most feral vampires in history. It was my arrow that took Quinn's life, and I'd watched as a bloodied Matteo gently lifted her in his arms, gave me a death stare, and vanished. I'd known in my gut he would turn her. But telling Mia what I'd done to our best friend was the hardest thing I'd ever done in my life. I'd sobbed in her arms as she held me, trying to comfort me.

"I'm leaving," Quinn's voice pulled me out of my reverie. "We're leaving. We're going to find a new home."

My instincts screamed at me to put another arrow through her heart. She was the very thing I'd been taught to hate. To hunt. But I'd come unarmed. Killing a creature that wore the face of my best friend wouldn't be easy. I'd declared us enemies, and we sat side by side in an awkward silence that hurt my soul. It was my fault she was a vampire, and she'd taken Mia from me in return.

I forced myself to meet her eyes, suppressing the shudder. They were still green, but the predator's gaze within them was unmistakable. There was nothing human about her anymore. "I think it's best that you do go," I said. "You can't stay here. I would hate to have to kill you. But you did kill the love of my life." She'd broken the accords, and it was on me and my family to eliminate vampires that did.

Mia. I hadn't even had a chance to say goodbye. She'd taken her last breath, lying on the cold ground, terrified and alone. Nothing more than a meal to our closest friend, who had shown no remorse at the time. I really didn't want to kill Quinn, but I wasn't sure how long I could endure before my grief won out and I went after her with a crossbow.

"You killed me first." Her words were like a punch to the gut.

Tears stung my eyes, and I clenched my fist. "Damnit, Quinn, I know, and I have to live with that for the rest of my life. That I'm the reason you're a goddamn vampire. Every time I close my eyes, I see that arrow hitting you in the chest."

That really would haunt me for the rest of my life.

"Are you expecting anger from me? Or hurt?" she asked. "I am what I am and have accepted my new existence. Your guilt cannot change what happened. Not that I'd want to. I chose this. I asked him to turn me, even before the arrow."

There was nothing of Quinn left. Again the urge to put another arrow in her heart fought its way to the surface. Did she really care so little?

"The Quinn I knew would never want that." I passed a photo across to her. It had been taken in Brisbane, the three of us arm in arm, cheering with sheer joy. Our dreams realised, our first tour ahead of us. As she glanced at the photo, I searched for any remaining sign of her. "When you chose him, this is what you gave up. You destroyed your own dream, and mine, and you took Mia's from her."

My words had no effect on her. The look she gave me was as if she knew I was trying to get to her.

"The Quinn you knew is dead." She stood. "I'm glad I got to say goodbye to you. All I ask is that you don't come after us." She walked away, leaving the photo on the seat.

I watched as she walked towards the black car with tinted windows. I could feel Matteo's eyes on me, but didn't move, until the car was gone, tail lights fading into the night.

The crushing pain of Mia's death closed around my heart, a tight fist. Tears wouldn't be held back this time, leaving hot trails down my cheeks as I returned to her grave. Quinn had left a daffodil at the headstone, and I picked it up, tearing the flower apart, throwing the pieces into the wind. A sob broke free, and I couldn't stand anymore. Dropping to my knees, I let the pain surge through me, not caring that I was ruining my mascara. Heaving sobs wracked me.

"Mia, I'm sorry," I murmured. "I should have kept you far away from all of this."

"It's my fault, I did go to the home of a vampire in the middle of the night," her voice came from above where I knelt.

My heart skipped, as icy fingers brushed the back of my neck. I frowned. The lack of sleep and grief must be making me hear things, I assumed. But I lifted my head anyway.

She was there, standing over me with her gleeful smile.

"Mia?" My voice shook, pain piercing my heart. Had someone made her a vampire? "Y-you're alive?"

"Well, no. A vampire killed me. I don't think there's any coming back from that. I'm dead. My body's in there." She pointed at the dirt. "So, I'm definitely not a vampire, in case you were worried about that."

I was on my feet, bitter tears turned to tears of joy. "How are you here?"

"Yeah, I don't know." She faced her grave, staring down at her headstone. "This is so weird."

I choked back a laugh. "You're telling me. I was here for your funeral. I saw them bury you, yet here you are."

"Am I a ghost?" she asked. "Ohh, there's soo many people I can haunt!"

Her excitement over the idea of haunting people was contagious, and we laughed over who deserved to be haunted the most.

"I'd like to pay a visit to Quinn to give her a piece of my mind," her smile faded. "I can't believe she really killed me. It hurt, in more ways than one. Have you spoken to her?"

"She's not Quinn anymore," I said. "I've known about vampires most of my life, I never imagined my best friend would become one."

I reached for Mia, only for my hand to pass right through her. "I'm sorry I wasn't there."

"Even if you were, what could you have done? You against two vampires, like that?" She pointed to the sling.

I yearned to touch her. To hold her in my arms. Tears welled up again. Words needed to be said while I had the chance. I didn't know why she was here, nor for how long. I opened my mouth to say the words.

"I know," she said, reaching for my face to wipe a tear away. Her hand made no connection with me. "Damn, this really sucks." she let out a sigh. "I don't know why I'm here if I can't touch you."

"I had a plan," I said.

She remained silent, waiting for me to go on.

"I planned to propose to you at the Melbourne concert." I pulled the ring box from my pocket. I'd carried it with me since she died.

I started to open the box.

"No, stop." Mia stepped back. "Don't open it."

I frowned. "You don't want to see the ring I got you?"

She laughed. "Oh, no I do. But I want to see what you would have done. How would you have proposed?"

My chest tightened. I was about to propose to my dead girlfriend for a wedding that would never happen. "I don't know…"

"No, don't do that Lil, please. I was cheated out of a proposal; this is my only chance."

Her eyes shone, and I gave in. "Okay." I took a deep breath and let it out. "You're there." I pointed to where she stood, then to the seat I'd sat on with Quinn. "Imagine my drums there, I'm sitting there." I pointed to another spot. "Quinn's there." The pain returned at the mention of Quinn's name. I would eventually have to face what she was, and probably find her to kill her. And Matteo. But for now, I pushed all that aside. "Quinn was going to be like, 'Tonight's a special night for us, and I want you all to know that the most important people in my life are right here,' and then point to us. 'Lilith usually stays at the drums, but tonight she is leaving her seat to say a few words.'"

Tears glistened on Mia's face, which surprised me. I didn't know ghosts could cry. Not that I knew anything about ghosts. "Quinn was in on it?"

I smiled. "Of course. She was so excited when I told her I was going to propose. Anyway, I was going to get up, and take the mic..." I held my hand up as if holding a mic. "I am a woman of few words. That's why I'm a drummer, and not a singer. However, there is only one way to convey what I want to say."

I dropped to my knee in front of Mia, opening the box as I did. Inside was a silver band with two stones set in it. One red, a colour that Mia loved and usually wore, the other deep blue. My own go-to favourite colour.

"Mia Wallace, I love you with all of my heart. We've all had one dream, to be here, on stage. Here we are. But I'm greedy and want more. I want you. I want to call you 'wife' and wake up next to you for the rest of our lives. To grow old with you." I paused, this proposal hurting more than I thought possible. I would never wake up next to her, nor grow old with her. "Mia, marry me. Be my wife, and I will make you happy."

Mia stood in silence, staring at the ring. She sniffed. More tears fell down my cheeks.

"That's a beautiful ring," she murmured. "It's you and me."

"It is," I said, laughing.

She held her hand out to me. "I would have done this," she said. "And waited for you to put it on my finger and kissed you so damn hard."

I pulled the ring from the box and pushed it over her finger,

447

even though we couldn't touch.

"It would have looked good on me." Mia started to sob. Again I wanted to hold her, my heart broken. "Oh Lil, I love you so much." She knelt in front of me. "My last thought as I died was of you. Of how much I love you. I was scared and in pain, but I thought about you."

We remained like that for a long time, grieving what had been taken from us. Occasionally, one of us would reach for the other. Only to put our hand down again. It wasn't until the early rays of dawn streaked across the sky that I realised she was gone. I climbed to my feet with effort, wiping my eyes. I glanced at her grave stone again, one last time. "Goodbye, Mia. I love you. Always have, always will."

I made the long walk back to my car and climbed in, letting out a shaky breath as I put my hands on the wheel.

"Okay, so I think I would have taken on your name but kept mine," Mia said. "So what sounds better? Mia Wallace-De Micheli, or Mia De Micheli-Wallace?"

I stared. She was in the front seat.

"Your mouth is open." She laughed.

"I thought you were gone," I said.

"Well I'm not. You're stuck with me. You think after a proposal like that I'd just leave?" She smiled at me, that beautiful smile that lit up her whole face and eyes. "Can we go home now?"

Stay tuned for more on Lilith and Mia.

Epilogue to follow

Epilogue

Matteo

T*wenty years later*

Quinn wore clothes almost identical to the first time I had seen her sing. Black jeans, a green shirt and black lipstick. Her fingers danced across guitar strings, the joy in her eyes unmistakable. Her love of music hadn't died, and I was as drawn in by her voice as the first time.

Her gifts as a vampire combined with those of her siren heritage had every human in the bar under her sway. They couldn't look away if they tried. Using it as a hunting technique, she would lure our prey to follow us. I loved to see her ability in action, appreciating the fact that while many had been drawn to her before me, I had been the first to fall under the influence of her irresistible voice. That I was the one her heart had chosen, Calling me to her, binding the two of us together in a way that neither of us could have resisted.

As I watched, it was clear that all connections to her band were gone. Songs that she'd sung twenty years before had not passed her lips since. Her way to eliminate all connection with her old life. With Lilith. The Hunter had come to Venice years before, but I'd picked up her scent in time to warn the clan. She'd left, finding no sign of us. The only song Quinn held onto was the one she wrote for me.

"I'll never tire of hearing her sing," I murmured to Carlos.

Her gaze landed on me briefly. Wordless affection from our blood bond surrounded me.

"She's bolder than she used to be," he said. "More daring in what she writes. As if the vampire and the siren allowed her to embrace that part of herself she wouldn't have been able to reach if she'd remained human. Her music is the very reflection of the vampire siren that she is. Darkness and desire."

Not so long ago, Quinn had discovered that Carlos had a musical talent of his own, and she was trying to convince him to join her on stage. Their conversations around music often went late into the night.

I caught her looking at a couple in the front with a smile.

"She's found someone," I told Carlos.

My hunger stirred.

"Be patient," he warned me. "Let her finish."

Finally, she finished singing and packed away her guitar. Humans smelling of desire surrounded her the moment she stepped off the stage, but Quinn stopped to whisper in the ears of those she had picked. A hum rose from her, echoing around us. Energy surrounded those she had chosen for tonight.

"The hunt is on," I told Carlos.

Quinn moved across the room and kissed me. I wrapped my arms around her, pushing my tongue into her mouth. I wanted to devour her and couldn't help the growl.

"Let's go." Carlos turned to leave.

"My beautiful siren," I murmured, kissing her again. "You know what your Siren Song does to me."

She licked my throat, sending a quiver through me. "Then it's best we get going, isn't it?"

We left the club, and Quinn cast a look over her shoulder, humming again from within. The humans she'd chosen started to follow. I carried her guitar case, and she slid her arm through mine. She leaned into me, her head on my shoulder.

Outside, the night was alive: Tourists walked past, shopping and taking in the sights. with excited voices. My heart burst. I had been forbidden to return to Venice for centuries, and while time had changed much about the city, it was still my home. Our walk took us past an art gallery with my name on it. This time I'd chosen to remain anonymous, but often went inside with Quinn to appreciate the art of emerging artists, and to listen to conversations about the mysterious 'Matteo Barone and his art.'

We led the couple to a quiet and dark alley where no one would bother us.

"Where are we?" The man asked with an Irish accent.

"Irish," I laughed. "You and your accents."

"Everyone here has accents," she told me. "The beauty of living in a city that attracts so many tourists."

It was a rule Carlos had made that we never feed from locals. Some of them even worked for us.

"I saw you sing," the human said as he gazed at Quinn. "Your voice, it's-" He didn't have a chance to finish before Carlos was on him.

The woman next to him didn't scream, only stared wide-eyed, her fear calling to me.

Quinn removed her arm from me. "Kiss her," she whispered. "I want to hear her moan."

I advanced on the woman, my hunger surging. Her eyes turned to me, wide with fear.

"Don't be afraid," I murmured.

"I'm not afraid," she replied, already under my influence.

I pulled her to me, pressing my lips to hers. She didn't resist and responded quickly to my kiss. Quinn circled around and attached her fangs to the human's throat from behind. The moan that escaped the woman was arousing, and I pulled away from the kiss, licking her throat and sinking my fangs in. Quinn's hand slid around the back of my head as we fed, fingers in my hair. Her pleasure of the feed spread to me. The red haze rose up, pulling me under, everything else fading into black.

'Matteo.' A voice pierced the dark, fingers caressing my neck, someone trying to pull me away from the human.

I growled, unwilling to budge, letting the blood take me further into my frenzy. Voices surrounded me, but I didn't care.

Someone started to sing, a song I knew. "I look into your eyes, they raise my pulse and I, am pulled to you and find

453

new strings control my mind."

I followed the voice from deep within my bloodlust and let the human fall to the ground, as Quinn continued to sing. "This beautiful abyss, I give myself to this. The dark eyes of a stranger."

Unable to hold myself back, I pulled her to me, kissing roughly. I hadn't killed in years, but often got close. Once she'd learned how to, she pulled me from my blood haze *every time*. It made things less complicated for our clan, not attracting Hunters.

"She'll need a hospital," Quinn said to Carlos without looking away from me. "Will you be joining us tonight?"

He picked up the woman. "I've been summoned to the bridge to attend to human matters. Perhaps tomorrow."

I grinned as he left, then pressed my forehead against Quinn's. "My song," I murmured.

A song she'd written for me. Once called Dark Eyes of a Stranger, she'd renamed it Blood Song.

"I will always sing it to you, my wild beast." She licked the blood from my chin, and I snapped my teeth at her playfully. Her laughter was like music, and we returned to the villa.

The descendants of my brother had occupied my family home when we'd arrived. I had compelled them to take a smaller villa on the other side of Venice, near where my own descendants lived. This opened a home for us, for our clan. Our den. Paintings from my days as a human lined the walls. Two portraits hung side by side. One, my only self-portrait, eyes full of hope for the future above those of my human wife and daughter. Next to it, that of my brother, older than me and a mischievous light shone from his face. He'd been dead for centuries, but the portrait I'd painted of him was a reminder of a life I'd long forgotten. Thinking of my human life was pointless. But I wondered about the life of my brother. And that of my daughter. I had missed seeing her grow up, marry, and have children.

I lay Quinn on our bed, hunger for her piercing me. She pulled her shirt off before removing mine.

"Bite me," she pleaded. "I want to see my blood on your face."

Instead, I lowered myself over her, to whisper in her ear. "I once told you that you'd be begging me for my vampire's kiss." I pulled her earlobe in between my teeth. "You know I like to hear you beg."

"Then bite me."

"Or what?" I lowered my nose to her throat, taking in her scent. "Mmmm, you smell delicious. Your lust."

The deep growl that came from her reverberated through my body as she wrapped one arm around me and flipped us over. She pinned my wrists, leaning towards me.

"Then I'll bite you," she insisted and lowered her mouth to my throat.

I tilted my head, waiting, wanting. She bit deep and I shuddered, our minds open to one another through the blood bond. She pulled back and I sat up, my arms tight around her. She moaned when my fangs slid into her throat, throwing her head back.

When I finished, I pressed my face between her breasts, and her cheek rested on the top of my head.

She lay back. A humming started from within her being, the sound wrapping around me. It was her way to express utter joy and contentment, her deep love piercing my own heart.

Straddling her, I gazed into those beautiful red eyes. *"Il mio piccolo cantante." My little singer.* I smiled. *"Mi amore."*

"Ti amo," she replied.

THE END

Carlos's story will continue in Consumed.

Dark Eyes of a Stranger

Tonight the room dissolved except for you and I
   I skipped a beat as my reply
   And from the stage all I could hear was one refrain
   The need to see you again

(chorus)
   I look into your eyes, they raise my pulse and I
   Am pulled to you and find new strings control my mind
   This beautiful abyss, I give myself to this
   The dark eyes of a stranger

You answered all my doubts, lit candles time put out
   A little hope can be a funny thing
   As I dove deeper in that moment than the oceans
   I felt that you were there with me

Now all the city lights bring whispers of your melody,
   Since tonight you walked into my song
   And though the streets may sleep I look for you,
   If you're a dream then please let me dream on

Lyrics written by Linda Joy

Acknowledgements

Jess, you're the first to read anything I write, and you were my sounding board on much of the story in my late-night writing sessions. When I was ready to write a vampire book, you helped me unlock who my characters were, from which their entire story flowed.

My FMC is a singer, and in this book she writes a song called Dark Eyes. This song plays such an integral role in the relationship between my main characters. I'm no musician, so thank you to Linda Joy for writing the lyrics.

My beta team, I will forever be grateful to you for getting me to the point where I felt ready to publish Bloodsong.

Thank you to Madeline and Joey Te Whiu and Roimata Hooper for the much-appreciated assistance in Te Reo translation and aspects of Māori characters, to provide representation while avoiding appropriation.

About the Author

Serra is an author of dark historical fantasy and paranormal romance books with stories that draw you in from page one. Within these worlds that she created, you will find unbreakable family bonds, darker aspects to humanity, shadow realms as well as passion, lust, strong FMC's and men who would risk anything for the women they love.

Serra's journey to becoming an author started from a young age, when her first creative writing attempt —a poem titled 'The Mighty Oak Tree,' —was published in her primary school newsletter. An avid reader with a vivid imagination, her Mum always encouraged her to keep writing. She proceeded to write poetry and short stories before discovering a deeper passion for novel writing and screenplays.

In 2021, she adapted a screenplay she'd been working on, into her debut novel 'The Shadow Within,' which was published in November 2023.

Serra is a Melbourne-based author from New Zealand. As a reader and a writer, she's drawn into the dark fantasy and paranormal romance genres. Like many authors, she balances her writing alongside a day job in which she works in the communications part of a marketing and digital team; by night, she's a weaver of words, creator of worlds bringing forth stories that hold readers captive.

If you wish to subscribe, please visit:

www.serrarosewrites.com

Be the first to receive updates and sneak peeks at character art, quotes, chapters, next projects and early access to pre-orders.

Also by Serra Rose

The Horsemen Chronicles:
The Shadow Within
Death's Shadow

Upcoming Titles in The Horsemen Chronicles:
The Whispers of War
The Echoes of War
The Scourge of Famine
The Plague of Humanity

The Bloodsong Series:
Bloodsong
Consumed

Upcoming Titles in The Bloodsong Series:
Bloodking

The Bloodsong Series Spin-offs:
Eternity
Lovestruck
Lovesong